"I think this house is perfect for both of you," Olivia said. **"You can build a deck in front and enjoy your meals with friends."**

"Would you come if we invited you, Olivia?"

"Of course." The way he was watching her sent a tiny thrill up her spine, but it also triggered wariness. She didn't belong here, yet his words created an irresistible picture.

"And I could put up Christmas decorations outside."

"You can do whatever you want. It's your land and it will be your home."

"Home," Gabe whispered. "It's been a long time since I had that. I don't think I'd have done this without you. I don't know how we'll ever repay you."

"Just be happy. Enjoy your home and Eli. That's payment enough." Her total focus was on Gabe, on how she'd only have to balance forward on her tiptoes to touch his cheek with her lips.

Been that route before, her brain warned. *Remember the pain.*

Olivia knew lots about Gabe, including *his* painful past. Which was why Gabe wasn't interested in her as anything other than a friend.

That was what Olivia want

Wasn't it?

Lois Richer loves traveling, swimming and quilting, but mostly she loves writing stories that show God's boundless love for His precious children. As she says, "His love never changes or gives up. It's always waiting for me. My stories feature imperfect characters learning that love doesn't mean attaining perfection. Love is about keeping on keeping on." You can contact Lois via email, loisricher@gmail.com, or on Facebook (loisricherauthor).

It took **Mindy Obenhaus** forty years to figure out what she wanted to do when she grew up. But once God called her to write, she never looked back. She's passionate about touching readers with biblical truths in an entertaining and sometimes adventurous manner. Mindy lives in Texas with her husband and kids. When she's not writing, she enjoys cooking and spending time with her grandchildren. Find out more at mindyobenhaus.com.

Rocky Mountain Daddy

Lois Richer

&

Her Colorado Cowboy

Mindy Obenhaus

LOVE INSPIRED
INSPIRATIONAL ROMANCE

Recycling programs for this product may not exist in your area.

LOVE INSPIRED®
INSPIRATIONAL ROMANCE

ISBN-13: 978-1-335-46127-8

Rocky Mountain Daddy and Her Colorado Cowboy

Copyright © 2021 by Harlequin Books S.A.

Rocky Mountain Daddy
First published in 2019. This edition published in 2021.
Copyright © 2019 by Lois M. Richer

Her Colorado Cowboy
First published in 2019. This edition published in 2021.
Copyright © 2019 by Melinda Obenhaus

This edition published by arrangement with Harlequin Books S.A.

For questions and comments about the quality of this book, please contact us at CustomerService@Harlequin.com.

Love Inspired
22 Adelaide St. West, 40th Floor
Toronto, Ontario M5H 4E3, Canada
www.Harlequin.com

Printed in U.S.A.

CONTENTS

ROCKY MOUNTAIN DADDY

Lois Richer

For Mom, who wrote her last chapter so well.
And for Oliver, who's just begun his own story.

What time I am afraid, I will trust in thee.
—*Psalms* 56:3

Chapter One

One minute Olivia DeWitt was happily steering her car up the hill toward home, the next minute she was heading for the ditch.

With a gasp of dismay she slammed on her brakes, managing to stay on the road shoulder—barely. She exhaled, slowly released her fingers from the wheel and then exited the car. The sight of the shredded tire made her groan.

"You couldn't have waited ten minutes before blowing?" Shielding her eyes, Olivia peered longingly at—was it still home?—The Haven, a massive stone house perched on the rocky mountain promontory above her. "At least it's summer," she consoled herself, then mocked the sentiment as a teasing breeze reminded her that June in the Canadian Rockies bore no resemblance to June in the eastern provinces.

For a microsecond Olivia considered calling The Haven and asking Jake, her foster aunts' handyman, to come and help her. Until a glance at her phone showed it was dead. Again. Not that it mattered, because she had no intention of calling.

Olivia never took the easy way out. She prided herself on being responsible and that included fixing a tire, even though she'd have to completely unpack her fully laden car to retrieve her spare.

"Nothing good comes easily," she reminded herself with a weary sigh.

Olivia had her hand on the trunk latch when a rumble to her right made her pause. A half-ton truck beetled toward her, leaving behind a massive dust plume from the bumpy dirt track—well, you could hardly call it a road.

Some might say you could hardly call the vehicle a truck. Rusted-out fenders, splotches of turquoise paint dabbed here and there—probably to contain the rust— and a cracked windshield numbered among its less noteworthy features.

"At least *his* vehicle is running," she chastised herself.

He was Gabe Webber, foreman of the Double M, the sprawling ranch next door to The Haven. Olivia knew him, but only casually. Gabe had been employed after she and her foster sisters Victoria, Adele and Gemma had left The Haven to attend university.

Years ago, when they were not quite teens, Olivia and the other girls had been brought here by Tillie and Margaret Spenser, former missionaries and aging owners of the huge stone house and pristinely forested estate known as The Haven. Despite their being dubbed *troublemakers* in the foster care system, the four girls had bonded while the Spenser sisters, whom they affectionately called "the aunties," sheltered and lovingly raised them as if they were all part of one big family. Those precious years had created a debt none of the four girls could ever hope to repay.

Over a year ago the aunties had come up with a plan

to sponsor an outreach program at The Haven, a way to offer respite to troubled foster children. Victoria had set that plan into motion. Then last fall, Adele, Olivia's second foster sister, came on board as the food and beverage manager. In a recent phone call to Olivia, Victoria had raved that the foster kids who now came to The Haven on a weekend, or for weeklong programs, loved the addition of trail rides to their activities, and she'd given a big part of the credit to the Double M foreman, Gabe.

Olivia was happy for Victoria and Adele and The Haven's success, but she didn't intend to become part of it. Olivia didn't do responsibility for kids. Never again.

Gabe's battered truck pulled up behind her car, motor purring smoothly. He climbed out. Six feet four inches and leaner than lean, Gabe Webber was always the image that came to mind when Olivia thought "cowboy." Handsome and hunky, his crisp dark hair glistened in the sunshine as he whipped off his black Stetson and smiled at her.

"Hello, Olivia. Nice to see you. Having trouble?" he asked in a low rumbly voice.

Funny that she'd never noticed how deep his voice was.

"Hi, Gabe." Olivia glanced at him and then quickly away, lifting one hand to make sure her hair covered her scarred cheek. Gabe had seen the scar before, of course, and never once had he made her feel uncomfortable about it, but her actions stemmed from a lifelong habit.

"My tire blew," she explained. "I was about to dig out the spare."

"I see that. I hear you're making a move to Edmonton." Gabe assessed the damage, running one gloved fingertip over the shredded tire. "Starting a new job, your aunts said?"

"That's the plan," Olivia agreed. "I need to find an apartment and get settled in before I start work, but first I wanted to stop by The Haven and see everyone."

"Organizing people, is that what you do?" Gabe clapped on his Stetson, then shoved it to the back of his head, sky-blue eyes darkening as he studied her nod.

"Sort of. My official title was systems analyst, but the job was more about being an administrative assistant to a colonel." She shrugged. "I was tasked with making his office run more efficiently." *Too much information, Olivia.*

"Uh-huh." Gabe blinked. "Been a long time since you were here, Liv. Your Aunt Tillie and Aunt Margaret miss you." His intense gaze shifted to scrutinize the other tires. Bald tires.

"I miss my aunties, too, but it wasn't always easy to get here from Ottawa," she defended. *Please don't say I should have bought new tires.* She'd used a hefty chunk of her precious savings to store her furniture and fund her move far away from the man to whom she'd given her heart, the one who'd lied about loving her. Edmonton would be her fresh start. "How've you been, Gabe?"

"Busy. Since the Double M started offering trail rides, Victoria keeps us hopping." His droll, dry comment didn't tell Olivia he was joking, but his slow, easy smile did. "I make time to come over to The Haven every week on Fridays, though. Doughnut afternoons." Gabe licked his full lips and grinned, white teeth blazing against his tanned skin. "Chef Adele makes the best glazed doughnuts. Besides, I enjoy her kids. Those twins are quite a pair."

"Yes, they are." Olivia barely knew her adopted niece and nephew, Francie and Franklyn, but that was by choice. If she didn't get too close to them, she couldn't wreck their worlds as she'd done to other kids. She pushed up her sleeves. "I guess I'd better change—"

Her words were cut short by the squeal of tires as a dusty white SUV barreled off the highway and around the corner. It slid to a halt mere inches from Olivia's back bumper. She and Gabe both stared as a woman got out and marched toward them.

"Lady, you have to slow down around here. There could be a horse wandering in the road and if you hit it, you'd be in trouble and so would it." Gabe sounded irritated, which Olivia thought was odd for what she'd always thought such an easygoing guy. But then this cowboy loved horses as much as other people loved their kids.

The woman seemed unfazed. "I'm looking for a Gabriel Webber."

"You found him." Gabe frowned at her. "What can I—?"

The words died on his lips as the woman racewalked around the front of her vehicle to the passenger side. She yanked open the back door and a moment later dragged forward a small boy and an equally small battered suitcase.

"This is your son, Eli," she announced.

"I'm sorry, lady, you've got the wrong guy." Gabe began shaking his head, but the woman interrupted.

"Eve's son. Your son." She stared at him hard. "Eli's almost six."

Olivia's head had been swiveling back and forth between them, trying to figure out what was happening.

At the word *Eve*, Gabe stiffened, but at the word *six* his face seemed to freeze.

"Impossible," he finally whispered, blanching.

"Possible." The woman nodded. "I'm Eve's sister, Kathy Kane. We've never met, though we might have if you'd had a proper wedding instead of dragging my sister to some unsavory elopement and then dumping her when she got pregnant." When she received no response to her angry criticism she continued. "I live in Calgary now. Where Eve lived."

"Lived?" Gabe squinted at her. His face tightened into a mask, giving away nothing. He glanced at the boy again. "She's not living there now?"

"Eve died a month ago. She had cancer."

Olivia knew less than nothing about raising kids, but she immediately knew it wasn't right that the woman said the words so baldly, without even a hand on the shoulder to comfort the boy. And yet, Eli seemed untouched by the remark about his mother's passing. He just stood where he was, staring at the ground, his little face pinched and sad.

"I'm sorry," Gabe murmured.

"Me, too. She left a mess behind." Kathy Kane was not a soft-spoken woman; nor did she make any effort to conceal her irritation. "I'll clean it up. But I can't stay and talk. I've got two kids at home and the neighbor will only watch them for a while longer. I've got to go. Wait." She went back to the car.

For a moment Olivia thought Gabe feared she'd leave because he leaned forward as if he'd go after her. But Kathy returned quickly, carrying a huge handbag into which she dug furtively for a few moments before producing a bedraggled envelope.

"Eve left you this. It'll explain everything. I wrote my information on the back, just in case you need to contact me, though I'd rather you didn't. I've done enough." She stepped forward, thrust the envelope at Gabe, her jaw tight. "Don't bring him back," she growled, her voice low and threatening. "I can't keep him. I got enough trouble raising my own kids and paying all Eve's bills."

"But—"

"You be good," Kathy said to Eli, her fingers clutching his shoulder.

Olivia saw the boy wince.

"This is your dad. You're gonna live with him, like we talked about. Bye." Without another word or even an embrace, Kathy wheeled around, climbed into her car and roared back to the corner. She disappeared down the highway.

Olivia remained silent, embarrassed that she'd witnessed the incident. Gabe's frigid expression kept her from offering her sympathy, but then as he studied Eli, his icy appearance began to melt and soften. Longing filled his blue eyes—as if he couldn't quite believe his dreams had just come true. Several long moments stretched until finally Gabe walked up to the boy and squatted in front of him.

"Hello, Eli. I'm very pleased to meet you. My name is Gabe Webber." He held out a hand, withdrew it quickly to strip off his leather work glove, then thrust it out again and waited.

Olivia caught her breath when Eli looked up, staring into intense blue eyes that were an exact replica of his own. Their jutting chins had the same hard line. Dark crisp curls flopped onto prominent brows in an identical manner. The child was a mirror image of Gabe. There could be no doubt that man and boy were related.

"Are you really my dad?" Eli's murmur barely carried over the freshening wind whispering across the foothill grasses.

"That's what your aunt said." Gabe let his unshaken hand drop. "I'll have to read your mom's letter before I know more." He gulped, then added very quietly, "But I guess I am your father, Eli."

Big fat tears began to course down Eli's cheeks. His shoulders sagged.

"Why didn't you come?" he asked, his voice breaking on a sob. "I prayed and prayed. Why didn't you come?"

Then, like a broken reed that just couldn't hold itself up anymore, the little boy collapsed in a heap, sobbing his heart out.

He had a son.

Gabe stared at Eli while his brain mentally regressed to the day he'd handed Eve a copy of their divorce decree. He could still hear her voice.

You'll be sorry, Gabe.

No, Eve. I won't. I wish our marriage could have worked out, because I loved you. But you don't want me. You only ever wanted what Dad's ranch could give you—money. Now you have it, though the stress and pain you've caused us will cost us a lot more than those few dollars you grabbed at. Goodbye, Eve.

Then he'd waited for her to leave. Had she already known she was pregnant?

"Gabe?" Olivia's soft voice cracked the mirror of his past. She moved closer to meet his gaze, her silver-gray eyes clouded as she glanced pointedly at the sobbing child. "Do something," she whispered.

"I don't know—" He spread his hands helplessly. The kid wouldn't even shake his hand. What was he supposed to do?

"Oh, for mercy's—" Obviously exasperated, she walked to Eli and squatted in front of him. "Eli? My name is Olivia DeWitt. My aunties live in that great big house up there. See it?"

Eli paused in his weeping, looked up and nodded with a sniff.

"It's called The Haven," Olivia continued. "My sister is making doughnuts there today. Would you like to go with me and have some?"

Gabe stared. He hadn't seen Olivia interact with kids much. She always seemed aloof, or perhaps *standoffish* was more accurate. Yet here she was offering to take his son—*his son?*—for doughnuts. Just another thing his brain couldn't seem to process.

"The thing is, Eli, my car has a flat tire. We'll have to ride up there with Gabe in his truck. Okay?" she asked.

"Uh huh." Eli scrubbed away the tears, which left dirt streaks across his face. He stared at Gabe. "Is he my dad for sure?" he whispered.

"I don't know, but why don't we forget about that for now and go enjoy the doughnuts. Maybe some lemonade, too. Deal?" Olivia held out a hand and, to Gabe's shock, Eli shook it.

They rose together. To Gabe it was as if some invisible bond stretched between them. A bond he hadn't been able to achieve. That stung.

"Could you drive us, please, Gabe?" Olivia asked,

locking up her vehicle. "I'll leave my car here for now. Gabe?" she prodded when he didn't respond.

"What? Uh, drive. Sure." He could hardly tear his gaze away from the boy. His son.

God, I'm going to need some help here.

He put Eli's small shabby suitcase in the truck bed without saying anything more, mostly because he couldn't think of anything appropriate. And yet, as he drove to The Haven, a million questions rolled inside his head. *Why?* That was the most pressing of them all. It seemed that his questions, like Eve's letter in his pocket, would have to wait till later.

Eve. Every nerve in Gabe's body tensed. Anger surged and the knot in his stomach tightened. *Deceiver. Cheater. Liar.* She'd been all of those, so why was he surprised by this? He clenched his jaw, braking a little harder than he should have in front of the huge stone house.

"Livvie!" Tillie and Margaret Spenser jumped up from the shaded cedar bench outside the back door. Both rushed toward them as Gabe parked and walked around to open Olivia's door.

"Another of our dear girls is home," Aunt Tillie gushed.

"Just for a week," Olivia said as she released Gabe's helping hand.

He thought that sounded like a warning.

"But—"

"My dear aunties, Victoria, and Adele have made their lives at The Haven and I'm very happy for them and you." Olivia interrupted Margaret as she hugged her close. "But Gemma and I are still the family's wanderers. I'm home for a visit, then I'll have to leave here to start my job. But having two of your four foster daughters living here permanently isn't bad, is it?" she teased.

"It's wonderful. All part of our God's glorious plan, my dear. Where's your car?" Tillie Spenser asked as she followed her sister in hugging Olivia.

"Bottom of the hill. Blown tire."

Olivia's unconcealed chagrin made Gabe smile, until Tillie released her and included him in the hugfest. Then she bent to study Eli.

"Hello, young man. Welcome to The Haven. It's doughnut day, did you know that?"

"She said," Eli responded, shooting a small smile at Olivia. The smile disappeared when he looked at Gabe.

"This is Eli," Olivia explained. "He'll be joining us," she managed to say just before being encircled by Adele's adopted twins, Francie and Franklyn, who'd come racing around the side of the house.

Gabe noted how quickly Olivia drew away from them.

"Hey, guys, you're kinda dirty," she said, nose wrinkling at the muddy streaks on her formerly pristine white shirt.

"Yeah. Choc'late mud pies." Francie grinned. "We gotta wash 'fore we c'n eat doughnuts," she told Eli.

"It's a rule," Franklyn agreed.

Gabe had loved the twins from the moment Adele arrived with them over six months ago. He couldn't have been happier when she'd married his boss, Mac McDowell, owner of the Double M, because it meant the cute pair now lived on the ranch. He loved kids, had always wanted some of his own, but Eve—*don't go there.*

He had a son. Gabe couldn't make that sink into his

brain. Nor could he comprehend why Eve hadn't told him, especially after she'd become ill.

"Come on." Francie grabbed Eli's hand. "Washup time. An' don't miss no dirt 'cause we can't eat nothin' till we get clean an' the doughnuts are yummy." She whirled to inspect the adults. "Uncle Gabe, you got dust on your cheek. You gotta wash, too."

"Yup, you do," Franklyn agreed. He grabbed Eli's other hand and drew him alongside, discussing crash-up cars. Eli went along with a confused look on his face.

"Let's do have some doughnuts," Aunt Margaret said. She and her sister followed the kids inside. Only Gabe and Olivia remained.

"I figured you wouldn't want to explain to them about Eli until you have everything sorted out," she said quietly.

"Thanks." He could feel her questions.

"I didn't know you'd been married, Gabe."

"At eighteen. For about three years." Because she'd witnessed the debacle with Kathy, Gabe figured he owed Olivia at least a rudimentary explanation. "Eve was the new girl in town and I fell hard for her. My dad didn't approve, though. We eloped, then she moved onto our ranch. I'd worked the ranch with Dad my whole life and I loved it, but Eve said it was boring and hated it. She started to cause problems—on the ranch and between Dad and me. I finally realized that when she looked at me, all she saw was a meal ticket."

"I'm sorry," she whispered.

"Me, too." He pursed his lips. Best to get it said and then forget it. As if! "Eve wanted out, so Dad agreed to sell off part of our land to pay her off. She took the money and ran, but Dad's treasure, our ranch, was decimated. We couldn't ranch on so little land, though he fought hard to make it work. Six months later he died from a massive coronary. I had to sell the land at rock-bottom prices."

"Oh, no." Olivia sounded genuinely upset. "What did you do then?"

"Enlisted. Did two tours, but I hated it. I worked at Wranglers Ranch in Tucson for a while. Tried to rebuild my faith in God." He heaved a sigh. "Then I got into equine-assisted learning. Eventually I came to the Double M and—" He shrugged. "That's my story. My stupidity in marrying Eve cost me my dad and my home."

"I'm so sorry. You never saw Eve again?"

"No. And I never wanted to," he muttered, tension building in his head. "Until today," he grated.

"You never fell in love again?" Olivia's hand went up in the automatic way she had of smoothing her hair over her damaged cheek. Funny, but unless she drew attention to it, Gabe never even noticed her scar.

"No." Even now, memories of that youthful over-the-top love and the gut-wrenching pain of knowing it wasn't reciprocated burned inside. "Eve ended my dreams of love and family. I grew up fast and I gave up dreaming." The words emerged sounding bitter. But then he had a right to be bitter, even more so now.

Why didn't you tell me we have a son, Eve?

"And that's enough for you?" she asked, a frown marring her beauty.

"I have a good job with horses, which I love. I live in a great community and I get to be part of The Haven's ministry. Someday I'd like to have my own spread, but…" He shrugged. "Really, why do I need a house and land?"

"I'm sorry, Gabe." Olivia's softly voiced words offered comfort, but he wouldn't take it.

"So am I. My stupidity in marrying Eve killed my dad. I'll never forgive her for that." Why had he told Olivia that? What good did it do? Out of the corner of his eye he saw Eli standing in the doorway. Surely the boy hadn't overheard his snarky comment? "Let's go enjoy those doughnuts," he said with forced cheerfulness.

"Wait." She stepped forward to rub the dust from his cheek. "Now the twins will allow you to eat doughnuts," Olivia said with a grin.

Truth be told, Gabe wasn't sure he could swallow anything right now. What he desperately wanted was to lose himself in the forest surrounding them and read the letter that burned a hole in his shirt pocket.

Later, he promised himself grimly. He'd read Eve's paltry excuses for keeping his son a secret later.

Chapter Two

"Is Eli staying here?" Victoria asked Olivia later that afternoon.

Olivia sat on the deck beside her sister, basking in the warmth of the sun, shielded from any breeze by The Haven.

"Not that he isn't welcome," Victoria backtracked. "Everyone's welcome at The Haven. But the aunties have some guests arriving tomorrow..."

"I don't have any answers, Vic." Olivia knew her sister's frown meant she'd demand some explanation, so she relayed the events of Eli's arrival.

"Gabe's a daddy?" Victoria grinned. "Couldn't happen to a nicer guy. He's great with kids."

"Well, he sure doesn't seem to know what to do with Eli." Olivia remembered the devastated look on the cowboy's face when Eli hadn't shaken his hand. Then she remembered Eli's pitiful sob. "There's something going on with that child, though I'm not sure what that is."

Victoria's adopted son, Mikey, was playing with Francie and Franklyn on the jungle gym equipment about six feet away. Eli stood apart, watching them.

"Probably after such a loss it will take him a while to feel his way. Most kids are like that." Vic smiled at her daughter, Grace, who was learning to walk. "Don't worry. Gabe will make him feel welcome. Meanwhile, your timing in coming home couldn't be better."

"Why?" There was a note in her sister's voice that worried Olivia. "What's going on, Vic?"

"The aunts' lawyers and accountants are coming to check out everything at the end of the month, to make sure The Haven's outreach program complies with all government rules." Victoria winced. "The office is a mess, Livvie. It just isn't my gift," she defended herself when Olivia frowned. "I can never seem to get the paper under control. I've been late filing a couple of forms, too." Her head drooped.

"I'll take a look." Olivia smiled at her sister's relief. "Why didn't you hire an assistant?"

"I did. She made things worse. Triple booked us at Easter. Forgot to mention she'd confirmed four military visitors were coming when we were already full. Can you say *nightmare*?" Victoria rolled her eyes.

"I'll set up some better systems, see if that— Hey, where's he going?"

"Who?" Victoria tracked her gaze. "Gabe? He has eyes like a hawk. Probably sees something down there. Maybe I'd better take a look." She lifted Grace and stretched as if to hand her over, but Olivia didn't move. She couldn't take her niece because warning bells filled her head.

"Leave Gabe, Vic. Eli's aunt gave him a letter from his ex. I'm guessing the poor guy needs a few moments to read it and figure out what's what." Olivia couldn't stop herself from chucking the darling little girl under the chin. "Miss Grace looks like Ben."

"Good. My husband is very handsome." Vic frowned. "Still have your aversion to kids, huh, Liv?" she asked sympathetically.

"It's not an aversion. How could anyone have an aversion to this sweetheart?" Heart aching, Olivia smiled at Grace and then sighed, knowing she wasn't fooling Victoria. "It's pure fear and you know it. I'm terrified to be responsible for any kid."

"Because of what happened years ago when you babysat in those foster homes." Victoria covered Olivia's hand. "Sweetie, the kid that died in the fire—you were too young to be looking after anybody back then, and his death was an accident. The child that drowned—that didn't happen because of anything you did, either."

Vic had pried the truth of Olivia's ugly past out of her when they were fourteen.

"But I was in charge—"

"The point is, you shouldn't have been, Liv. The authorities even said so. You were a strong, competent and responsible kid, yes, but you weren't the adult in that home. Those parents were wrong to blame you. *They* should have been watching their kid *and* you *and* the pool. It wasn't fair to expect you to be in charge. The fire was an accident and it was not your fault." Vic patted her shoulder.

"Maybe. But it doesn't change anything inside my head, Vic. Caring for kids, being responsible for them still terrifies me." Olivia rose, uneasy with those awful memories and unwilling to revisit them. "It's just the way I am. Sorry." She made a face at Grace, who only giggled.

"But to keep avoiding children means this fear robs you... Livvie, don't you want to have your own children someday?"

"No!" Seeing that her sharp response had drawn frowns from the kids, Olivia smiled at them reassuringly before resuming her seat. She wasn't going to tell Vic about Martin or that she'd given up on marriage because he'd pretended he wanted to marry her even though he was already married to and living with someone else. *Betrayer.* "I just want to start my new job, prove myself and earn the things I've never had."

"Things are worth more than family?" Vic sounded disapproving.

"No, and it's not a competition. It's just—it's best for me." She shrugged, relieved to see Gabe emerge from the woods, though he wasn't alone. "Looks like he found some stragglers," she mused.

"Those two again." Victoria stood, her lips pressed tight together. "That pair has caused more than enough problems today."

"I doubt they've done anything as bad as what we did at that summer camp, before the aunties brought us here," Olivia reminded. "We four girls terrorized everyone."

"True. Think this is my payback?" With Grace in her arms, Victoria straightened her shoulders before striding forward to meet the threesome. She listened to what Gabe said, shook her head at the pair and ushered them to the meadow where they were supposed to be learning to rock climb with their group.

Olivia watched it play out, marveling at her sister's ease in handling these troubled youth. Judging by the slump of their shoulders as they walked down the path with her, the two had been strongly chastised.

"Vic's good at this job, isn't she?" Olivia murmured, her gaze now focused on Gabe. His attention seemed riveted on his son.

"Vic's like your aunts. A dragon lady lives under that big generous smile of hers." Gabe glanced at her, then back to Eli. "Any trouble?"

"With Francie and Franklyn in charge?" She rolled her eyes. "Not yet, but there will be. Did you read your letter?"

"Didn't get a chance before I found those two."

"What are you going to do about Eli?" Olivia was curious to hear his plans.

"Ask the aunts if he can stay here, I guess." He shrugged at her surprise. "I live in a bunkhouse, Olivia. There's barely room to turn around let alone fit in a kid. It never mattered before, but—"

"It does now. You need to start looking for a home." She could see the idea surprised him. "He's a little boy, Gabe. He's been pulled from the only place he knew. He needs his own home. With his father."

"What kind of a home?" He shrugged at her confused look. "I'm clueless. I've been saving for my own spread for years, but—"

"Buy it," she interrupted.

"Can't. I've never found what I want. But even if I had, I have to consider…things."

"Such as?" Why did she feel he was hesitating?

"Such as—it might be dangerous for a kid from the city to live on a ranch. Maybe a temporary place in town is better." Gabe's suddenly narrowed stare made

Olivia uncomfortable. "You wouldn't have time to help me look, would you?"

"Me?" Olivia blinked. "What do I know about finding a home for a little boy?"

"Probably more than me. It doesn't have to be right away," Gabe quickly added. "Eli could stay here for a while. Your aunts wouldn't mind. In fact, it might be better if he settled in here."

"No, it wouldn't." Olivia wasn't sure why it felt so important to get Eli into a home of his own with his father. Maybe it was because she'd sensed an inner angst in the child. Or maybe it was because at Eli's age she'd always longed to belong to someone. Or maybe it was Gabe himself.

Granted, she didn't know him well, but she'd always thought him too easygoing, too laid-back, too prepared to wait for things instead of making them happen, like staying in a bunkhouse instead of getting the spread he obviously wanted.

Kathy had said Eli was almost six. Hadn't father and son waited long enough?

"Why wouldn't it be good for him to stay here long-term?" Gabe frowned at her.

"Because though he's welcome, Eli's a visitor here. Kids need a place where they feel secure. Being shunted around, not having a permanent parent in his life, nothing to call his own—that's no way to start off your life together. That boy needs a home of his own, with you, his dad. Pronto."

"Strong feelings much?" Gabe's blue eyes twinkled. "So, you're offering to help?"

She'd fallen right into that. Olivia sighed.

"Fine. I'll help you look for a place to live, Gabe. But

that's all. I won't help you decorate it or buy furniture for it or any of that stuff." As if she had any clue as to how to make a house into a home for a cowboy and a kid. Organizing systems, creating efficiency, that was her specialty. Not helping somebody belong.

"Okay," the big cowboy agreed easily. "I can always ask salesclerks about furniture."

Oh, brother.

"This home is for you and Eli. You should make the decisions about it together. You do know I'm leaving soon, probably next week, but for sure no later than the end of June."

"When do you want to start looking? Tomorrow?" And she'd thought Gabe laid-back. "I'm off in the afternoon." He looked very eager now.

After her first glance at Eli, Olivia had wanted to help him. But she didn't do kids. Fear of the past happening again, of being responsible and failing, kept her from interacting with her own nieces and nephews. What was so different about Eli that he made her feel he needed her?

Olivia exhaled. She had no idea why this child tugged at her heart. All she knew was that she had to do what she could. And the sooner she helped Eli, the sooner she'd feel okay about leaving The Haven to get on with building her future. Alone. As usual.

Helping Gabe had nothing to do with it.

"Tomorrow afternoon is good," she agreed.

Gabe,
First, I apologize. I should have told you about Eli years ago. But you had your dad and your ranch. Eli was all I had. I guess I wanted to pun-

ish you for not making me stay with you, so I kept the two of you apart. That was stupid and selfish. All I did was cheat my son of knowing his father, someone he's asked about since he first learned to speak. I cheated you of knowing him, too, and I'm so sorry. He's a wonderful boy, Gabe. So curious, so generous. His heart is so tender. Now he's hurting, worried that I'm dying, and he'll be left all alone.

I wish I'd eaten my pride ages ago, but now it's too late. I'm too ill to come and find you. I'm in hospice and there are days I can hardly lift my head. I can barely hug Eli, so I tell him that I love him and that one day you'll come for him. I don't know where you are, Gabe, but I pray that somehow God will bring you and our child together. God is my best friend now. You're the one who first introduced us, remember? My favorite Bible verse is, "He hath made everything beautiful in His time." God will do that with you and Eli, I know it. Forget about me and how I ruined things between us and concentrate on this wonderful little boy who needs your love so badly. He needs a dad, too, and I know you'll be a great father. Love him, Gabe.

While I've been ill I had to let my sister care for Eli, but please don't leave our son with Kathy. He has a tender soul and she'll crush him, just as she did me at that age. Contact the lawyer on the card I've included. On my death you'll receive permanent custody of Eli. I so wish I would have told you this in person, but since I can't, this is from my heart. Please, I beg you, love our son.

*Even if you never forgive me, Gabe, love Eli. He
desperately needs you.*
Eve

Sitting on his bed in his bunkhouse that evening,
Gabe reread Eve's letter several times. Every time he
did, the knot of bitterness inside him wound tighter.
Simple for Eve to say she was sorry. She was gone. She
didn't have to face him; she'd never answer for what
she'd done. But he'd lost almost six years of his son's
life, six years when he could have watched Eli learn to
walk, to talk, call him Daddy, share baby kisses and
birthdays.

Forget the past. Focus on Eli, his logical brain ordered. Probably good advice, but Gabe doubted he could
ever forget or forgive Eve for what she'd done.

So now what?

Lips pursed, he folded Eve's letter and slid it back
into its envelope. He selected a new envelope and wrote
Kathy's address on it. He filled out a check, signed it
and slid it inside. Then he added a note. *Use this for
whatever you need.* A father should be responsible for
his kid's expenses. Better late than never. He sealed the
envelope and set it on a shelf, ready to mail.

Eve's letter went into a small bronze box with a lid
that Gabe snapped shut before shoving it into a drawer.
Though the letter was hidden from his sight, it felt viv-
idly alive in his seething brain.

Head and heart aching, Gabe went outside and sank
onto the step, peering into the half-lit sky. Summer
nights in the mountains never really got dark. Sunset and
sunrise would meet soon. What would tomorrow hold?

"I know the thoughts that I think toward you, saith

the Lord. Thoughts of peace and not of evil, to give you an unexpected end." That verse had been Gabe's life's motto for years.

You've known about all of this for a long time, Lord. But I'm stunned, he prayed silently. *I've tried to follow You as best I can, but—a son? I never imagined—show me the best way to win his heart. Show me how to be Eli's father, Lord.*

Gabe prayed until there were no more words left. But nervous worry, concern that he'd mess up and perhaps hurt this little boy he didn't even know, plus uncertainty about his suddenly shifting world, did not abate.

His pastor's Sunday-morning sermons last winter had been all about trusting God. Gabe had been so certain he'd been doing that. But Eli's appearance today had rocked his world and shaken his faith. Almost six years—why had Eve done it? But more importantly, why had God let her? How could he trust God now?

Because a sense of futility hung over him, Gabe shifted his thoughts toward practicalities. How would he know what kind of a place to get for Eli?

Olivia's image flickered through his brain. She didn't seem to hesitate when making decisions. Maybe he could lean on her, let her take the lead in this house-hunting business. After all, she'd grown up at The Haven, certainly the best home in the area. She'd know all the things a good home should have.

The knot inside Gabe eased. Yeah, he'd follow Olivia's lead. Could it be that's why God had brought her back at this particular time? To be a friend? To help him?

Startled by awareness that he was allowing a pretty woman he barely knew to become so involved in his personal life, in direct opposition to everything he'd resolved after Eve's departure and in the years since, Gabe's brain whirled. He'd take Olivia's help, he decided, but he would not allow anything more than friendship between them, because though she was very attractive, romance wasn't for him. Never again would he let himself be that vulnerable.

When he finally retired, sleep was elusive because Gabe knew that no matter how great Olivia was at organizing things, the fact remained that Eli was not a ranch kid. He'd even shied away from Spot and Dot, the Spenser sisters' mild-tempered dogs. What would happen when the kid met a horse?

Horses were Gabe's world.

Were. But now he had a son. With whom he had nothing in common.

"This could be doable." The following day Gabe tilted back on his cowboy boot heels, surveyed the interior of the tiny rental house he'd been told about and gulped.

"You're kidding, right?" Olivia bristled with indignation. "You and Eli would have no time to spend together because you'd be constantly repairing something."

"It's a rental, Olivia," he muttered. "*They're* supposed to look after all the maintenance."

"Looks like they're doing a bang-up job," she muttered in disgust, flicking a finger against the peeling countertop, nudging a toe against a loose floorboard and obviously struggling not to inhale the overwhelming odor of too many cats. "Come on, Eli. Let's get out of here," she muttered, and headed out the door, stumbling on the faulty step.

Gabe steadied her before following to stand beside her in the long grass outside, next to Eli, who studied the tilted bilious green house with disapproval.

"That house stinks," his son said, the first words he'd spoken since he'd climbed into Gabe's truck after lunch.

"We'll clean it out," Gabe assured him, striving for a positive tone.

"Not without removing the carpets, curtains and wallpaper, which is what I like to call a gut job." Obviously repelled, Olivia strode toward the truck. "Moving on."

So they did move on. And again, several times. After the fourth house, Gabe began to lose hope in his wobbly dream of a home for his son. Olivia found problems with every single rental they viewed. Not that the problems weren't there. They were, and Gabe knew it. But he had to find a place if he was going to keep Eli with him, if he was going to be a real father.

"Can we stop for coffee, please?" Olivia licked her lips. "I need a break."

"Sure." Gabe pulled up in front of the local diner, shoved the gearshift into Park and climbed out. He reached to help Eli, but the boy veered away from him and exited on Olivia's side. It was one of several signs that Gabe interpreted to mean his son was upset with him, though he couldn't figure out exactly why that should be.

Inside Olivia chose the best booth in the place, halfway between the entrance and the kitchen with a street view. It was like her to have automatically selected the best one, Gabe thought. She seemed to possess an inner ability that almost unconsciously prioritized every decision she made. Maybe it came from her years of working for the military.

He paused to admire her in the stream of sunshine. She looked lovely. Efficiently lovely, he corrected. Her navy slacks and coordinating navy-and-white sweater set were perfect for an afternoon of house hunting. Businesslike casual, Gabe would have termed it.

As usual, her hair covered the left side of her face to fall over the scar and tuck under her jaw. For a minute he wondered about that scar and how it had gotten there. Then her glossy dark hair recaptured his attention. On the other side of her face it entwined behind her ear revealing silver-hooped earrings, a perfect complement to the two thin silver chains around her slim neck. Her rust-brown boots looked like they'd be comfortable in whatever terrain they happened upon.

"Do you want milk to drink?" she asked Eli.

"Pop." Eli didn't seem to be requesting.

Olivia glanced at Gabe. He nodded at the server and waited until Olivia ordered coffee, then requested a cup for himself.

"And a large plate of fries, please," he added.

"You're hungry already?" Olivia's eyes stretched wide. She checked the slim silver watch on her wrist. "Lunch was only an hour ago."

"Didn't get any lunch. One of the riders decided he didn't want his lesson to end." Gabe smirked. "But Betsey didn't like it when the kid dug his heels into her side and wouldn't get off. She decided his ride was over."

"What happened?" Eli blinked as if he'd surprised himself with the question.

"Betsey, uh, let him down." Gabe winked at Eli.

"She bucked him off?" Eli's eyes grew huge.

Gabe was about to launch into a full-fledged tale of the event when Olivia cleared her throat. He glanced at her. She shook her head, just once.

"The trail riding horses at the Double M don't buck off their riders. Do they?" she asked Gabe pointedly.

"Uh, no. They're way better trained than that." Gabe smiled at the boy. "Betsey just moved against the rails and rubbed so he had to let go and slide off. But he pretended he was hurt so we had to get him checked out. That was my lunch hour."

"Oh." Eli frowned as he considered that.

"Would you like to learn to ride, Eli?" Olivia smiled as their server brought their drinks and a huge plate of golden fries.

"Uh-uh. Horses are *huge*." Eli helped himself to a fry after Gabe nudged the plate toward him. "How old were you?" he asked his father.

"When I first rode a horse?" It was the first time his son had addressed him directly. Gabe tried to conceal his pleasure and treat the question matter-of-factly. "I was raised on a ranch, Eli. My dad told me he first put me on a horse when I was two. But I don't remember that," he added lest the boy feel intimated.

This fatherhood thing was treacherous. A guy had to be so careful not to say the wrong thing. What should he say next? While he thought it over, Gabe squirted ketchup on the edge of the plate and dipped his fries into it, hoping his stomach would stop that embarrassing growling. He hid his smile when Eli copied his actions by dipping into the ketchup, too.

"Not everyone rides the full-size horses, Eli. There are miniature horses at the Double M, just your size," Gabe explained. "Francie and Franklyn like to ride them."

Eli thought that over as he ate more fries.

"What kind of things would you like in the house you live in, Eli?" Olivia's question startled Gabe, but then he figured it was probably one he should have asked himself. Maybe the kid had preferences.

"Windows." Eli popped another fry into his mouth and chewed thoughtfully. "So I can see to draw."

"You like to draw." Olivia nodded. "I see. What else would you like?"

"Grass. Mine." Eli fell silent for a moment. The sad look he gave Olivia tore at Gabe's heart. "Not just a park."

"It's not the same, is it? I lived in an apartment in Ottawa and I loved the park, but having your own yard is way better. Did your aunt have a yard?" she asked nonchalantly.

Not nonchalantly enough, Gabe figured, watching Eli's face close like a clamshell.

"No." Eli said nothing else.

And here I've lived my life surrounded by grass. I could have... Inside Gabe the nugget of bitterness toward Eve hardened.

"Too bad." Olivia sipped her coffee. "What other things would you like, Eli?"

"Nobody beside us?" Eli peeked sideways at her, as if he doubted this could be accomplished.

"You mean no neighbors?" When he nodded, she added, "You don't like neighbors?"

"Yelling."

Was it fear that made the kid's eyes so huge? Gabe wondered.

"I don't like yelling, either. What about a pet? A

cat maybe?" Olivia ignored Gabe's vigorously shaking head.

What was the woman doing? A house, a kid *and* pets? Gabe cleared his throat, but she ignored him.

"No cat," Eli said firmly.

"Okay. A dog? A horse?" she added, even though Gabe shook his head.

"A canary. I like canaries." Eli licked the ketchup off his fingers, then dug in his pocket. "Like this." His small fingers spread out a sheet of paper on the table to reveal a carefully drawn canary with even the tiny claws sketched out.

"Eli, this is beautiful." Olivia leaned nearer to study the delicate strokes. "Did you used to have a canary?"

"Aunt Kathy did. It died." The words sounded ominous.

"It's a very good drawing," Gabe said quietly. "So you like to draw birds?"

"Uh-huh." Suddenly Eli came alive. "In the house?" he said in a rushed tone.

The house, not *my* house or *our* house, Gabe noted. "Yes?"

"Could I get one of those seats in front of a window to sit and look out? An' maybe a tree?" he added wistfully. "Then when birds come an' sit in the tree, I could draw 'em. I really like drawing birds."

"We'll put that on the list." Gabe pulled out a small notebook he kept tucked in his shirt pocket. He opened it to a fresh page and dutifully noted *window seat, canary* and *tree*. "They're such small things to want," he said softly to Olivia, who was watching him.

"And such important things," she agreed with a funny smile that half mocked, half shared. Then she said briskly, "That was great coffee. Ready to start looking again, Eli?"

"'Kay." He drank the rest of his soda, ate one more ketchup-laden fry, wiped his fingers carefully on a napkin and then slid out of the booth.

After a rest stop they were back in the truck. Gabe felt a little better about this search now that Eli finally seemed interested, but everything they saw was too small or too dirty or out of his price range.

"I'm sorry," Olivia said as she watched Eli climb back into the truck. "I guess Chokecherry Hollow is such a small town that there aren't many rentals. I should have realized that. Just for curiosity sake, let's drive past the Realtor's office and see what's in the For Sale window."

"Sure." Gabe had already checked the advertisements in the huge picture windows last night, but he pulled up to the curb anyway.

"Maybe we'll see something here that will suit," Olivia murmured.

Gabe doubted that. Most all the ads were for massive spreads with fancy homes and lots of cattle, starting well above seven figures. Way beyond his means. But he would look with her because he knew Olivia well enough now to know she'd insist they leave no stone unturned in their search. Since Eli had fallen asleep, Olivia eased free of him, stepped out of the truck and quietly closed her door. Gabe did the same. They met in front of the windows.

"I had no clue ranch land sold for this much," Olivia gasped after scanning the display, obviously taken aback by the prices.

"They're big spreads. I wouldn't be able to work

at the Double M and manage so much land or cattle," Gabe told her.

"You don't want to raise your own herd?" She looked at him with those big silver-gray eyes, as if trying to fathom why he would settle for less than his own animals.

"It takes a while to build a really good herd and lots of money to cover the lean years so, no, I don't. But it's mainly because my interest has always been horses." He shrugged, adding before she could question him, "That also takes lots of cash and time to build your stock."

"I see." She turned back to survey the window once more. A long time passed before she finally faced him. "There's nothing here for us?"

Us. He liked the sound of that. As if he wasn't alone in this new and uncertain world. *But only because she's a friend*, his brain reminded.

Olivia frowned at him, waiting for a response.

Gabe simply shook his head. Together they walked to the truck. He held her door until she was inside, then gently closed it. Once he was behind the wheel again he looked at her.

"I guess that's it," he muttered.

"You're giving up already?" She glared at him, eyes shooting silver sparks. "We've only been looking for what?" She checked her watch. "Three hours. And you still need a place to live with your son. Let's go for a drive."

"A drive?" He wanted to ask why, but faced with her implacable glare, Gabe obediently shifted into gear. "Where to?"

"In the country," was her only directive.

That was fine by Gabe. He never tired of the densely

verdant rolling hills, thickets of green trees, lush meadows and rocky peaks where granite foundations thrust into the light.

"It's beautiful, isn't it?" Olivia breathed reverently. "Ottawa's lovely, too, but I never realized how much I've missed all these wide-open spaces."

"Quite a Creator we have," Gabe agreed.

"Look at that house, nestled against the hillside. It has a wonderful view."

"That's the Browns' place, Evensong. Not much more than a few acres now." Sadness crept through Gabe. "They bought a big spread five years ago to live out their retirement dream, but they've been slowly selling off bits of land to neighbors. Since Mrs. Brown got sick Art just can't handle it all and look after her."

"Mavis? Isn't that her name?" Olivia smiled at his nod. "I think the aunties mentioned this morning that she's having treatment in Edmonton."

"Yeah. Would you mind if we stopped for a few minutes? I'd like to see if there's anything Art needs help with. I think he's home today to catch up."

Relieved when Olivia nodded her agreement, Gabe pulled into the yard. He usually stopped over to check the few head of cattle grazing in the pasture and sometimes curried the last two horses the Browns owned. The house looked worse than usual in the bright sunlight. It sure could use a coat of paint. Maybe he could manage that this summer. Somehow.

After he'd figured out fatherhood.

As they pulled into the yard, Art Brown emerged from the shed carrying a gas can and a wrench. To Gabe he looked weary beyond belief.

"How are you doing?" he asked after he'd introduced Olivia. Eli was still sleeping.

"Okay. Hated to leave Mavis in Edmonton alone, but she must be close to the hospital for her treatment and I've got to tend things here. All this back and forth is wearing me out," Art admitted, heaving a sigh. "But you don't want to hear my woes. Come on inside and I'll make you a cup of coffee. Place isn't very tidy but—"

"You have the most glorious deck. Do you mind if we sit out here for a bit? Then Eli, that's Gabe's son, will see us when he wakens. And we had coffee earlier so don't go to any trouble on our account." Olivia's smile seemed to put the fatigued man at ease.

"Okay. Have a seat. Son, huh? Good for you, Gabe." Art sat down gratefully. "Thought maybe I'd mow the yard today. Sure does need it, but that beast won't start." He shook his head at the ancient green ride-on mower sitting in the long grass. "Guess it's getting old, just like me."

"Mind if I take a look?" Gabe asked. He shot Olivia a questioning glance, relieved when she nodded. "Stay here and relax," he ordered Art with a grin. "I'm better if I work alone. Or at least I'm less embarrassed when I can't figure it out."

"Join my club. Have at it." Art stretched out his legs when Gabe stepped off the deck and bent to look at the mower.

"My aunts, Tillie and Margaret, send their best wishes to you and Mavis. They're praying for both of you," Olivia said quietly. "Is there anything we can do to make things easier for you?"

"Everybody's already doing so much," the man said,

tears welling at the corners of his eyes. "Embarrassing to ask for more."

"That's what friends are for," Olivia assured him.

Gabe listened in unabashedly, liking the way Olivia deflected the man's concern.

"We'd like to help if we can, Art," she said now. "Please tell us how we can best do that."

Gabe already knew most of the issues at Evensong. He'd been trying to rectify them since the couple had left, but the list seemed to increase daily.

"I'm most worried about the house roof," the retired man admitted. "God's blessed us so far this summer and we haven't had a big deluge. But the next downpour is going to cause huge problems inside." Art hung his head, obviously ashamed he hadn't been able to fix it.

"Don't you dare go up there, Arthur." Gabe called his warning loudly, hoping the older man would heed him. "Climbing on roofs won't help that knee of yours." He glanced at Olivia, surprised to see her writing in a tiny notebook. "We'll get it done," he assured his friend with a grin while wondering, *When?*

"What else needs doing, Art?" Olivia glanced around.

"Well, the cattle and the horses are a worry, of course. Gabe's been great at taking care of them while I'm gone but we can't keep relying on him. Guess I'll have to sell them, though Mavis raised that mare from a foal and she's attached to it—"

"You know I don't mind caring for the animals, Art." Gabe fiddled with the carburetor, then flicked the starter switch. The mower sputtered momentarily but finally came to life. He let it run for a few minutes as he added gas from the nearby can. "I'm going to give it a whirl," he called to the pair on the deck.

He noticed Art start to rise, saw Olivia restrain him with a gentle hand on his arm. Then, heads bent together, the two chatted and Olivia wrote some more in her book. Gabe was curious about that book, but he concentrated on grass cutting until he saw Eli's head pop up inside the cab. Then he parked the machine, got off and went to his son.

"Ever ridden on a mower?" Gabe asked. Eyes wide, Eli shook his head. "Come on, you can ride with me while we cut this grass for my friend." He explained the rules about riding to Eli, then sat him on the back of the long seat. "Hang on to me now," he ordered, a tiny rush of pleasure surging through him when the small hands wrapped around his waist.

Just then Gabe happened to glance up. Olivia was watching them. She smiled and nodded her approval. For some reason that made him unreasonably happy, and he returned to his mowing with a light heart.

Whatever You have in store for me, God, I thank You for my son and for a friend like Olivia. Underneath that reserve, she's got a good heart.

Chapter Three

Back at The Haven, Gabe accepted Tillie and Margaret's invitation for supper. He always enjoyed the camaraderie around their table and envied the easy pleasure this family took in being together, welcoming whomever joined them. Tonight Gabe especially enjoyed how Eli seemed to relax and even laugh with Victoria and Ben's adopted son, Mikey, who was about the same age. Yet Eli still avoided his father, which bugged Gabe no end.

"Where's Francie and Franklyn?" Eli asked.

"At home on the Double M where they live. Saturday night is pizza night at their house. Then they go on a family ride. Francie and Franklyn ride their miniature horses, and Adele and Mac ride on the big horses." Victoria glanced from Olivia to Gabe. "What did you three do today?"

Gabe let Olivia explain about their house search and the subsequent visit to Art.

"There are one or two ways we could help there, aunties," she ended quietly.

"We'd love that. Art and Mavis have become very

dear souls in our community. Tell us what they need, Livvie," Tillie demanded, leaning forward.

Victoria got the boys busy with a board game while Olivia consulted her notes and then spoke, astounding Gabe with her perception and quick assessment of the situation.

"Eli needed the bathroom so I took him inside Art's house and noticed the house needs a cleaning. With all the outside work, I don't suppose Art's had much time or energy. When Mavis comes home, I'm sure cleaning will be the last thing on her mind as she recuperates."

"We'll have a cleaning bee. We love bees, but our ladies' group hasn't had one in forever." Tillie beamed. "We'll go Monday morning. I know Art plans on returning to Edmonton tomorrow, so we won't upset his plans. Done."

"Next?" Margaret, not to be outdone by her sister's enthusiasm, waited impatiently.

"Well." Olivia glanced at Gabe as if to ask his opinion.

"You're doing fine," he assured her.

"It's just—" She glanced at her list, then around the table. "The way Art spoke about Mavis and their stay in the city made me think neither of them are eating properly. I doubt if she's well enough to cook and he said he can't, so perhaps a few frozen meals would be in order?"

"Adele has plenty of them in the freezer. Tillie and I will deliver some this evening. Art can take them with him to Edmonton." Margaret smiled. "Good thinking, Livvie." The Spenser sisters smiled at each other, but those smiles faded when Olivia cleared her throat.

"I wasn't finished." Her cheeks pinked when everyone looked at her in surprise. "The place needs a second work bee."

"For?" Margaret was busily making her own list.

"The outside. Art mentioned the roof leaks. Gabe warned him to stay off the roof because of his knee, but apparently it must be fixed before the next rain or considerable damage will occur inside." Olivia looked around the table. "Their hardwood floors are lovely. It would be a shame for rain leaks to ruin them."

Gabe had noticed those gorgeous floors many times, but he hadn't given a thought to their shape if a leaky roof damaged them. Full marks to Olivia the organizer.

"Our men's group from the church can reroof the house. We have the cash to pay for it and we've been looking for a way to use those funds locally." Ben, Victoria's husband, mused aloud. "It's not a large house so it shouldn't take long. I'll ask the guys, see if Tuesday works."

"That's more than generous." Olivia noted his offer in her book before inhaling. "Then there's the painting," she added in a rush.

"Painting?" Tillie leaned forward. "Inside, you mean?"

"It could certainly use a refresh inside, but I was thinking more of the outside. The siding is peeling and looks so shabby. It would be disheartening for Mavis to come home to."

"I've been meaning to paint the house," Gabe admitted, "but I never gave a thought to Mavis's feelings." He smiled at Olivia. "Your perceptions intrigue me."

"I like organizing things in a way that makes sense to those who'll be using them." She shrugged. "It's what I do—did. Will do, in my new job."

"It's what she's doing in our office and she's amazing," Vic praised. "I never dreamed bookings at The Haven could be so easy. My phone is now linked with our system. It doesn't matter if I'm out, I can still see our openings at a glance. You have a gift, Liv, one God blessed you with abundantly. I wish He'd given me just a little of it."

"He blessed you with other things," Olivia said with a quick glance at Victoria's husband and daughter.

"Yes, He has. Is that everything on your list, Olivia?" Ben asked.

Gabe noticed Olivia's face redden before she ducked her head to consult her notes once again.

"There's more," he guessed with a wry smile.

"I do have a few other suggestions," Olivia admitted, looking embarrassed.

"Such as?" Gabe couldn't stop gazing at her, admiring the glistening fall of her dark hair against her newly sun-kissed cheek. "Hit us with them, Olivia."

"It's just—I wondered if it would be possible to get some roses planted at the corner of the deck. Art said Mavis used to have some there and she loved them, but what hasn't been winter-killed has been eaten by deer." She tugged out a small sheet of paper and laid it on the table. "Maybe something like this? Eli drew it for me."

"Eli drew this?" Gabe stared at the perfectly shaped rosebuds on a rosebush and the scattered shorter flowers beneath the bush that hugged the deck post. An almost invisible fence protected the flowers and, of course, birds fluttered nearby.

Gabe knew zip about art, but he recognized that his son was talented. How was he supposed to nurture that here, far away from teachers and special schools that knew how to encourage artistic stuff? Had Eve done anything about Eli's talent?

This fatherhood thing—he'd ask Olivia's advice. Again.

"We know the very person to create a lovely garden." Tillie studied the paper. "May we take this, Liv?"

"If Eli agrees," Olivia said, and asked the little boy.

"It's okay. I can draw more," Eli said. "I like drawin'. 'Specially birds."

"Thank you, dear. Our Jake is the most wonderful handyman we could ask for, but he's an absolute master at gardening. His specialty is roses. This would be the perfect project for him to show off his gift." Margaret leaned closer, peering through her bifocals. "You're very talented, Eli."

Eli shrugged and went back to playing.

"When the house gets painted, it might be nice to give the outbuildings a coat, also," Olivia murmured. "That way when they arrive home—Art said perhaps in two weeks—everything will look fresh and welcoming."

"We have a credit with the local painter. We'll ask him to paint the house," Aunt Tillie declared.

"Yes," Margaret agreed. "But I doubt our credit will cover more than the house."

"I'll paint the outbuildings," Gabe said, thrilled that his friends would be so well cared for.

"But you're already looking after Art's livestock. And you have Eli." Olivia frowned. "How are you going to have time for all this?"

Gabe didn't stop to think it over. He wasn't even sure where the idea came from. He only knew he liked it. A lot.

"Eli's going to help me," he announced. "We're going to paint those buildings together. Right, Eli?"

Eli blinked. He set down his game piece, thought for a moment then shrugged. "'Kay."

"Great." Olivia's smile was something to behold. It made her eyes sparkle. She glowed so much Gabe couldn't stop gawking at her. "Then the only thing left on my list is to find you and Eli a home."

. "We need to pray on that," Tillie said firmly.

"Yes. God has a plan. That's why he sent Olivia and Eli to us." Margaret folded her hands. "Now we must discover that plan. Let's pray."

Gabe closed his eyes, but truthfully he didn't hear much of the aunties' prayers. He was too busy thinking about how Olivia fit in so perfectly with The Haven's ministries. Victoria certainly seemed delighted with her help, and in one afternoon she'd set things in motion that he'd struggled with for months.

How sad that she'd be leaving soon.

"How goes the search for a home for Eli and Gabe?" Victoria asked the following Thursday as she strolled into the office. She stopped, gulped. "What a mess!"

"The house search does not go well," Olivia said from her sitting position on the floor. "This mess is your old system of filing bills. But by tomorrow you'll be doing things differently and much more neatly."

"Okay." Victoria crunched on her apple as she watched her sister sift through the mass of files. "Did you take a call from social services about a weekend in July?"

"Yes."

"And they booked it?" Victoria asked, frowning when Olivia didn't immediately answer. "Liv?"

"I talked them out of it."

"You did what? Why?" Victoria's easygoing manner disappeared. "Olivia, the whole summer schedule revolves around—"

"That's the problem. It shouldn't." Olivia exhaled and rose, ready to calm her frustrated foster sister.

"But we—Olivia!" Vic exploded, staring across the office. "My wall. My charts. Everything's gone. What are you doing?"

"Making it better. I took your stuff down and painted this wall with chalkboard paint. When it's fully dry I'm going to draw a year's worth of calendars and mark in the bookings. Here's an idea of what it'll look like." She tapped the computer and a calendar appeared.

Victoria looked, frowned, but said nothing.

"See how you were always losing Friday night between groups? But everybody wants that night to start the weekend, right?" Olivia was so excited she barely waited for her Victoria's nod. "If we check out one group Friday morning and check in the next one that afternoon, the cabins don't stay idle overnight. You can accommodate more kids."

"But then I won't get a break and we'll have even less time to clean the cabins." Victoria's frustration was evident in her tone. "I need those few hours off, Liv, to spend with my kids and my husband."

"You need more than a few hours per week. That's why I've fitted in full days off for you." Olivia showed her the days marked in pink. "And you won't be cleaning the cabins, Vic."

"I won't?"

"Uh-uh. Each camping group and counselor will be responsible to clean their own cabin." Delighted with her plan, Olivia explained, "We'll have a contest and award prizes so they'll be eager to do a good job. One of your staff can do the final checkout."

"But who will handle the guests when I'm off?" Victoria's tone grew thoughtful.

"Again—your staff. They should all know how to deal with stuff like that anyway. You're the director, Vic, not the do-it-all girl." She grinned. "Another thing. We're going to change up the schedule so that everybody gets an occasional weekend off."

"Then we'll have to hire, train and house even more staff." Vic sighed. "Livvie, I know you mean well, but this is going to be expensive and cause so much more work for me—"

"No, it's going to streamline things so that you don't have to work so hard. Trust me, Vic. This will work." Olivia tamped down her frustration at her sister's dubious expression. Didn't Victoria realize that she knew what she was doing, that she'd handled far bigger and more complex scheduling issues than this? "I need you to call a staff meeting for this afternoon so I can explain how things are going to change. Is two o'clock okay?"

"Yes. But if this doesn't work, it's on you, Liv," Victoria warned. "You'll have to stay and pitch in. I can't take on any more."

"I know that. You're doing too much now, and you're worn-out. My schedule will fix that," Olivia reassured her gently. "Isn't that why you asked for my help? Please, trust me."

"I'll try." Clearly still troubled, Vic left.

Trust me. Such an easy thing to ask for, Olivia thought. She used the words over and over each night at Eli's bedtime, trying to encourage him to talk about his past. But the child had yet to divulge details. His words from that first day still troubled her.

I prayed and prayed and he never came.

Why had Eli been praying for his father to come for him? What had his life with his mom, his aunt and her children been like?

Those questions whirled around without answers until Olivia finally forced them from her mind. She finished entering everything on the chalkboard, then checked and double-checked her work before deciding to take a break. It was lunchtime and she was starving. She strolled to the patio where Adele was busy grilling a picnic lunch. Olivia's stupid heart rate sped up to double time when Gabe sauntered up.

"Hi, there." He threw her that lazy-cowboy, knee-knocking smile of his and reached up to rub something from her scarred cheek.

Olivia jerked away, shifting her head so her hair covered the scar.

"Sorry. You had some blue chalk there." His smile didn't alter, which allowed her to relax a little. "Are you able to go house hunting this afternoon? I have a lead—"

"Victoria and I have a staff meeting at two o'clock," Olivia explained. "It should take about half an hour." Funny how much she wanted to go with him to look for a house. Why did it matter to her where Gabe lived?

For Eli's sake, she told herself. Her brain scoffed. *Eli. Right.*

"Meaning you'll be free after two thirty?" Gabe smiled at her nod. "Good." He stood there, studying her.

"What?" she demanded, suddenly uncomfortable.

"You know you want to ask," Gabe shot back with a smirk.

"Oh, brother." Olivia rolled her eyes. "Okay, the aunts say everything else is progressing well, so how's Eli doing with his painting on Art's outbuildings?" Truthfully? She was very curious, especially now because Gabe had insisted she see nothing until they were finished the entire job.

"Doing well." He burst out laughing at her disgust. "Patience isn't your strong suit, is it, Olivia?"

"Usually I'm a very patient person," she insisted. "You have to be when you work with logistics. It must be your effect on me."

"Sure," Gabe said.

Ignoring his amused chuckle, Olivia turned her back and sauntered toward the picnic table to fetch herself a hamburger. It didn't seem as if Adele had an overabundance of cooked burgers ready for the growing crowd of kids. She'd just selected a charred burger, intending to eat only the center when a long arm reached around her and replaced her meat patty with a less burnt one.

"What are you doing?" she demanded, whirling to glare at Gabe. "I like well-done burgers."

"That one passed well-done and moved into the 'ash' category a while ago. It's inedible." His grin somehow made her day brighter. "Mustard?"

"No, thanks. I prefer relish on my burgers." She moved her plate when he offered a scoop of raw onions. "No, thank you."

"Your loss." Gabe selected a serving of every single condiment offered, added a bag of chips and a glass of lemonade before following her to a grassy spot in the shade under a tree where Eli was eating with Mikey.

"Olivia, did anyone ever tell you you're not very adventurous?" Gabe asked in a mocking tone.

"No," she assured him, hiding her smile when he bit into one of the hot peppers her sister always served.

Gabe's eyes stretched wide. He stopped chewing, gulped, then grabbed his drink and downed the entire contents.

"Mostly people compliment me on avoiding the pitfalls of taking chances," she said smugly before holding out her own untouched glass. "Go ahead."

Gabe didn't refuse, simply took her glass and emptied it. She calmly ate her hamburger while he regained his breath. Then he carefully set aside the rest of the pepper. Finally, voice hoarse, he spoke.

"I still say you miss out on all the fun parts."

"Like you just did?" Olivia giggled. "Some things are missable, Gabe. Like Adele's ultrahot peppers. Is your painting going well, Eli?"

The child managed to utter about three words before Gabe reminded him that the painting was supposed to be a surprise. Eli shrugged at Olivia before returning to his lunch and Mikey's explanation about monster trucks.

"Good try," Gabe murmured. "Plying innocent kids with questions isn't very nice."

"Why is it such a secret? It's just an outbuilding." Frustrated by his refusal to tell her anything, Olivia huffed a sigh and concentrated on her lunch.

"Your strong suit is patience, huh?" Gabe laughed, then finished his hamburger. "Can I ask you a question?"

"Plying me with questions isn't nice, either," she shot

back, surprised to find she enjoyed verbally sparring with him. "But you will anyway."

"Why don't you like to try new things?" Gabe set aside his empty plate and leaned back on his elbows.

"I am trying new things. I'm starting a new job in a new city, finding a new home and learning new skills. You're the one stuck in a bunkhouse, remember?" She shouldn't have said that, but Olivia knew exactly where his questions were leading. And she didn't like it.

"You've helped a lot with the program here. Don't you want to stay at The Haven and be part of the foster kids' ministry?" Gabe pressed curiously.

"I don't belong here. I'm only staying long enough to streamline things for Vic. When I'm finished, I'll go." She crunched on her chips as she surveyed the groups of kids chattering around them. "I'm not good with children, Gabe."

"Not true," he asserted. "You're very good with Eli." They watched as Eli and Mikey ran off.

"Not really. Eli's mostly self-sufficient. He doesn't tell me much. When we're alone together he doesn't talk about whatever's bothering him, and though I've tried, I haven't been able to elicit any information about his former circumstances."

"Me, neither," Gabe said glumly.

"You will." Olivia shrugged. "But kids and I just don't mesh. Never have."

"I think you could, but you won't let yourself unbend enough to get close to them." Gabe's blue eyes narrowed as he studied her. "I can't help wonder why that is when you're so competent at everything else."

"You know I'm competent how? Because you've seen my fabulous sewing and cooking skills? As if!" She hooted with laughter, hoping to divert him. "You don't know that much about me, Gabe."

"I know some," he defended. "Your aunts told me you took a nothing job in the military and turned it into an example for other administrative assistants. I know the colonel you worked for was so impressed with your work that he signed off on you taking a bunch of courses that others were not offered. I know you were awarded several service honors and that you set up two other offices—"

"Enough. Let's agree that the aunts told you some stuff about what I do. Did." Olivia looked directly into his eyes. "Now add this to your knowledge. I freeze up around kids. I do stupid things and sometimes they get hurt. I'm lousy with responsibility for children so I avoid them. That way they don't get hurt." Irritated, she glared at him. "Can we drop it now?"

"For now." He grinned. "What kind of houses do you think we'll find this time?"

"I already know." She smiled triumphantly. "I've done some research."

"Ah, so you were intending to go house hunting with me again." He looked a little too pleased with himself.

"I was hoping you'd locate something you'd consider buying so Eli could have a home," she corrected. There was something about this cowboy with his pretense of slow-wittedness that annoyed Olivia no end because she knew Gabe was smart as a whip. "As I've said before, that kid needs his own home. And I need to get to work if I'm going to be able to leave with you after the meeting. Excuse me."

She rose and walked toward The Haven, fully aware that Gabe's blue eyes followed her and eager to escape that pensive stare. But the aunties stopped her before she could enter the office.

"Livvie, dear, we fear we may have bragged on you a little too much with Gabe," Tillie said, looping her arm through Olivia's.

"It's just that we're so proud of you. But, well..." Margaret's voice dropped away.

"We know you like your privacy," Tillie finished.

"Yes, I did prefer that when I was with the military. And Gabe's just informed me of all the details you shared." She smiled at their worried looks. "Don't worry, Aunties. It's fine. But, please, don't tell him anything more, okay?"

"Why not?" Margaret frowned. "If he already knows most—"

"A girl should have some secrets." The moment she said it, Olivia wished she hadn't. Her aunts glanced at each other, speculative looks filling their faces. Looks Olivia knew too well. "Not that it matters one little bit," she quickly backtracked. "There is no relationship between us. I don't know Gabe very well and—"

"Not to worry, dearie. You'll get to know him a lot better now that you're home. Meantime, your secrets are safe with us." Tillie made a zipping-the-lip motion and winked.

"So, you're going house shopping—with this man you hardly know? How exciting." Margaret chuckled aloud as Olivia rolled her eyes. "We do love having you girls back with us at The Haven. It's such fun."

"I'm only home for a short while, remember. I can't stay." Given her aunts' glazed expressions, Olivia could only hope her cautioning words sank in.

"We know that's what you *said*, dear. Later." Tillie

looped her arm in Margaret's and the two strolled away, whispering and giggling like girls.

"Olivia, you need to learn to shut up," she scolded herself. To enforce the words, she closed the office door and forced herself to concentrate on finishing the schedule plan. She intended to hand it out at the meeting later.

But it wasn't that easy to muffle the giddiness that burbled inside when she thought about the upcoming house hunt with Gabe. He was going to be so surprised.

Something was up.

After a quick glance at Olivia's face, Gabe took the back road as directed. She looked smug, too satisfied with herself.

"This track leaves something to be desired," he muttered as his truck almost bottomed out on the ruts.

"Once you're living here I'm sure the county will maintain the road." Olivia pressed her lips together firmly, stifling her smile.

Definitely something up, Gabe decided.

"Turn left here."

He obediently turned, rounding a huge grove of massive spruce trees. His foot fell off the gas pedal.

"Isn't it gorgeous?" Olivia whispered. "Forty acres. On the crest of the hill, protected against the north winds, facing south so you get the best light—well?" She studied his face eagerly.

Gabe parked, got out of the truck and soaked in the view. Green rolling hills undulated all around, perfect for a few horses to graze in. Trees, deciduous and evergreen, lay scattered in bunches here and there, offering shade. A small river dissected the land on the lowest level. Outcroppings of granite rock someone had piled here and there added to the variety of the scene.

"Outbuildings?" he managed to croak, shocked that he hadn't known about this lovely piece of land. "House?"

"There's a barn there." She pointed.

The reserve in her voice made Gabe study Olivia's face.

"Needs work," he grunted after a quick appraising glance. "And the house—" Words failed him at the sight of a burned-out black skeleton of what might once have been a two-story home. "Talk about a fixer-upper." Gabe frowned at her. "You were the one who said I need time with Eli. If I bought this place I'd spend ages building a house and we couldn't live here in the meantime, so—"

"That's the beauty of my plan." Olivia looked anything but defeated. "You don't have to."

"Good thing Eli didn't come," Gabe muttered, squinting at the charred ruins. "The kid would be terrified imagining living in that horror house. So am I."

"It's a teardown for sure." Olivia grinned as if that was perfect. "Come on. Let's take a closer look and I'll explain."

"This had better be good," he warned, slightly annoyed that they'd wasted time driving here.

"Oh, Gabe, it's very good." She stood in the sunshine, eyes sparkling, trim and neat in her jeans and red cotton shirt, looking as if she belonged on this land. "Look around. The ranch part is perfect, right?"

"Yes, but—"

"Great, we agree on the land. And the price?" She named a figure that made him blink.

"That can't be—"

"It's correct." She grinned, obviously delighted with her find. And why not? The setting was gorgeous.

"Great. Except for the house," he muttered.

"True. But what if you moved in a house, one that's mostly completed?" The silver sparkle in Olivia's gray eyes transmitted her enthusiasm. "A ready-to-move house."

"An RTM?" Gabe struggled to visualize it.

"It wouldn't be hard to move one onto the foundation once that road was taken care of." She held up a hand, forestalling his next comment. "RTMs aren't prohibitive costwise and they're well built. In fact, I got the idea from the aunts when they mentioned a man in the congregation who builds them. Apparently, he's trying to cut down on his stock to get some cash flow. Here, look at these."

Gabe stepped forward to look at the tablet she'd lifted from her purse.

"I chose two different styles that I thought might suit what Eli wants and what you need. Eighteen hundred square feet in the first house and twenty-five hundred in the second." She pointed out a variety of features in each, ending with, "Both have a big wall of windows that would overlook the valley and that magnificent view."

The cost was printed beneath each house.

"Affordable, right?" Olivia shrugged at his raised eyebrows.

"How—?"

"I did some research." She grinned. "It's what I do."

"Very well done, too." Gabe couldn't believe she'd gone to all this trouble for him. And Eli.

"The price may be negotiable if inventory is high," she suggested as if she knew his focus was on the price and whether he could swing it.

In the end, Gabe didn't get fixated on the money side of it. He grew entranced by the acres of land, virtually isolated, with not one single neighbor in view. In his brain a dream was forming of what he could create here, with Eli.

"Is this anything like what you wanted, Gabe?" Olivia murmured.

"Yes." Except that he hadn't known he wanted it so badly, hadn't known he'd ever be able to find something as special as this property. He faced Olivia. "Thank you," he murmured.

"You'll buy it?" she asked eagerly.

"I don't know. It's something to think about." Gabe watched her excitement fade. "What's wrong?"

"A beautiful piece of land like this isn't going to last," she said quietly. "Once it goes on the market, it will be snapped up in a minute."

"How did *you* find out about it?" he asked curiously.

"The aunts. They'd been visiting the fellow who owned this place. He moved into the nursing home in Chokecherry Hollow after the fire ruined his house. That's why the remains of the building haven't been cleaned up." As Olivia gazed into the valley, the sun highlighted her face. "He passed away last week. Tillie and Margaret talked to his only son, Edward, at the funeral. They learned he wants his father's estate settled immediately. Edward lives in Australia. He wants to get home to his family and his business. This is his phone number." She handed him a card with a number printed neatly on it. "I'm guessing this place will be listed before the end of the week. If you want it, you need to call immediately, Gabe."

"I have to think about it," he protested. "I can't just buy this place on the spur of the moment."

"Why not, if it's what you want and you feel it's a good price?" She gazed at him, utterly unaware that the wind had mussed her hair and left her scar revealed.

Not that it mattered to Gabe. He thought Olivia one of the most beautiful women he'd ever seen, elegant, sophisticated, talented and very clever. What he didn't get was why she wasn't married, or at least engaged. She must have had plenty of chances while working with the military.

"Gabe?" Her soft voice broke through his musings.

"I understand what you're saying." He struggled to gather his thoughts. "I'm still going to need a bit of time to think this over, check into some details."

"Of course," she agreed, walking back toward the truck with him. "But, Gabe?"

"Yeah?" He had to tamp down his reaction to the intensity of her expression as she studied him.

"Don't wait too long. Eli needs a home. So do you." She walked away.

Olivia thought he was needy? Or indecisive? He didn't like that. Not at all.

Gabe double stepped until he caught up to her at the truck.

"Have you got a few extra minutes?" he asked as they drove away.

"To do what?"

"Might as well take a look at those houses." He shrugged. "We'll detour through town on the way back to The Haven."

"Now you're talking," Olivia cheered. "Onward to the RTM builder."

"I wonder what Eli would think of the place," he mused.

"There's certainly a lot of grass." She winked at him, ticking it off on her slim fingers. "No neighbors to yell. He'd be able to have his tree wherever he wanted it. And he could even raise canaries if you made him a cage."

Gabe figured her delight was worth the effort of quashing his inhibitions about moving forward so fast.

Who knew organizing, scheduling, bossy Olivia would be the one to help him make a home for his son?

For the first time in years, Gabe was anticipating the future.

Chapter Four

Oblivious to the beauty from her favorite perch overlooking the gorgeous valley spread below her, Olivia tapped her phone several times, trying to make it come on. Finally the calendar flashed on screen. She stared at it in disbelief.

That couldn't be right. She'd now been at The Haven almost two weeks? That was well past her self-imposed deadline.

She studied the snowcapped mountains to her left. The days had flown past in a rush of activities and she'd loved every minute of being here. But she was getting too involved, and not just with The Haven's outreach to foster kids. Her heart ached for the quiet, solemn little boy who'd shown up the same day she had.

"Why the frown?" a voice behind her asked. "Phone out again?"

"For such a tall man, it's amazing how you creep up on people, Gabe," she snapped, startled by his sudden appearance.

"I *do not* creep." The cowboy's blue gaze narrowed. "I don't think I've ever heard you cranky, Olivia. Something must be wrong." He sank onto the grassy knoll beside her and, after a quick study of her face, turned his gaze on the lushly forested valley below them. "Want to share?"

"No. Thanks." She turned the question on him, so she wouldn't have to explain her sudden inexplicable yen to stay here. "Did you buy that land yet?" One look at his face said everything. "Gabe! It'll probably be listed soon, if it isn't already." Understanding dawned. "You couldn't get funding," she murmured sadly.

"The money's in place." He stretched out, legs in front, leaning back on his elbows to support his upper body. He looked completely relaxed. "That's not the issue."

"Then what is? Won't Edward sell it to you?" Reasons for his failure to act multiplied in her head. "Has he changed his mind about selling?"

"Nothing like that." Gabe's slow drawl, something Olivia usually enjoyed, suddenly irritated her.

"Then why in the world haven't you bought it?" she demanded.

"Because I'm not sure that's the right thing for Eli."

Gabe's soft-voiced response killed her irritation. This man was acting like a responsible father, putting his son's welfare first. How could she fault that?

"What specifically are you worried about?" she asked quietly.

"I work long hours at the Double M, Olivia. That won't change if I intend to keep my job, and I do." Gabe's pensive tone told her he'd given a lot of thought to this change. "I'd probably have to hire a housekeeper to maintain the house anyway, but I'd also want whoever that is to watch Eli until I get home. It's a lot of time for a kid to be alone."

"Or he could take the after-school bus with Adele and Vic's kids here to The Haven," Olivia mused aloud. "My sisters hired an after-school sitter who watches over the kids and plays with them until five or so. Maybe you could chip in for her pay and Eli could wait here for you to finish work," she proposed.

"It's an idea." He thought about it for a few minutes. "Probably better than him being at our home, or what could be our home."

"What makes you say that?" She couldn't understand the comment.

"Olivia, Eli has never lived in such an isolated place."

"But he said he wanted no neighbors," she protested, thinking she should have put more research into after-school care for kids, though she'd been very busy reorganizing the office and the schedule and a myriad of other details that had cropped up. "He wanted grass," she remembered.

"Eli can have all the grass he wants." Gabe laughed, then quickly sobered. "The rest—I'm not so sure. In theory, having no neighbors sounds great. Until you're alone and the coyotes are howling, or a blizzard is blowing in." Gabe shook his head. "Scary, especially if you're a little kid."

"You've really considered the angles," she said, unable to mask her admiration. "Good for you, Dad."

A tinge of red colored Gabe's jutting cheekbones before he tilted his Stetson down, which meant she couldn't read his expression.

"It's my job. I'm responsible for Eli now. I'm all he has. I want him to have a home, but most of all, I want him to be happy." His voice changed, grew sadder. "I don't think the kid had much of a life before Eve got sick, let alone after. I'm only guessing that since Eli hardly says a word, but a couple of his comments make me think somebody bullied him."

"I've wondered that, too." Olivia reached out and squeezed his hand in commiseration. "But that's the past. He's here now, Gabe, and you're not going to let that happen again. Eli's going to be very happy here. Especially when you get into your new home. *If* you get into it," she added with emphasis.

"Maybe." His dithering drove her crazy.

"You've come to The Haven every night to have dinner with him, to read him a bedtime story and say goodnight. That's all good," she said, nodding. "But it doesn't make The Haven Eli's home."

"No, it doesn't. And it doesn't make me his father, either. That's clear because he always asks you to listen to his prayers, even though I'm sitting right beside him." Gabe's face was a picture of hurt and confusion. "That's another reason I'm hesitating. I'm hoping that with a little time he'll get more used to me."

"Or maybe he'll get so used to staying at The Haven that it will become his home, instead of one you both live in together—eventually. Time will only make it harder when you move him." Olivia shook her head. "I doubt that's what you want, Gabe."

"What I want is for Eli to be happy." The low-voiced comment made her pay attention. "Even if it isn't with me," he added.

Mentally, Olivia cheered that Gabe was willing to deny himself for his son. He was going to be a great dad. But she also wanted him to be practical.

"That is all very selfless, until you remember the day Kathy dropped him off." Olivia couldn't explain why she felt compelled to help father and son bond. She only knew they couldn't—wouldn't—do that when they were mostly apart. "Eli said he *prayed* you'd come, Gabe," she reminded softly. "That doesn't sound like he doesn't want his dad. The two of you just need your own place and time alone together to figure out how to mesh."

"You make it sound like a marriage," he grumbled. "Bad comparison."

"Not all marriages are bad, Gabe." Olivia giggled at his glower.

"I've been told," he shot back, face grim. "But mine was bad enough that I'm not going to repeat the experience."

"I feel the same about marriage myself, though I never actually made it to the altar," Olivia agreed, then wished that hadn't slipped out.

Gabe sat up. "Why didn't you? Make it there, I mean?"

There it was, the question she'd been avoiding. She unclenched her jaw.

"Because I could never marry a liar."

"What did he lie about?" Brows pleating, the cowboy dad studied her.

"Everything. His love, me being beautiful, a future together. Most importantly about already being married. That kind of turned me off matrimony." She met his gaze and shrugged. "Doesn't matter now. It's over, finished, in the past. I do *not* want to talk about him or remember my stupidity in being so gullible that I believed every lie he spoke."

"I don't think it was a lie to say you're beautiful,

Olivia." Gabe's soft voice and gentle smile reached inside her and warmed a cold, hard place, but his words made her furious.

"You think this is beautiful," she demanded, pushing her hair off her cheek so her scar was on full display.

"It's a scar, sure." Gabe didn't flinch or turn away. In fact, he looked totally blasé. "I've got a few of my own. That's the cost of living. Visible or not, Olivia, everyone has scars."

"The point is, it's not beautiful," she muttered, half to herself. "And Martin didn't love me. He couldn't have."

"Why not?" Gabe was not going to let this go. She wished she'd never brought up the subject. "Olivia?" he pressed when she didn't answer.

"Because he was already married," she blurted. "He has two children. Can you believe I didn't know that, didn't guess?" Disgusted with herself, she tightened her arms around her knees. "Olivia, the great organizational expert, didn't have a clue she was being duped until her boss told her the ugly truth."

"Was Martin unhappy at home or something?" Gabe asked.

"Who cares? He was still living there, *with his wife and family.*" She blinked fast and furiously to suppress the tears. "Anyway, it didn't matter."

"Why not?"

"Because even if he'd got a divorce, I wouldn't have anything to do with him. I never want to be the cause of a family breakup. Besides that, I would never be first in his life. I don't want to be someone's second best." She glared at him. "Don't you dare say a word about this to anyone, Gabe Webber. It's not for public consumption."

"Of course not." His moue of disdain somehow made

her feel better. "What a pair we are with our terrible taste in the romance department."

They were a pair?

"Back to the point," Olivia said after a moment, uncomfortable with the picture his words drew in her brain. "I still believe you and Eli need to get into your own place as soon as possible."

She hesitated, wanting to say more. But to do so meant she'd risk offending Gabe. And yet, maybe it was worth it if it would get this cowboy and his son to begin bonding.

"You know, it's none of my business, but I was thinking. Maybe part of what went wrong between you and Eve," she began tentatively, not liking the way his whole face tightened, "was not being alone together. Maybe if there'd been just the two of you, you'd have been forced to work things out."

"You're wrong," Gabe said flatly. "Lack of togetherness isn't what went wrong with my marriage. Our failure wasn't due to my father's presence. He never interfered. In fact, he made it a point to be away most evenings. Actually, so did Eve." His face tightened; his lips pinched together. "I told you—all she wanted was good times and money. Period."

Olivia sighed. Gabe sounded so bitter, so hostile when he spoke about Eve. That couldn't help with his attempts to bond with Eli.

"Are you thinking it was a hardship for Eve to live on our ranch?" he snarled a moment later. "It wasn't. My father did very well. We had a huge house, several vehicles, everything we needed."

She waited, somehow knowing he wanted to vent.

"Married to me, Eve had a respected name in the

community, a nice home, somebody who loved her like a fool," he added, blue eyes blazing. "She threw it away for money, money my dad gave her, so I could be free of her. It was my fault he died. I married her against his wishes and he paid for it."

"Oh, Gabe." Olivia's heart ached for the young man who'd been so disillusioned by love and was still hurting. Not that she'd done much better. But at least she'd been able to write off Martin's pretense of loving her and move on to embrace a new life.

Have you really?

"I do not want to talk about Eve." Cold and hard, the words seemed dragged from him.

"Me, neither. Let's talk about Eli." Olivia squared her shoulders and faced facts, as she always did when dealing with a problem. "Have you watched him with the other kids? He never just grabs a toy and joins in with them. He always waits until all the toys have been chosen, and then he picks up one and tries to amuse himself with it."

"So?" Gabe arched an eyebrow.

Lord, help me say this so it helps him. Olivia inhaled and let the words flow.

"So, I know exactly what that's like. Every single foster home I was ever in gave me the same feeling," she said as grim memories assailed her. "It wasn't always that someone was mean to me or wouldn't let me use the toys. It was mostly that I didn't feel like anything was mine, that I had a right to play with their stuff."

"Why did you feel like that?"

"I guess because it wasn't my home and they weren't my things. Because no matter what anyone told me, I knew I didn't belong there." She paused. "I wonder if Eli feels the same?"

"He'll get over that once he gets used to everyone here," Gabe said with a shrug.

"Not necessarily."

"Why not?"

To explain she had to tell him a little more about her past.

"I didn't. I went through the motions of living here at The Haven, but it wasn't my home. My foster aunties tried to help me understand that no one was going to come and take me away. That I could stay here, that I could let myself love them and my sisters." Frustrated that Gabe hadn't seemed to notice his son's aloof behavior, Olivia struggled to gain his understanding. "Aunt Tillie and Aunt Margaret kept at it, and I did finally relax, but sometimes I still don't feel like I belong here, that The Haven is my home."

"You're saying Eli needs ownership of where he lives."

"Yes." She exhaled. "Once he's at home, other kids can come over and he can be the one to say, 'Play with anything you want. It's my stuff and I don't mind sharing.' That's when he'll gain confidence." Olivia hadn't thought about it for eons, but suddenly the feeling of not belonging anywhere returned full force. Where did she belong now?

"I'm not sure—" Gabe's nose wrinkled, showing his disbelief.

"I was left at a hospital as a baby. I never knew my parents, never knew where I came from or where I'd be sent next. It's a horrible feeling for a kid, Gabe. In a way, Eli's going through the same thing. His mom's gone. His aunt dumped him off. You leave him at The Haven. He doesn't know what to expect next. He needs control and stability in his world. He needs a home to come home to."

"I guess." Gabe studied her as if she were a total stranger. "I knew your aunts fostered you. I didn't know the rest."

"I don't like to talk about those days." Wasn't that the truth?

"I'm glad you told me. It helps me understand some of Eli's issues." His gentle smile made her feel better about blabbing her life's history.

"That land is what you want, Gabe. You said so. If you and Eli choose the house together, it would make it seem more like you're a family and that you value his opinion, that he has some say in what's happening to him. It will give him ownership in the place he'll eventually call home."

"I guess you're right."

"Good." She exhaled, then blurted out the next part. "But you have to act. You can't keep waiting for the perfect situation to happen along because it won't. And you'll have lost this opportunity."

"Okay, okay. I get it, Olivia." Gabe straightened from his lounging position and held up his hands in surrender. "I'll call the guy and make an offer."

"Now?" she pressed, afraid he'd come up with more excuses once he left.

"Can we say pushy?" He rolled his eyes at her before pulling out his phone. Then he frowned. "I don't have the number with me."

"I memorized it." Olivia recited the numbers, thrilled that Gabe was finally doing this.

"I should have known you would, Ms. Organizer," he muttered, flicking the phone on to speaker. When it was answered, he gave his name and said he was interested in purchasing the land.

Olivia sat, elbows on her knees as she listened to the back-and-forth discussion, trying to stem her excitement when they agreed on a price and a possession date.

"I'm really happy to see Dad's land go to someone with family," the seller, Edward, told Gabe. "I have so many wonderful memories of times there, with my dad. My mom left us when I was little, so the two of us were on our own. But Dad made the place a wonderful home for a kid. It's good to hear you intend to do the same with your son, Gabe."

After discussing details, Gabe finally hung up looking bemused.

"Congratulations. You've taken the first step to making a home for Eli." Olivia tried to hide her delight, but judging by his expression, Gabe saw her satisfaction.

"You're the one who got me into this," he grumbled, tucking his phone into his pocket. "You better not leave until Eli and I are settled in that house."

"No guarantee of that. But I can probably stay another couple of weeks." *You weren't going to get involved, remember? Fresh start in Edmonton?* She shoved away the nagging voice in her head.

"Why are you grinning like that, Olivia?" Gabe grumbled.

"Because I just had a great idea. Let's go get Eli and show him where his home is going to be." She jumped up and held out her hand. "Come on, Gabe. Smile. This is a happy day."

He did grasp her hand, but it wasn't for help to get

up. He rose on his own, his fingers tightening around hers as he studied her face.

"If this doesn't work out," he began, but she wouldn't allow it.

"Enough with the naysaying," she ordered, and yanked her hand from his. She had to, in order to stop the electric current shooting up her arm. "This is going to be the best decision of your entire life, cowboy."

The best decision of his life?

Gabe wasn't so sure when he saw Eli's lack of response to the land he'd just purchased.

"Can you just imagine it, Eli?" A very excited Olivia pointed out features. "Your dad could hang a tire swing from that tree. And you could make a hideaway place in the caragana hedge over there. I used to do that."

Gabe grinned. The woman was like a kid herself as she outlined possibilities for what would be Eli's home.

"Do you think you'd be okay to live here?" Gabe finally interrupted, worried when Eli kept looking around without saying a word.

"It's very—big." Eli gulped.

"There's lots of grass," Gabe reminded. "You said you liked that."

"Yeah." Hesitant or afraid?

"We'd need a dog." Stark fear filled Eli's face at Gabe's comment. He immediately revised. "Maybe a puppy would be better. Where I work they have a dog who's going to have puppies soon."

"A little dog?" Eli asked timidly.

"The puppies would be small at first, but they'd grow. Just like you," Gabe added. Maybe this was all too much for the kid. Maybe he should have done some work on the place first.

"It can't hunt birds?" the boy insisted.

"We'll teach it not to." Was that his imagination or did Eli's shoulders relax a little?

"There's lot of trees." Eli wandered over to a row of poplar trees that lined the driveway. "Birds live here, right?" he asked Olivia.

Gabe's heart sank. *I'm right here, son. Talk to me.*

"I don't know much about birds, Eli." Olivia hunkered down to look into his eyes. "But your dad has lived around here for a long time. You should ask him."

Eli looked at Gabe soundlessly.

"Owls, chickadees, robins, swallows, geese on the pond, blue jays. Those are just a few of the birds that live in these parts." Gabe watched Eli digest that.

"Are chickadees like canaries?" His son's blue eyes sparked with interest.

"Not exactly. Sometimes they have a bit of yellow on their stomachs," Gabe explained. "But mostly they're kind of gray and brown so they can hide in the bush. Sometimes in the summer we get a bird that looks a lot like a canary, though I think they're a variety of finch. They usually come if you feed them niger seed, but they always leave for the winter."

"They gotta eat." Interest flared in Eli's eyes. "So I can draw 'em."

"Sure. We'll build a feeder. No problem." Gabe heaved a sigh of relief. One hurdle over.

"Then I think it'd be good," Eli said quietly. "'Cept I don't like that house."

"It will be gone. There will be a new one in its place,"

Gabe assured him. "But we'll have to pick it out before they can deliver it."

"Oh." Eli fell silent, apparently intrigued by a house moving.

"We'll have to leave pretty soon," Olivia said. "The party for Art and Mavis is supposed to start in an hour." She mussed Eli's hair with a smile. "I can hardly wait to see your painting."

"The secret will be over then." Eli looked at Gabe, his little face very serious. "It's okay?"

"It looks beautiful, son. You did an amazing job." Gabe's heart sang at this first bit of father-son sharing. "Before we leave, let's walk around where our house will go. You can tell me if you think we need to add some other things."

Eli turned to survey the road they'd driven in on, then looked at him with a question in his eyes. Gabe burst out laughing.

"I agree. Getting that road graded should be number one on our to-do list." He caught Olivia's glance on him. Her gray eyes shone approvingly, and that sent a ruffle of warmth shooting through him.

Surprised by this unusual reaction, Gabe asked himself why. Olivia was a friend, a good friend. He wasn't interested in anything more. Was he?

They spent the next half hour chatting about possibilities. Olivia had many suggestions, some outlandish, but most extremely practical. She was a natural at organization, at seeing possibilities. She was the one who'd encouraged him to take this step. Gabe needed to think of a way to thank her.

"We've got to get a move on if we're going to make it

to the housewarming," she chided him after he'd fallen into thought.

"Okay. Wait a minute." Gabe reached out and plucked a leaf from her hair, then brushed a ladybug off her shoulder. "Okay, good to go."

"Thanks." She seemed to suddenly withdraw though he was fairly certain she never moved a muscle.

"Olivia?" he asked, confused. "Is something wrong?"

"Of course not. Let's go." Whirling away, she raced Eli to his truck, helped the child into the middle and climbed in behind him. The slam of her door made Gabe stir. He gave her a quick glance after he'd started the truck, but Olivia was turned away, her face hidden.

It felt like something had changed between them.

But what?

Chapter Five

"Ta-da." Gabe ripped away the paper covering their artwork on the outbuilding.

"It's marvelous!"

As Olivia gushed over their painting at Art's ranch, Gabe stood with the paper balled in his arms, grinning like an idiot.

"Where did you learn how to do this?" she asked Eli. "Those baby birds in the nest and the little squirrel carrying an acorn—they're beautiful." As if aware she'd excluded him, she twisted to smile at Gabe. "Your painting is nice, too," she offered.

"Nice." He burst out laughing. "Timid praise indeed, Olivia." In the moment that his gaze held hers, he noticed she was blushing. She quickly turned away. "Eli and I make a good painting team."

"You sure do. In fact, this whole place looks amazing." She clasped her hands like a kid awaiting Christmas. Just another thing Gabe appreciated about Olivia. She wholeheartedly delighted in another's joy. "I can hardly wait for Art and Mavis to get here."

"Don't have to wait. Here they come," he said, just

loudly enough for the assembled group to hear. Everyone stilled, watching the elderly couple's car slow and then stop in the driveway. Eyes wide, Art took it all in before helping Mavis out of the car.

"Welcome home," Aunt Tillie said as she hurried forward to welcome the pair.

"We hope you won't mind that we took some liberties," Margaret added, matching her sister step for step.

"Some? You've done so much," Mavis breathed. "Roses! They're stunning. And the house." She took in each of the changes with little gasps of joy. "Look what they've done, Art," she crowed. "Just look."

"I see it, girl. New paint, new roof, deck's fixed—oh, it's too much." Tears welled and rolled down his weary face. "How can we ever thank you?"

"You don't thank friends for helping out, Arthur." Gabe stepped forward and shook his hand.

"He's right." Tillie smiled. "You're our friends. We love you. We don't want you moving away from us because of a few little problems."

"A few? Oh, my!" Mavis gaped at the outbuildings that Gabe and Eli had painted. "Who did that?"

Gabe watched as Olivia eased Eli forward and explained. Mavis wrapped her arms around the boy and hugged him fiercely.

"If you knew how often I've sat here, wishing for something prettier to look at. I just love those birds, Eli," she said softly. "Thank you."

"Welcome," Eli answered politely, looking, Gabe thought, a little shocked by all the attention.

Duty done, Gabe now encouraged his son to join the other kids, which Eli did, though he stood to one side until Mikey grabbed his hand.

"It's a glorious day, so come enjoy your deck, my dears," Margaret enthused. "The men built this ramp for you to get up and down more easily." She hooked her arm in Mavis's and, with Tillie on the other side, walked the woman slowly up the incline and escorted her to one of the big wooden chairs with their gaily striped cushions.

"Those cushions weren't here yesterday." Gabe glanced at Olivia, knowing they were another of her "ideas."

"I only finished them last night. Adirondack chairs are comfortable, but according to Aunt Margaret, a little padding doesn't hurt." She tilted her head to one side. "Are the fabrics too bright? I pieced from Aunt Tillie's quilt stash to make the cushions and the hanging."

"I think they look amazing." He studied the *Welcome* hanging for a minute. "You used the dark green of the trim—was that color your choice?"

"The painter asked the aunties. They asked me and, well—" She blushed but nodded. "I heard Mavis loves green. It seemed appropriate."

"I don't know how you do it." He stared at her. "I've known this couple for ages and I never knew about Mavis's preference for green. Yet you're here for a couple of weeks and…"

"Something the aunts mentioned." As usual Olivia shrugged off his praise though she looked pleased. "Aunt Tillie suggested using the same tone for a feature wall in the living room. I checked, and it looks stunning with that wood floor and the cream walls."

"The cream was also your choice. And perfect," Gabe added, seeing the truth on her face.

Everyone paused as the pastor asked a blessing over

their picnic. He then invited folks to savor the lemonade and fresh cherry pie.

"Adele?" Gabe guessed.

"She wanted to contribute. Since the cherries are early this year and very plentiful..." Olivia blushed again at his knowing look. "I thought it would be a shame not to take advantage of the bounty, that's all."

"That's all," he agreed with a grin.

"Want to get in line?" she asked, ducking her head in that way she had that hid her expressive eyes.

"Of course." He panned a droll look. "When have you known me to miss out on pie, Olivia?"

"Right, silly question." She glanced around. "I love the benches scattered here and there. One under that big maple, another beside the roses and a third near the garden. Who built them?"

"Ben conned me into helping him do it. *After* he saw a sketch *you* left lying around." Gabe's admiration for the way her brain brimmed with ideas had grown exponentially in the past weeks.

"Not much of a sketch compared to Eli's work," she demurred before speaking to a burly man in front of them. "Thanks for making those metal picnic tables, Victor. They're amazing."

"Welding part was easy," the man said with a grin. "The wife painted 'em with enough coats of weather-resistant paint they should be good outside for many years. I'm glad you thought of a way I could help. I can just see Art and Mavis feedin' their grandkids on 'em."

"Me, too," Olivia agreed with a—wistful?—smile. Something glinted in her eyes. Longing? For this? Well, no wonder. He thought a do like this was pretty special, too.

After they'd retrieved their pie, Gabe's coffee and her lemonade, they found a lush grassy spot under a flowering lilac and sat down together. He ate in contented silence, occasionally glancing around to greet friends and neighbors who'd come to welcome the couple home. For Gabe this was what life was about—communities caring for each other. He was thrilled his two friends would now find life much easier on their beloved ranch.

"Is there anything you don't think of, Olivia?" Gabe asked, noticing several burgeoning planters strategically placed here and there. That had happened sometime after his departure yesterday, too. Good thing he'd covered Eli's painting. "You have your fingers in a lot of lives around here. Chokecherry Hollow, The Haven, the church. Our whole community is better off for you being here, receiving your special touch."

"I haven't done much, but that's nice of you to say. You like it here a lot, don't you, Gabe?" Her silver-gray eyes studied him.

"I do. I chose Chokecherry Hollow because it's very much like the small community I grew up in. Neighbors caring for neighbors. Like today." Satisfaction bloomed inside at the sound of laughter and happiness filling the yard. How could Eve *not* have wanted this life?

The same old flare of antagonism threatened to spoil his afternoon, so Gabe tamped it down. Memories of Eve couldn't be allowed to tarnish one second of his time with Olivia.

"I've loved my holiday here." She looked around as if she was fixing the scene in her mind to take out and remember later. Her gaze lingered for a moment on Eli, who still hadn't joined in playing with the other kids. She moved as if she was about to go to him but then the dreamy expression in her eyes drained away. That fear of getting too close to children again, Gabe guessed.

"You love it here, but you'll still leave The Haven?" It wasn't really a question. He could see the resolve fill her face.

"Of course. I start a new job in September, remember?" Olivia calmly finished her lemonade.

"September?" Gabe frowned in confusion. "I had the impression it started next month."

"Nope. September 21," she said.

"But this is only June. What's the rush to leave? Summer is very busy at The Haven. They could use an extra pair of hands," he said with a frown. "Especially your organizing hands."

"I've already stayed longer than I intended to, Gabe. I need some time to organize my new life. I don't know Edmonton anymore after so many years living in the East. It will take time to find a place to live. Also, I'm not as familiar as I'd like to be with my new employer's business, so I need time to prepare with some research."

"You and your research." He caught her watching Eli's attempt to befriend a child afraid of Art's dog.

"Research is what I do, Gabe," Olivia said absently. A slight smile curved her lips. "Look at your son. He's making friends."

"That's also thanks to you," he said quietly. "You've helped Eli feel comfortable when I couldn't. I appreciate it. But there's so much more he needs to figure out and I'm not sure how to help him or what to do to get him to truly trust me."

"You *do* know, Gabe. It's all in here." She tapped his chest, right over his heart. "Just be his dad, day in, day out. Love him. No matter what. You'll figure it out." She shrugged as if it was simple. "Anyway, it's not like I'm leaving tonight. I have a few more days here."

"Good." He grinned. "In that case can you come with Eli and me to look at houses tomorrow?"

"What's the rush?" Olivia said, but he sensed her approval. "I had to nag you to buy that land. You were very reluctant."

"Now the decision's made I want to get on with creating a home for Eli." Gabe arched one eyebrow. "I think it would be good to get him settled before school starts. Don't you agree?"

"Wholeheartedly," she assured him with a smile.

Had she agreed only for Eli's sake? Or did she really believe in his ability to be a good dad?

They spent the next two hours visiting with others who'd stopped by to welcome Art and Mavis home. Then Olivia said she needed to get back to The Haven.

Gabe didn't want to hear that. He enjoyed her company and didn't want it to end. Not enjoyed her company in the romantic sense, he told himself, but because he had nowhere to go except back to his bunkhouse, where he'd be alone again since Eli was going to a new friend's house for something called a playdate, which Olivia had arranged.

Pathetic life, cowboy.

Nevertheless, he asked her, "What's the rush to leave?"

"I'm rebooting The Haven's entire computer system tonight so the new programming can take effect. That means going offline," she explained after they'd said goodbye and Gabe was driving toward The Haven. "Probably at midnight since Vic doesn't need anything then. But once it's back up and running, I have to go through everything, make sure there aren't any glitches before they start using it again."

"Sounds like a big deal," he mused, wishing he was more computer literate so he could understand exactly what Olivia was doing.

"It won't be a big deal if my new program runs as planned. If it doesn't—" She made a face. "Let's just say I intend to have everything running smoothly by the time The Haven wakes up tomorrow morning."

"Meaning you'll be up all night—again." Eli had told him how he'd woken last night to see Olivia walking her Aunt Tillie up and down the hall to work off some type of severe leg cramp.

Gabe admired Olivia's stamina. She couldn't have had much rest last night. She'd had a full day with Victoria's office to-do list, and he was pretty sure she'd already made several trips to Art and Mavis's before he'd met up with her at noon yet still looked fresh and ready to take on more challenges.

"I'm a little nervous about the reboot. Pray that all goes well, will you, Gabe?" she said quietly as they pulled onto The Haven's circular driveway.

"Sure." He wondered about the uncertainty in her voice. "Do you pray about your work a lot?" he asked, then grimaced. "Sorry. Too personal."

"It's okay." Olivia shrugged. "I pray a lot about everything. I just don't feel like I get answers very often." She grimaced. "Don't tell my aunties that."

"I'm sure they've gone through the same thing," he said quietly, surprised Olivia had doubts about her faith. He'd never have imagined this competent woman doubted anything.

"Maybe when they first became missionaries they

had doubts, though I doubt it. I'm pretty sure the aunties' faith is rock solid now and has been for years." She tilted her head to one side. "What about you?"

"What about me?" Gabe didn't want to talk about himself when she watched him so closely.

"When you pray, do you feel like you get the answers you need, Gabe?"

He inhaled. It was an honest question. He couldn't just brush her off, but he didn't have a good answer, either.

"Sorry. Too personal." Olivia shook her head, her face rueful. "Never mind."

"I don't always feel like I get the answers I want," Gabe admitted quietly. He switched off the motor and silence yawned between them. Olivia had asked for his help and he wanted to give it, to give back something in return for all she'd done for him and Eli. "The pastor did a study on prayer a while ago," he mused aloud. "It really made me think about how I pray, not that I'm great at it, but it did bring a new perspective."

"Go on." Olivia studied him as if she needed to hear his answer.

"I don't know if I can recall everything he said." She waited, hands folded in her lap, so Gabe shrugged and repeated what he remembered. "Basically, he started with trust. If we trust God, really trust Him, we can live without worry because we'll expect He'll take care of us. The 'cast your cares' verse figured into that lesson a lot."

"Because?" Olivia's intense scrutiny made him want to get it right.

"Because true trust means we don't worry and fret." Gabe watched her frown. "It's not easy to trust, but I remind myself every day that God's in control, that growth takes time. If I'm still worried, then I tell Him that. That's when peace comes." *Usually.*

"Right away?" Olivia asked, eyes wide.

"Sometimes." Gabe shrugged.

"I've struggled with this for so long," she admitted, her voice tight. "I want to trust God, but nothing happens when I pray."

"Nothing happens immediately, you mean? Or you don't see anything happening?" Gabe cautioned himself to be careful. He was no spiritual leader, but the strain in her face made him want to share what he'd learned. "It's funny, but since Eli's appearance I think I understand certain aspects of God a bit more."

"Really?"

"It sounds weird." Gabe hesitated before deciding to just say it and let Olivia make of it what she would. "Those words of Eli's—that he'd prayed and prayed for me to come—they stick in my head. I got thinking about how I've prayed and prayed for something."

"And?" she nudged verbally, eyes wide.

"I think sometimes God doesn't answer right away because He's trying to stretch our faith." Though he felt silly trying to explain something he'd never articulated, Olivia seemed eager for him to continue. "It's not that He can't do whatever we ask. But it's like when you were a kid at Christmas and you so desperately wanted something—a doll, maybe?" He looked at her to see if that made sense.

"A laptop," she murmured.

"Of course." He made a face. "You dreamed and thought about and planned all the things you'd do with that laptop, right? And all the while you waited, expecting your aunts would put it under the tree for you because you knew they loved you and wanted you to be happy." He stopped, uncertain if this was a good comparison.

"They gave me a lovely silver one. I used it until I finished university," she told him.

"You trusted them with your desire because you knew they loved you, but you had to trust and believe and wait until Christmas." He sighed. "What I'm trying to say, badly, is that I think sometimes God makes us wait so we can really think about what we're asking for, because we often say, 'I want this, I want that,' but it's really only a momentary fleeting thing that we forget about in a few minutes, or as soon as the next thing strikes our fancy."

"I've done that." Olivia flushed as if embarrassed by the admission.

"Me, too." Gabe nodded, a little distracted by her sad expression. "So, if we believe God is good and just and faithful, then we can be confident and rest in the knowledge that He will answer our prayers—but in His own time. We don't have to worry and struggle over things we don't control. We can rest in God and let Him work it out."

She stared at him as if surprised.

Gabe gulped, felt his face burn. "I sound like some kind of preacher," he muttered.

"You sound very smart." She kept watching him.

"Why did you ask me about this, Olivia?" he asked after a few moments had passed. And then he knew. "It's this thing you have about kids getting hurt around you, isn't it?"

She nodded, tears welling and spilling over her cheeks.

"I love my nieces and nephews so much and I want to be close to them, to have them hug me and be able to hug them back, to take them on walks and find special bugs or pretty stones or watch a doe and her fawn. But then I remember the past and fear takes over and I'm terrified I'll cause them harm." She looked at him, eyes huge and glossy in her lovely face. "What if God never answers my prayer to be free of that, Gabe? What if I'm always going to be afraid?"

Gabe didn't really understand all she was suffering, but he couldn't stand to watch Olivia weep, to see her quiet desperation. He slid his arm around her shoulders and drew her close, allowing her to cry out the worry and fear that dogged her while he silently prayed.

"I'm sorry." She sniffed as she drew away a few moments later. "I've soaked your shirt."

"Olivia, have you talked to anyone about this?" When she shook her head, he frowned. "You should at least talk to your aunts."

"I don't want them to see how spiritually weak I am," she whispered.

"You're not spiritually weak," he said firmly.

"Then—?" She frowned at him, raised her shoulders helplessly.

"I'm no psychologist but I think inside you're afraid that God won't give you what you want, that is, freedom from this fear you carry." Gabe wasn't sure where the knowledge came from. He only knew it seemed right. "I don't know much about your past, but I'm guessing you became an organizer because you felt you had to take care of yourself, because nobody else would."

"How did you know?" she gasped.

"I didn't, but—that's how Eve was." He did *not* want

to talk about his ex-wife, but some distant memory flickered in the recesses of his mind. "Even though I loved her, when I think about it now I realize that no matter how many times I said it, she never really seemed to believe me. And the reason she didn't was because she didn't trust me." The burst of knowledge burned like fireworks in his brain.

"Does knowing that make it easier to forgive her?" Olivia murmured.

Gabe stared at her and in that instant the gut-burning fury flared again.

"No," he snapped.

"Sorry." Olivia drew away, opened the door and stepped out of his truck, her face thoughtful.

"Wait," Gabe chewed himself out for not wording that properly. "I was trying to say that God tells us He loves us, but if we don't believe it and trust in it, it doesn't do us any good."

"You're right. I need to think about that." She gave him a funny smile. "Thanks for sharing, Gabe. See you tomorrow—after lunch?"

He nodded, watching as she closed the truck door, walked to The Haven and disappeared inside. He drove to the Double M with the pastor's words from that study on prayer echoing inside his head.

You're afraid to trust God because you don't ask for His will to be done. You want Him to do your will. That never works. Trust only comes when we want God's will more than we want our own.

While you're thinking about that, consider this. Maybe your prayers aren't answered because God's waiting for you to take care of something that gnaws and festers inside you.

Obviously, God wanted Gabe to forgive Eve.

"I can't," he said bitterly as he shoved the gearshift into Park and climbed out of his truck. "I can't just forget everything she cost me. Dad. Our ranch. Love. Eli."

He'd forgotten that kids from The Haven were coming for an evening trail ride. They would end the event with a big campfire. Gabe changed clothes and then went to chop wood. Maybe if he wore himself out he wouldn't have to think about Eve and the past and everything he'd lost.

Maybe.

Two nights later, weary from the reboot but satisfied that The Haven's systems were working properly, Olivia perched on the edge of Eli's bed to finish his bedtime Bible story and wondered where Gabe was. She hadn't seen him last night. Was he upset with her? Was he angry at her for asking about forgiving Eve?

"David was brave, right, Livvie?" Eli watched her closely. "He wasn't scared of that big giant." His solemn face studied her. "Do you get really scared?"

"Yes." *I have my own giants.* Immediately her mind time traveled back to her childhood and the day of the fire. With those memories came the usual blanket of guilt. Why hadn't she searched just a minute longer? Tried a little harder?

"Why d'you get scared?" Eli wanted to know.

"Somebody got hurt because I couldn't help them," she said brusquely, not wanting to elaborate and leave him with bad thoughts before he went to sleep. Actually, she didn't want to remember at all. "I tried, but I was so scared I couldn't help. That's why they got hurt."

"Is that why my mom died? 'Cause I was scared?"

His voice dropped. "I tried to be a good boy. I din't tell when Bobby pinched me real hard or when April hitted me with the belt 'cause Mommy said I had to be a good boy so she'd get better." Tears rolled down his cheeks. "But I musta not been good enough 'cause she didn't get better."

"No, Eli, that's not right." Olivia ached to wrap him in her arms and rock away his sadness and guilt, but she couldn't. Fear kept her frozen in place. Better not to build the bonds and make herself responsible. All she could do was try to dispel his sad thoughts with words. "You didn't do anything wrong, sweetheart."

"But you said—"

"It isn't the same." Olivia now wished she hadn't brought up the past. Going back only added to her culpability.

"Why?" Eli was obviously struggling to comprehend.

"Well." How was she supposed to word this so the kid wouldn't feel responsible for his mother's death? "Your mom needed to know you were okay with your aunt."

"How come?" He wrinkled his nose.

"Because if she knew you were okay, she wouldn't worry about you and that made her feel better. You kept her happy by not telling. The only thing is…" She paused, struggling to find the right words. "If someone is nasty like Bobby and April were, I think you needed to tell someone, Eli. You couldn't tell your mom, I know that. She was too sick." She rushed to reassure him, anxious to dispel his worry. "But if someone hits you or pinches you like that again, tell your dad or me or someone, okay?"

"But you're goin' away." His frown matched the sinking of her heart.

"Not forever and, anyway, your dad will be here. He'll always protect you, no matter what." Of that at least Olivia had no doubt. "Promise that if anything bothers you or makes you uncomfortable, you'll tell your dad about it right away. Okay?"

"'Kay." Eli relaxed against the pillow, his face thoughtful. "Who'd you tell?"

"Pardon?" Olivia blinked, surprised by his question.

"When the person got hurted 'cause you din't help." He studied her unblinkingly. "Who'd you tell 'bout it?"

"Nobody," she whispered.

"But you said—"

"It's bedtime, sweetie." She pulled the covers up to his chin and smiled. "Want me to listen while you say your prayers?"

"Yes, please." Eli squeezed his eyes closed and began talking as if God was sitting right there beside her in the armchair.

Olivia marveled at the simplicity of his prayers, and the sincerity with which he thanked God for his new friends, The Haven, and, of course, the birds he was learning to identify. He stumbled a bit when he came to the end of his *God Blesses*, hesitating before he added Gabe to the long list. He did not say *Dad*. There was an uncertainty underlying his words that said he wasn't quite sure how to pray for the man now in his life.

That hesitation pained Olivia. Her arms ached to enfold the little boy, to hold him close and assure him that Gabe wouldn't allow anything bad to happen to him ever again. But nobody could guarantee that. More than anything she wanted to promise to be there if Eli needed her. But she couldn't say that, either, because she wouldn't be here. Her future didn't lie at The Haven, and, anyway, forming the bond between this child and his father was the most important thing.

Eli had just whispered, "Amen," when Gabe added his own "Amen" as he set his Stetson on the floor.

"I'm sorry I'm so late, Eli," he apologized. "Some cattle broke through a fence and I had to round them up."

Olivia moved so Gabe could kneel at the side of Eli's bed. He, at least, had no hesitation about touching his son, his hand smoothing unruly strands so like his own, his smile lifting the corners of his lips.

"That was a good prayer," he said softly. "I think God likes it when we thank Him for all the things He gives us."

Eli watched him.

Gabe finally kissed the top of his head, murmured a good-night, then rose and switched off the main light, leaving a tiny night-light burning. Olivia preceded him out of the room and waited until he'd closed the door before walking down the stairs.

"I'm sorry I had to cancel our house hunt. It's been crazy busy, and now I've got to get back to the Double M," he said apologetically. "We have a couple of sick horses. Can I let you know about looking at houses— maybe tomorrow?"

"Sure." Tears welled as he left. Gabe had driven over to say good-night to his son. What a great guy. Gabe deserved to be a dad.

He deserved to be happy, to love and be loved. She couldn't stay, but while she was here she would help him however she could.

Chapter Six

"I'm sorry you're hurt, Eli." The hall clock had just chimed twelve noon the following day when Olivia finished pressing the adhesive strip to the child's arm. She winced in empathy at the ugly red scratches the length of his arm, but said only, "I'm sure it will heal quickly, honey."

"Thanks, Livvie." Gabe's son flung his arms around Olivia's neck and squeezed tightly, obviously needing comfort.

Maybe it was his use of her family's nickname, or perhaps it was the way Eli's hold tightened. Or maybe it was her own silly yearning to share a bond with this little boy. Whatever the reason, Olivia hugged him back despite her brain's protests. She was getting too emotionally involved, but she needed this contact as much as Eli did, needed it to soothe her aching heart. But what if—? She eased away from him.

"Don't climb on sharp rocks anymore, okay?" she advised, gulping down the rush of emotions his warm hug had caused.

"I won't." Eli's bottom lip trembled for a moment as

he studied the plaster bandage and the few angry red marks it didn't quite cover. Then he summoned a smile and, with shoulders back, pronounced, "I'm a big boy."

"You sure are, sweetheart." Concern for the children's safety made her ask, "Where were you playing, Eli?"

"There."

Olivia followed the direction of his pointing finger through the window. Every nerve went on high alert. There were no rocks over there, unless... She had to check this out.

"Show me exactly where." She followed Eli out of the office, her worry growing as they tromped through underbrush and straight to a pile of jagged rocks Jake had gathered from the property. "But there's a sign here, Eli. See." She pointed to each printed word, saying them distinctly. *"Keep out!"* She saw his blue eyes widen in surprise. "This little gate shouldn't be open. Did you do that?"

"Uh-huh." His head dropped to his chest.

"Why?" Olivia couldn't understand his disobedience.

"I needed a rock. Vic said we're gonna paint 'em after lunch." He frowned. "I gotta have a really nice rock. To give—someone."

A rock—the truth suddenly dawned. Sunday was Father's Day. Eli wanted to give his painted rock to Gabe. The significance of that action built a lump in her throat that she had to gulp down. Voice wobbling, she reached out and patted his shoulder.

"We'll find you a nice rock, Eli. But not in here." She firmly relatched the gate and double twisted the wire to make it very difficult to open. "When the sign says to stay out you must obey. The signs are to keep you safe."

"'Kay," he mumbled, eyes downcast. Something in his response bothered her.

"You did read the sign, didn't you?" she asked, but he darted away. She stood there, confused, studying the rock pile, trying to work it out.

"Something wrong?" Gabe's quiet question caught her attention. Olivia faced him.

"Do you think this sign is too small?" she asked, struggling to decipher a niggling warning that wouldn't be shaken.

"Hardly. You could read it from the kitchen window." When she didn't respond, Gabe set a hand on her shoulder, his voice concerned. "What is it, Olivia?"

"I'm not sure yet. I need to think about it some more." She forced a smile. "Ready to go house hunting?"

"Ready as I'll ever be." His tone made her do a double take.

"Are you getting cold feet?"

"No." His blue eyes held hers. "Just worried I'll miss some detail that's important to Eli."

"Then we'll take him— oh." Olivia stopped in her tracks. "He can't come with us today."

"Why not?" Gabe wore a confused frown.

"There's, um, an activity planned for this afternoon that he really wants to be part of." She shrugged. "It's not a problem. We'll scout out the houses and when you see a couple you think are suitable, we'll get his opinion. Not that I think he'll notice much except the windows. He's sure big on watching birds."

"Very big," Gabe chuckled. "When a bird arrives, he stops midsentence and stares. It's unnerving."

"Maybe we should find out what got him interested in them," she mused.

They walked to The Haven. Gabe said he'd have a word with his son while she got her purse. When Olivia returned, Gabe looked upset.

"What's wrong?" she asked. "Oh, you saw his scratches. Did you ask him about them?" When he shook his head, she explained what had happened.

"That's why you were asking about the sign." Gabe helped her into his truck, closed the door and walked to the driver's side. When the truck was rolling down the hill, he said, "Eli must have seen it. Why would he disobey?"

"We'll ask him later," Olivia temporized, not wanting to reveal the secret of Eli's Father's Day gift. "Now let's concentrate on finding your new home."

"I'm glad you're with me to help."

"Me, too." Olivia felt her stomach butterflies begin their dance at Gabe's grin.

This man was generous, kind, so loving to the son he'd only known for a few short weeks. Gabe was clearly a family man. It was such a shame he couldn't let go of the past and find love again. But no matter how much she wished it for him, Olivia simply couldn't envision exactly the right woman for Gabe.

Because you don't want to? Though she mentally scoffed at the thought, it persisted and wouldn't be silenced.

Delighted to see prospective customers, Harry St. Ames, the builder, took them on a tour of the yard where houses sat completed, waiting for families. Olivia tuned out the men's discussion about insulation and R-values of windows to scan the newest homes, comparing each to the vision in her head. The models that she'd shown Gabe online still seemed the best options, although she preferred one above the other. For now she'd keep that preference to herself.

"Roam around, look through each one," Harry invited. "Make sure you think about how you'll use your home."

They entered the first house. Olivia didn't care for the floor plan, but she followed Gabe without speaking, listening as he mulled over possibilities.

"I don't think this is it," he said after about five minutes. "What do you think of the one next door?"

"Let's look." She was determined not to reveal her partiality. Yet, as they studied the open plan, the large kitchen, the huge bank of windows off the living room and the sweet reading nook tucked into the corner, she couldn't help remarking, "Eli would love that spot. He loves it when someone reads to him."

"I noticed." Gabe mulled it over. "He doesn't seem interested in reading for himself, though. I remember when I was his age. I devoured books, even if I had to sound out every letter."

"Maybe when he has his own room, you can build a bookshelf and fill it with some of your favorite books," she suggested as they walked through the master suite.

"This is pretty nice," Gabe said with a grin. "Lots roomier than a bunkhouse."

They toured several other houses, however they kept returning for another look at the second one they'd viewed.

"I think this is it," the big cowboy said after they'd toured it again. "What do you think?"

"Let's walk through it one more time and see if we can find any faults," Olivia suggested, pleased that their tastes were so similar. "The kitchen seems perfect."

"Lots of room but still homey," he agreed. "Those windows will give a great view. I could stand at the island and look into the valley while I'm washing dishes."

"No dishwasher?" she teased. His droll look made Olivia chuckle. "The laundry room is handy. Which room will be Eli's?"

"He can choose, but I have a hunch he'll like this." Gabe walked into the blue bedroom. It featured a small turret-like jut out with a window seat beneath a huge window. "Plant a tree outside, set up a couple of bird feeders and it should have everything Eli asked for."

"Then I think this house is perfect for both of you," she murmured. "You can build a deck off the front from those French doors and enjoy your meals or a barbecue with friends."

"I never thought of entertaining." Gabe turned to stare at her. "But I could. Would you come if we invited you, Olivia?"

"Of course." The way he was watching her sent a tiny thrill up her spine, but it also triggered wariness. She didn't belong here, yet his words created an intimate picture that echoed a longing she'd kept suppressed inside since—no! Gabe was nothing like Martin. "You could watch a full moon and stars on a summer's night from the deck's vantage point."

"We could have fireworks in that valley on Canada Day. And I could put up a Christmas tree and decorations outside." Gabe's bemused tone made her smile.

"You can do whatever you want. It's your land and it will be your home."

"Home," he whispered. "It's been a long time since I had that." His eyes focused on her. "Thank you, Olivia."

He touched her cheek, the one with the scar, with his

fingertip, and for once she didn't flinch away. Couldn't. The intensity of his penetrating gaze held her in place.

"I don't think I'd have done this without you," Gabe said very softly. "I don't know how we'll ever repay you."

"Just be happy," she said around the lump in her throat. "Enjoy your home and Eli. That's payment enough." The quiet words slipped out. Her total focus was on Gabe, on how she'd only have to balance forward on her tiptoes to touch his cheek with her lips.

Been that route before, her brain warned. *Remember the pain.*

Only too well Olivia remembered gut-wrenching feelings of betrayal. But Gabe wasn't like that. Gabe had integrity and scruples. He wasn't trying to deceive her. She knew all about his world at the Double M, knew his friends, even his predilection for pie. He was everything she'd looked for in love and—

"Eve would hate this place."

That drew Olivia out of her daydream. Yes, she knew lots about Gabe, including his painful past. She especially knew how he was snagged in his anger toward his ex-wife. Everything in Gabe's world seemed tainted by angry memories of Eve.

Which was why Gabe wasn't interested in her as anything other than a friend.

That's what Olivia wanted, too.

Wasn't it?

Eve would hate this place.

As soon as the words left his lips, Gabe knew he shouldn't have said them and not only because the words cast a blemish on what had been a fun afternoon. Olivia's big smile had disappeared.

"Is that why you like it?" she asked.

"I really like the open layout and the way things seem to flow naturally. She liked—" He caught himself. "It doesn't matter."

"It really doesn't," Olivia agreed, her face somber.

"You want to say something." Because Gabe was learning to read her expressions he knew her next words wouldn't bode well for him. "Go ahead, Olivia."

"It's not my place," she began, but he shook his head.

"We're friends." He shrugged. "I know you're trying to help Eli and me. So be honest. Say it."

It took Olivia a few moments to summon her courage and speak.

"It's just—you keep bringing up Eve. Negatively," she added. Her soft gray gaze held his unrelentingly. "That can't be good for Eli. She was his mother after all."

"I don't speak about Eve at all around him," he objected defensively. Olivia cut him short.

"You do, Gabe. Not in words maybe, but in your manner. Whenever the subject comes up it's like an invisible cloak of fury falls on you." Her face seemed to soften as she stared at him. "I know it's painful for you, and I'm guessing that gets worse when you look at Eli and think about what you missed, what she took from you."

She saw a lot, this former foster girl. Maybe too much? Yet Gabe was determined to really hear what she was saying because this was about his son, the kid that he couldn't seem to relate to. And he wanted to— desperately.

"I'm not trying to negate your pain, but—" Olivia exhaled quickly as if for courage, then blurted, "I wonder if you're subconsciously holding Eve's misdeeds against Eli."

"That's not true!" Gabe stopped, reconsidered. Eli's words that first day replayed. *I prayed and prayed you would come.*

Why hadn't Eli said something to someone or run away?

Ridiculous! Where's an almost six-year-old kid whose mom is dying gonna go? To whom? That was why God made parents. All those years—why didn't you check on Eve? You should have made sure she was okay. It's your fault the kid had no place to go.

Gabe sagged. His fault? Could it be?

"I'm probably wrong," Olivia said somberly. "But your anger isn't helping ease the barrier between you and Eli."

"What do you suggest I do?" Gabe felt humbled and ashamed by her perception that he was the cause of the distance between himself and his son.

"Let's go get Eli, involve him in this." Olivia's silver eyes began to sparkle. "Somehow we've got to get that kid talking."

"First let me speak to Harry about buying this place. Then we'll go." Gabe wasn't going to dally over this decision any longer. That feeling of guilt and Olivia's insistence that they have their own house as soon as possible drove him. It made sense.

"Smart move." Her wide grin made Gabe even more certain of his decision.

When they returned to The Haven to pick up Eli, Victoria needed her sister's help. Rather than wait around until Olivia was free, Gabe thought of a plan. He whispered it to Eli and they left to put it into action, returning just before the supper hour.

"I wondered where you two had gone." Olivia ruffled Eli's overlong hair and smiled at Gabe. "Staying for dinner?"

"Uh, no." He didn't dare look at his son lest he blurt out their surprise. "We've had a look at the house. Now we're going out to the acreage to let Eli see how the house will fit there. Want to come?"

Olivia paused, glanced at the group of children filing into the house for supper and shrugged. "Sure."

Gabe caught himself grinning as he drove to what would soon become home. Eli, too, was smiling. For once they were going to surprise Olivia.

First the three of them walked the area. Gabe pointed out different aspects of the place to Eli, who seemed underwhelmed by the whole exercise.

"Is something wrong, son?" Gabe finally asked.

"There's no birdhouses." Eli's flat voice bothered Gabe.

"That's because we have to build them. But we won't put them up until they move in our house." Eli nodded as if he understood, but his gloomy look didn't dissipate.

New father or not, Gabe knew there was something else going on in that little head when the boy barely touched their surprise picnic for Olivia. Even she couldn't coax a smile from him. Her frown told Gabe she was as perplexed as he was by Eli's lack of response.

Gabe watched his son carefully while they ate their picnic. When he could stand the boy's silence no longer, he blurted, "What's wrong, Eli? Don't you want to live here? With me?" he added after a momentary hesitation. "You can tell me the truth."

Eli only stared down at his hands.

"You need to tell us what's bothering you, honey," Olivia encouraged. "If you don't tell us, we can't help."

After a tense pause that made Gabe clench his teeth, Eli spoke.

"How long will I live here?"

"How long?" Gabe figured he'd clearly overestimated his progress in figuring out this kid. "I don't know what you mean."

"This will be your home, Eli." Olivia's soft voice made Gabe think she was following a hunch. "It's going to be your home forever. Even when you grow up and someday move away, you'll always come back here because it's your home."

"I don't want to move away." Eli's ragged whisper tore at Gabe's heart. "I want to stay here and maybe—" He lifted his head and looked straight at his father. "Maybe I could learn how to work with horses, like you."

"Maybe you could," Gabe said around the lump lodged in his throat. "That would be a lot of fun."

"Yeah." Eli managed a smile and Gabe grinned right back. Progress at last.

But apparently Olivia wasn't satisfied. She touched Eli's arm.

"Tell me about your life with your mom, Eli," she said quietly.

The boy glanced at his dad half fearfully. A rush of shame filled Gabe. He'd put down Eve once too often for his son to be comfortable talking about her.

"We'd really like to hear," he said with a broad smile

of encouragement. "Where did you live? What did you do for fun? Did your mom have a job?" He kept his tone as neutral as possible.

"She had lots of jobs." Eli frowned. "It was nice when we had our own place. Sometimes we went to the park and I got to fly a kite." He smiled momentarily before it was gone. "Then we couldn't live there no more."

"Why was that?" Olivia voice was thoughtfully reassuring, the way a parent should be.

Gabe couldn't decide what she hoped to elicit from Eli, but he was content to listen and wait for answers. Maybe they'd help him understand his son better.

"When Mommy couldn't work we had to move out." A shudder rippled across his shoulders. "I din't like it then."

"Because your next home wasn't very nice?"

"We din't have no home," Eli said sadly, gazing into the distance.

"Oh. So where did you live?" Olivia glanced at Gabe, her gaze troubled. "With your aunt?"

"Not then. We stayed with some other people in funny kinda places. Sometimes we got to sleep outside. We had a big fire in a barrel when it was cold," he explained. His eyes lit up. "I liked that."

Gabe didn't. Was Eli saying they'd been homeless?

"A campfire *is* fun," Olivia agreed. "Could you cook hot dogs over that fire like we do at The Haven?"

"Mommy said no 'cause it smelled funny. Kinda like cars." He glanced at Gabe sideways, as if fearing his father would criticize his mother. "I had to stay with the loud lady sometimes 'cause Mommy was trying to get a job so we could find a place with real beds where it was warm and people didn't yell. But Mommy coughed too much."

"That must have been very hard, Eli. I'm sorry." Olivia hugged him close. "Were you hungry sometimes, too?"

"Uh-huh." He studied his shoes for a moment, then grinned at her. "But not when we went to the big church with the bells. We got to eat lots there. An' they had birds, lots and lotsa birds. A man in a funny dress showed me where the birds lived up in the bells. It was cool. I drawed a picture for Mommy, but Bobby teared it up." Again Eli glanced at Gabe fearfully.

"That's when you went to live with your aunt, right?" Olivia shook her head at Gabe when he would have interrupted. "Bobby and April are your cousins. Your aunt's children," she explained when Eli's face wrinkled in confusion. "I don't think they were very nice cousins, were they?"

Eli risked a quick look at Gabe before he shook his head.

"They were bad," he whispered. A tear fell from his downcast eyes. "But I din't tell."

"You can tell me," she murmured.

"Mommy had to go 'way 'cause she was sick. They said it was 'cause I was dumb, too dumb to help her. They said—" He sniffed and then a sob broke out. "They said I made her sick."

"But that's not right, Eli." An infuriated Gabe had to speak or blow up. "You didn't make your mom sick."

"I didn't?" Confusion filled Eli's little face. "But that's why Aunt Kathy said she had to lock me in the room an' I had to stay there all day 'lone. 'Cause I made Mommy sick."

"She was wrong, Eli. She lied." Gabe couldn't help it. He picked up his son and gathered him onto his lap. "I don't know why she lied, son. Sometimes people do that. But it was wrong, and it was not true. You are not dumb. And you didn't make your mother sick."

"How'd you know?" Eli's big eyes peered into his, waiting for an explanation.

"One time when we were married, your mom got sick. She had to go to the doctor because she was coughing so hard. The doctor told me your mommy had that cough for a long, long time, even when she was a little girl. He gave her special medicine that he said she'd have to take whenever she got the cough. You didn't make her sick, Eli."

"Oh."

Gabe couldn't tell whether it was relief or confusion flooding his son's face. All he knew was that he had to make this better, even though it meant praising Eve.

"You were a good boy and your mother loved you very much. It wasn't her fault that your cousins were mean. She wouldn't have left you there if she'd known about that."

Gabe suddenly recalled several disparaging comments his ex-wife had made about her sister and the treatment she'd received from Kathy when they were kids, before they'd both gone into foster care. Eve must have been desperate if she'd left Eli with Kathy. But why hadn't she come to him? If only— Anger made his jaw clench.

"Eli, when they made you stay in the room, did you miss school?"

Surprised, Gabe twisted to glance at Olivia. He'd never even thought of that. Eli slipped out of his grasp and moved about four feet away before he sank onto the ground, shoulders slumped in defeat.

"It's okay, son. It doesn't matter. We will—"

"Gabe?" Olivia's tone forced him to stop and look at her.

Those expressive eyes of her were trying to tell him something. But what?

"May I ask Eli a couple of questions?"

Hesitant, afraid he'd missed some key thing that he, the boy's father, should have noticed, Gabe nodded, and wondered, *What now?*

Fully aware of how important her next questions would be, Olivia sipped from her water bottle as she organized her thoughts. She had to ask, though she was almost certain she already knew the answers. The point was to get Eli's fears into the light where they could be dealt with.

"When you cut yourself today, could you read the sign that said to stay out?" she asked Eli after she'd shifted so she was seated cross-legged beside him.

"I know some of the letters," he mumbled, head hung low.

"But not how to make them words, right?"

He shook his head, obviously ashamed.

"Bobby and April said I'm stupid." A tear plopped onto his T-shirt. "I guess I am stupid 'cause I can't read words."

Olivia could feel Gabe's irritation building. She knew he wanted to gloss things over, make everything all right. What father wouldn't? But she knew that wouldn't help Eli.

"Am I stupid, Eli?"

"No." His eyes widened. "You're really smart, Liv. You do lots of things."

"Well, I can't read Spanish books, so that means I'm stupid, doesn't it?" She risked a glance at Gabe and saw his shoulders relax just a bit. "And I don't know how to make a spaceship or fly an airplane, so I guess I'm very stupid."

"No. You never learned that." He paused, staring at her as he absorbed it. "I never learned reading," he said slowly. "So, you mean—I'm not dumb?"

"Of course you're not!" He was so sweet. Olivia just wanted to embrace him and, like Gabe, make life perfect for this little boy. But she wouldn't be here long enough and besides, when she got involved with kids, bad things always happened.

"How're we gonna make me read, Liv?" Eli looked at her so trustingly. She couldn't disappoint him.

"We'll figure out something, don't worry. And don't be sad about it." She gave him her biggest smile and brushed his cheek with her knuckles. "April and Bobby should never have called you those names, but just because they did, it doesn't make them true. Okay?"

"Uh-huh." His big smile back in place, Eli jumped up and raced across the grass to inspect a robin's nest he'd spied earlier.

"Homeless. They were homeless, Olivia. Even then Eve didn't contact me." Lips pinched tight, his face taut with anger, Gabe glared at her. "I've never been without a place to live. Why didn't she call me?"

"She didn't know where you were? She didn't have money to find you? She was too proud?" Olivia shrugged. She had to make him understand. "It doesn't matter, Gabe."

"Doesn't matter?" He sounded outraged.

"No, it doesn't. There's nothing we can do to change the past, no way to find answers to your questions." She touched his arm, drawing his attention from Eli to her. "All we can do now is help your son. That means making sure he doesn't start school behind other kids his age."

"How do we do that? School will be out soon."

"He has to get to his grade level. I don't know how to do that, and I doubt you do, either. But I promise you this, Gabe. Getting that child ready for school is hugely important, if only so he won't feel he's what his cousins called him, what his aunt called him," she growled, a fierce protection rising inside. "Eli is not stupid."

"I thought the most important thing was getting us a home," he said, obviously confused.

"It is. But starting school at or above the other kids in his class will also help heal Eli's insecurities and help him settle into his new life."

"Olivia, I am deeply moved and very grateful for all your help with my son, but— " He frowned. "Neither of us know what or how to teach him."

"Correct. But I can find out who does." Her phone pinged. She checked her texts, then jumped to her feet. "It was a great picnic, but I have to leave. Now."

"What's wrong?" Gabe demanded, senses ramping to high alert. "Must be bad. Your face is pale and those tiny lines of strain around your eyes are back."

"Victoria fell while she was rock climbing. She's at the hospital. She has several broken bones, nothing life-threatening, but they'll put her out of action for a while." She stared at him. "The aunts need me to take over for her while she recovers."

"Okay." He waited. "Now tell me what's really bugging you?"

"I'm not sure I can do this, Gabe." She chewed her bottom lip, grateful she could talk this out with him before being inundated by her aunts. "But I can't say no, either. Summer is The Haven's busiest time. Disappointing all those kids who are planning to come?"

"You can do this, Olivia. You've already got the staff organized and scheduled. You've worked with Victoria, you know how things operate. And I'll do whatever I can." Gabe grinned at her. "I guess you won't be leaving here anytime soon."

"I—" She hadn't really considered what this would mean to her own plans.

"You'll be giving up your summer in Edmonton, but being at The Haven has lots of compensations." He grinned. "Including the kids you'll get to work with."

"Yeah." Olivia gulped. That was exactly what she was so worried about. She'd be the one in charge. What if she messed up and another child was hurt because of her?

When I am afraid I will trust in Thee.

I'm trusting You, God, she prayed silently as they drove back to The Haven.

At least Gabe would be around. The next few weeks would show if her judgment had improved, if the tall, lean cowboy really was a man you could count on if things got bad.

Don't let me mess up, she begged as worry filled her mind.

Chapter Seven

In Gabe's mind the July First Canada Day festivities at The Haven were a complete success.

Olivia seemed to have thought of everything and invited everyone in Chokecherry Hollow. The Haven was teeming. From sack races and fishing ponds to bouncy castles and a live theater presentation about the history of the Rockies, Olivia had planned something for every age.

For Gabe, however, the best thing was that he was part of it. Between watching and encouraging Eli's participation, Gabe judged several relay races, chose the winner for the bean bag toss and adjudicated the best carved-watermelon contest. He didn't much care for helping with the face painting, but since there was a shortage of makeup artists available and an excess of children who wanted their faces decorated, and because he'd been promised a massive slice of lemon pie, he chipped in. Thankfully, the kids didn't care if his work was weird and lopsided.

Gabe loved being part of the celebrations instead of standing on the sidelines watching, as he had for so many years. Helping Olivia was an opportunity to pay back a little of what she'd done for him and Eli, so Gabe took the job seriously, ensuring she stopped for lunch, had coffee or a cool drink when she sagged, and insisting she take a few minutes to rest when possible.

Gabe also went to great pains to be ready to assist whenever he saw a tiny frown mar the smooth skin of her brow, whether that meant rescuing some weeping child or solving a new dilemma. By the end of the day he was weary but very pleased with his efforts and thrilled that Eli had enjoyed himself.

"You've outdone yourself today, Olivia," Gabe murmured as they sat together on a quilt hours later, watching the fireworks display. He glanced at his son sitting with Mikey. The two gaped at the colored flashes in the sky, oohing and aahing like everyone else. "Everybody enjoyed themselves, especially the kids."

"I hope so." She wrinkled her nose. "Thank you for saving my bacon with that bingo game. Don't ask me how I could have forgotten to get prizes," she muttered in disgust, cheeks pink. "My only excuse is that my phone went dead, again, which took out my schedule plan and I had to wing it."

"Which the aunts did very capably." Gabe chuckled, enjoying cool, competent Olivia's embarrassment. "The kids thought the ladies' prizes were fantastic."

"Except for Eli. I'm pretty sure he guessed I'd messed up after Aunt Tillie gave him her orange knitted hat." She winced. "At least he didn't tell everyone I forgot to charge my phone. I thought I'd done that last night, but—"

"Okay, your phone died. Cut yourself some slack, Liv. You did an awesome job taking over for Victoria. I doubt even she wouldn't have thought of throwing together that hike after you found out supper was going to be late."

Olivia shivered then so Gabe laid his jacket over her shoulders. True to form, this ultra organizer hadn't taken time to fetch a sweater for herself. She'd been too busy ensuring the kids were all warmly clothed and that her aunts were cozily ensconced in their lawn chairs with jackets and woolen blanket coverings to bother about herself. That was Olivia—selfless.

"That hike was not my smartest brain wave," she mumbled.

"What do you mean?" Gabe knew, but he sensed she needed to talk it out.

"That girl falling. That was my fault for letting her go along." She winced as the bang from a huge red fireball resounded through the valley. "Thank God you were there. I don't know what I'd have done otherwise."

"You would have picked her up, kissed her knee and carried on, of course. That's what you do, Olivia." He chuckled at her dour expression. "What?"

"I wouldn't have kissed her knee." She looked so sad he had to tease back her good humor.

"Because it was so dirty?" Olivia had a way of rolling her eyes that expressed her thoughts about his attempt at humor better than any words. Gabe tried another tack. "You'd have consoled her somehow if I hadn't been there."

She frowned. "I'm not very good at interacting with kids. I shouldn't—"

"Olivia, her falling was *not* your fault. She insisted on wearing those crazy boots despite your advice to wear sneakers. You kept checking that she'd suffered no ill effects and she, like all the others, had a great time dipping her toes in the stream." He chuckled, remembering the splashing. "On top of that, the hike helped them work up an appetite for Adele's delicious al fresco dinner. Couldn't ask for a better day."

"If it was, it was only because you and the aunties had my back. Thank you, Gabe." Her words sounded like a sigh as she leaned her head against his shoulder. "I couldn't have done this day without your help."

"That's not true," he insisted, liking the way her head fit against him. "Your middle names are *confidence* and *organization*. You're a natural at this job because you're a ways-and-means person. What you don't know you figure out."

"Ha! Look how I messed up with the kite races." She ducked her head so her reddened cheeks were hidden.

Gabe tried, but he couldn't suppress his laughter.

"It is *not* funny," she insisted, drawing away. "Someone could have been hurt."

"By a runaway kite?" He snickered at the disgusted look she tossed his way. "It's not as if you could have known the wind would kick up, Livvie. Nor is it feasible that one of those kids was light enough to be carried away by a gust of wind. Anyway, you soon got them interested in something else and it worked out."

"Yes," she murmured. "But next time it might—"

Gabe placed his fingertip against her lip and shook his head.

"'Sufficient unto the day is the evil thereof,'" he quoted as he slid his palm to cup her cheek. He winced when she immediately drew away, puzzled until he realized he was touching her scar. "Don't borrow trouble,

Olivia. Though if it does come, I still have every confidence in your ability to turn it into something good."

"Thank you." She tipped her head to study him in the gloom. "You're a good friend, Gabe."

As they sat together watching the afterglow of the fireworks die away, Gabe found himself disliking that word. *Friend.* Somehow it didn't quite encapsulate whatever this was that he and Olivia shared.

"Is that all there are?" Eli murmured after the last boom. He yawned, then crawled into his father's lap. Mikey was already asleep on their blanket.

"And now to bed," Olivia said as everyone around them rose. "Is he asleep?"

"Pretty much." Gabe stood, hoisting his son into his arms. "Feels like he's put on ten pounds. How much watermelon did he eat?"

"Not enough. Adele says there are five of those monster things left over. We'll be eating it for days." Olivia folded the quilt and slung it over her arm.

Ben had brought the aunties and Victoria to the site in an ATV. Now, having retrieved Mikey, they were loading everyone into the buggies for the return ride. Gabe glanced at Olivia.

"Since they're full I guess we're walking back." He didn't mind in the least that they'd have a few moments together, on their own. Well, alone if you didn't count Eli.

Gabe deliberately slowed his pace to allow people to pass. With sunset falling soon after ten, parents were anxious to tuck their children into bed. The counselors from The Haven also shepherded their weary charges toward their cabins. There would be no campfire tonight. Everyone was worn-out. Except him. Oddly, Gabe felt completely alive.

"It was a perfect evening for fireworks." Olivia licked her fingertip and held it out with a grin. "Not even the tiniest breath of wind for the fireworks. Exactly what I prayed for after the kite fiasco."

"Proof that God answers even the smallest prayers." Gabe enjoyed the way moonbeams lit her expressive face.

"I like the way you include God in everything." Olivia's smile held a hint of wryness. "I try but often find myself fussing over things right after I've prayed about them."

"I'm no saint," Gabe protested, though he was flattered by her comment. "But his arrival," he said, glancing down at the boy sleeping in his arms, "has made me more aware of God's sovereignty."

Without a word spoken between them they entered The Haven, climbed the stairs and put Eli to bed. Gabe kept a close eye on Olivia as she tucked in the covers around his son, her hand lingering above his cheek before she quickly drew away. Something—longing?— washed across her face as she stepped back to give him room.

"Your turn," she whispered.

"Good night, son." Gabe brushed the flop of curls off Eli's forehead and pressed a kiss there, his heart full of love for this child, this blessing that had come from such a painful past. "Sleep tight." If only he'd been there from the beginning.

And the bitterness was back.

"Let's let him sleep." Olivia tugged on his arm, urging him from the room. She led the way downstairs and then outside to the patio, where solar lights beckoned them to enjoy the night's beauty a little longer. She sank into a chair and tucked her feet underneath her, her face troubled. "Just now, after you kissed Eli. You were thinking of her, weren't you? Of Eve?"

Gabe sat down across from her, uncertain of where this conversation was leading and uncomfortable with admitting the truth. "Yes."

"I could tell."

"How?" he asked, puzzled by her words.

"I don't know if I can describe it properly." Olivia shoved her hair behind her ear and leaned her head against the chair back to peer at the stars above.

Gabe doubted she realized her scar was clearly revealed in the moonlight.

"Try," he urged, liking that she felt comfortable enough to talk to him about it even though she knew he didn't. This must be important.

"It's not any one thing that gives you away, Gabe." She shrugged. "It's a combination of the way your face tightens, and you go kind of stiff for a moment, as if you're remembering she hurt you and are waiting for the next blow."

"That's a pretty apt description of how I feel," he admitted starkly. "How did you get to be so smart, Olivia?"

She chuckled as if he'd made a huge joke, but the laughter quickly died away as her face grew sad. "I know because that's how I feel sometimes," she confessed.

"When you get too close to kids," Gabe guessed, keeping his voice very quiet. "What happened, Olivia? Can you tell me what causes you to withdraw like that?"

Her internal fight was obvious.

But perhaps because she found her new job so stressful, perhaps because she was around children more than she had been, or perhaps because she was just plain tired of the past interfering with her present—whatever the reason, Olivia closed her eyes and began to speak.

"I was a foster kid for as long as I can remember."

Olivia blurted out the words, desperate to release the miasma of emotions whirling inside. She needed to talk to someone other than her foster sisters and her aunts. They were too close and might be hurt by what she so desperately needed to say.

Hurting those she loved was the last thing Olivia wanted. She knew Gabe would listen. His quiet "uh-huh" brimmed with understanding, proving she was right.

"All I know is that I was left as a newborn at the hospital in Edmonton with my name pinned to my blanket. I have no past, no history, no family. I have no memories and no records of who I belong to or where I come from. I just—" she shrugged "—am."

"But you've defined yourself since then, Olivia," he objected with a frown. "You've become a woman with a past, with history, with a family. You are loved. You belong at The Haven."

"I'm not decrying anything I've been given, Gabe," she assured him, striving to make him understand. "I'm just trying to explain how growing up was for me back then, how I always knew I never belonged anywhere or to anyone. That I always understood that wherever I was, it was only temporary. That it wasn't home."

"Until you came here." Gabe waited, frowning when she took a long time to answer.

"Yes." Olivia sighed. Maybe unloading on Gabe wasn't a good idea.

"I keep interrupting. Sorry. Please continue." Gabe's grin gave her the courage to push on.

"I was thinking. Maybe my lack of family history was the reason I always felt like an outsider, why I needed to belong," she murmured. "Without even realizing what I was doing, I began to define Olivia DeWitt by being ultra-responsible."

Gabe's empathetic nod helped her relax. His dark eyes revealed no condemnation. Just acceptance. Of course, that might change, but she had to take the risk. The feelings boiling inside demanded an outlet.

"In every foster home I looked for ways to make myself indispensable, to be someone they could count on in a pinch. So that they wouldn't want to let me leave," she added, aware that her tone had dropped.

"Understandable." Gabe grinned. "It also explains a lot about who you are now, Ms. Competence."

"Whatever. It didn't work, though, because I still got sent from one home to the next."

"Which meant you tried harder. You became increasingly responsible, maybe babysat even though you were too young?" He smiled at her blink of surprise. "Stands to reason and you are, above all things, a logical person, Olivia."

"I guess." She sighed, hating the next part. Though if he was to understand, it had to be said. "That's how I got in trouble."

Gabe arched one eyebrow in surprise, and suddenly she couldn't do it.

"This is silly. It's late. You have as hectic a schedule as I do." She jumped to her feet, forcing a yawn as if to prove her tiredness. "We should say good-night, Gabe. We can reminisce another time."

Only Olivia did *not* want to go back to that sad pathetic girl, to remember, to feel the guilt all over again.

"This is a perfectly good time. I don't have to be anywhere else." Gabe's steady voice told her she wouldn't get off so easily. "And I'm not in the least tired."

"You should be, after all the running around you did for me today. I do appreciate it, you know." She was surprised by the wry smile lifting his lips.

"Okay, you've thanked me profusely and used those good manners the aunts taught you. Now can you just say whatever it is?" he added in a soft murmur.

"I don't know," she admitted. "I'm—afraid."

"Of me?" he demanded, eyes wide with consternation.

"Not of you." Olivia wished she'd gone to bed and let sleep drown out the memories. "It's me. It's my past. It's—pretty bad," she warned.

"You were abused." The words sounded pulled from him. "Olivia—"

"No." She rushed to stop him. "That's not it. I almost wish it was."

"What? Why?" Poor Gabe looked so confused.

"If I'd been the one who'd been hurt, I could deal with that," she explained. "But to know that someone else was hurt because of me?" She shook her head. "That eats at me. You see, I'm the one who should have died."

Gabe stared at her. "I don't understand."

"How could you?" Olivia inhaled deeply, then sat

back down to quickly relay the details of her past, beginning with the fire when she was eight and then the drowning a year later. Accidents that had taken two of her young foster siblings.

She bared her soul, told him all the issues of blame and accusations that had followed, how the parents had hated her, because she'd lived and not their child. How after that she'd been shuffled from place to place, unwanted and in the way and growing increasingly bitter, acting out that bitterness until no one wanted her.

"I even beat up another girl once."

"You were an unhappy kid lashing out, Olivia," Gabe said softly.

"Yes. After those kids died—they sent me to therapy. I've been told many times by many people that those two deaths weren't my fault," she admitted. She lifted her head to study him. "It doesn't help. Psychologists, psychiatrists, counselors, ministers. They all say the same thing." Olivia made a face. "Forgive myself for not saving my foster siblings and get on with my life." She sniffed her disgust. "Trust me, I've tried."

"And?" Gabe frowned as he watched her face.

"I can't." She couldn't meet his gaze.

"Because?" As always, Gabe went straight to the point.

"Because I don't understand why I'm alive and they aren't. Because I can't figure out the reason they had to die and I didn't," she whispered brokenly. "They had family, people who loved them, needed them, wanted them. I didn't. I didn't matter to anybody. So why did God let me live? What's so special about me?"

"I finally get it. That's what drives your need to organize and find order. You're trying to make sense of your world." The understanding filling Gabe's voice made her study him. "You're trying to prove you deserve to be alive, Olivia."

"Am I?" She mulled it over. "Maybe. I am trying to be the very best I can be."

"Because?" He was pushing her to look deeper.

"It's stupid, but if I'm good enough—" Olivia hesitated, his gaze holding hers "—maybe then I won't be responsible for another child being hurt?"

"That's why you avoid kids, to protect them." Could he see into her heart? "And that's getting harder to do because you've taken on Victoria's job and responsibility for kids scares you. It's like being thrust into your childhood again." His dark eyes glowed. "Am I right?"

"I've always tried to do my best, Gabe." She reconsidered her life in Ottawa. "I volunteered where I could. I tried to make my life meaningful…" She let the sentence trail away, hating the pathetic sound of desperation in her words.

"All of that is great, Olivia." Gabe crouched in front of her. His hands closed over hers, warm and comforting. "But you're putting too much pressure on yourself. You can't keep living your life avoiding contact with kids without it adversely affecting you. And what you're saying now proves that is already happening. You're constantly checking yourself lest you get too close."

"Avoiding them is the only way I know to protect them from me. What else am I supposed to do?" Tears rolled down her face. "Tell me, Gabe, and I'll do it."

"You can't *do* anything to fix the past, Livvie—" He stopped and shook his head. "You have to let it go."

"How?" she demanded, angry that he made it sound so easy.

"By accepting that the deaths of those two kids so long ago were not your fault." His unflinching gaze held hers. "There's a verse I really like from Psalms 56. 'What time I am afraid, I will trust in Thee.'"

"I've tried that," she muttered. "Repeating biblical verses doesn't help me."

"Of course not." He chuckled at her glare. "Because repeating them doesn't reach the heart of the issue. You have to *believe* the words you're repeating." He reached up to brush a wisp of hair from her eyes. "Sweet Olivia, you're trying to take responsibility for something that's not in your power."

"Huh?" She struggled to concentrate on what he was saying, too aware of his warm fingers and how much she liked his touch against her skin.

"Those children living or dying—whether *you* lived or died—that was not your decision, Liv." Gabe's gentle voice soothed as much as the brush of his fingertips. "Trusting God means believing He knew what was happening, He was there, and *He* decided when those children died. It was never up to you. You mattered to somebody. You mattered to God and He wanted you to live. It was His choice."

"But maybe if I'd—" The big strong cowboy's gentle fingertips smoothed across her lips to stop the words.

"Uh-uh. You don't get to second-guess God's choices," he said in the most tender voice she'd ever heard. "God never put young Olivia in charge back then. He knew you wouldn't save those two kids. He didn't expect you to. He doesn't expect that now, either."

Olivia remained still a long time, long after he drew his hand from her lips.

"Then what does He expect?" she asked miserably.

Chapter Eight

Olivia's words fell like raindrops, almost silent in the hushed evening. But in them, muted though it was, Gabe heard her unspoken desperation to be free of the long-time load of guilt she'd been carrying. He sent a silent prayer heavenward for the right words to offer this precious woman.

"I think He expects you to trust that He had and still has it all under control, to rest assured that He has a plan, even though it's one you may never understand." Gabe felt as if he was treading on shaky ground. He was no Bible scholar, no expert on the thoughts of God. But helping Olivia understand that she couldn't keep blaming herself for the heartbreak of her past was like a physical need inside him. This beautiful woman's sadness reached in and gripped his heart so strongly it scared him.

"Continue, Gabe. Please?" Her trusting silver-gray eyes gazed into his and he knew he had to keep going.

"Either you believe God is in control of everything, or He's not in control at all. There's no halfway with trust." He had to get this right, had to help her understand. "Either you believe God does what is best for us or…"

Gabe deliberately let it hang, praying that she'd finally absolve herself of the blame. But Olivia wasn't there yet.

"It sounds too easy to just blame it on God's will," she murmured.

"Not blame. Trust." Gabe's emotions were running wild. He couldn't stay so close to her, but he couldn't walk away, either. He'd sort out these crazy reactions later; now he needed some space between them. He rose. "The past, as painful as it was, happened. You can't change it. But you can change your future."

"How?" she demanded with a glare.

Typical of this organized woman. She needed a plan, an organized, detailed strategy. But most of the time life didn't have one.

"Trust," he said gently, watching as the words penetrated. "Stop being afraid."

She was silent for a long time. Gabe glanced at his watch. It was after one in the morning and he had a full riding day tomorrow. He should get home. And yet he was loath to leave and end these special heart-sharing moments with Olivia.

He was about to say good-night when she spoke.

"Is trust how you recovered from your divorce, Gabe?"

There was no malice in Olivia's question, but in his head her words condemned his self-righteous advice, because even after all these years he still could not get past Eve's perfidy. Though she was no longer alive, his anger at her would not abate. It was a familiar ache. Too familiar. Why couldn't he forget her?

Gabe did not want bitter thoughts of Eve to taint this special new relationship with Olivia, so he brushed it off with a glib response.

"I'm still working on the trust part. Maybe I always will be." He cleared his throat. "I need to get home and you need your rest. Good night, Olivia." He turned to walk away, but suddenly Olivia was there beside him, touching his arm.

"I didn't mean to hurt you, Gabe," she said, her voice gentle. "I'm so sorry if I did. You've been a great friend to me. Thank you." She wrapped her arms around his waist and hugged him with a fierceness that surprised him.

And yet it felt right. It felt as if Olivia *belonged* in his arms. Without a second thought, Gabe embraced her, holding her close in the intimacy of the evening's darkness.

"I know you're trying to help me and I appreciate it," Olivia whispered into his shirtfront. "But I don't think I'm going to be able to trust God very easily."

"We all work at it," Gabe murmured into her hair, noting the fresh citrus scent of it even after a hot day spent racing around The Haven. "But the kids that come here need you, Olivia. They need your leadership, your perspective, but most of all, your love. You've been where they are. You can empathize with their struggles as no one else can. Maybe that's why God brought you home to The Haven."

"Just temporarily." She burrowed closer.

Somewhere in the hills surrounding them a coyote howled. The trees rustled with a light breeze that rifled through her hair, tossing those strands against his cheek. Gabe lifted one hand to smooth the silky threads, filled with awe at the wonder of God's creation, and of this special woman who thought he was some sort of hero.

As if.

"Maybe you don't know your family history, Olivia, but you know God." Gabe rested his chin against her hair. "You've known Him for a long time, haven't you?"

"I thought I did, but—God doesn't change, so I guess you're basically saying that now it's time to put my faith where my mouth is." She drew away, sobering. "It's time for me to walk the faith I talk. I agree with you. It's way past time."

Gabe's arms felt empty now that she'd stepped back. Odd how absolutely *right* that embrace had felt when he'd sworn he'd never let a woman get close again.

He so did not want to think about Eve now. Yet he'd chastised Olivia for her lack of trust. Was it the same for him? Did he doubt God's ability to heal his heart? Was he clinging to the anger because he was afraid God would let him get hurt again?

What about Eli? This was no time to be thinking about romance. Not when Gabe still hadn't figured out fatherhood.

"Gabe? What are you thinking?" Olivia watched him with those all-encompassing eyes that took in far more than anyone realized.

"That tomorrow's going to be here before we know it," he growled. "And that you don't need any beauty sleep, but I do."

True to form, Olivia tilted back on her heels to study him. "I think you're very handsome."

"Sure." He brushed the words aside like a joke.

"I mean it. You're a very good-looking man, Gabe. But what I like best is that there's more to you than simple good looks. You have a quality, an inner integrity, that drives most everything in your life. You're utterly honest and that's refreshing. Lots of men aren't who you think they are."

Meaning the guy she'd fallen for, the one who already had a family? Comparing him to that creep did not sit well with Gabe.

"Don't crown me yet. The reason I don't tell lies is because you always get caught." He shrugged, brushed her nose with his lips, then stepped back. "It's late. I have to go. See you tomorrow."

"Good night, Gabe. And thank you again."

He nodded. He didn't want Olivia's thanks.

What did he want?

Gabe walked to his truck, climbed inside and drove away, knowing she stood there watching until he disappeared from her sight.

I don't tell lies, he'd claimed.

Yeah, right, cowboy. You're telling the biggest lie of all and it's to yourself. If you told the truth, you'd have to admit that hanging on to your anger at Eve allows you to forget that not everything about your marriage was awful, and that some of the awful part was your fault. You didn't love your wife enough and that's why she left.

Uncomfortable with that, Gabe tried to put the past out of his head by mentally forming a list of all the things he needed to do before the house was moved at the end of the week. It didn't work.

In the wee hours of dawn, he was still wrestling with the bitterness that wouldn't go away.

"C'mon, Livvie. I got my stuff. We gotta go see my house moving." Raggedy suitcase bumping against his skinny legs, Eli tugged at her arm, urging her toward the car.

"It won't be there yet, Eli. Houses get moved slowly." She smiled at the excitement blooming in his face. So like Gabe. One fingertip touched her cheek, remembering how he'd held her. *Stop it!* "Do you like going to Miss Erma's now?"

"Yeah. At first I didn't want to go when you tol' me 'bout her. But she's nice an' she has lotsa games," the boy said. He threw in his suitcase, then buckled himself into the back seat. "I really like games."

"I do believe you've told me that once or twice," Olivia teased as she checked the belt, then fastened her own. "Which game do you like best?"

"The cookie game." Eli giggled when she rolled her eyes.

"Figures. My sister says you're like the cookie monster in her kitchen." Judging by the chocolate smear on Eli's shirt, Olivia figured she'd probably hear it again.

Olivia had discovered Ms. Erma Nettleworth's private tutoring class thanks to the aunties. Though neither Tillie nor Margaret had said so, Olivia was almost certain the two ladies had been instrumental in helping retired teacher Erma start her remedial summer learning program. Newly widowed, Erma was struggling to pay down the mortgage on the lovely cottage she and her late husband had built for their retirement. Her program was fast gaining notoriety for her unique and extremely effective methods of helping kids succeed scholastically, and Eli loved it.

Thrilled that Gabe's son would start school well-grounded in the basics and that she'd been able to talk Erma into taking one more student under her already

bustling wing with the simple exchange of a week at
The Haven for her grandson, Olivia reveled in a rush of
joy. Finally, after all Gabe had done for her, she'd been
able to do something to help ease his burdens. Now if
she could only find a way to erase the tight lines around
his mouth whenever he mentioned Eli's mother.

Half-listening to Eli outline how Miss Erma's cookie
game worked, Olivia drove to Gabe's acreage while
hoping she'd covered all eventualities that could occur
at The Haven in her absence. The staff were rock-solid,
and her earlier insistence that they be able to take over
different facets of the ministry when Victoria couldn't
be there was beginning to pay off, as was her hard-
fought scheduling plan. Olivia was mostly happy with
that part of her job.

She wasn't as satisfied with her own efforts at running her aunts' program. That kid, Skylar—she'd let
him go on the ride today even though she'd known in
her heart of hearts that he was lying about his previous
riding experience. She'd purposely questioned him several times and watched him carefully on the ride yesterday, expecting trouble. Since he'd done all right, she
couldn't very well hold him back from going with his
group this afternoon, but—

"Liv?"

"Yes, sweetie?" She glanced in the mirror at the
young boy who'd wormed his way into her heart despite her resistance to getting too involved with him.

"D'you think I'll like it in my new house with…
Gabe?" That slight hesitation was painful to hear after
all this time, but it also told her Eli had been thinking
about this for a while.

"Don't you?" she asked.

"I dunno. It's kinda funny." He kicked his sneakers up and down for a minute while he thought about it. "I never had a whole house of my own before."

"Funny good?" she asked.

"I guess." He didn't sound convinced. It would be up to Gabe to prove it to him.

"I'm sure you and your dad will have a great time in your new house."

"Yeah." Eli's bottom lip trembled. He dashed a hand across his eyes, then turned his head to stare out the window. "My mom won't be there," he whispered.

"No, she won't." Uh-oh. Olivia pulled into the yard site and parked well beyond the area needed to manipulate Gabe and Eli's new home into place. "But she'd want you to be happy with your dad. She'd want you to enjoy your new house and all the birds that will come."

Eli looked at her as if he thought she was making it up. "How do you know?" he asked when she got out and began undoing his seat belt.

"Because she told your aunt that you were to come here and live with your dad. She wanted you to be happy, so she made sure your dad would look after you." Olivia stopped herself from hugging him though her heart yearned to ease his sadness. "You told me about all the things your mom did. I think she always did her best for you, didn't she?" She waited until he'd nodded his head. "Oh, sweetheart. I wish she could be here to see you now, to watch you riding a pony and learning to read and flying that kite. She'd be so glad to see you being happy."

"But if she was here—that wouldn't be good." Eli stopped, a catch in his voice. "My dad hates her."

"Oh, no, Eli. Gabe doesn't hate your mommy." Olivia paused. She had to get this right.

"Well, he gets a mad face when I talk about her. An' when I tol' him the funny story about how one time our popcorn got burnt on the fire, his hands went like this." He formed his little hands into fists.

"Sweetheart, I'm going to tell you something. You'll have to be a little bit grown-up to understand, but you're so smart, I think you can do that." Olivia exhaled, hoping she was doing the right thing. *Help me*, she prayed silently.

"Well? Tell me, Liv." Eli's scared voice emerged in a whisper.

"I will, but I was thinking that first we should get out our blanket and sit on the grass. We can watch while we talk." When they were seated on the hillside with the house-moving panorama spread out before them, she tried to explain. "Your mom and dad got married when they weren't very old. They didn't know lots of things about being married so I think they made lots of mistakes. Those mistakes hurt your dad. Sometimes people can't forget getting hurt by somebody they love."

"Huh?" Eli's confusion had her sifting through her brain for a better explanation.

"It's like with you and Mikey," she said, wondering how she'd gotten into this. Involvement so wasn't her thing. And yet... Trust God, Gabe had said. "You two are good friends, right?"

"Uh-huh. 'Cept when he tells me I gotta do sumthin'. I don't like that."

"I understand." She smiled. "I think it was kind of like that with your mom and dad. He loved living on his ranch because he really likes horses. But maybe your mom never lived on a ranch before. Maybe she was used to living in town and she didn't like having so much change. Some people don't."

"Oh." Eli's tanned forehead furrowed as he considered that.

"Maybe your mom and dad couldn't agree about lots of things. That would make it hard to live together. Maybe they argued. Lots of people do and that makes being together even harder, like when you and Mikey argue and then you don't want to play with him for a little while."

"The man in my class at church said you're not 'sposed to argue," Eli muttered, peeking at her as if he wasn't sure he should mention that. "God doesn't like it."

"God doesn't like arguing," Olivia agreed. "But sometimes people get angry and they do argue. Sometimes they stay angry." She could almost feel herself drowning here and all because she'd taken on the responsibility of this child. *Not your business*, her brain reminded. But she'd started. She had to finish it.

"You mean my mommy and him din't want to fight so they din't live together no more?" Eli slowly put the pieces together.

"You'd have to talk to your dad to know for sure, but I think maybe that's what happened," she said, wincing at her oversimplification. "But people change. Just because your mom didn't like to live on a ranch back then doesn't mean she wouldn't like it that you're here now, Eli."

"Really?" Hope made his eyes glow.

Keep going, something inside Olivia encouraged. *Make staying here with Gabe in this house okay for him.*

"I'm pretty sure that if your mommy could see you and your dad living in this new house and enjoying it, she'd be very happy."

"How'd you know, Livvie?" he asked, big eyes searching hers for assurance.

"Because moms always want the very best for their kids, and this place, with all its trees and birds, plus a snug house that will keep you warm in the winter— I think this is the kind of place that would make your mom smile." She waited, breath suspended.

"She liked trees an' grass." He sniffed, then nodded. "An' she liked to be warm. She *was* scared of horses, but maybe she'd get used to them, like me," he said hopefully.

"I think so." Olivia loved that Eve had showered her love on this little boy. Poor kid. How awful to be left totally alone with his horrid cousins after knowing his mother's wonderful love. "It might take some time to get used to things with your dad, but I think you're going to like it here, too, Eli. Let's ask God to help you."

She quietly prayed a blessing on Eli and his dad.

That done, they shared a smile as they sat together, surveying the area below them. The burnt-out shell of the old house had been completely removed since Olivia had been here last, and a new cement pad poured. Assorted mechanical pipes and outlets awaited hookup. Her gaze automatically searched for and found Gabe. He spent ages speaking with someone, but then he waved and jogged up the hill to talk to them.

"Very smart to park over here, Olivia," he said after ruffling Eli's hair. "It's well out of the way." He crouched down and explained to Eli what was about to happen. Then he produced a small camera, a sketchbook and some pencils. "I thought you might like to make some memories of today."

"Thank you." Eli listened to his explanation about the camera, took two practice shots and then assembled his pencils in perfect order. After a second look at the site, he began to draw.

"That's a great idea, Gabe." Olivia admired his tall lean figure in the bright sun. This cowboy always looked ready to handle anything which was just one of many things she admired about him.

"He's always reciting memories about Eve. I want to have a record of our memories together, too," Gabe murmured, his gaze meeting and holding Olivia's. "Thank you for bringing him. I know you have a lot on your plate, but I appreciate you taking the time to be here with him."

"Well, of course I want to see your home moved in." Why did it feel as if his blue eyes saw past her bland comments to the nervous quiver in her stomach? "It's a big day for you both."

"It is." His gaze shifted to Eli, who was busily re-creating the gorgeous summer afternoon with swift, sure pencil strokes. "The first of many, I hope."

"Hmm. Who was it lecturing me about faith—was it only last week?" she asked, miming an innocent blink.

"Guilty." Gabe shrugged. "I'm trying to do better, but I'm a work in progress."

"Me, too." She shared a smile with him before someone called and he strode away as the first truck bearing a wide-load sign rounded the bend. "Here it comes, Eli."

They sat entranced as the white house rolled into view. After much discussion, various movements backing up and going forward, the house was finally ready to be moved onto its footings.

"It's perfect," Olivia mused to herself as it slowly, gently moved over the ground. She felt an undue delight in how the house didn't take away from the stunning landscape around it but made the entire setting more beautiful.

"It belongs here, right, Livvie?" Eli said softly.

"It belongs, and so do you," she said with a gentle smile. "You and your dad."

Eli tipped his head back and stared at her without saying a word. But Olivia was getting better at translating the expressions fluttering through the dark eyes so like Gabe's. She saw hope and longing in those dark eyes. Then Eli focused on the movers.

"What's that big hook for? An' why do they have ropes? An' what does that yellow machine do?" His questions came at a rapid pace as he snapped pictures, but Eli quickly grew disgruntled with her lack of illuminating answers. Eventually, he stopped asking.

"Don't you have any more questions?" Olivia studied the little boy who was always curious.

"I'll ask my dad." He offered her a glance brimming with pity. "You know lotsa stuff, Livvie, but I don't guess you know much about moving houses."

"I guess I don't," she admitted, and tucked her smile behind her hand.

It seemed to take forever before the house was finally settled in place and being expertly fastened down. Olivia had brought along two bottles of juice, an apple and a granola bar, which she and Eli shared as the afternoon grew warmer. Gabe, she noticed, never seemed to pause in his inspection of the house, constantly checking that everything was done correctly.

The afternoon grew late. Olivia knew it was time for her to get back to The Haven and her job, but she couldn't just leave Eli. A quick check via her cell phone ensured no one had left a message about any major issues. Maybe she could stay a little while longer.

To pass the time, Olivia made up a game where she quizzed Eli on the letters he'd learned, made up words with them, then watched him painstakingly print them on the tablet Gabe had given him. Finally, the movers seemed to be finished. They left just as a huge truck drove in.

"What in the world—?"

"It's our stuff." Eli jumped to his feet in his excitement. "We got lotsa things. I even got a bed with drawers underneath it. Can we go watch them put it in my room?"

"*Your* room, huh?" Delighted that he'd laid claim to his new home, Olivia thought about it for only a moment. If they needed her at The Haven, they'd call. "We'll ask your dad."

Worried he might rush into the chaos of vehicles, Olivia took his hand and they walked toward Gabe. Well, she walked. Eli almost danced. It was the most excited she'd ever seen him.

Inside Olivia was dancing, too, because finally Gabe would be home with his son.

By the time Eli went to school she'd be leaving. The thought sobered Olivia like a douse of cold water.

But she didn't want to stay.

Did she?

Chapter Nine

Gabe divided his time between watching the men load in furniture and housewares and watching Olivia and Eli. But mostly he watched Olivia. He wanted—no, needed to see her approval for his choices, though he wasn't exactly sure why.

"My son's bedroom first," he directed the movers. "Then he can be in there while we fill the rest of the house."

As promised, the men assembled the captain's bed and put it in place. A chest of drawers, a small desk and a chair followed.

"Gabe, you had them build in a window seat for Eli!" Olivia's gray eyes shone like polished silver as her fingers brushed his arm, though he knew she wasn't aware she'd done it. "It's perfect."

"There should be a cushion—ah. There it is." He took the long, tailored rectangle and, enlisting Eli's help, set it in place. "Try it out, son," he encouraged, loving the sound of that word "son."

Eli carefully took off his sneakers, then climbed onto the seat and peered out the window.

"It's good," he said. "But there's no tree."

"Not yet. You and I will plant one this weekend," Gabe promised.

"An' then the birds will come." Eli stared at him so trustingly. Gabe vowed then and there that he'd never do anything to betray that trust. "An' birdhouses?"

"Soon as we build them." He ruffled Eli's already messy hair before asking, "Eli, can you do your drawing in here while the movers bring in the rest of the furniture? I don't want you to get hurt by something."

"I'll draw stuff," the boy said proudly. "Then we can hang it on the wall."

"Good idea. Call out if you need anything." Gabe doubted that would happen soon since Eli seemed enraptured by his new surroundings. He sprawled across the bed, tried out the desk, raced to the window seat and then started all over again.

Gabe surreptitiously beckoned to Olivia to follow him.

"What can I help with?" she asked as they stood behind the kitchen island watching the movers carry in furniture.

"How about if you tell me if you think things need to be moved around?" he suggested. "That chair, for instance. I'm not sure—"

"It's a bedtime story chair," she told him without batting an eyelash. "It should be by the fireplace. No, that table can't be in front of the windows. It blocks the view."

Gabe smiled to himself. Olivia had told him she'd help find the house but that she would not get involved in decorating it, and yet here she was, directing the movers to rearrange his purchases in a much better configuration than he'd come up with. Exactly what he'd wanted.

She caught him smiling and blushed.

"I'm so sorry, Gabe. I didn't mean to take over. Wait," she called to the moving men, but Gabe shook his head. "It's perfect as it is," he told them.

Wrought iron stools fit perfectly at the kitchen island, and even better, they were heavy enough that Eli could climb onto them without fear of tipping. Appliances, bedroom furniture, a table and chairs, two loungers for the patio—all were set in place and, where needed, connected.

"The water should be hooked up by now," he told Olivia. "But it will take a bit for the hot water tank to reach capacity, so I'll wash our new bedding later." He grinned when she pointed to a box that sat in a corner. "That's Eli's, but he's not getting it. Not yet." He stopped her from calling out to Eli with a hand on her arm. "They have to put up the blinds. Then he can open it."

Gabe almost laughed out loud at the curiosity filling Olivia's expressive face. He wondered when the last time was that this ultra-organized woman had been kept in suspense. Following on the heels of that thought was a decision to arrange a surprise for her before she left.

"Everyone moves so fast." She watched as the blind hangers finished in the living room and kitchen and moved on to the rest of the rooms. "You can hardly tell anything's there," she marveled, trying to peer behind. "How do they work?"

"Remote control." Gabe loved seeing her astonished face when he pressed a button and the shades on the massive living room windows lowered. "I can even program them to close when I'm not here. And I had a skylight installed in my bathroom that will close at the first sign of rain."

"Wow. You're a surprising man, Gabe Webber." She looked suitably impressed.

"Because I bought a house with some toys?" He made a face. "Well past time, don't you think?"

Just then Amy Andrews, the daughter of local hardware store owners, pushed her way inside, lugging two gigantic boxes.

"Let me help," Gabe insisted, and lifted them from her arms. "More?"

"In the truck," she said with a grateful smile.

"You start unpacking. I'll bring them in." He glanced at Olivia. "You could help Amy, if you want."

"Sure." She opened one box. "What have we here?"

"Kitchenware." Amy grinned. "Gabe wanted his home functional from day one."

Satisfied that he'd surprised Olivia, Gabe began carrying in Amy's boxes. When he returned with the final box, Olivia had found his dishes.

"These are my favorite pattern," she told him, fingering the pale gray-on-white check. "They fit in perfectly with the decor."

"He said they reminded him of you." Amy chuckled as Olivia's brows rose. "I understand what he means now. It's like you said, Gabe, dainty but sturdy." She continued working, apparently unaware of Olivia's red face. Soon the island was laden with what she'd assured him were necessary kitchen essentials. "How do you want these things organized?"

Gabe blinked. Though he hadn't a clue, he knew who would.

"Ask Olivia," he suggested. "She's the most organized person I know."

"But it's your house, your kitchen," Olivia protested.

"And I'm asking for your help. I'm going to check on Eli." Gabe knew that if he left, she'd take over, so he stayed away a good half hour, grateful for the precious moments of sharing time with his son. They discussed all the things they would do together in the future.

Then they went outside together to watch as the last details on the house were completed. Finally the seller, Harry, handed over the keys.

"Welcome home, Gabe. You too, Eli," he said with a grin for the little boy. "I hope you enjoy your new home."

"Thanks a lot. We appreciate everything." Gabe shook his hand firmly. "Buying from you was so easy. You made the sale a pleasure."

"A lot of that was due to Olivia, you know. She's the most detailed person I know. Even gave me a checklist." Harry chuckled. "It was a good one, too."

Gabe was surprised by the information, but then he realized that's what she did. She'd been part of this from the beginning. Of course, she'd want to ensure the move went smoothly. For Eli's sake.

Gabe and Eli sat on the patio and chatted about birds and bugs and bedtime. Then he remembered Eli's box.

"Let's go inside." His heart racing with anticipation, Gabe glanced around.

The kitchen was now completely organized. Everything seemed to have a place, and the whole effect was bright, cheery and efficient. Though his appliances, large and small, were all in a stainless finish, there were bright splashes of orange here and there. Amy had asked his preference for accessories and he'd blurted orange because it made him think of Olivia. She always wore an orange scarf, an orange hair clip or some other item in that shade.

Gabe saw a bright orange pitcher and matching glassware behind the glass-doored cabinets. He didn't remember buying that.

"Amy says those are a thank-you gift from her parents," Olivia explained. She looked perfectly at home seated at his kitchen island, laying out bright orange woven place mats on the white stone counter.

"To say thank you for your business," Amy explained with a wide grin.

"Thank *you*. Both of you. What you've done looks amazing," he complimented, overwhelmed by his magazine-worthy kitchen.

"It's mostly Olivia's doing. I just put things where she said. Now I must go. Thanks, Gabe." After a wave at Eli, Amy gathered up her three bags of packing refuse and left.

"Hey, Eli. What's up?" When Eli shrugged Olivia glanced at Gabe.

"It's time for Eli's box." Smothering his excitement, Gabe picked up the box and carried it to a spot on the hardwood floor not covered by the new area rug. "This is for you, Eli."

"It's not my birthday yet," his son protested.

"It's for all your birthdays when I wasn't there. And Christmases, and Easters." Gabe stopped because the same old surge of anger at Eve blocked him from speaking. Enough! He was not going to allow it to ruin this moment. He cleared his throat. "It's from me to you."

"Th-thank you." But Eli just stood there, staring at the box.

Gabe hadn't anticipated his uncertainty, wasn't exactly sure about the proper way to handle it. He shuffled awkwardly until—

"Don't you want to see what it is?" Olivia walked to a corner of the rug near the box and sank onto it. "I do. Come on, Eli. Open it."

"Okay." Still Eli hesitated. Then he moved next to Gabe and slid his hand into his father's. "You help," he said quietly.

"We'll do it together." His heart so full it felt like he'd explode, Gabe sank down beside Eli and removed the first piece of tape, then let him do the next.

"It's a—a train?" Eli lifted his head to stare at Gabe. "It's old."

"Just like me," Gabe told him with a grin. "It was my grandfather's and then my dad's. They both passed it on to their sons and now I'm passing it on to my son. You."

"Oh. Thank you." Eli carefully lifted out one piece after another, examining each thoroughly before moving on.

"What a great idea, Gabe," Olivia whispered. Gabe saw tears in her eyes. "A welcome-home gift from father to son."

"How does this train work?" Eli asked, both hands full of train tracks.

"Let me show you." Gabe lay on his stomach and demonstrated how to put together the antique train that he'd once loved so much. He got it running and then Eli took over, laughing out loud every time the engine whistled and the caboose rattled around the track. Gabe moved to sit beside Olivia, content to soak in the sight and sound of Eli enjoying something without reservation. A muted noise made him glance at Olivia. He quickly did a double take.

What was the woman bawling about?

"What did I do wrong?" he demanded with a frown.

"Nothing. You did everything perfectly." She leaned over and kissed his cheek. "You've done a wonderful, wonderful thing here, Gabe. The house, Eli's room, the window seat. That's amazing. Passing on a bit of his history to give him a sense of connectedness, to make him feel he belongs—it's the perfect end to a wonderful day."

With Olivia's head resting on his shoulder and his son giggling nearby, Gabe thought so, too.

Nearly perfect.

Only what was he going to do when Olivia left for her new job and he was all alone?

Olivia cradled her cup of mint tea against her cheek and sighed. Mid-July. She loved this time of year.

She also loved that The Haven's latest youth group was gathered in the meadow below them, joyfully belting out songs as they roasted marshmallows over the campfire. Seated beside her on the patio, Gabe stretched out his long legs.

If only...

"Why the frown?" he asked.

"I thought it would get easier," she admitted softly, hesitant to tell him that.

"Hasn't it?" He studied her. "You looked very competent and in command today when you were organizing the kids into search teams for that girl who wandered off."

"I wasn't competent. I was a nervous wreck. It didn't help that my stupid phone died again."

"The new battery didn't help?"

"Maybe I didn't let it charge long enough," she admitted sheepishly. "I do know that I've never in my life prayed so hard as I did today. The relief of finding Sara lying in that field of wild clover, studying cloud shapes…" Olivia rolled her eyes, fairly certain her heart rate would never be normal again. "I had to give her a lecture about wandering off. This place is fenced, but that doesn't mean wild animals don't occasionally get through. What she did was foolhardy. And against our rules."

"Agreed." He arched one eyebrow. "But you straightened that out, didn't you?"

"As best I could, though I'm not sure I got through. Her reason for needing space didn't make sense to me. As usual. I just don't 'get' kids sometimes." Olivia tried to stifle her feelings of inadequacy.

"But it wasn't just Sara, was it?" Gabe asked.

"No. Skylar acted up again. He got into a fight with Jeffry, who is the sweetest kid." Olivia pursed her lips. "This is Skylar's third visit here, and I honestly don't know why that center in Edmonton keeps asking if he can return when we have to keep reporting his misbehavior. I don't think he's learning anything from being at The Haven."

"He's probably learned way more than you realize. They all have. You *are* making a difference here, Olivia. Even if you can't see it right now." Even in the gloomy twilight, Gabe's smile blazed white. "God's using you. All you have to do is trust."

"Now where have I heard that before?" she muttered,

then slumped, ashamed as silence stretched between them. Gabe was always so encouraging. It wasn't fair to unload on him just because things hadn't gone according to her plan. "Sorry."

"Hey, I can take it. But I hate to see you so down. And grumpy," he added with a cheeky grin.

"Lately I'm always grumpy," she admitted.

"No, you're not. What's changed?"

"Nothing." *Everything.*

He just kept staring at her, waiting. Olivia sighed. It was useless to prevaricate. Gabe could see right through her.

"Today Victoria told me she needs additional physiotherapy, in Edmonton. That means I'm going to be running this gig for at least another month."

The thought of overseeing so many children for even one more day set her teeth on edge. She'd accepted that she would have to stay at The Haven until her sister was able to return to work. She'd tried hard to trust God knew what He was doing sending the toughest kids here. But she'd never imagined she would be in charge for so long. That she hadn't yet goofed and ruined some kid's summer seemed like it was only a matter of time.

Besides that, Olivia still didn't have a place to live in the city, nor had she done any background work to prepare for her new job. She was worn-out, unsettled and totally out of her groove. And she didn't like those feelings. They reminded her too much of her past.

"You know you'll miss The Haven and the kids when you leave, Liv. But it's not really about this job, is it?" Gabe's blue eyes held hers, waiting.

"Not totally." She checked over one shoulder to be certain there was no one to overhear. Then she admitted in a quieter voice, "Managing the office is fun. I feel competent, like I can do it with one hand tied. But problems with the kids—that drains me. I'm totally, utterly ill-equipped to handle all the issues that keep cropping up."

"Discipline, you mean?"

"Not just that. Some of these kids are very troubled. They need someone to talk to, someone to advise them." She chewed her bottom lip. "How can I be sure I'm not making things worse for them?"

"The fact that you're even asking yourself that question is a great sign." Gabe shrugged. "You're smart and resourceful, and I doubt you have to worry. But you do have trained counselors you can call on if you need to. You're not alone in this." His mouth quirked into a smile. "You know what I'm going to tell you."

"Trust God." She let her breath out in a whoosh. "Easy for you to say, buddy. You're getting a handle on your world. You're all moved into your gorgeous new house and you told me you now have full legal custody of Eli. By the way, where is he tonight?"

"Home. I put him to bed before I came over. Amy's child sitting. I've been told she's very trustworthy." Gabe frowned. "But don't think everything's right in my world just because I'm in a new house, Olivia." His lips tipped down. "I have my own battles to fight, one of them being Eli's continued silences, even when I offered to get him a pony. The kid just won't confide in me the way he does with you."

"Maybe he's still scared of horses," she offered.

"Doubtful, given his over-the-top response to riding the miniatures at the Double M last weekend. It's something else." His jaw clenched. "I think it's tied up with Eve."

"Eli mentioned her the day you moved in." Olivia relayed the conversation as best she could remember. "It seemed to me he was feeling guilty because she isn't here and doesn't get to enjoy his new home."

Given Gabe's glowering expression, it probably wasn't the right thing to say, but she was tired of skirting around this issue.

"Look. If you want Eli to open up to you, you've got to encourage him to talk, no matter what the subject. And you have to listen."

"I already do that," he shot back sharply.

"Really? Well, if you get all tense and angry like you are now, it's no wonder the kid clams up. I'm no child expert, but even I can see that." She wanted so desperately to help this sweet, kind cowboy, but there was only so much she could do if he wouldn't break free of his cycle of bitterness. "Sooner or later you *are* going to have to forgive her, Gabe."

"I've tried, but—I don't think I can." The whisper-soft confession was punctuated by his bowed shoulders that expressed his defeat. "Believe me, I'd love to be free of the memories of what she did, to stop thinking about how much time I've lost with him, to stop mourning all the things we never got to do together. But I can't. What am I supposed to do?"

"I don't have the answer." Olivia's heart ached for his obvious pain. "I guess we have to keep praying for God to intervene, to work it out in your heart. Otherwise—" She was not going to finish that.

Gabe did.

"Otherwise I'll never get to be the father I want to be,

to have the relationship I want to have with my child," he finished. "I know Eli's probably the only kid I'll ever have, and everything's so messed up with him." Gabe now looked angrier than before.

"You know that's not what God wants. Trust that He has something better planned for both of you. But you have to do your part, too, Gabe." She leaned forward, earnestly desiring to help him.

"What's that?" He glared at her.

"Stop dwelling on it. Every time a negative thought comes, confess it and give it to Him. Don't cling to it and rehash it over and over. It's done." She knew her situation wasn't the same, but she was desperate to help this man she liked. "I was talking to the aunts this morning about how inadequate I feel to deal with these kids, how much I want to escape when they come to me with their issues. The aunts gave me a verse. Maybe it will help you, too."

"I'll accept all help." Gabe shuffled his feet on the patio, obviously restless.

"It's from James, first chapter, verse five. 'If any of you lack wisdom, let him ask of God, that giveth to all men liberally, and upbraideth not; and it shall be given him.'"

He mulled it over while Olivia studied him, loving the way he was so determined to be the father Eli needed.

"You don't know how to rid yourself of the bitterness, Gabe, but God does. Ask Him to show you."

"I'll try," he said, but there was an edge to his voice that told her he didn't think it would be that easy.

The group in the meadow was climbing up the hill toward them now, heading for their cabins and some rest. Olivia wanted that, too. She'd been woken before four this morning to drive a sick child to the hospital and the lack of sleep was catching up.

"You're yawning," Gabe said, a smile in his voice. "I should go. Amy's curfew is soon."

"Okay." She rose and found she was very close to him. "Try not to worry too much," she consoled quietly. "I doubt God would have brought Eli here if He didn't mean for the two of you to be happy together. Hang on to that."

"I guess." He stood blocking her way, thoughtfully studying her face. "Ever wonder why He brought you here, Olivia?"

"To step in for Victoria," she said more airily than she felt. There was something about being so close to Gabe that was unsettling, though why that should be puzzled her. He was the best friend she'd ever had.

"A stand-in? You think that's all God intended?" His tone amused, Gabe fiddled with his black Stetson. "In working on the trust factor, one thing I've noticed is that God often has something else going on. We think it's about one thing, but it often turns out to be a much wider scope that we thought."

Olivia couldn't smother another yawn. She blinked in surprise when Gabe bent and brushed his lips against her scarred cheek.

"Good night, Olivia. See you at church tomorrow."

"Good night," she finally managed to whisper, but Gabe was long gone. And so was her tiredness.

She went inside to retrieve Aunt Tillie's bilious purple afghan, wrapped herself in it and curled into the big wrought iron chair on the deck to think about what Gabe had said.

She *was* only staying at The Haven to fill in. She certainly didn't belong here. She wasn't sure she belonged in Edmonton, either, but that's where her new job would take her.

"I don't know about the future," she murmured long after the kids had retired and only the night sounds of the woods echoed around her. "But now that I'm here, I want to do what I can to leave a mark on these kids' lives. Please show me how to do that."

Gabe's handsome face, hurt and angry, swam into her mind.

"And please help Gabe. Show him a way to forgive Eve so he can concentrate on his future with Eli. Use me to help them if You want."

Olivia wasn't exactly certain why she felt compelled to ensure the father and son's reunion. She only knew she wanted the very best for them.

"Help us both to trust You, Father."

When Olivia finally climbed the stairs, she felt a new courage infusing her. There would be more tests to come, but with Gabe's, the aunts' and her sisters' help, by trusting God to guide her, surely she wouldn't mess up any of the troubled kids who came to The Haven.

"On my own I probably would fail, maybe even endanger some kids," she whispered. "I'm scared stiff I'll do that anyway. But You must have me here for a reason. Can You give me some clue to what that is, please?"

Olivia's sleep that night was fitful. She fell into a dream where Gabe and Eli were playing a game outside their new home. Somehow it was a sad dream.

Because she wasn't there.

Chapter Ten

"Today we're going to see the school you'll attend when summer's over." Gabe studied his son's bent head, bothered that Eli barely looked at him. "Aren't you excited?"

A shrug.

"Well, I am. I believe you're going to enjoy meeting all the kids and teachers and learning new things." He paused, waiting for some reaction.

Eli lifted his head to study his father. For Gabe, it was like looking in a twenty-five-year-old mirror. Strange how much Eli looked like him, and yet, had he ever been so...closed up? He had to get Eli talking.

"Did your mom ever talk to you about going to school?" Eli's nod made Gabe purse his lips. Would this child ever speak normally, blurt out things like other kids did? Why was it always such an effort to get any information about the past? "What did she tell you?"

Eli took his time answering. "To not be scared," he finally murmured.

"Why would she think you'd be scared of school?"

And why did a comment from Eli about Eve get Gabe so bent out of shape?

Eli stared at him for a minute, then returned to eating his cereal. "I dunno," he whispered, tucking his chin into his neck.

From Eli's reaction, Gabe immediately guessed that he'd said something wrong. Or done something wrong. But what? *Oh, Lord, I just don't get this kid.*

In his brain he carried on a conversation with Olivia.

You have this tone when you speak about Eve, Gabe. Her brows would be drawn together as she studied him with that penetrating silver gaze.

What tone? Did he have to be so sarcastic?

That tone you just used with Eli. Olivia would glare at him. *Eve's gone, Gabe. She can never be part of Eli's life again.*

Thank you. I had realized that, he'd shoot back, irritated by her criticism.

Then why are you so afraid, cowboy?

The question ended his pretend discussion. He wasn't afraid.

Was he?

"Is Livvie comin' to my school with us t'day?"

The question drew Gabe out of his contemplation and annoyed him.

"Olivia's working at The Haven today, like she always does."

"Oh." Eli's shoulders sagged until he was almost hunched over, like a fearful little ball.

Feeling like a bully, Gabe was ashamed.

"She couldn't come to our supper last night, either," Eli murmured. "I wish she coulda."

"I'm sure she wishes she could have, too. But she

had an emergency, remember?" He remembered how excited Eli had been to serve the meal they'd prepared, recalled, too, how utterly devastated Eli had been when Olivia phoned to say she had to return a homesick child to Edmonton. So now Gabe repeated the paltry words of comfort he'd offered last night. "Olivia can't help it if she has to cancel her plans. Sometimes some of the kids she works with need her."

"I need her, too." At least that's what Gabe thought Eli mumbled.

"Won't I do?" he asked, gutted when Eli shook his head in a firm no. "Is it private?" He hated that Eli would keep something private from him.

"Kind of. Sometimes I tell Livvie 'bout stuff." Eli peeked at him, as if worried his father would object to that.

"I'm glad you can talk to her, son." Gabe couldn't discourage Eli from speaking to the one person he trusted, but he felt compelled to warn him. "Olivia's helped us both an awful lot because she's our friend. But the thing is, she's very busy. We don't want to take up too much of her time."

"Isn't Miss Victoria's leg never gonna get better?" Eli asked, his frustration evident.

"It will. But it takes time. So Olivia has to do all the things Victoria would do. Because we are Olivia's friends, we don't want to make even more work for her. Right?"

"I guess." Eli blinked, but Gabe figured he'd understood most of it.

"That's why I don't want to ask her to come on our tour of the school today," he explained. *Also because I'll be better able to focus on what your teacher's say-*

ing if Olivia isn't there to distract me. "Maybe we'll have time to stop at The Haven. Then you can tell her about it before you go to Ms. Nettleworth's place this afternoon. Okay?"

"Okay." Eli's eyes blazed. He straightened up, finished his cereal and tucked the bowl into the dishwasher as Gabe had shown him. "Should I go brush my teeth?"

At Gabe's nod, Eli dashed away to complete the task. Gabe squeezed his eyes closed.

Eli's not the only one who wants to see Olivia. So do I. But every time I'm around her I get all these feelings and it reminds me of the past. I don't want that to happen again.

Please, God, help me understand how to deal with this churn of emotions inside.

I can't love Olivia!

And yet he did. The knowledge had been lurking in the corners of Gabe's brain for a while now, waiting for him to stop lying to himself. He was in love with the lovely organizer. But he didn't want to be, didn't want his heart vulnerable, and he sure didn't want to ever feel that gut-wrenching sense of betrayal again. Bottom line, Gabe did *not* want to reexperience the weakness that love brought. The cost of being vulnerable was too high.

But what he wanted didn't seem to matter. He still loved Olivia. He tried to push it away.

Okay, so he was supposed to forgive Eve. He'd talked to the aunties by phone yesterday, told them the whole ugly story. The aunties had texted later offering their sympathy but insisting that God expected Gabe to forgive Eve. They said only forgiveness would get rid of this iron lump of anger festering in his gut. But how exactly was he supposed to do that when even her name made him uptight, never mind thoughts of her betrayal with Eli?

Olivia would tell him to suck it up. No-nonsense Olivia. Even thinking about her made him smile. She'd become such an integral part of his world. Of Eli's, too. In fact, she was the one who made Gabe's world with Eli work. She was the buffer between them. The odd day when he didn't see her seemed gray and lackluster. Olivia made life worth living.

He loved her.

Stunned by the absolute rightness of that thought, Gabe swallowed the rest of his coffee. But the dark bitter brew couldn't erase the truth that rang through his brain. He loved her, but he would never act on it.

And yet—life without Olivia? He couldn't wrap his brain around that without his stomach sinking to his feet.

Unsettled by his inner conflict, Gabe drove Eli to the school. The tour explained who his teacher would be and which rooms Eli would be in, however, none of it dislodged his thoughts from Olivia.

Sweet Olivia, who feared getting too involved with any of The Haven's youth lest she hurt them. Olivia, who went out of her way to keep from hurting everyone. Olivia, who put her heart and soul into whatever she did.

Gabe drove Eli to The Haven with his jaw clenched, feeling caught between a rock and a very hard place. Yes, he loved her. Seeing her was like having the sun slide out from behind a cloud.

But love was a vulnerability he couldn't afford. The cost was too steep.

"So how did school go?" Olivia smiled at him, then hunkered down to Eli's eye level.

"Okay." Eli eyed the picnic table loaded with food and drink, then surveyed the kids lounging around enjoying their lunch. "Can I have some of that?"

"Of course. Help yourself." She waited till he hurried away. Then she scowled at Gabe. "What happened?"

"Nothing. We went to the school, Eli met his teachers, saw where he'd be sitting, and we left." Gabe itched to follow his son and sample some of those golden chicken drumsticks before they disappeared, not because he was hungry but because that would put some distance between him and Olivia. Maybe then he could convince his brain that he couldn't care for her. "It's all good."

"No, it isn't." She glared at him. "Eli's not talking, not even to Mikey, and Eli always talks to Mikey. What happened?"

"Nothing." Gabe edged toward the table. "Can I beg some lunch, too? Once I drop Eli at Ms. Nettleworth's I'm going to have to work double time to catch up on my chores if I am to take that group of yours on a ride."

She stared at him. Gabe could feel her gaze probing his soul.

"Chicken," she accused darkly, glaring at him.

"Olivia—"

"Forget it. I don't want to hear your denials again. Go eat." She waved a hand. "I can talk to Eli later. On second thought, maybe I'll get something, too. I missed breakfast."

Once again the familiar concern for her he so often felt flared inside him.

"You can't afford to do that, Olivia," Gabe chided. "You've got to keep your energy up."

"What energy?" she muttered, rolling her shoulders as if to ease tension. "I think I'm too old for this."

"Eat. You'll feel better." The mundane subject allowed him to breathe. When Olivia put so little on her plate, Gabe piled up a second one to temp her. He followed her to an empty table away from the mayhem and watched her sink onto the bench.

"What I really want is this tea. I'm so thirsty." She sipped the icy beverage, ignoring her plate, and closed her eyes. "Perfect."

That's when Gabe noticed the two dots of color on her cheeks.

"Are you feeling all right, Olivia?" he asked.

"No. I think I'm getting a cold. A summer cold. The worst." She wrinkled her nose in disgust before taking a tiny bite of carrots. "Also, I messed up again. One of the counselors believes I erred by not hugging Skylar after our latest discussion, the one where he agreed, again, to follow our rules."

"What difference would you hugging him make?" The remark irritated Gabe. Olivia didn't mess up. She was meticulous about her work and he hated that someone dared criticize her and made her doubt herself. "You were trying to make Skylar realize that he and everyone else have to obey the rules. That doesn't require hugging."

"She suggested hugging him might get through to him better than lecturing him." She gave him a dour glance, silver-gray eyes narrowed when he snorted in disgust. "She's a counselor, Gabe. She's had lots of training. I'm sure she knows more about kids than I do."

"Maybe," he allowed. "But not about running The Haven. You're taking care of every aspect that has to do with these kids because that's your job. Hers is to work directly with the kids." He noticed that she kept glancing around, scanning the children. Something else was going on. "You're worried. About anything specific?"

"No." But he knew she was because her gaze rested a long time on the boy named Skylar.

"Stop worrying." Gabe held out his extra plate. "Eat."

"Yes, sir." She made a face, but when he continued to hold out the plate, she finally took half a sandwich and a slice of watermelon. After sampling each she grinned. "Thanks. Guess I was hungrier than I thought. What's your afternoon look like?"

"Same old." Gabe shrugged, not wanting to tell her of his phone call to the aunties. Then he'd have to tell her that this morning's conversation with Eli had shown him he was a fool if he kept believing everything was going to work out. Gabe prided himself on not being a fool.

Clearly the past was coming between him and Eli, and even though Gabe wasn't convinced it was possible to forgive Eve, he was beginning to accept that he had to try.

"I'd better get Eli to Ms. Nettleworth's," he said after checking his watch. "Thanks for lunch."

"No problem. See you later?" When Olivia smiled at him like that, brushed his arm with her fingertips as if she really did want to see him later, Gabe felt strong, important, confident—all the things a man aspired to be, if only because he wanted to be worthy of a wonderful woman like her. All the things Gabe wasn't because he couldn't get past his past.

"Yeah." He savored one last look at her lovely face, then went to find Eli. And maybe later, when he returned, he'd have another chat with Tillie and Margaret. There had to be a way to forgive Eve, even if he didn't want to.

Olivia watched Gabe leave. She wanted to call him back but then decided she had nothing to substantiate her concerns about Skylar. Gabe was an expert with horses. He would handle whatever the boy threw at him.

Thrusting aside the worry that had clung all morning, she returned her dishes to the kitchen, checked with Adele about the trail ride dinner planned for tonight, then took attendance of each child climbing onto the bus that would drive them to the Double M ranch to attend Gabe's riding group this afternoon.

Skylar smiled as he passed her. If there was acrimony on his part, it didn't show. Olivia silenced her concern as she watched the bus leave. There was a lot to do today. She didn't have time to waste on what-if.

She spent the next two hours teaching a class on hand-building pottery. What a pleasure to instruct the three girls who seemed to have no ulterior motives.

"You've done a great job," she congratulated, admiring their displayed items. "Now you need to smooth off the edges more because when these dry, they'll be very difficult to work on."

"How fast will it dry?" Sari, a bright-eyed girl who'd blossomed into a chatterbox after the first two silent days, asked.

"Typically, we'd cover it tightly and then smooth it off in several stages as it slowly dries. But with this heat and all the wind we've been having, I'd suggest double covers. Tomorrow it should be dry enough to skim off a first layer. If you leave it too thick it will probably crack."

Olivia loved teaching pottery. She'd offered this hand-building class because she'd noticed that as The Haven's ministry grew, some youth didn't wish to pursue riding. Some needed more personal attention or were unable physically, and some were eager to learn hobbies that they could hopefully pursue at school later.

That's why she'd persuaded Aunt Tillie to teach a knitting class and, after much coaxing, gotten Adele's agreement to give simple cooking lessons. Olivia strove to find each child's niche in hopes they'd eventually open their hearts and share their struggles.

Olivia was becoming more comfortable in this area as she realized The Haven's ministry wasn't about her fears, but about the troubled kids who came here, about reaching them however she could. Now she was learning to pray for guidance, shove back her hesitation and grasp whatever opportunity she found while God worked things out. Slowly she began to enjoy the challenges, though each day was still a test. But thanks to her fosters aunts' support, she was learning how to be used.

The pottery girls' giggles filled the air. Fresh scents of mountain wildflowers and Adele's delicious baking tickled Olivia's nose. The murmur of her aunties' voices as they shared tea on the patio—all these things made Olivia aware of how bleak and barren her former life had been. Avoiding kids, pouring her energy into organizing to forget her past and the guilt that still lurked in the nether regions of her mind—those past actions had never tested or fulfilled her like this work.

In her new job there would be no concerns about

whether a child needed someone to listen, whether she'd failed a needy child, caused a problem or endangered some poor kid. Maybe she wouldn't have to trust God as much, either.

Silly little daydreams about staying at The Haven had filled her head lately. Not just because then she'd see Gabe constantly, or for the blessing of having her family's fellowship every day, or for the delight of watching Eli grow, but for reasons that encompassed everything about this place. She loved it here.

She couldn't stay, she knew that. Victoria was in charge. There wasn't enough work for them both and, anyway, Olivia didn't belong here. She wanted to belong with Gabe but that, too, was a pipe dream. But couldn't she at least stay long enough to see just one of her labors succeed? To see one child completely change for the better?

When she was gone, would the dreams stop? Olivia wondered. Dreams of Gabe and his life with Eli in their snug new home, sharing all their father-and-son firsts— first day of school, first Thanksgiving together, first Christmas. Sadness engulfed her knowing Eli would forget her as he built his place in the world, a world she wouldn't be part of. And Gabe—did he ever wish she'd stay, be part of his world permanently? Of course that was silly. Gabe was still stuck in the past.

The girls laughed and worked together on their clay, leaving Olivia with her thoughts.

Would Gabe miss her? When the stars came out and he needed a second opinion, would he find someone else to bounce ideas off of? Would he care if he never saw her again? Would he keep praying for her after she left? Would the bond they'd built hold up when she came back for Christmas, Easter, the aunts' birthdays? Probably not.

But Olivia knew now that wherever she went, part of her heart would remain here with Gabe. The realization that she was falling in love with him had dawned slowly over the past few weeks. Now it was rooted deep inside. Gabe was the man she loved, the real love of her life. She desperately wanted him to love her back.

Olivia knew Gabe cared for her. But each time she thought he'd finally declare his love, his bitterness against Eve came between them. She knew his long-held bitterness wouldn't let him trust her, not as a man should trust the woman he loves. The way she yearned to be loved.

I guess I need to learn to trust You with Gabe, too. She smiled sadly. Everywhere she turned the lesson was trust.

"Olivia? I think something's wrong." Sari's troubled voice drew her from her thoughts.

Jake, The Haven's hired man, raced toward their pottery shed. Olivia hurried to meet him.

"What's wrong?" she demanded.

"Don't have all the details," he huffed, trying to catch his breath. "Gabe phoned, said a kid, Emmet, fell off his horse and hit his head. Gabe's at the hospital. It had something to do with that kid, Skylar."

"I knew he was up to something." Olivia glanced at the girls. "Can you girls clean up? Jake will help you store your pieces and take you back to the main buildings."

"We know what to do in an emergency because you made us practice." Sari grinned cheekily. "Go. And send Skylar home." She was one of the kids Skylar had publicly mortified.

"Jake?" Olivia glanced at the hired man.

"Go," he ordered.

Olivia hurried to her car, praying as she went.

Please take care of Emmet. I'm trusting You, she repeated over and over, but every time she said *I'm trusting You*, her heart sank a little further.

I should have stopped Skylar.

Chapter Eleven

Where was Olivia?

Gabe paced the hospital corridor, thankful his boss, Mac McDowell, had insisted that copies of permission slips for every rider from The Haven be kept on file at the ranch. Being able to bring it along meant there had been no delay in treatment of this kid.

"Gabe?" Olivia raced toward him, hair flying back, her scar puckered and reddened against the whiteness of her face. "What happened?"

"That kid, Skylar, loosened the cinch on Emmet's saddle. They'd just begun to canter when someone yelled and next thing I knew Emmet was lying on the ground. He hit his head on a fence rail and cut his hand." He grabbed her shoulders and hung on, hoping to soothe the terror he saw written on her face. "Emmet's fine, Liv. The doctors are with him. I only brought him here as a precaution. I called but your phone is off," he added, knowing he sounded testy.

"No, it isn't—" She dragged her phone from her pocket and stared at it. "It's dead again."

"You need a new one." *Nothing like stating the obvious, cowboy.*

"This is the second new battery I've put in it. I'll order a new one tomorrow." She shoved it back in her pocket. "Skylar again. I thought that kid was up to something."

"Wish I'd—" Gabe cut himself off when the doctor appeared.

"Emmet's fine. He'll have a bump on his noggin, though. I want him to rest for another fifteen minutes before he leaves. The nurse will give you a list of things to watch for. Nothing serious, just precautionary."

Gabe listened as Olivia extensively questioned the medical professional, like an overprotective mother. He finally intervened so the doctor could answer a page.

"Emmet's fine." He blinked in surprise when strong, capable Olivia's face crumpled. She threw herself into his arms and started crying. "Hey. It's okay," he murmured, smoothing a hand down her shiny hair. "It's all good."

"It's not good at all," she sobbed against his chest. "I knew Skylar was up to something."

"You couldn't know that, Olivia," he protested, loving the way she fit in his arms. Where she belonged.

"I knew. He has this way of looking at you," she asserted, lifting her head to frown at him. "When Skylar's smile doesn't reach his eyes, trouble always follows. I've seen it before and I should have warned you."

"Olivia." She moved as if to pull away, but Gabe held her arms.

"Yes?" She looked at him in puzzlement.

"How could you have warned me?" He had to reassure

her that no one could have foreseen the boy's actions. "What would you have said? Be careful. Watch out?"

"Maybe." Frustration chewed at the edges of her response.

"But we were already doing that. Every time we allow someone to sit on our horses we do that. We check and double-check. We always watch as closely as we can," he insisted.

"I know. But—"

"No." Gabe shook his head. "You can't be their babysitter, and neither can we, Liv. They have to follow the rules. Unfortunately, they suffer the consequences if they don't."

"But that's just it. It's not Skylar suffering," she shot back with a glare.

"Isn't he?" Gabe raised his eyebrows. "Isn't that why he keeps acting out? Because somewhere inside him something hurts, and he can't make it better? Because he needs you and The Haven to help him figure it out?"

"I'm not good at figuring out kids or trying to be a parent." Tears streaked her lovely face as she gazed at him. Her voice dropped to almost a whisper. "I want to be. I wish so desperately that I could be like their mother and protect them. But I'm not. I'll never be a mother."

That threw Gabe off balance. He'd never suspected to hear such a depth of longing in Olivia's voice, never suspected that she yearned to be a mom.

"Why not?" he demanded. "You're great with Eli. You're great with the kids at The Haven. Just because you had a tough childhood doesn't mean you wouldn't make a great mother, Olivia."

"Two kids died, Gabe."

"Stop," he snapped, hating to see her suffer. "Both were accidents. Let go of the past." The funny little smile tilting up the corners of her mouth surprised him. "What's funny?"

"This advice of yours." She shook her head, eyes crinkling at the corners. "Earlier today I was thinking the same thing about you."

"Huh?" Olivia thought about him?

"Do you remember when Eli started to tell you about his mom and you cut him off? Your anger at Eve always gets in the way between you and him," Olivia said in a very quiet tone. "I'm wondering why you don't let the past go, just as you've told me to do."

"It's not the same."

"Isn't it?" Her honest stare made him flinch. "Things happen to all of us. But I'm learning the past is past. You and I can't change it. If you want a future with Eli, you have to let the past go." Her smile darted back to her lips. "I do, too."

He loved that about Olivia, her chipper, take-it-on-the-shoulder-and-come-back-fighting air that squared her posture and lifted her determined chin. But it was her silver-gray eyes that wouldn't let him off the hook.

"I can't. It keeps coming back," he muttered.

"Because you let it." She eased away from him, tossed her head and blew her nose. "I've been doing the same thing with my fears. But I'm not doing it anymore. Life's too short to be constantly living in the past."

"Meaning?" He didn't think he liked where this was going.

"I have a job to do for as long as I'm here. Then I'll move on. I believe that's God's plan for me and until He shows me differently, I'm committed to obeying

Him. The aunties texted me a verse this morning. 'For I know the thoughts that I think toward you, saith the Lord, thoughts of peace, and not of evil, to give you an unexpected end.'" She tugged her shirt and straightened her shoulders. "I've got to believe God will keep His word. So no more weeping, no more whining over the past for me. It's time, past time, for me to trust God completely."

"That's what I love about you, Olivia." The words tumbled out of Gabe before he could stop them. Stunned and a little embarrassed by them, he hurried on. "You never run away from challenges. You keep pushing forward. You're an admirable woman."

He stared at her, mesmerized by her quiet beauty. Then, without conscious thought and following an overwhelming impulse, Gabe leaned forward and kissed her the way his heart had been demanding for weeks now. Olivia startled, then eagerly responded. Gabe eased his arm around her waist and drew her closer, deepening the kiss as he tried to show her how much she meant to him, completely forgetting his vow not to love.

When Olivia's arms twined around his neck. Gabe thought he'd never been happier, until someone cleared their throat.

"Sorry." The amused nurse couldn't conceal the glimmer in her eyes. She winked at the boy standing beside her. "Emmet has been discharged. You may take him home."

"Thank you." Olivia slipped away from Gabe and knelt beside the little boy. "I'm so sorry this happened, Emmet."

"It was Skylar's fault," the boy insisted quietly.

Gabe frowned. Emmet didn't sound angry or upset with Skylar. He wondered why. Apparently, Olivia did, too.

"What do you think I should do about that?" she asked.

Emmet took his time considering while the nurse ushered them out of the hospital. He walked between Gabe and Olivia across the parking lot, his dark eyes narrowed.

"You gotta talk to him and find out what's making him so mad," Emmet finally suggested. "'Cause that's why he does stuff."

"You are a very smart boy, Emmet." Olivia brushed her hand over his bristly hair. She smiled at Gabe, then her eyes widened. "Oh. Your truck. My car."

"Yeah. How about if you take Emmet back to The Haven. I need to get to the ranch. I've got stuff to do." Not that he wanted to leave Olivia. But Gabe needed some time and distance from her to think about that kiss, about what it implied.

About where he wanted it to go. And where it couldn't.

"Sure. Thanks, Gabe." She pointed to her car. "Over here, Emmet."

"Thank you for helping me, Gabe," the little boy said.

"My pleasure. Feel better, okay?" Gabe smiled as the kid nodded.

Olivia shepherded Emmet into her car and ensured his seat belt was fastened before she opened her door. After a moment's thought she turned and called, "See you later?"

"I'll be there to pick up Eli, as usual." But man, Gabe wanted to go with her now, to sneak a few more moments holding her, kissing her again. His brain held him back.

Remember Eve, cowboy? Think carefully about what you're about to do, about where this could leave you.

"Then thanks again." Olivia gave him a big smile before she got into her car and drove away.

Gabe figured there were probably a hundred jobs waiting for him back at the Double M, but he stood exactly where he was for several minutes, watching Olivia's car disappear.

He couldn't love Olivia. But he did. He wanted to be with her, listen to her dreams and fears, tell her about his own. He wanted to ask her opinion about his birthday party idea for Eli and make sure she'd be there for it.

He wanted her to stay. Forever.

But loving Olivia scared him. To be so dependent? To need someone as badly as he needed her in his world, to once again invest himself in love? What if it didn't work out? What if she couldn't or wouldn't stay? What if loving him wasn't what she wanted?

His phone chimed with a text from his boss. How long will you be?

On the way, Gabe texted back. Thrusting away all thoughts of Olivia and what they might share if she loved him, he drove back to the ranch and concentrated on work for the rest of the day. But Livvie was never far from his thoughts.

Olivia's one-on-one with Skylar produced several results. But the best one was that after apologizing to Emmet, the two became best friends. Emmet made Skylar face his feelings instead of brushing them off. And Skylar taught Emmet confidence.

Three days later, watching the two of them roasting marshmallows, Olivia knew she'd been right not to send the boy home. Her heart sang with joy at the changes God was working in *her* kids.

Funny how they'd become hers, each one special, unique and loved. She'd taken the aunts' advice and initiated these smaller-sized get-togethers, times to sit around a campfire and talk about what returning home would be like for them. Slowly their deepest fears emerged.

Olivia's heart ached as they discussed how scary it felt to be moved from a familiar place to a new one where no one understood anything about you. She could empathize with those who spoke of how hard it was to be the only one who felt they didn't belong. Their pain touched her deepest soul as she whispered a prayer for those who'd lost families or couldn't find the love they longed for. Most of all she prayed they'd experience a deepening of the faith in God they were just learning about. Sometimes kids begged her to let them stay. Those were the hardest times of all for Olivia.

"Everyone at The Haven loves you so much, kids," she said gently, forcing back tears as she studied the faces peering at her so trustingly. "That's why we wanted to make your vacation here special. But soon you'll be leaving because " she paused, imprinting each face on her mind to pray for later "—vacations don't last forever."

"They do for you," Skylar yelled. Olivia had just learned that Skylar was in a horrible home situation where he was basically ignored. He needed attention, any kind of attention to acknowledge him. "You belong here."

"You're wrong, Skylar." Olivia smiled at his astonished look. "I came here for a visit before I start my new job in Edmonton. I'm just helping out until my foster sister Victoria gets better."

"You mean you were a foster kid, too?" Tyler and the rest of the group stared at her in disbelief.

Never once had Olivia felt comfortable sharing her past. But tonight her heart went out to these kids. They thought they were alone in the world. They'd leave tomorrow and perhaps never return. This would be her last intimate interaction with them as a group, and she longed to send them away with hope, to show them they weren't alone.

She wanted them to know that she had gone through the same longing and survived. No, better than that. She'd flourished. Maybe if she let God's light shine on them, her fears would be healed. For good.

"I was a foster child," she said. A sense of peace filled her and somehow it was okay to admit the truth, to let out all the awful secrets that had bound her spirit for so long. "When I was just a few days old, I was left in a hospital with only my name pinned to my blanket. I never knew my parents. I don't know if I ever had a family."

"But you got to come here," Skylar pressed.

"I came to The Haven when I was twelve." Olivia gazed at their sweet faces. "But before that I lived in lots of different homes. Some bad things happened to me along the way. Maybe things have happened to you, too."

"You never told us this before," Skylar accused. Not all the hard edges had been softened from him, but at least now Olivia understood a little of where he was coming from.

"No," she admitted.

"Why not?" He glared at her.

"I don't like to talk about my past. It hurts." No going back now. "Foster kids learn how to do lots of things, don't we? We learn not to cause a fuss. Maybe then we'll get to stay. That didn't work for me."

No child moved. Eyes remained on her face, and oddly enough that gave Olivia the freedom she needed.

"I became really good at being the babysitter, the one in charge, the person my foster parents asked to help with everything and depended on. But then something bad happened."

"What did you do wrong?" a little girl named Esther asked.

"I don't know." For the first time in eons, Olivia let herself relive that awful inability to free her foster sibling. Was there something she'd forgotten to do, something she'd missed? Despair hovered like a blanket waiting to drop.

"Livvie didn't do anything wrong." Gabe's quiet voice came from behind her. He sat down on the tree stump beside her, cradling a sleeping Eli on his knee while his other hand clasped hers. "Sometimes things happen that aren't anyone's fault."

"But *you* get blamed." Skylar nodded, his face miserable. "I know about that."

Esther ignored him. "What happened, Livvie?"

"A fire." Olivia clung to Gabe's hand as a flood of memories cascaded into her brain. *Let me say it, Lord. If it will help even one of these children, I need to say it.* "I got out of the house, but I couldn't save my foster brother. He died."

"Where were his mom and dad?" Skylar demanded.

"I—I don't remember." She glanced at Gabe, surprised by a new thought. "I don't remember them being there."

"Did they go somewhere and leave you in charge?" he asked, squeezing her fingers as she searched the awful memories for an answer.

"I don't know. It was night and I wasn't old enough to babysit. I was just a kid. Like you guys." Olivia squeezed her eyes closed, framing that horrible time in her mind. "The parents came after," she said, slightly bemused by this revelation. "They were angry. They asked me how I got out and he didn't."

Gabe met her stare while truth filtered through her brain. In that moment those parents had wished her dead, but not because she was bad or because she'd *let* him die. They were just bereft parents aching to have their beloved son back.

"It was grief talking, Olivia. Grief."

She nodded with new understanding. But she couldn't speak. Not yet.

Esther knelt and laid her head on Olivia's knees. "I wish I could take away the hurt like you sometimes take our hurts."

"Thank you, Esther." Olivia's heart overflowed with love for this dear child. For all of them. "Thank you for listening. God is still taking away my hurt. I'm learning that sometimes if we talk to other people about the bad things that have happened to us, that also helps heal our hurt. Does anyone want to talk?"

It was as if a dam broke. One by one, in hushed voices with halting sentences the children began to reveal bad things they'd experienced, feared and endured. As if sensing the preciousness of this moment, no one interrupted. Each child waited, listened and comforted.

For Esther that was through touch. For Skylar that was by encouragement. For Emmet that was simply sitting next to the sufferer, being there.

Through it all, Gabe's hand held hers, an anchor in a storm of emotion Olivia had neither anticipated nor prepared for. All she could do was silently pray.

Complete darkness had fallen when the last child's story died away. The group sat silent, contemplative and yet at peace, as if nothing could ever be so bad again.

"When you go home, and life seems too hard to bear, I want you to remember this evening," Olivia said into the tender silence. "I want you to remember that we are never, ever alone. We have a heavenly Father who loves us more than we can ever imagine. We can always talk to Him and He will always listen. He knows all the sad, hurt things about you, and He knows how to make it better."

If they were so precious to her, how much more so to God?

"I always kept my hurt and fear tied up inside. Don't do that. When you need to tell your story to someone, do it. Tell your foster parents, or your social worker or your teacher. If nobody else will listen, I'll always listen. You all know how to email The Haven?"

Nods all around.

"If no one will listen, email me," she told them. "I will listen. I promise."

"Olivia." Gabe's hand tightened, his tone full of warning.

But Olivia was tired of holding back.

"Thank you all for sharing. You've made this a wonderful evening I will never forget. Now it's time for bed."

Counsellors shepherded their groups to their cabins. Olivia heaved a sigh.

"That was amazing," she said, feeling lighter, freer than she had in years. She hugged Gabe, careful not to disturb Eli. "Thank you for sharing it with me."

"But—"

"Hi, Livvie." Eli's eyelashes fluttered up. A big smile stretched across his face. "I was having this dream about my mom—" Seeing Gabe's mouth tighten into a forbidding line, he froze.

"That's wonderful, sweetheart," she said cheerfully, ignoring Gabe's fierce expression. "We should always remember those we love in our dreams. You can tell me all about your dream sometime."

"We need to go home now. It's late." Gabe dropped her hand and rose, setting Eli on his feet, but offering no reason for his impromptu visit. "Good night."

"Eli, honey, can you go up to the house with Marina for a minute." Olivia waved over the senior counselor. "I need to talk to your dad about something."

"Okay." Eli peeked a second look at Gabe, then hurried toward Marina.

"What is it?" Gabe demanded brusquely.

"The other day—you said you loved me. Was it true?" Might as well get all honesty in the open tonight.

"I don't say things I don't mean."

As declarations went, that left something to be desired. But Olivia persisted.

"Do you love Eli, too?"

"Of course," Gabe was obviously irritated. "You know that. Why would you even ask?"

"Because you just hurt your son, the child you claim

to love. He wanted to tell you about his dream of his dead mother and you cut him off."

"I didn't say anything," he sputtered.

"You didn't have to. Your expression was enough." Olivia hated doing this, but she had to. Facing the truth hurt but it was less costly than ignoring it. She feared that Gabe would pay dearly one of these days and she so wanted to prevent that. "I love you, too, Gabe. You're honest and generous and caring, all the things I always longed for when I thought about loving someone." When he would have embraced her, she held him off. "Problem is, I don't believe you truly love me."

"What? Why not?" He glared at her.

"My darling Gabe. When I think about loving you, it takes all the room in my heart. I know who you really are. There are no shadows, no memories of anyone else, no fears that you'll hurt me as I've been hurt before. There's only you, the man that I love with every part of my heart. Can you say the same?"

"I don't know what you mean." His blue-eyed gaze searched hers.

"You can't love me, Gabe, not the way I need. That's because there's not enough room in your heart for me. I come in second." Though tears rolled down her cheeks, she ignored them and laid her palm on his chest, trying to soften her words. "It's too crowded in here with the past and with anger and bitterness toward Eve. If we were together you'd constantly compare us. You'd always be afraid I was going to do what Eve did to you and you'd hold back to protect yourself." She paused, caressed his cheek. "That's not love, Gabe. That's fear and it's a horrible way to live."

This would end everything they'd shared, but now

that Olivia had faced her past, she couldn't go into the future with anything less than complete honesty.

"The Bible says perfect love casts out fear. That's what I want, what I need, Gabe. Perfect love, for me, Olivia. Love that's not tainted by the past or anger or bitterness from someone else. I won't accept anything less." She stopped, suddenly aware that he hadn't said a word. *Lord?* "Perfect love is what Eli needs, too, Gabe. That's what he deserves. I believe it's what his mother gave him, no matter what you think of her."

She could see Gabe didn't like that. But she couldn't, wouldn't apologize.

"God has wonderful things planned for you and me and Eli. But you can't see it, Gabe. You're too busy looking back, reliving the pain and anger repeatedly. Please, if not for me, then do it for your son. Forgive and trust that God has something amazing planned for your future. I love you. Goodbye."

After one last, painful study of his beloved face, Olivia walked to The Haven. She put on her happy face, teased her sisters, laughed with the aunties and bade Eli a sweet good-night before his father silently shepherded him out.

But once in her room she couldn't stop her tears.

"It hurts, God, more than I ever thought possible. But I won't settle for less than your best. It's time for a new day, a new life, with You in charge. Help me?"

One more week and then she'd leave behind The Haven, and the man and boy who'd carved a special place deep in her heart, but the memories were carved inside forever.

Chapter Twelve

As the end of August approached, Gabe deliberately altered his times of visiting The Haven to mesh with times when Olivia was busy elsewhere. He figured that out thanks to her big scheduling chart on the office wall.

Avoiding her worked until Friday evening when he went to pick up Eli and read, "Last event for Olivia."

Gabe's heart took a nosedive when he perused her notes about tomorrow's treasure hunt hike for a group of ten-year-olds. He knew she'd been nervous about hosting it since the two brothers who were experienced counselors and would have accompanied her had left yesterday for a family emergency.

Gabe figured being responsible for seven young kids with two newbie counselors would test Olivia's determination to trust God, but he also knew there was no way she would cancel and disappoint the kids, especially given the aunts' oft-repeated insistence that each of their guests must experience the beauty of The Haven's wooded surroundings.

But the schedule wasn't the only source of Gabe's knowledge about the treasure hunt. For the past week

Eli had nagged incessantly about going along, insisting it was the only gift he wanted for his upcoming birthday. So far Gabe had refused, but today he'd learned The Haven's hired hand, Jake, would be accompanying Olivia. Jake had been working with the program since its inception. He had plenty of experience with the youth groups who visited and with The Haven's surroundings. He could be counted on to watch out for Eli. Today Gabe had promised Eli he'd ask Olivia's permission for his son to accompany her on the treasure hunt.

"Lose someone?" The object of his thoughts stood framed in the doorway. Olivia's voice was friendly as always. Her usual smile welcomed him. But there was a reticence in her silvery gray eyes he'd not seen before. "Eli's playing with Mikey on the climbing apparatus."

"I saw him, thanks." The thought of her leaving made Gabe's stomach clench. "I'm actually here to talk to you."

"Oh?" Olivia's glance didn't meet his. Instead, she walked to the desk, sat down behind it and folded her hands. "What can I do for you, Gabe?"

"Eli's been bugging me to go on your treasure hunt tomorrow. I know he's way younger than the others and I've told him no a hundred times, but he keeps saying that's the only thing he wants for his birthday, so I was wondering…" This wasn't as easy as he'd expected. Because of that invisible wall between them?

"Ah." Olivia chuckled. "He finally got to you." She grinned at his surprise. "He's been bugging me, too. I said he had to ask you."

"His birthday is next week—do you think he'd be okay? It wouldn't be too much?" The fatherhood business was filled with potholes of doubt that left Gabe uncertain about his decisions. He met Olivia's amused glance. "Say no if you think he can't handle it."

"Ordinarily I would. But as it happens, I had a call from the youth center in Edmonton. They're sending the kids we'd scheduled plus two eight-year-olds and one seven-year-old. Also, Mikey wants to join us, so I've modified the trip. Eli should be fine. Have him here at eight thirty please."

"He's not all that strong," Gabe fussed. "He says Jake is going. I can go, too, if—" Olivia's glare stopped him.

"If what? I can't manage." She arched one eyebrow. "We'll be fine, thanks."

"That wasn't—"

"After all this time, even though you claimed to love me, you still don't trust me." Her voice tight, Olivia pinned him with a look as he was about to backtrack. "I am not Eve, Gabe. I'm not going to break your heart and run away with your child," she said through gritted teeth.

"I never said—"

"You don't need to say it," she snapped. "It's evident in everything you do, in the way you act toward me and Eli. The past controls you. You cling to your unforgiveness and foresee so many problems that it blocks out the wonder of your son."

"I see Eli just fine." Gabe so did not want to go through this again, to hear her denunciation. "You cannot possibly know what it's like," he muttered.

"To know that a wonderful little boy has come into your world and that now you're not alone anymore? To be given the gift of fatherhood to a sensitive, artistic child who only wants to love and be loved?" Her ragged voice grabbed at his heart, reminding him of her comments about wanting to be a mother. "No, Gabe. I don't know what that's like. I wish I did."

"Olivia." He could hardly stand to hear the pain in her words, to see her wounded eyes. He stepped forward, wanting to comfort her, to make the hurt go away, but she held up a hand. The loss of the closeness they shared annoyed him, and he blurted out the first thing that came to mind. "He talks about her all the time as if she was perfect."

"Because to Eli, she was." Olivia shook her head. "Kids usually think of their mother that way. Didn't you?" She smiled as if reminded of her own childhood. "I had many foster mothers and they all had their faults. But some of them really tried to be my mother, to love and care for me. None more than Aunt Tillie and Aunt Margaret." Her chin thrust out. "What's wrong with loving someone because they loved you? The Bible says we love God because He first loved us."

Gabe couldn't object, not with all that passion and conviction in her voice. But she hadn't known Eve. His ex was nothing like the women she was describing. She'd been self-centered and grasping and—

"Why can't you shelve your view of Eve long enough to see how much your son loved his mother? I mean, who else did he have? His aunt Kathy?" Olivia was furious. Her voice oozed scorn. "Don't you get it? Who cares what you think of Eve? The fact is she adored that little boy, and he knew it. She left him a legacy of love. Whatever else she was, Eve was an amazing mother."

A bell rang somewhere on the grounds of The Haven. Gabe's jaw unclenched. It didn't matter that Eve had ruined his life? This woman didn't have a clue.

"That bell is for me, for my crafting class." Olivia

rose and walked past him to the door. There she paused, turned back and asked in a very solemn voice, "Sounds like you wanted perfection. Were you the perfect husband, Gabe? Are you positive you're the best father Eli could have? Will the legacy you leave him be something he'll cherish when you're gone?"

Her gaze held his for an interminable time. A thousand defenses rushed through his brain, but somehow Gabe knew Olivia would shoot down every one of them. And somewhere deep inside, he knew she was right. Eve had done well with Eli. Gabe needed to move on.

God knew he wanted to. If only…

Olivia walked out the door. It seemed to Gabe that all the joy and happiness he'd recently found in sharing his life with her left, too.

"It won't be an easy walk, Eli," Gabe warned early the next morning as he made sure his son's boots were securely tied. "You'll have to keep up with the others and do everything Olivia and Jake tell you to. No arguing."

"I know." Eli flung his arms around Gabe's neck and hugged as hard as he could. "Thank you," he whispered. "It's the bestest birthday present ever."

Better than anything your mom gave you?

Instantly ashamed, Gabe smoothed the unruly hair. They needed to fit in a haircut day before school started, he thought, startled by the rush of love that filled him.

Eli's first day of school.

How many more firsts would there be for them?

Would they all be without Olivia?

"Thank you very much." Even in this moment of gratefulness, Eli didn't say *Dad* or *Daddy*. Would he ever?

"You're welcome. But listen carefully now." Gabe lifted Eli onto one of the stools at the kitchen island and sat down beside him. "I know you're very strong and we've been practicing hiking. You've done well. You're an excellent hiker."

"Yep." Eli's grin revealed the tooth that had fallen out yesterday. "I am."

Gabe smiled while his mind searched for exactly the right way to phrase what he needed to say.

"I'm sure you'll enjoy yourself today. To celebrate, I have a gift for you. It's your own phone." He pulled a brand-new cell phone from his pocket. "We're going to put this in your backpack."

"Why?" Eli looked confused.

"Because that's what people do with their phones. They take them everywhere they go."

"Oh." Eli studied the item. "Why do I need it?"

"Well, let's say you get tired and don't want to keep going on the hike today. Maybe you want to quit because your boots hurt or because Mikey doesn't want to walk anymore. Here's what you do." He showed the boy how to press a button that immediately dialed his own cell phone.

"Your phone is ringing," Eli said, eyes wide.

"Your phone is calling mine." He ended the call and handed the new one to Eli. "Now you try it."

Eli's forehead pleated as he stabbed the key he'd been shown. Immediately Gabe's phone began to ring.

"Now what?" Eli asked blankly.

"Now you talk into it, to me. I'll go into the other room, okay?" Gabe walked to the bathroom, smiling at Eli's heavy breathing. "Are you there, son?" he asked when nothing was forthcoming.

"Yep. I can hear you," Eli shouted.

"Shh. Use your quiet voice now. Pretend you're in the woods and there are some lovely birds nearby. If you yell they'll fly away and you won't be able to take their picture or draw them."

"Oh." Eli waited. "Is this better?" he murmured.

"Perfect." Gabe returned to the kitchen. "So that's how it works."

"Cool." Eli studied the device with wonder. "Mikey hasn't got a phone."

"Well, this one is only for special occasions. Like today." He wanted to reinforce its intended use. "Do you remember what it's for?"

"Uh-huh. If don't wanna be on the treasure hunt no more then I phone you."

"And then what?" Gabe pressed.

"I dunno." Eli shrugged.

"Then I'll come and get you."

"In the woods?" Eli's blue eyes expanded.

"Wherever you are. Doesn't matter," Gabe assured him solemnly. "If you want to leave, you call me and I'll come get you. I'll always come if you ask me to, Eli," he emphasized. "Whenever you need me. Because you're my son and I love you very much."

"I love you, too." Eli initiated a second hug and Gabe hung on a little longer than strictly necessary. He was beginning to understand that he needed to cherish every one of these precious moments spent with his boy.

"Wait till Livvie sees my phone." Eli tucked it into a special pocket inside his backpack. "She'll be happy. Anyway, she's always happy."

"Um, maybe, just for today, we won't tell her about

your phone," Gabe murmured, irritated that he hadn't thought of this before.

"Why?" Eli's innocence grabbed at him.

Because she'll think I don't trust her. And phones were not allowed on her hikes. Eli would be breaking her rules.

"I think it would be better if you didn't tell her about the phone until after your hike is over." Seeing Eli's frown, Gabe quickly added, "We don't want her to think that you don't want to go on the hike," he said. "Or that you can't finish," he added.

"No, 'cause I'm a big boy." Eli's thin chest pushed outward. He nodded. "I know how to keep a secret," he said proudly.

"It's not exactly a secret—"

But Eli had already raced out of the house, yelling "C'mon," as he went.

Gabe followed. Was he too overprotective? Was he becoming one of those helicopter parents the news had talked about last night, trying to protect his kid from life?

"He's younger than the others," he mumbled as he grabbed his keys. "And he's never been on a real hike in the woods." And then as he headed for his truck, he added, "He's *my* kid."

As if that had exempted Eli from any of life's harsh realities.

At The Haven the treasure hunt group was assembling. Eli, backpack flopping, raced up to Olivia and hugged her leg.

"I'm here," he squealed.

"Really?" To Gabe's surprise she giggled as she bent

to pick him up and swung him around. "I hadn't noticed." Olivia usually didn't pick up the kids.

"Yes, you did," Eli laughed.

"Yes, I did. Did you bring everything on the list?"
she asked as she glanced at Gabe.

"Yes. An' I brought—" Eli stopped, looked at Gabe,
then shook his head once. "I got everything," he said.

"Good." She looked questioningly at Gabe. He
shrugged as if to say, *Kids*.

After a moment she turned her attention to the group,
introduced Jake and the two accompanying counselors while she laid out the guidelines. She then gave
each person a small plastic zipper bag to store the items
they would seek while on their treasure hunt. The same
old rush of love sprang up inside him for this amazing woman.

If only—

"We'll leave in five minutes," she announced.

Gabe had hoped to ask her about his ideas for Eli's
birthday party, but Olivia avoided him. Perhaps that
was for the best. She'd be leaving soon. Once she was
in Edmonton, the ties between them would be cut. He'd
have to manage on his own.

Why did that feel so final, so horrible?

Gabe accepted Eli's goodbye hug, reminded him
softly about the phone in his backpack and nodded
at Eli's assurance that he wouldn't need it. Then he
watched the group leave, singing a happy song as they
went. He stood there watching until he couldn't see either Eli or Olivia anymore.

"Separation anxiety, dear?" Tillie threaded her arm
through his. "Olivia's a fantastic director. She'll take
care of Eli, don't you worry."

"Yes, she will." On his other side, Margaret sighed. "I wish she could stay. It's been so wonderful to have her logical brain smoothing out all the issues that snarl things up."

"Then what would Victoria do?" Gabe asked, reminding them of their other foster daughter.

"Oh, my dear. There's so much to do. Victoria would be over the moon if Livvie stayed. She'd like to share the job, leave the office running to Livvie." Tillie's voice died away.

"But Olivia wants to go to her job in Edmonton," he guessed.

"You know, I don't believe she does." Margaret shook her head. "I believe she's found her confidence here. That's why she can take that group today. Her fear is gone. She's trusting God to meet her needs and direct her. She's grown so much."

"We've been praying for our Livvie to let go of the past and allow the love she keeps bottled inside to spill out." Tillie smiled at him. "Isn't it wonderful to see it happening? Especially with your little Eli. My, she does love that child."

"I think leaving him behind will be hardest of all for her. And you, of course." Margaret smiled. "You're fond of her, too, aren't you, Gabe?"

"Yes, I am." What was the point of denying the truth? Gabe swallowed. Though "fond" hardly seemed strong enough for what he felt. "I love Olivia."

"But there's a problem." Tillie nodded. "I've seen it."

"We both have," Margaret agreed. "And from what little our dear girl has confided, we think it has to do with your past. Is there anything we can do to help you?"

Gabe was fed up with feeling like he'd done something wrong. His anger at Eve wasn't wrong. It was well deserved. But here was his chance to get some more advice and he wasn't about to waste it.

"I talked to you about forgiveness before and you suggested some things, but, well, they don't work. I can't forgive my ex-wife."

"Oh, my dear boy." Tillie laid her head on his shoulder. "You must."

"Why?" he demanded. "She doesn't deserve it. She lied, cheated, stole Eli's childhood. Because of her I've missed all the milestones in my son's life," he blurted, desperate for a sympathetic ear that would understand his battle.

"My dear man. Forgiving isn't about her," Tillie said with a shake of her head. "It's about you. It's about freeing yourself from that burden."

"Besides, it's because of your wife that you have a son," Margaret said, her tone just the tiniest bit severe. "A boy whose mother made certain he knew he was loved. Do you understand what a legacy that is to a child, Gabe? Do you understand how many children never receive such love?"

They didn't understand his position, either.

"Olivia says it doesn't matter what I feel about Eve," he snapped.

"No, it really doesn't. God says forgive. You don't get to pick who." Margaret looked quite severe.

"The thing you must keep foremost, my dear, is to balance what you gain by forgiveness against what you lose." Tillie shrugged. "It's really no contest."

"But forgiving Eve means she gets off scot-free."

"And not forgiving her means you're punishing her?"

Margaret raised her eyebrows. "She's beyond your reach, dear. You're only punishing yourself."

Frustrated, irritated and feeling alone in his misery, Gabe made an excuse and went home. Of all the days off he'd longed for, this wasn't one he wanted. He cleaned the house, did the laundry and made a popcorn dessert his dad used to make for him. It was one Eli loved.

But thoughts of Olivia filled every moment. In Eli's room he dusted the treasure box she'd made him from an old shoebox covered with gold foil and decorated with stars. Gabe unloaded the dishwasher and stared at the big white platter she'd given him as a housewarming gift because she'd said he'd need it for his Thanksgiving turkey. He watered the tubs of cascading red petunias she'd helped Eli choose and plant.

Chores completed, Gabe sat in his living room with a steaming cup of coffee, trying to come up with something else to keep busy. That's when it hit him. He was alone and that's how it was going to be from now on. Eli would grow up, play with his friends, make a whole world for himself. And Gabe would be alone because Olivia was leaving.

He'd have nobody to talk things over with, to help make decisions, to laugh with at Eli's goofiness. No one to encourage Gabe with a salty comment or a challenge. No one to press him on whether he'd based his decision biblically.

Loneliness swamped Gabe as he realized that Olivia was rooted inside him. Whether she was present or not, the aunts' organized foster daughter now filled every niche and corner of his world. The artwork he'd chosen at Chokecherry Hollow's local fair reminded him of her smile. The stove reminded him of her laughter when he'd burned an expensive roast in it. His mind repeated the prayer he'd overheard the day he'd moved in. She'd thought she was alone and had asked God to bless him and Eli as they became a family.

How could they be a family without her?

Olivia was a necessary part of Gabe's world. Avoiding her this past week had proved just how integral she'd become to his life. He thought about her when he made coffee exactly as she'd shown him. He thought about her when he was making dinner, whether she'd approve of his meal plan, and if she'd approve of the new school clothes he'd bought for Eli. It was Olivia who'd made this home a reality for him and Eli.

But mostly Gabe thought about what she'd said, how she'd dissed his claim of love.

There's not enough room in your heart for me. It's crowded with the past and with hate for the woman who left you. I think you'd always be afraid I was going to do what Eve did. That's not love, Gabe.

If only he could shed this unyielding chunk of bitterness inside, but even the aunts couldn't help him with that.

Chapter Thirteen

Olivia was ecstatic. The treasure hunt hike was going so well. Of course, it hadn't been without its issues, but she'd handled them with Jake and the newbie counselors' help. Her pleasure grew as the kids laughed with each discovery. She was thrilled to hear their giggles when they took time to shed their shoes and socks and dip their toes in the cool creek. It felt so good to share these moments without worrying.

"I know we had lunch, guys, but it's so warm I think we need another break. Let's share a snack. Then you can lay out all the items you've collected so we can make sure everyone has one of each. After all, we need every single item on our lists if we're going to get that treasure."

"You've done an amazing job here," Jake praised as the kids finished off their juice boxes and the cereal treats she'd brought. "There's a big variance in age in this group, yet you've managed to make it fun for all of them."

"It's nothing," she demurred breezily. But Jake wasn't buying.

"Yes, it is, Olivia. You relate to every kid. You make each one feel appreciated and that gives them a sense of accomplishment. You've done an excellent job for The Haven." He crushed his box and put it in the trash bag they'd brought. "You have a lot to offer your aunts' ministry. Why not stay?"

Olivia noticed Eli had curled up on his backpack and was now sleeping. So were three of the other younger children. The rest of the group seemed content to quietly discuss their treasures, comparing them and musing about what the final treasure might be.

"There won't be anything for me to do when Victoria returns," she murmured.

"But you wish you *could* stay?" Jake pressed, then nodded. "This place does that to you. You think that you're only here for a little while and you end up staying."

"That's what happened to you?" Her curiosity rose. Jake was such a major part of The Haven that it was hard to remember he hadn't always been here. The aunts had never explained why Jake had come or why he'd stayed, and Olivia had never asked.

"I was just going to help out for a while, to pay the aunts for caring for me." He shrugged. "I guess it's never seemed like quite the right time for me to leave."

"It never will be," she said, aghast at the thought of Jake leaving. "This is your home."

"It's yours, too," he said quietly.

"Yes." She shrugged. "I've struggled to forget my past. I always thought leaving here, getting as far away as I could, was the answer. But being here, the responsibility of having to take over this ministry while Vic gets better—that's what has helped me deal with the dragons in my past and learn to depend on God."

"That's The Haven effect. And your aunts'." He twiddled with a thread on his shirt. "Somehow they seem to just know what each of us needs."

"They'd tell you that's the God effect," Olivia said with a chuckle.

"Will it be hard for you to leave? Especially Gabe and Eli?" he asked soberly.

"Very."

"He loves you," Jake said quietly.

"But not enough," she returned sadly. "I'm trying to trust that God has a plan for my life. I guess Gabe and Eli aren't part of it." She checked her watch.

"Yeah, time to go." Jake pulled a bit of straw and stuck the stem between his teeth. "Sometimes it takes a lot to knock sense into the heads of stubborn cowboys," he mused in a twang straight from Texas, then smiled at her.

"Well said. I—"

A noise from the shrubs ahead of them made Olivia freeze. She recognized that sound. Jake did, too.

"Stay put," he whispered. "Tell the kids to do the same while I check it out." He unzipped his pack to show her the butt of his rifle.

"But a black bear—" she began, but Jake read her thoughts.

"I know. The law says I can only shoot if it attacks us. If we don't do anything threatening, I doubt it will. But I'll have a better idea what we're dealing with when I get a look," he finished. "Call the wildlife authorities and explain our situation."

"Okay. Be careful, Jake."

"Pray," he murmured, then crept away, his steps almost soundless in the green underbrush.

Olivia quickly made the call, grimacing when she was told the officers were attending to another call and might take a while to arrive. As quietly as possible she gathered the children around her, heart thudding as she wakened Eli and cuddled him close.

She was the one responsible here. With her Father's help, she was not letting one of them be hurt. *Please, God, help us.*

A moment later Jake returned. His tight face said all she needed to know.

"A mom and her cub. They're right in the middle of our path, feasting on the berries. We can't back up or go around so we're going to have to wait it out."

"Okay. Thanks." She quietly addressed the children. "I need you to pay close attention. There is a mother bear nearby with her baby. They're eating berries to fill up before they have their long sleep all winter." The children's eyes grew huge.

"What do we do?" one of them asked, voice panicky.

"Will that bear eat us?" Eli asked.

"No. This is a mommy bear with her baby. She isn't interested in us. She just wants her baby to eat his berries so he'll be able to sleep during the winter. If we're quiet and leave her alone, she doesn't care about us. She only wants the food," she emphasized.

Jake stepped away to the edge of the clearing. He peered into the forest. Olivia knew he was monitoring every moment of the bear and her cub. Because *she* was watching him, the kids were watching him. She could feel their fear mounting.

"The first thing we're going to do is ask God to help

us," she told them, and then began praying. Several children added their own prayers. When silence fell, she lifted her head and smiled. "God has heard us. We can depend on Him to help us. Now, I'm going to tell you some of the things I know about bears while we wait for the people I've called to come and help us. But you must remember to be very quiet. We don't want to scare the mother."

Olivia told them story after story, everything she'd read about the Rockies wildlife, studied in school, learned from the aunties and later from Jake. As she did she thought of Gabe, trusting her to watch the son he'd only just begun to know. Her heart sent up another plea for help when she remembered how she'd chided him for doubting she could handle this treasure hunt. Why hadn't she asked him to come along instead of attacking him?

Please, God, help us. Please send someone.

"They're coming closer," a little girl whispered.

"It's going to be dark soon," one of the eldest kids noticed.

We need to get out of here, God!

"We'll be fine." Olivia met Jake's glance. She tried to place a second call to the wildlife service and found her cell phone was dead, despite the new battery she'd installed and fully charged since her new phone hadn't yet arrived. Jake had no cell phone, but he had a walkie-talkie to reach The Haven, but it made a lot of noise and he was hesitant lest it startle the bears.

Lord, I'm trusting You to keep these children safe. Please help us. I'm the responsible one. I suggested this treasure hunt as a way for the younger kids to participate in The Haven's program. Don't let me be the

*cause of this ministry failing, of children getting hurt.
I'm trusting in You to deliver us.*

The words spilled from Olivia's heart in a steady stream until a very soft, very plaintive voice penetrated her consciousness.

"Daddy? There's a bear. Can you help?"

Olivia blinked. Eli held a tiny cell phone. Two things hit her at the same time.

Daddy. He said "Daddy".

He's asking Gabe to help us.

Olivia's heart swelled with praise. Two answers to prayer.

"Sweetie, let me—" She froze when Eli clenched the phone tight to his ear, listened and then nodded his head.

"Okay, Daddy. I'll do it. Then can you come and get me?" the plaintive request came. "I want to go home." Another nod, then Eli handed her the phone.

"Gabe?"

"Tell me where you are, Olivia. Exactly." His gruff voice made her heart swell. She trusted him, knew he'd save his son. Gabe loved Eli.

"There's a little map on the wall in my office. Just follow it." She recited the landmarks they'd passed, the small glen and the path they'd taken to get here.

"You know the rules," he said, sounding angry. "Stay quiet, in one place and together. And wait. I'll get there as quickly as I can."

"What am I waiting for?" she asked, confused.

"You'll know," Gabe said.

She wanted to thank him, to tell him she loved him, that she needed him in her life forever.

But Gabe had hung up.

"Olivia." Jake's urgent whisper got her attention.

She twisted, saw the mother bear lurch to her hind feet and sway for a moment before her eyes fixed on Olivia's little group.

"Oh, Lord—help!"

Stark fear overtook Gabe as he grabbed his truck keys and drove to The Haven. He took the map, had a short conversation with Victoria, then climbed on a quad and set off on the path Olivia had charted for the treasure hunt. Heart in his throat, he drove quickly, offering desperate prayers for the little group's safety.

For as long as he lived he would never forget Eli's scared voice calling him Daddy. How sweet that sound. Yet how terrorizing to hear his son beg him for help. No way was he going to disappoint his child.

Branches slapped Gabe in the face as he drove. The sting against his cheeks, the damp of a light rain trickling down his neck and the discomfort of jarring over the trail barely registered as truth began to dawn inside his hardened heart.

Olivia was right. The past didn't matter. Eve, her deceit, all the wrong she'd done him—they were immaterial now. Gabe could lose the future with his son, could lose the woman he cared for more than his own life. He'd gladly be hurt a hundred times over if it would protect Eli or Olivia. Nothing mattered as much as they did.

So what if loving Olivia broke his heart? Wasn't that better than never loving her? And anyway, who said he'd get hurt. Olivia didn't hurt those she cared about. She protected them. She would gladly lay down her own life if it would save any one of those children she was with.

That couldn't happen!

Gabe couldn't lose her or Eli, not now, not when he'd finally realized the past didn't matter. God had gifted him with two special loves, a future, a chance to watch his boy grow up, to teach him about God and love. A chance to love Olivia and be loved. Was he going to lose his chance to grab happiness because he couldn't let go of the past?

"You're a fool, Webber," he muttered, jaw clenched in determination.

Olivia was going to leave because he hadn't told her that nothing mattered more than her, that she would always be the most important person in his world. Could he stand back and let her go? Could he live each day without remembering the memories they'd made, thinking of new ones they could make? No! But he'd messed up so badly. Would she forgive him, take a chance on him? Was there a way to make it up to Olivia and Eli?

Love them.

Gabe smiled at the voice in his head. Love was always the answer. How silly to forget that.

"Hang on, Eli. Hang on to Olivia. I'll be there soon." It was slow going now. The quad didn't fit on the walking path, which meant he sometimes had to ride leaning to one side. But Gabe wouldn't even consider giving up on his beloved ones.

"Forgive me for being so stupid, Lord," he prayed as he traveled. "You are love and forgiveness. I lost sight of that for far too long."

As Gabe asked for forgiveness, the rock-solid nugget that had lain in his heart since Eve's departure from his life began to melt and dissolve until he felt only freedom and joy. Okay, and a little fear.

"But I'm trusting You," he said out loud to conquer it, and then he quoted, "'What time I am afraid, I will trust in Thee.'"

The rain fell harder, soaking him. But Gabe didn't feel it because he was on a mission.

A mission of love.

Olivia wanted to grab the kids and hug them as close as she could. But she knew moving now was the wrong thing to do, so she fixed her gaze on the bear and maintained eye contact.

Clearly agitated at finding them so near her feeding spot, the mother bear growled menacingly. From the corner of her eyes, Olivia saw Jake take aim.

"Please help us, God. She's just a mom protecting her baby. I'm trusting You."

The bear sank onto all fours. She was going to charge. Olivia held her breath.

A shrill whistle pieced the afternoon. Once, twice, three times. The mother bear jerked her head from side to side, trying to locate the sound.

"Again, Eli," she heard Jake say. And Eli blew twice more. "Get out of here, bear," Jake yelled. "Everyone, stand up as tall as you can and yell really loud."

Each child did as they were asked. Confused and obviously concerned about her cub, the mother grunted loudly, then swung her head to one side. After surveying them a moment longer, she nudged her cub and together they lumbered off into the woods.

The entire group burst out cheering.

"I'll make sure she's gone," Jake murmured. "Stay here."

Olivia nodded. She felt wilted, as if her knees were

jelly. "Thank You, God," she whispered. A few minutes later Jake returned. "Gone?"

"Yes. The wildlife guys will have to catch her and her cub and move them outside the fence. Then we'll need to get that fence inspected. We can't have that happening again." He heaved a sigh. "Let's get back to The Haven. I could use a big mug of your sister's strongest coffee."

"Me, too. How did you know to bring your rifle?" she asked.

"I was out riding last night and thinking about this path and decided I'd bring it just in case. Didn't want to alarm anyone. I should have run the perimeter before we left." He wore a grim expression. "I won't make that mistake again."

"You always look after everyone at The Haven so well." Olivia smiled. "The aunties are blessed to have you. Thank you, Jake."

"My pleasure." With his rifle tucked away in his bag, he began encouraging the kids to pick up any trash they'd dropped.

"Did I blow it okay? Daddy said to be real loud." Eli studied his whistle.

"Honey, you were amazing. I didn't know you had a whistle," she said, smoothing his hair with a trembling hand. *Or a cell phone.*

"I din't know neither," Eli said with a grin. "Daddy said he put it in in my backpack in case I got losted, so you could find me in the woods. But I didn't get losted." He stopped, listened and then grinned so wide Olivia couldn't help but smile in return. "He's coming! Do you hear? He's coming just like he said he would."

"Of course. Your daddy will always come if you ask

him, Eli. He loves you very much." Eli wasn't the only one who'd learned a lesson today. Olivia had learned she could trust Him in every situation. Always. Even when she had to leave here and move on.

At that moment Gabe barreled through the brush and stopped in the middle of their resting spot.

"Daddy!" Eli raced to his father and laughed with glee when Gabe jumped off the quad and swung him into his arms. "I blew the whistle just like you said, Daddy, and the bear runned away."

"Good man." Gabe pressed his lips against the dark hair so like his own, then gazed into his child's face. "You scared me, Eli."

"Why?" Eli rubbed a hand against his dad's bristly jaw, reveling in the experience.

"Because I love you very much. I don't ever want anything bad to happen to you."

"But nothin' did 'cause Livvie prayed and I blew the whistle an' Jake said God sent the bear away." Eli hugged his father, then leaned away and said very gently, "I love you, too, Daddy. I won't talk about Mommy no more 'cause it hurts you an' Livvie says we shouldn't do stuff to make other people sad."

"Oh, Eli." Olivia was pretty sure those were tears in Gabe's eyes, though he quickly ducked his head into his son's neck. "You can talk about your mom whenever you want," he said, his voice very quiet. "I want you to tell me all about her. I'd like to know about such a wonderful mom like yours."

"Really?" Eli asked, then grinned when Gabe nodded. "Well, she always smelled really nice." He sniffed, then wrinkled his nose, obviously not getting the same vibe from Gabe.

Olivia smothered a chuckle as the boy wiggled to be free. Gabe set Eli down, one hand resting on his shoulder as if he couldn't quite let go. Her aching heart eased a little at the sight of Gabe's fierce love.

"Can I ride home on that bike with you, Daddy?"

"If Olivia says it's okay." Gabe's eyes met hers, but she couldn't read the expression in them. "Are *you* all right?" he asked very quietly, his gaze intense.

"Yes. God took care of us." She smiled. "But thank you for the whistle."

"Hey, Gabe." Jake slapped him on the shoulder. "The wildlife people are probably using that old road to the west to get here. Can you go back that way and tell them to head toward Flinder's Crossing? I tracked that mother and her cub in that direction."

"Sure," Gabe agreed, but his gaze remained on her.

"We'd better head back, too," Jake said, glancing from him to Olivia. "Before daylight's completely gone. At least the drizzle has stopped."

"Yes. Let's go." She smiled at Eli. "See you back at The Haven," she said, meeting Gabe's solemn gaze.

"You will."

There was something different about him, she decided as she herded the little group toward home. Something softer?

"Probably worry about his son," she told herself and focused on helping Mikey, who wouldn't go with Eli, navigate the rougher spots. "You're in charge now, so do your job and stop mooning over something you can't have."

"Are you talkin' to me, Aunt Livvie?" Mikey frowned. "'Cause I don't know what mooning means."

"Nor should you, Mikey, my boy. Let's see who can

go up this hill the fastest?" She smiled as he dashed upward. Kids were so precious. Kids and families. That's
what made life worthwhile.

*And tall lean cowboys who didn't smile much and
yet still managed to say a thousand things with their
intense blue eyes. If only...*

Chapter Fourteen

Back at The Haven, a very frustrated Gabe stayed for supper and endured the children's repeated accounts of their treasure hunt as he waited for an opportunity to talk to Olivia. But the woman seemed intent on avoiding him.

"Hey!" Mikey's frown expressed his dissatisfaction. "We never got no treasure!"

Victoria tried to suggest they needed rest and could get it in the morning, but that didn't fly. Every child in the room began demanding to see the "treasure." Gabe fully expected Olivia to agree and lead them to it; instead, she beckoned to him to follow her outside.

"What's wrong?" he asked, surprised by the deep, dark flush covering her face.

"The treasure. The stupid treasure," she muttered. When he simply stared at her, she snapped in exasperation, "I forgot to bury it."

Gabe couldn't help it. He burst out laughing. It was such an anticlimactic event and the opposite of Ms. Organization's usual style that he took a moment to simply enjoy her discomfiture.

"Well? Are you going to help me or not?" she demanded grumpily as she slapped her hands on her hips in annoyance.

"Sure." He shrugged, loving the way her gray eyes turned silver and shot sparks of lightning when she was displeased. "What do you need me to do?"

"Tell them we can find it in the morning?" she begged, arching her neck.

"Too late for that, Olivia." Gabe inclined his head toward the kitchen where a chant of "treasure, treasure" emanated through the open windows.

"I didn't think it would work." She was tired. Who wouldn't be after such an experience?

Gabe's heart softened as he gazed at her. He would do this and anything else she asked of him, anytime, anywhere. He loved this woman so much and he was going to tell her so, only not now when a bunch of kids were yelling, demanding her attention. He was going to tell her when nothing and no one would interrupt.

"Just tell me what you need me to do," Gabe said tenderly.

"There's a wooden box in my office, under the red pillows. In it there are several bags of those little chocolate coins wrapped in gold foil and some small toys. You need to dig a hole and put our treasure chest in it."

"Okay." *I'd do anything for you, my darling.*

"That's not all, Gabe. The box has to be buried on the north side of the pottery shed because that's where the instructions will lead them." Olivia brushed pine needles off her sweater with a disgusted look. "Dig underneath that great big poplar tree. Oh. But before you bury the box, you need to tie a belt around it."

"A belt?" He blinked.

"Yes. It's part of the rhyme I wrote, but then I couldn't find a belt, and then it was too late to rewrite the rhyme and we had to leave and that's why I didn't get around to burying the treasure. I thought I could do it while they ate, but…"

Gabe figured his face must have shown his confusion because Olivia exhaled in a long-suffering sigh before resuming her explanation.

"Their clues specifically say they have to unbuckle the chest and open it to find their treasure."

"Ah." He nodded. "So where do I find a belt?"

"I don't know. Improvise." The noise from the kitchen was deafening. Olivia looked like her last nerve was in danger of fraying. "I'll go keep them busy, but it won't be easy. Please, Gabe, don't take too long." She hurried away.

"Find the chest and a belt and dig a hole." The chest was easy to locate, and the stuff was inside just as she said. That's when Gabe had the idea. But by the time he'd completed his secret task, the noise was deafening, and he still didn't have a belt. He caught a glimpse of himself in the office mirror.

Really? You're willing to do that? his brain demanded.

Yep. Truth was, he'd do almost anything for Olivia.

Gabe lugged the box to the spot she'd mentioned, ran back for a shovel, found a soft spot and started digging. Ten minutes later the hole waited. He undid his belt, fastened it around the box and lowered it into the earth. He felt funny without the familiar weight around his waist but he backfilled the hole anyway. There were clumps of weeds nearby. He pulled a bunch up and replanted them under the tree. Then he smoothed the area. Hopefully the kids wouldn't notice the disturbance he'd made.

Then he hurried back toward the house, losing the shovel on the way. Olivia and Jake were struggling to engage the kids in a game, but the response was lackluster. Olivia lifted her head as he entered, a question mark in her lovely silver-gray eyes. For a moment Gabe stood transfixed, staring as he imagined all the futures they could have together. *If* she'd agree.

"Gabe?"

He swallowed hard before nodding.

"All right, children. You may now open your last clue." Olivia moved toward him as the sound of rustling paper filled the room. "Ideas? Anyone?"

"'Birds love my open arms,'" the eldest read, face screwed up in thought. "Nests?"

"Birdhouses?" another suggested.

The kids looked at each other, uncertainly.

"Trees." Eli smiled. "Birds like trees. That's where they build their nests."

"He's right. What's the next part of it?" one child said.

"'Kids like my shade for lunch.'" Again the eldest child spoke. He looked at Eli.

"Which tree?"

Gabe watched Olivia's face, saw the love in her eyes as her glance slid from one child to the next. She was perfect for this job. His heart grew impatient, but he wasn't going to rush things. He tilted back on the heels of his boots, waiting, praying, trying anything to chase away his doubts about his impetuous actions.

"We had our sandwiches under a tree," Eli murmured, brow wrinkled in thought. His eyes searched for and found Olivia. "You brought me lemonade when mine got spilled."

Olivia smiled and nodded. Then her glance swerved

to Gabe. There was something unspoken there, something he wanted to know more about—when they were alone together.

"Good thing you came along, Eli," one of the kids cheered. "We wouldn't know where to look. Show us, Eli."

His chest proudly thrust forward, Eli led the way out the door and toward the pottery shed, the other kids following.

"Where's your belt, Gabe?" Olivia's voice came from just below his left shoulder, soft, filled with—affection?

"It was needed for a higher purpose." He so badly wanted to kiss her, to speak from his heart. But he wanted more than that for her. He wanted to make this so special she'd never forget. "You'd better join them," he said, letting her beauty soak into him. "This is your treasure hunt."

"And yours. Thank you, Gabe." She smiled and it was like fireworks went off. Then she joined the children, who were now pawing at the freshly dug earth.

Content to watch, Gabe held back, unable to stop smiling. Moments later there was a shriek of excitement as the box was unearthed.

"There's the belt, just like it said."

"Open it. I want to see what's inside."

He waited, almost breathless as the box was opened and the treasure distributed.

"Hey, this says Livvie's name." Eli held up a white envelope.

Olivia turned to look at Gabe, a question in her eyes. He simply watched her, saw the way she hesitantly took the note, slid her thumb under the seal and pulled out the slip of paper. She read it, then looked at him, eyes wide. With hope?

If only she still loved him.

The next few minutes passed in a blur for Gabe. Someone—Victoria?—urged the children to save their treasure for tomorrow and sent them scurrying for bed, insisting Eli and Mikey needed a sleepover. Gabe let his gaze slide off Olivia just long enough to embrace his son and kiss him good-night. He thought it was Jake who filled in the hole he'd dug, but then he, too, disappeared, leaving Gabe and Olivia alone on the tiny hill just above the house with the full moon shining on them.

"What does this mean?" she asked, holding up the note.

"Exactly what it says." Gabe took a step toward her, loving the fragrance of her hair on the night breeze. "You're my treasure. I love you."

"But—" A furrow appeared on her forehead.

"I'm free, Livvie. I've forgiven Eve, if there was ever anything to forgive." He took her hands in his just to make sure she heard him out and didn't run off before he'd said everything he needed to say. "When you and Eli were out there with a black bear—let's just say I got my priorities straight."

"And they are?" She wasn't quite sure of him. Not yet.

"That you and Eli are what matter most in my life. My marriage failed, but it wasn't all Eve's fault. It was mine, too. Given my heartless dismissal of her, it's no wonder she didn't tell me about Eli." He paused, stared into her eyes, loving the clarity he saw there. "But whose fault it was doesn't matter anymore. It's in the past. I'm more interested in the future."

"Which is?" Something in those silvery eyes warned Gabe to be very clear.

"I love you. I want to be with you. Always. And I don't care where that is." He inhaled silently, praying for the right words. "If you still want to live in Edmonton, I'll move there."

"But your new house—?"

"I don't want to be there if you won't share it," he said firmly.

"Your job, the horses, Eli's school?" He knew Olivia was listing them because she still wasn't certain about him. That was okay. If she loved him they would have the future for him to prove his love.

"There are lots of jobs, lots of horses, lots of schools," he said with a smile. "But there's only one you. You're the one I want in my life. You moved into my heart, Olivia, and now you own it. Wherever you go, Eli and I go. I love you."

"But—" She frowned as tears welled.

Gabe lifted one hand and gently smoothed a thumb under each eye, pushing away the tears.

"Darling Olivia, I have finally gotten my priorities straight and they are you. I love you, though I'm surely not good enough for you. I'll make mistakes and hurt you and not be half the man you deserve. I'm grumpy and selfish and disorganized and I've lost my belt which cowboys never do—"

"And you love me?" she added with a beatific smile. He nodded.

"I can't fathom why God would batter down my wall of bitterness, why He would take the time to make a dumbbell like me see how wrong I've been. And I'm so, so sorry that He had to use you and Eli to make me see sense. When I think of what could have happened—"

"God was in control, Gabe. We were in His hands." Her arms crept around his neck. "There is no better place."

"No." He liked the way she traced the curls at his nape and touched the tips of his ears and the corners of his eyes. But he needed more. "Olivia?"

"I love you, Gabe. I want us to have a future together, too. You and Eli and me. A family. It's what I've always wanted, even when I didn't know it. But God knew. It's been hard to learn to trust Him completely, but knowing you love me is so very worth it—"

"Olivia, please." Gabe caught his breath at her beauty as she tipped her head back to stare at him. "Can I kiss you now?" he asked.

"I've been waiting and waiting," she whispered.

Olivia stood on her tiptoes and Gabe met her halfway, his lips touching hers with a promise that came from the depths of his soul. Without using a single word he told her that she was his beloved, the most important thing in his world.

"You don't need to worry, Olivia. You are and will always be first in my heart," he whispered when at last they drew apart. She smiled and nestled her head against his chest.

"And you'll always be my cowboy knight in shining armor, minus his belt," she teased with a giggle. Then she gazed at him, her silver eyes memorizing each angle of his face. "You're always there for me, Gabe, from the first day I came home. You've helped me realize that here at The Haven is where I belong."

"Just to be clear—you don't want to move to Edmonton?" he asked hesitantly.

"No," she whispered, her smile wide. "I want to be part of this amazing ministry. I want to trust God to show us how to help kids. I want to be here, so I can see their transformations. I want to be with you, Gabe, for as long as He gives us together, with Eli. I love you. If you love me, I have all I need."

He traced a fingertip over her lips, stunned by what God had worked out in his life. He didn't deserve it, but he was going to grab it and squeeze out every precious second of the time God gave him with this amazing woman.

"When can we get married, Olivia?" For the first time, when he cupped her face in his hands, his fingers tracing the scar in a gentle touch, Olivia didn't move.

"Well, you haven't actually asked me yet, Gabe," she giggled.

He immediately went down on one knee. He was dumb but not that dumb. When God gave you something wonderful, you hung on to it.

"My darling Olivia, I love you more than you will ever know. I want to marry you and share our wonderful future together. So, will you?"

Her fingers smoothed across his face, memorizing each detail as she studied him. For a moment Gabe's heart quaked, but then he remembered in whom he trusted and waited. At last a smile flickered across Olivia's face.

"Yes," she said, head tilted to one side. "I'm thinking October. Any objections?"

"Not a one," Gabe said as he rose and embraced her. "Fortunately, I already have a place for us to live."

"A very nice place," she agreed. "And a son we can love and raise to trust in God. Thank you, Gabe." She kissed him. "Suddenly I'm not tired at all."

"Me, neither. Let's sit here for a while and watch the stars."

So they did.

Chapter Fifteen

Gabe and Olivia chose to be married on Thanksgiving Monday at The Haven. Both the bride and groom wanted a simple family-centered event, outside if possible, in the splendor of the autumn-toned woods.

Overwhelmed with her new job as codirector of The Haven's outreach program, Olivia had only one weekend to shop for a wedding dress, but thanks to her aunties' preparation, that was more than enough to choose a beautiful shantung suit in purest ivory with matching heels.

The aunties also located the most perfect bridesmaid dresses with swirly chiffon skirts featuring Olivia's signature orange tones among multi hues of autumn greens, grays and browns. Once the dresses were chosen, Tillie and Margaret ordered gorgeous russet mohair yarn and hand-crocheted shrugs for each sister to provide a bit of extra warmth if the day turned chilly.

But, of course, it wasn't. Monday dawned a glorious day with a warmly glowing sun that turned the hills into a splendorous setting, certainly a day for Thanksgiving.

As Olivia waited for ring bearer Eli to finish his walk

down the aisle to his father, she thought about how full her life was. The aunts, her sisters, their children, the youth who came to The Haven, and now Gabe and Eli.

Trust God? Always. He had given her the desires of her heart.

"Are you ready, dear?" Aunt Tillie's arm slipped through hers on the left, Aunt Margaret's on the right.

"Ready, aunties." Her gaze riveted on Gabe's face, Olivia walked down the aisle, certain that whatever their future brought, she could trust her Lord.

The couple repeated the vows they'd chosen with friends and family as witnesses and God's spectacular creation in the background. Olivia was lost in her first kiss as Gabe's wife when she felt someone tugging on her skirt.

"Congratulations," Eli said with careful enunciation.

"Thank you, darling." She bent and hugged him, hid a smile as the little boy shook his head. "Is everything okay, Eli?" she asked when his blue eyes, so like Gabe's, locked with hers.

"Yeah. I was just wondering. Are you my mommy now?"

Olivia felt Gabe's fingers tighten against her waist. She stood on tiptoe and kissed his cheek for reassurance before bending to address Eli.

"You had a wonderful mommy, Eli. I wouldn't ever try to take her place." She brushed her fingers against his cheek. "I'm just Olivia, same as always."

"You can't be." Eli shook his head firmly. "Daddy said today makes us a family. I got a daddy." He grinned at Gabe. "But I hafta have a mommy, too. My other mommy would be happy," he assured her seriously. "'Cause she loved me."

"So do I, Eli, and I would love to be your mommy. Thank you." Tears filled her eyes at the wonderful gift of this little boy.

"You're a lucky kid to have the two best mommies in the world." Gabe swung his son into his arms, then threaded his other arm around Olivia's waist. "Now we're a family."

"Ladies and gentlemen, may I present Mr. and Mrs. Gabe Webber. And family," the pastor added, after Eli glowered at him.

The bride and groom laughed, hugged and enjoyed the afternoon. Though they were eager to be off on their short honeymoon, they were delayed by questions about their plans for the future.

"What will you do now?" people asked Gabe.

"Settle in to Trust Farms, that's the name of our spread. Keep working at the Double M and with the foster youth who come to The Haven for respite." He winked at Olivia. "In our spare time, I'll start a petting zoo with my wife and son and try to do whatever God asks of us."

Later, as they lifted off in an aircraft that would take them on their honeymoon to Maui, Olivia leaned her head against Gabe's shoulder.

"Aside from falling in love, getting married and finding your son, what's changed with us, Gabe?"

He thought for a minute.

"We've put the past in the past, where it belongs. Now we're focused on our future together, with God, whatever it is."

"Yeah." She smiled and nodded. "I finally figured it out."

Gabe arched an eyebrow, waiting.

"Home isn't where you are. It's who you're with."

"Now you're talking." He stole a kiss. Then she giggled.

"I forgot to ask if you liked your first wedding gift."

He patted his flat waist. "Love it, though I've never had a belt made of rope before."

"I'm thinking it might be a good craft when we're snowed in this winter. We always need a good craft to keep the kids busy."

They leaned back into their seats and began planning for their future.

Together.

* * * * *

HER COLORADO COWBOY

Mindy Obenhaus

For Your glory, Lord.

Acknowledgments

Thank you, Allison Wilson,
for helping me brainstorm this story
and find the outcome it deserved.

Many thanks to Steve Wicke
for sharing your roping expertise.

Betty Wolfe,
you're one of my favorite residents of Ouray.
Thank you for all your help.

To my loving husband, Richard,
where would I be without you?

Weeping may endure for a night,
but joy cometh in the morning.
—*Psalms* 30:5

Chapter One

Lily Davis had lost her mind.

She loathed horses. Yet, somehow, she'd allowed her children to talk her into taking them horseback riding. What was she thinking?

Knuckles white, she guided her luxury SUV across the cattle guard of Abundant Blessings Ranch and Trail Rides, her gaze darting from the majestic mountains that backdropped the picturesque setting to the menacing red-and-white metal building that sat a short distance from the road.

She swallowed hard. Any other time she would have put her foot down, but she was desperate. They'd only been in Ouray for three days, and already her kids were begging to go back to their friends and electronic devices in Denver.

Okay, so it was her ten-year-old son, Colton, who did most of the complaining. He thought everything was boring. On the contrary, her seven-year-old daughter, Piper, had proclaimed Ouray, Colorado, the most beautiful place ever. Which was good, because returning to Denver before the end of the summer was not an option. Not if she wanted to save her son from following in his father's footsteps.

She eyed her firstborn in the rearview mirror. With his sandy brown hair and green eyes, he favored her, though his blatant lies were a hallmark of his father. Something Lily found increasingly disconcerting. But learning of how he'd bullied another boy at school had spurred her into action. Because despite what Wade Davis might believe, the fact that they had money did not make them better than anyone else.

He'd agreed to let her take the kids away for the entire summer, instead of splitting the time the way they usually did. Whatever deal he was working must be big. She could only pray he wouldn't change his mind before August 15, the date they'd agreed upon for the kids' return.

Easing to a stop between another SUV and a sedan, she shifted into Park. Why couldn't they have just gone on another Jeep tour?

The kids were out of the vehicle before Lily even turned off the engine.

"Hurry up, Mommy." Piper's excitement had her blonder-than-blond ponytail swishing to and fro. The perpetually cheerful child had always been eager to try new things. A trait Lily usually admired. Until she suggested horseback riding.

Too bad Lily hadn't had the guts to say no.

Setting her booted feet onto the gravel, she rubbed her arms, eyeing the two chestnut-colored horses staring at her from the adjacent paddock. Did they know? Were they able to sense that another horse had once gotten the best of her?

"Aww…" Piper noted the pair. "Aren't they cute?"

Lily cleared her throat. "Horses are some of God's most beautiful creatures." Not to mention frightening. Her kids didn't see it that way, though, so she wasn't about to pass her fears on to them.

She drew in a deep breath, the once-familiar odor of horse and hay tightening her stomach. How was she ever going to pull this off?

"This is boring." Colton shuffled toward the entrance. "I want to ride them, not look at them."

Lily's gaze lifted to the mid-June sky. *God, please help me.* She glanced at her son. *In every way.*

Inside, the walls of the small but tidy lobby were lined with rustic wood planks. A couple with two boys who looked to be a little older than Colton sat on an old wooden church pew that hugged one wall.

"Mommy, look." Piper pointed above the doorway of what appeared to be an office. "A horseshoe."

"It's a horse barn." Arms crossed, Colton rolled his eyes. "They probably have, like, a million of those things."

"I don't care, Colton." Hands on her hips, his sister glared at him. "I still like them."

Before Lily could intervene, the sound of footsteps on concrete drew their attention.

She turned, feeling as though she'd suddenly stepped into a country music video. From his boots and Wranglers to the shiny belt buckle and straw Stetson perched on his head, this guy was all cowboy.

He stopped to address the other family. "If you all will head straight down this corridor—" he pointed to the long aisle behind him "—and to the right, Amber and Jackie are waiting with your horses."

As the group departed, he turned his attention to

Lily and her children. "Welcome to Abundant Blessings Ranch." Tall and clean shaven, he tipped his hat back just enough to reveal dark brown hair and even darker eyes, like a rich espresso. He was older than she would have expected. Perhaps even older than her thirty-eight years, but not by much. And while his smile was pleasant enough, it did little to put her at ease. "I'm Noah Stephens. How can I help you folks today?"

Pressing one hand against her stomach, she fingered the silver chain around her neck with the other. "Um—"

"We want to ride horses." Piper stared up at the man, looking very matter-of-fact.

"You do?" His smile grew wider, forming creases around his eyes. "Well, I guess you've come to the right place then." He reached for one of a series of clipboards that hung on the wall. "I'll just need your mother to sign these papers." He handed the clipboard to her, along with a pen.

The knot in Lily's stomach grew even bigger as she filled in the required information. Why was she putting herself through this? She should have simply said no in the first place.

But then Colton and Piper would have wanted to know why. She couldn't bear the thought of telling them she was afraid. After all, she was their mother. The one who was supposed to be strong. And she was, most of the time. Right about now, though, she felt like that four-year-old girl who'd just been bucked off her first, and last, horse.

"How much riding have you kids done?" The cowboy looked from Colton to Piper.

"I've never been on a horse." Piper's blue eyes sparkled. "But I can't wait."

"That's good to know, because I want to make sure I pair each of you with the correct horse for your level of experience."

"What does it matter?" Colton shrugged. "It's just a stupid horse."

The cowboy straightened to his full six-foot-plus height, and Lily froze. What would he do? Everyone knew cowboys didn't tolerate disrespect. And her son had plenty. Would he tell them they couldn't ride?

Wishful thinking on her part.

Arms crossed, the man stared down at Colton, his expression stern. "Actually, horses are quite smart." His deep voice left no room for question. "And they're able to sense what kind of people are riding them." His gaze narrowed. "So you might want to keep that in mind, young man."

Under different circumstances, Lily might have chuckled. But by the time she handed the completed paperwork back to the cowboy, her stomach was churning.

His brow lifted. "Are you all right, ma'am?"

"Yes." However, the more she tried to psych herself up for this endeavor, the worse things became.

She grabbed a white-water rafting brochure from the rack against the wall and fanned herself, wondering when it had gotten so warm. All the while, the tossing and turning in her belly intensified.

This was not good. Not good at—

Just as the cowboy turned to talk with Colton and Piper, Lily bolted out the door. She rushed to the side of the building, her stomach in full revolt. Not once, but twice.

Standing there, doubled over, she heard someone behind her. *Oh, no. God please don't let it be—*

"You look like you could use a little help." That deep voice definitely didn't belong to Colton or Piper.

Mortified, she glanced at the cowboy and managed to eke out, "Don't let my children see me," before hurling again.

When she finally collected herself a short time later, she leaned against the metal building, feeling more than a little embarrassed. And all over the mere thought of riding a horse. She wiped her mouth, praying she wouldn't have a repeat performance.

Returning to the stable, she spotted Piper and Colton halfway down the wide corridor that ran between a small arena and some horse stalls.

"Where were you?" Colton eyed her suspiciously.

"I had something I had to take care of." She forced a smile, hoping she didn't look as pale as she felt.

Fortunately, the cowboy reappeared with two horses before her son could ask any more questions.

It pleased her that one of them was nothing more than a Shetland pony, and she wondered if they might have another for her.

The man stopped in front of them, looking far too serious. "We have a slight problem."

Oh, no. Her kids were so looking forward to this, and now they weren't going to be able to ride. All because of her. Her silly fear had blown it for all of them.

The cowboy continued, "We had another family that arrived just before you. Typically, we prefer not to have any more than six guests on a trail ride. With you three, that would be seven."

Piper's bottom lip pooched out. "You mean we don't get to ride?"

"Man, we finally get to do something cool…" Colton kicked at clump of hay.

Lily's stomach tightened again. If only she hadn't panicked. Now she'd ruined everything.

"Of course," the cowboy finally said, "if one of you would be willing to stay behind, the other two could still go."

Lily jerked her gaze to his.

His dark eyes were directed right at her.

He was giving her an out. But why? Was he afraid she'd get sick again while they were on the trail? Or did he know she was afraid?

"I'm not staying," said Colton.

"If Colton doesn't hafta stay, I don't want to, either." Arms crossed, Piper peered up at Lily.

Looked like it was up to her to take one for the team. Something she was more than okay with this time. Thanks to Noah Stephens. However, it presented her with a new problem.

Mr. Stephens was a stranger. Colton and Piper were her greatest blessings. A gift from God she cherished with every fiber of her being. Could she trust this cowboy with her children?

Clearing her throat, she looked at her kids. Saw the disappointment etched on their faces. "I wouldn't want the two of you to miss out, either." She eyed the cowboy. He looked responsible. And he'd already shown he wasn't the type to stand for Colton's shenanigans. "Would it be all right if they went without me?"

He nodded. "So long as you signed the consent forms."

She looked at her children. "Are you two okay with that, or would you prefer to wait until later when we can go together?" Not that she'd be any more enthusiastic, but she'd settle for less nauseous.

"I can watch Piper," offered Colton.

"Yeah, Colton can watch me."

Lily couldn't help but laugh. For once her children were in agreement. "Okay. But I want you to be on your best behavior."

"We will," they said in unison.

The cowboy tipped his straw hat in her direction. "I promise to take good care of them."

To her surprise, she actually believed him. Probably because he'd come to check on her when she was outside. Something she found very chivalrous. And as they walked away, she couldn't help wondering what it would be like to be taken care of by someone like that. Someone strong, caring... Not self-serving like her ex.

She quickly shook away the thought. God and her children were her only priorities. Not love or any notions thereof. Especially with a cowboy.

"Mom, you should have seen it." Colton met his mother in the lobby, his enthusiasm obvious. And that made Noah happy.

The kid was far too young to have the kind of attitude Noah had witnessed prior to their ride. Angry. Disrespectful. The type of kid Noah hoped to help. Not that troubled kids were the focus of his soon-to-open rodeo school at Abundant Blessings Ranch. Still, Noah knew firsthand the difference horses could make in the lives of troubled kids and adults dealing with loss. They're what helped him get past the deaths of his wife and unborn child. And he had a feeling the root of Colton's anger had to do with some sort of loss, too. During their ride, the kid had mentioned that his parents were divorced. Was his father involved in his life?

While Noah's parents had loved each other until his mother succumbed to cancer three years ago, he'd had many friends whose lives had been impacted by divorce. He understood the pain and anger that came from such an experience. Especially when it was something they hadn't chosen and there was nothing they could do to fix it.

If only he could help those kids deal with their feelings by giving them a way to channel their emotions into something else. Or perhaps the kids would simply benefit from spending time with a good listener. He knew for a fact that horses were very good listeners.

"We got to ride on the mountain," Piper said.

Cute kid. Happy, smart, energetic... If his child had been a girl, he'd have hoped she'd be like Piper.

"Can I get a soda?" Colton watched his mother hopefully. "Noah said there's a machine around the corner."

The woman—what was her name? Some sort of flower. Lily? Yes, that was it—pulled a series of ones from the pocket of her jeans. "Okay, but no caffeine. And get one for your sister, too."

She looked at Noah then, her green eyes void of the anxiety that had been there before. "Thank you for taking them. I...hated to disappoint them."

"No worries, ma'am. I'm pretty sure they enjoyed themselves." He turned his attention to her daughter. "Right, Piper?"

"Right!"

They both chuckled at her daughter's exuberance.

He eyed the woman again. She'd tucked her long reddish-blond hair into a crude ponytail, making him wonder if she'd gotten sick again after they left. "I trust you're doing all right?"

The pink in her cheeks heightened as she tugged on the hem of her fitted gray button-down. "I am. Thank you again."

"Good." Suddenly uneasy, he glanced down the corridor. "If you'll excuse me, I have something I need to tend to."

"Of course."

With the voices of Lily and Piper echoing in his ears, he rounded the corner and headed down the corridor. Passing the alcove where the soda and snack machines were, he saw no sign of Colton.

Weird. Had Noah been so lost in thought that he'd passed him without even realizing?

Continuing on to the tack room, he spotted the boy. And his heart sank.

There, beside the bridle rack, Colton was stooped over a bucket of horseshoes. Horseshoes meant to be given to kids as souvenirs. Instead, Colton grabbed two, stuffing one into each of the pockets of his Nike hoodie.

He was stealing.

"Colton." Noah kept his voice firm, all the while keeping it void of any accusation.

The boy jerked his head up. "I...couldn't find the soda machine."

"And the horseshoes?"

Colton looked everywhere but at Noah. "I was just looking at them."

"If you want one, all you have to do is ask."

The kid's green eyes narrowed. "They're just stupid old horseshoes. Who'd want one of those?"

Noah shook his head. He'd hoped the kid would at

least acknowledge his curiosity. Instead, he'd lied. And there was no way Noah could tolerate that.

He took hold of Colton's arm. "Let's go see your mother."

"Why?" The boy's voice held a note of terror as he jerked free and started down the hallway.

"I think you know why." Noah could understand the kid's attitude, but lying was a different ball game altogether.

Rounding into the lobby with Colton in tow, he saw the bewildered look in Lily's eyes as she rose from the old pew.

Grateful no one else was present, he said, "I caught this young man stealing."

"I didn't steal anything!"

Noah glared down at the boy. "Care to show me what's in your pockets?"

Colton promptly turned his pants pockets inside out to show them empty. "He's lying, Mom. I didn't take anything. See?"

A confused Lily looked from her son to Noah.

Undeterred, Noah said, "And your jacket pockets?"

The boy hesitated then. "This is stupid, Mom. I didn't take anything. You believe me, don't you?"

His mother's confused and seemingly pained gaze moved between Colton and Noah. Once. Twice.

Finally, "If there's nothing there, then you should have no problem showing us, Colton."

After a few moments, the boy pulled out the horseshoes and thrust them at Noah, the clanking of metal echoing through the small space. "They're just stupid horseshoes. You have a ton of them."

The look on Lily's face flitted between horror, disappointment and panic in a matter of seconds.

What saddened Noah the most was that he would have given the kid the horseshoes if he'd asked. But Colton hadn't asked. He'd simply taken something that didn't belong to him. Then compounded matters by lying.

Noah knew what he would do if this were his son. Question was, what would his city-slicker mother do? Offer to pay for it? Call it a misunderstanding?

That was the problem with today's world. Too many parents eager to bail their kids out instead of letting them face the consequences for their actions.

"Colton...take your sister to the car and wait for me there, please." With her arms crossed, Lily's eyes never left Noah's.

Yep, she was going to pay for her son's transgressions.

"But, Mom—"

"*Now*, Colton." She watched as the two moved slowly out the wooden door, then faced Noah. "Any chance we could work something out?"

All that was missing now was the checkbook. "Depends what you mean by 'work something out.'"

She hesitated. "I don't want my son to grow up thinking that money is the answer. He made a bad choice. He needs to learn that there are consequences for bad choices."

Her words had Noah taking a step back. He cleared his throat. "Yes, of course."

"Some parents are all too happy to pay for their kids' mistakes, but I'm not one of those people. I want Colton—and Piper—to know that every choice has a consequence. And I want them to learn now, while they're young."

Hmm… He couldn't have said it better himself. "That's commendable."

She glared at him. "I'm not looking for any commendations, Mr. Stephens. I simply want my children to grow up to be good people."

Okay, so he'd definitely underestimated her. "All right then. What if we had him work it off?"

The light in her green eyes shifted. "I like that." She hesitated then. "Depending on what you have in mind."

Ah, now he got it. Pay the consequences without really paying the consequences. "I was thinking he could come by tomorrow morning and muck out the horse stalls."

Lily choked back a laugh. Something he found rather cute. "That's perfect."

"Really?"

"Yes. Of course, it'll be 'stupid.'" She made air quotes with her long fingers.

"Of course."

Her expression softened. "But I think it'll drive home the message."

"That stealing is wrong."

"Among other things, yes."

The heel of his boot scraped across the concrete floor. "Okay, so what time can I expect him?"

"The earlier the better. How about seven?"

"In the morning?" Humph. He would have taken her for a not-before-ten kind of girl.

"You don't think I'm going to let him sleep in, do you?"

"I…obviously wasn't thinking. My apologies."

She studied him, a smile playing on her lips. "I believe in teaching my children values. So I will see you in the morning." With that, she turned and marched out the door, passing his father as she went.

Moving beside Noah, Clint Stephens watched after her. "She's pretty."

Noah made a quick left into the office. "Is she?" He grabbed the day's consent forms. "I hadn't noticed."

His father followed him. "Since when have you been blind?"

Noah chose to ignore the remark. He wasn't blind at all. But his heart belonged to his late wife, Jaycee. Now and always.

Dad paused beside the desk. "Newspaper called. Wanted to know about the ads for the rodeo school."

Noah scrubbed a hand across his face. While the new building should be completed in time for Ridgway's annual rodeo on Labor Day weekend, now that summer was here, he'd barely had any time to think about the grand opening that was supposed to coincide with the Ridgway event.

"Oh, and that Realtor called again." Dad watched him. "Have you given any more thought to renting out the cabin? Might bring you some extra income."

Noah tossed the forms into the file cabinet and threw the drawer closed with more force than he'd intended. He didn't need the extra income. He'd earned plenty during his rodeo days, made wise investments and lived modestly. Dad knew that.

And you've put all your savings into the rodeo school. Even so, how the old man could think that he would allow strangers into the home he and his wife had once shared boggled his mind.

"Son, you know I've never been one to tell you and your brothers how to live your lives, but Jaycee's been gone twelve years now. Don't you think it's time you started living again?"

"Living?" He gestured to the stacks of papers and plans for the rodeo school. "What do you call this?"

"Oh, you're going through the motions, all right. It's just…"

"Just what?" Hands on his hips, he tried to get a handle on his annoyance.

The man looked everywhere but at Noah, then let go a sigh. "It's been a long time since you've been happy." He didn't miss the sorrow in his father's tone.

"Dad, I love this place, you know that. And the horses… I can't wait to get the rodeo school up and running."

His father held up his hands. "No need to get defensive. I believe everything you've said. I'd just hate for you to be so stuck in the past you close yourself off to the future God has in store for you."

Noah chuckled, wondering what had gotten into his father. After all, he was a widower, too. Perhaps spending so much time with his old classmate Hillary Ward-Thompson was finally getting to him. But Noah wasn't about to head down that road again. He'd loved and he'd lost. And he never wanted to feel that kind of pain ever again.

Chapter Two

Clouds dotted the sky as Lily passed under the arched metal sign that read Abundant Blessings Ranch late the next morning. She could hardly wait to hear about Colton's experience. Lord willing, three hours of mucking out stalls would teach him a lesson.

A shudder ran through her as she approached the stable, though this time it had nothing to do with equines. Hands tightening around the leather-wrapped steering wheel, she stared straight ahead. Colton was becoming so much like his father it was scary. The lies, the bullying, now stealing...

God, please help me to train my son up in the way he should go.

Something that wasn't always easy for a single parent. Especially when the other parent didn't share your faith. Not that Wade ever spent any time with his kids. Even during their visitation, they were often left in someone else's care. Because Wade didn't care about anything but himself and having a good time.

Unfortunately, it was Colton who suffered the most. Like most young boys, he wanted his father's approval.

And, apparently, he thought that behaving like him was a means of getting it.

Only one of many reasons she'd wanted to get the kids away from the city. And while they usually took an extended summer trip, this year she hadn't wanted to go somewhere exotic or to some exclusive resort. That was Wade's style, not hers. She wanted something simpler. Something meaningful.

Okay, so it hadn't even been a week since they arrived in Ouray. Still, she'd never expected things could actually get worse.

By the time she and Piper stepped out of their SUV, Lily had determined that there would be no TV, handheld devices or computers of any kind for Colton for at least a week. And if he pulled another stunt, or she caught him lying, his sentence would be even longer.

That should provide the perfect opportunity for plenty more Jeep rides and family hikes. Maybe the kids would enjoy exploring some of the old mining towns that dotted the area. Anything that didn't involve horses was fine by her.

Inside the stable, she spotted her son midway down the wide corridor, standing on the bottom rung of the pipe fencing that surrounded the practice arena in the center of the building. His arms were draped over the top of the fence as he watched something or someone inside the arena. Whatever it was had certainly captured his interest, because not only had he not noticed her or his sister, he was completely engrossed. Something Lily had rarely witnessed outside of his video games.

Evidently noticing her brother, Piper let go of Lily's hand and ran ahead of her, sending dust flying from her sneakers. "Colton!"

He looked their way and, to Lily's surprise, actually smiled. He hopped down off the fence. "Mom, you wouldn't believe all the horses Noah has."

Funny, if Piper had made that same remark he would have belittled her the way he had yesterday when she pointed out the horseshoe.

"Wanna see them?"

That would be the last thing she wanted to do on such a beautiful day. Or any other day, for that matter. Still, she was happy to see him so animated.

"He's even got one that can do tricks."

"Oh." Piper's eyes widened. "I wanna see the horse that does tricks."

"And look at that, Mom." Colton pointed into the arena, where Noah was standing beside a young man on horseback.

"What are they doing?"

Her son's gaze never left the horse. "Noah's teaching him how to rope."

"What does that mean?" Piper poked her head between the rungs for a better view.

"Just watch," said Colton.

Noah stepped away from the boy then. "Go!"

Suddenly, on the other side of the dirt-covered ring, an all-terrain vehicle sprang to life, driven by another cowboy, pulling something that looked like a small cow with horns, except with a wheel at the front. As it moved around the ring, the hind legs bobbed as though it were running.

Behind that, the horse and rider took off, the rider swinging a rope in one hand. As they approached the makeshift cow, the rider sent the rope flying.

"He did it!" Colton thrust a fist into the air as the

rope fell around the horns. He looked at Lily, his smile wide. "That guy's been practicing all morning. He finally got it."

She loved teachable moments like this. "Like they say, practice makes perfect. If you want something, you have to be willing to work for it."

He looked toward the rider, who was getting ready to go again. "He's sure been working, all right."

"And all that hard work paid off." She draped an arm around her son's shoulder. "How did things go today?"

"Good."

That was vague.

Just then, she saw Noah coming across the arena, looking all cowboy and sending a wave of unease rippling through her. She hoped Colton had done the work he was assigned. But what if he hadn't or if he had been a problem?

"Hello again," Noah said.

"Hello." Lily watched as he deftly climbed the fence, swinging one long leg over, then the other, as though he'd done it a million times before. Next thing she knew, he was beside them.

"You'll be happy to know that Colton did a real good job. Did everything I asked him to, didn't argue much."

Her son's head shot up. "I didn't argue. Did I?"

The man grinned. "No, you didn't. I just wanted to see if you were paying attention."

Colton relaxed then. "Good. 'Cause I can't wait to come back."

Lily's smile faded, her stomach muscles tightening. "Come back? You mean you want to go riding again?"

"Yeah, kinda. But what I really want is to learn to rope. With Noah."

"Oh." Uncertain how she felt about that, Lily's gaze drifted to the cowboy.

His dark eyes held an air of guilt. Had he been planting ideas in her son's head? "In addition to trail rides, we also offer riding and rodeo lessons."

She felt her own eyes widen. "Rodeo?" The last thing she wanted was to see her son bucked off some unruly bull or equine the way she had been all those years ago.

"Well, that's kind of an overarching term. Roping is only one part of rodeo. One that starts with learning how to use the rope correctly. It takes patience and discipline, but if he's persistent…"

"I'm sure I can learn."

Had she ever seen her son this enthusiastic about anything? Especially something that involved work? While she didn't relish the idea of spending so much time with a bunch of horses, patience and discipline were things Colton desperately needed to learn. Perhaps this sort of training—any training—could be good for him. Give him something to focus on besides himself.

Tucking her fear aside, Lily addressed Noah. "How much do the lessons cost?"

He tipped his cowboy hat back with a smile. "They won't cost you a thing."

She bristled. "Nothing is ever free, Mr. Stephens." In her experience, people always expected something.

"I said it wouldn't cost *you* anything."

She eyed him curiously, waiting for him to explain.

"Colton tells me you're in Ouray for the summer."

"That's correct."

"Well, he's the one who wants lessons." He turned his attention to her son. "And we could use another hand around here. What if we worked out a trade? You muck out the stalls three days a week in exchange for three days of lessons."

The elation on her son's face only added to her dilemma. "Can I, Mom? Please?"

She studied the rafters overhead, uncertain how to respond. If she said no, she'd be the bad guy. But while she liked the idea of Colton working and appreciated his excitement, she was still skeptical. And not only about the horses.

Her gaze shifted to Noah. Why was this long, tall cowboy being so nice after Colton stole from him? Was he simply trying to get some free labor or did he genuinely want to help her son?

No matter which way she looked at it, she couldn't help wondering what this arrangement might cost her in the long run.

"That's good, Colton, but you need to twist your wrist like this." Standing alongside the boy in the arena the next morning, Noah demonstrated. "Which also turns the rope so it will lie properly as you're coiling it."

"Like this?" The boy ran a gloved hand down the length he held, then twisted his wrist outward the way Noah had.

"Now you're getting it." Noah's gaze inadvertently veered toward the aluminum bleachers outside the arena where Lily and Piper had been throughout Colton's lesson. Why had Lily been so cynical when he offered to teach Colton in exchange for some work? As if he was trying to take advantage of them. Wasn't his word good enough?

The kid looked up at him. "It feels kinda weird."

He again gave the boy his full attention. Or at least

tried to. He sure hoped Colton's mother wasn't planning to be there for all of his lessons. Given her fear of horses, though, Noah had a feeling she'd be front and center for each and every one.

"At first, yes. But as you practice, it'll become second nature."

Colton tossed out his rope again, and a few moments later, he had it perfectly coiled. "Look, I did it." He held it up. "It looks just like yours."

His enthusiasm warmed Noah's heart. This was what he loved about teaching kids. Sharing in their sense of accomplishment.

"Remember what I said yesterday about practice, patience and persistence?"

"Yeah."

Noah lifted a brow, careful not to look too stern. "How about we say 'yes, sir'?"

A hint of pink crept into the kid's cheeks. "Yes, sir."

Noah smiled then. "You exercised both patience and persistence as you practiced coiling that rope until you finally got it right."

The kid was quiet for a moment. "Can I keep practicing?"

"Not only can you, you have to." Noah tossed his rope out. "The more you practice—" he began to reel it in —the more used to it you become." He held up his freshly coiled rope.

"Awesome." Colton practically beamed as he made another attempt.

Noah, however, found his thoughts preoccupied once again by the boy's mother. Why did it chafe him so that Lily had questioned his integrity?

He glanced from Colton to Lily to one of the hands

who was tending to the horses. Because in his world, integrity was everything. A man without honor was nothing but a coward in his book. And for some strange reason, he wanted Lily and her children to see him as honorable.

He shook his head. Ridiculous. Why should he care what they thought? They were strangers. Which made his reaction even more preposterous.

"How come I'm not on a horse?"

He jerked his gaze back to Colton, annoyed that he'd allowed himself to be distracted. "There are two parts to roping. Rope handling and horsemanship. You have to learn both, though we won't put the two together for a while yet. We'll work with a horse during your next lesson."

"Next lesson? You mean we're done already?"

"We've been working for almost two hours." And Lily had been watching them from the second row the entire time.

Colton's eyes widened. "Really?"

"Time flies when you're having fun."

"Yea— Yes, sir."

Noah ruffled the kid's sandy brown hair. "Good boy."

Out of the corner of his eye, he saw his father take a seat beside Lily.

She smiled as they talked, making Noah uneasy. What were they discussing? Colton? The weather? After Dad's little talk the other day, not to mention his comment about Lily being pretty, there was no telling what the old man was apt to say.

Noah cringed at the possibilities.

"Okay, Colton, how about we plan to meet again Monday morning?"

"Aww, but I'm just getting good."

"All right then, you can keep practicing while I go talk to your mother." Because the more he saw Lily laugh, the more he wanted to know what she and his father were discussing.

A few minutes later, he hopped the fence to join the three of them. "What's going on?"

Hands clasped, forearms on his thighs, his father looked up at him. "Lily here was just telling me that she plans a lot of charity events back in Denver."

"That's nice." He glanced at Lily. Dressed in jeans and riding boots with a navy blazer over a white T-shirt, she looked ready for English riding. Something she wasn't likely to find at Abundant Blessings Ranch.

"*Big* events." Dad's dark brown eyes glinted with pleasure. "Like *grand openings*."

Noah glared at his father, knowing good and well what he was up to. He wanted Lily to help them. Well, Noah wasn't biting.

"Mommy gave me the best princess birthday party ever." Piper moved behind her mother, snaking her arms around Lily's shoulders.

"I see." Birthday parties. Kids' parties, at that. Not exactly the kind of event he had in mind.

"She also hosted Denver's Oil Baron's Ball," said Dad.

Noah lifted his hat to scratch his head. Okay, so that was a little higher up the scale. Still, that didn't mean Lily should help him.

Straightening, his father twisted to give Lily his full attention. "Did you know that Noah is in the process of expanding our little riding school?"

She peered up at Noah. "I heard mention of rodeo lessons."

Noah cleared his throat. "Actually, we're expanding to a year-round rodeo school." He shifted from one foot to the next. "The new arena is still under construction, but it should be ready sometime in August."

"Is that the building going up next door?" She pointed in the general vicinity.

"Sure is," Dad answered before Noah even had a chance. "The grand opening is set for Labor Day weekend to coincide with the annual rodeo in Ridgway. Problem is that Noah doesn't have any time to promote or plan the event." He shrugged. "Not that he really knows much about that sort of thing."

Noah shook his head. He knew the old man was trying to help, that he wanted the rodeo school to succeed every bit as much as Noah did, but sometimes he just didn't know when to shut up.

"Dad, I—"

"Mom could help you. She knows all about planning stuff."

Noah jerked his head to discover Colton standing beside him. "I thought you were practicing."

The boy lowered his gaze. "It wasn't as fun without you."

Noah's heart swelled, though he quickly tamped it down. "Your mom is on vacation, Colton."

"I know, but she always says parties and stuff aren't really work." He looked at Lily. "Right, Mom?"

The poor woman seemed to be at a loss for words. She was no more interested in giving Noah her help than he was in receiving it. Yet while he'd come to accept that he did, indeed, need some sort of help, he'd prefer to hire someone local. Someone familiar with rodeo. Not a city girl who was afraid of horses.

He set a hand on Colton's shoulder. "Colton, that's not fair to your mom. You all are here because she wants to spend time with you and Piper, not some grungy old cowboys."

"That's okay," chimed Piper. "We can help, too."

"Yeah," said Colton. "We'll still be together."

Dad stood then. "I'm afraid Noah's right, kids. It's not fair to volunteer your mother like that."

Noah's brow lifted. Dad was the one who started this whole discussion.

"Thank you for understanding." Lily reached for Colton's hand. "This summer is all about my kids."

"As it should be." Ignoring the unexpected wave of disappointment that came over him, he studied the woman laughing with her children. Lily might know how to put on a good party, but she was the wrong candidate for this job.

Chapter Three

Lily stood at the top of Hurricane Pass the next afternoon, savoring the breathtaking view. At more than twelve thousand feet, it felt as though she was on top of the world.

Brown, barren peaks stretched out before her as far as she could see, while lush green mingled with patches of snow across their rocky slopes. She drew in a long breath of crisp mountain air. Simply glorious.

This was exactly what she'd envisioned when she decided to bring the kids to Ouray. Jeep rides in the mountains, exploring God's creation…togetherness.

"What do you guys think?" She eyed her children, who had finally stopped throwing snowballs at each other long enough to join her.

"Spectacular!" Her daughter tossed her arms wide in typical Piper fashion.

"It's okay." Hands shoved in the pockets of his hoodie, Colton squinted against the sun. "It would be cooler on a horse."

Lily tried to keep her groan to herself. She was beginning to regret ever having taken the kids to Abundant Blessings Ranch. All she'd heard about the past four days was horses, riding, roping... Not to mention how she should help Noah with the rodeo school's grand opening.

Her gaze drifted to the glacial blue waters of Lake Como just below where she stood. She was not here to plan an event. Especially the grand opening of a rodeo school. Spending this summer as a family, teaching her children to enjoy the simple things in life was what was important to her.

What could be simpler than spending time on a real ranch with good, hardworking people and beautiful animals?

Horses might be beautiful, but she still didn't want to be around them. Or their cowboy owner.

You could at least consider helping Noah.

The thought stiffened her spine. And allow herself to be taken advantage of, the way she had when she was with Wade Davis? No, thank you.

When they returned to town a few hours later, Lily walked along Main Street with her children, allowing them to peruse a couple of souvenir shops while she relished the remarkable view. Unlike most towns where the mountains sat in the distance, Ouray was literally enveloped by them. No matter which way she looked, the mountains were right there. Only part of what made this town so appealing. Throw in the gorgeous Victorian-era buildings, friendly people and colorful baskets of flowers hanging from every lamppost, and she was smitten.

"Afternoon, Lily."

She turned to see Clint Stephens. "Hello, Mr. Stephens."

Hands dangling from the pockets of his Wrangler jeans, he glanced around. "Where are Colton and Piper?"

"In the gift sho—" She spotted the pair exiting the store. "Make that right here."

"Hi, Mr. Stephens." Their collective greeting revealed how genuinely happy they were to see him.

"What have you kids been up to today? Did you do anything fun?"

"We went to the top of the world," said Piper.

"Top of the world?" Clint eyed Lily as a motorcycle rumbled past.

"We took a Jeep tour up to Hurricane Pass."

"Oh." He looked at Piper again. "Then I guess you were way up there."

"I'm hungry." Colton moved beside Lily. "What's for dinner?"

She was surprised he'd gone this long without asking. Save for a small snack, he hadn't eaten since lunch.

"Honestly, I haven't given it much thought, but I'm sure we can find something at the house."

"I'm on my way over to Granny's Kitchen to grab some dinner." Clint looked at each of them. "Would you three care to join me?"

Piper gasped while her brother's eyes and smile grew wide.

"Could we?" said Colton. "We haven't eaten there yet."

Beside him, Piper prayed her hands together. "Please…"

Lily noted the sun hovering over the town's western slope. "I guess it has been a while since we've gone out to eat." Besides, she really wasn't up to fixing a meal tonight. "Are you sure you don't mind, Mr. Stephens?"

"Course not. It'll save me from eating alone."

"Okay then."

Inside the quaint restaurant situated on a corner farther down the street, the four of them sat down in a booth by the window, allowing them to enjoy the view.

"Granny's Kitchen is as close to home cooking as you're going to get." Clint removed his cowboy hat and slid in beside Colton. "And everything on the menu is good." He ran a callused hand through his thick salt-and-pepper hair.

A waitress approached. Blonde, closer to Clint's age and very well put together, from her perfectly styled short hair to her chic red patent leather ballet flats. "Looks like you've got some company, Clint." She set four waters on the high-gloss wooden table top, then handed menus to each of them, along with crayons for the kids, before laying a hand on Clint's shoulder.

"Hillary, this is Lily—" he gestured "—and her children, Colton and Piper."

Lily held out her hand. "It's nice to meet you, Hillary."

The woman took hold, her grip firm. "Are you in town on vacation?"

"For the summer, yes."

"Well, we're glad to have you." Hillary eyed each of them. "I'll give you minute to look over those menus." With that she was gone.

Noting the familiarity between the two, Lily watched the older man. "Is that your wife?"

"Hillary?" Clint blushed. "No, she's just an old friend. My wife died three years ago."

"I'm sorry to hear that."

"I won't try to kid you, it was rough. But God has a plan."

"Yes, He does." Reaching for her water, she eyed the waitress behind the counter. Either Clint was unaware of Hillary's feelings toward him or simply refused to acknowledge them. Whatever the case, Lily suspected they were more than just friends.

After turning in their orders, Lily rested her forearms on the edge of the table, curiosity niggling at her brain. After all, with Colton taking lessons, she owed it to herself to learn as much about his instructor as she could.

"Tell me about this rodeo school Noah plans to open."

The man smiled like any proud father. "Noah's always had a gift for teaching and a heart for kids." He unwrapped his silverware and set the napkin in his lap. "This school has been his dream ever since he left the rodeo circuit."

"He was a bull rider?" Lily regretted the surprise in her voice.

Clint's amused grin was worth it, though. "Yes, but horses were always his specialty. He gets that from his mama."

"Why was the rodeo school Noah's dream?" Colton watched the older man intently.

"He…went through some hard times." Fingering the unopened straw atop the table, he continued, "The rodeo—horses, in particular—helped him get back in the saddle, so to speak."

Hard times? That could be almost anything. Drugs. Alcohol. But she wasn't about to pry.

"What kind of hard times?"

"Colton!" Lily cringed.

"It's all right." The corners of Clint's mouth tipped upward once again. "Can't blame the boy for being curious." He looked at Colton. "Noah lost some people that were very special to him."

"Like his mommy?" Crayon still in hand, Piper looked up from her colorful place mat.

"That's right." Clint turned his attention to Lily. "Rodeo helped him cope."

She watched the man across from her. "Was he any good?"

Clint's grin seemed laced with as much sorrow as pride. "When you have nothing to lose, you tend to put it all out there."

Nothing to lose? What did that mean?

Curious, Lily wanted to know more. So after the kids went to bed that night, she searched the internet for Noah Stephens and came up with a plethora of articles, photos and videos.

She clicked on the first link.

After the deaths of his wife and unborn child...

Lily found herself blinking back emotion. Though her ex-husband was still very much alive, she understood how it felt to lose someone you love. But to lose a child, too... She couldn't imagine how painful that must have been.

She clicked on another link. *The man had no fear. Every time he went out there, it was as though he was challenging God to take him, too.*

When you have nothing to lose, you tend to put it all out there, Clint had said. *Rodeo helped him.*

She swiped at a wayward tear that trailed down her cheek. No wonder the rodeo school was so important to Noah. And he did seem to be good with the kids. In fact, Colton had rarely responded so well to a stranger.

Still...

She drew in a breath. That didn't mean *she* had to help him.

* * *

Monday was a busy one for Noah. Aside from lessons and numerous people wanting trail rides, he still needed to run into town to drop off his ad for the July Fourth edition of the newspaper. Next week, thousands of people would flood Ouray for its annual Fourth of July celebration, which was as unique as the town itself. Giving Noah the perfect opportunity to let everyone know about the rodeo school. Some of those visitors might even be persuaded to return in September for the school's grand opening and Ridgway's Labor Day rodeo.

But first he needed to concentrate on helping Colton with his riding lesson.

Boots firmly in the dirt, he watched as Colton made a practice run around the arena. He was surprised by how quickly the boy was catching on. The fact that he had a positive attitude was a big help. It seemed that whenever Colton showed up, whether to work or learn, he was ready to give it his all. A far cry from the cantankerous, smart-mouthed kid Noah had met last week. Sure, there'd been a few complaints, but overall, the kid was as eager to help as he was to learn. Like he'd found his calling. Or just someplace to direct his pent-up anger.

And Noah was more than happy to help.

He took hold of the quarter horse's bridle as the kid approached. "Good job, Colton."

"That was fun." The boy leaned forward to stroke the animal's mane.

Sonic nickered in response.

"You hear that? I think Sonic likes you."

"He's a good horse."

"Yes, he is." Not to mention experienced, which was

why Noah had chosen him. "Now, when you're roping and riding, you're going to need your hands to control the rope."

The kid cocked his head, his brow marked with confusion. "So how do you hold on to the reins?"

"You don't." Noah couldn't help grinning. "Let me show you something." He moved beside the horse. "Let go of the reins."

Colton complied.

"Now pull your legs together so they're pressing into Sonic's sides."

"Like this?"

Noah knew the boy was doing it correctly when Sonic dropped his head and began to back up.

The kid's eyes widened. "Did I make him do that?"

"You sure did."

"That is so cool." His excitement echoed from the rafters.

"When roping, a rider has to know how to control the horse without using his hands. We'll work on that more next time."

"Aw, we're done already?" He reached for the reins, slapping them against his leg.

"Afraid so. I've got something I need to take care of in town."

"Okay…" The boy reluctantly dismounted, the leather of the saddle creaking.

"Why don't you take ol' Sonic here back to his stall while I talk to your mom?"

"Can I give him some horse cookies?"

"A couple, yes."

While Colton headed off with the horse, Noah made his way to the opposite side of the arena to talk with

Lily. She was sitting alone in her usual spot on the bleachers.

"The kid's a natural." He hopped the fence.

"Really?" Lily stood, her long hair spilling over her shoulders. "He must get it from his grandmother then, because it certainly didn't come from me."

"Mommy?" An excited Piper skipped toward them, her ponytail bobbing, while Noah's father followed a short distance behind.

"What is it, Piper?" Lily laid a hand on her daughter's back as if to settle her.

"Mr. Stephens said I can have a soda if it's all right with you. Can I?"

"Piper's been working hard, helping me clean the riding helmets." Dad grinned at the child. "Would it be all right if I rewarded her with a soda?"

"Of course." Lily looked at her daughter. "But nothing caffeinated."

"Okay." Piper took hold of his father's hand.

Noah couldn't help smiling. She was a cutie with a personality to match. And just like his nieces, she brought out the best in his old man.

"Newspaper called." Dad's voice pulled him from his thoughts.

He looked at his father.

"They said you missed the deadline for advertising in the July Fourth edition."

"No, I didn't." He shook his head. "The cutoff is tomorrow. I'm planning to drop the ad by the newspaper office in just a little bit."

"The deadline was noon today."

"Noon?" He looked at his watch. It was almost three. Then he remembered that they'd moved the deadline up a day this week due to the holiday. His stomach clenched. How could he have forgotten something so important? His life savings were riding on the success of the rodeo school.

He glanced in Lily's direction to discover her watching him.

Just what he needed. Why'd his father have to bring that up in front of her?

"Mom, did you see me out there?" Colton approached, his smile wide.

"Yes. You looked very handsome."

"Mr. Stephens said I could have a soda." Piper peered up at her brother. "Maybe he'll let you have one, too."

"Can I?" Colton looked to the older man.

"Sure. Come on, you two."

As the trio headed down the corridor, Noah sensed Lily was still watching him. But he didn't dare turn around.

"You know—" he heard her boots against the bleachers before she stepped in front of him "—an interview with the newspaper might garner more attention than an ad. Besides, you have to pay for advertising. Interviews are free."

He stared down at her, still frustrated. "What would they interview me about?"

Her expression went flat. "You're a former rodeo champion who's opening a rodeo school. And not just any rodeo champ, but one of the best champions ever."

He studied her, his gaze narrowing. "How do you know that?"

She shrugged. "The internet."

She'd googled him? Why? "Don't believe everything you read." He turned, ready to leave.

"Well, unless somebody made up those stats…"

He paused then and faced her again. "Do you really see me going to the newspaper and asking them to interview me?"

"No." She crossed her arms over her chest. "First you have to create interest. Say, in the form of a press release." She was talking way over his head.

He set his hands on his hips. "Lily, I don't even know what that is."

"Maybe not—" she inched toward him "—but I do."

He wasn't in the mood for games. "What is that supposed to mean?"

"It means—" with only a short distance between them, she dropped her arms to her sides "—that I'm willing to help you promote the rodeo school and get ready for its grand opening."

"Why would you do that?"

Seemingly frustrated, she gestured around the arena. "My kids are completely enamored with this place. And you." Her sideways glance hinted at annoyance. "Meaning we'll likely be spending a lot of time here this summer. Especially now that Piper wants to take lessons. So I may as well make myself useful."

A woman who was scared to death of horses wanted to help him promote the rodeo school? That had to be one of the craziest things he'd ever heard.

She was right about one thing, though. With both of her kids becoming more and more entrenched in events at the ranch, she'd likely be here a lot. At least helping with the rodeo school would give her something to do besides hover during the kids' lessons.

He contemplated her a moment. What if she did help him? In the last two minutes alone, he'd seen that she knew way more about publicizing something than he did. Still, her fear of horses gave him pause.

"Perhaps I could give you riding lessons, too. I mean, if you're helping me with the promotion."

She straightened, her shoulders rigid, her expression pinched. "That's highly doubtful, Mr. Stephens."

Her quick response almost made him laugh. Because there was nothing he enjoyed more than a good challenge. And getting Lily comfortable around horses was a huge one.

Of course, he also knew when to loosen the reins. "Okay, then I will take you up on your offer, on one condition."

One perfectly arched brow lifted in question.

"That you call me Noah. Mr. Stephens is my dad."

Chapter Four

Lily aimed her SUV north on Highway 550 just before noon the next day. Passing the Ouray city limits sign, she tried to figure out what had compelled her to take on the role of promoter for the rodeo school. She'd even gone so far as to talk Noah into it. And, in the process, she'd taken a giant step out of her element. What did she know about rodeo? What about the panic that threatened to set in whenever she was around horses?

She eyed the rushing waters of the Uncompahgre River to her left. Perhaps it was the pride in Clint's eyes when he talked about Noah's dream that had persuaded her. Or maybe it was the tough-but-tender manner Noah had with Colton. Encouraging him and gently correcting, instead of belittling him the way Colton's father so often did.

Her grip firm on the steering wheel, she maneuvered her vehicle past the red sandstone walls to her right. She'd seen the sadness in Noah's dark eyes on more than one occasion. Yet it couldn't have been the sudden knowledge of what he'd gone through that had spurred her.

No, she simply needed something to keep herself occupied while the kids were busy at the ranch.

"Mommy, when am I going to start *my* riding lessons?" In the rearview mirror, she noticed Piper watching her.

"I'm not sure, honey. Noah had to check his schedule." A schedule that seemed to be getting fuller all the time, making Lily wonder when she'd be able to sit him down for a little Q and A. Because whether she wanted to or not, she was going to have to learn more about this rodeo school. Something that inevitably meant spending way more time with Noah and those horses than she cared to. However, if she was going to tackle this job to the best of her ability, she had no other choice. Her reputation was at stake.

That's it!

Smiling, she bumped her vehicle over the cattle guard at Abundant Blessings Ranch. She'd simply think of this job as a challenge. Something that would stretch her and help hone her skills. After all, she'd already been thinking about turning her enjoyment of event planning into a business. This would be one event she could add to her résumé that would be different from anything else she'd ever done. However, she prayed she'd never have to do anything with horses ever again.

Excitement filled her as they pulled up to the stable. If she could bring about a successful launch for the rodeo school, she should be able to tackle anything.

Under a cloudless sky, she shifted her SUV into Park, turned off the ignition and exited, noting the numerous other vehicles parked in the area, even overflowing the small gravel parking lot onto the grass. Why were they so busy?

She released a frustrated sigh. Busy didn't bode well for her plans of a meeting with Noah.

Inside the stable's rustic lobby, at least a dozen people stood waiting while Noah passed out paperwork and pens.

He spotted her. "Colton's practicing in the arena." He nodded in that direction before disappearing into the office.

She followed him. Watched as he added paperwork to two more clipboards. "I have several questions I need to ask you about the rodeo school."

"Such as?" He grabbed a handful of pens from a small basket.

"For starters, I'd like more information about your rodeo days so I can start getting some interviews set up. I could take the kids to get some lunch and come back. Perhaps things will have slowed down."

"Sorry, Lily, but between lessons and fully booked trail rides, I'm busier than a termite in a sawmill." He nudged the brim of his cowboy hat, tilting it up ever so slightly as his eyes met hers. "Any chance you could come back this evening? Say around six?"

"Oh." Disappointment had her gaze falling to the concrete floor. "Sure, I can do that." Lifting her head, she sent him her best smile. "I need to do some more research on media outlets, anyway."

He grinned then. "Great. I'll see you this evening."

While Lily had every intention of doing that research, those notions came to a screeching halt once she and her children returned to town. Suddenly, Colton was the one ready to do some exploring. It was an opportunity she wasn't about to pass up. So, after a quick round of sandwiches at the mountainside cabin she'd rented for the summer, the three of them went to Box Canyon, where they hiked deep into the gorge to see a powerful waterfall, then climbed up the hillside to the high bridge that not only spanned the gorge but offered the most incredible view of the town she was quickly growing to love.

By the time she was finally able to drag Piper away from all the chipmunks that called the area around Box Canyon home, it was almost four o'clock, leaving them just enough time to grab an ice-cream cone and enjoy the views on Main Street before heading back to the ranch.

Clint was there to greet them when they pulled up to the stable at six o'clock, and she couldn't help wondering if he was there to run interference for a still-busy Noah. He waited beside the front door as they got out of the SUV.

"I wasn't expecting to see you all this late in the day." He tipped his hat in greeting.

Shielding her eyes from the sun, Lily tucked the electronic tablet she used to take notes under her arm. "I'm here to meet with Noah."

"Well." The older man chuckled. "I was just coming to get him. We're having a family cookout up at the house tonight."

Noah hadn't said anything about a cookout. Then again, he had been pretty busy when she stopped by earlier.

"Why don't you and the kids join us for supper?"

While her children's eyes went wide, Lily hesitated. "We don't want to interrupt a family meal."

"Nonsense." Clint waved off her objection. "We just call it a family supper, but that doesn't mean other people can't come. There's always plenty of food." His gaze moved between the children. "Besides, my grand-daughters are here, and they'd enjoy having someone else their age."

"How old are they?" Colton appeared as curious as he was apprehensive.

Clint rubbed his chin. "Let's see. I believe Megan is eleven now—she's turning into quite the horsewoman—and Kenzie's five."

Right about her kids' ages. And while it would be nice, they hadn't come for dinner.

"Can we, Mom?" Colton's interest had definitely been piqued. "We haven't had dinner yet."

"No, but we're here so I can meet with Noah."

Just then, the wooden front door creaked open, and the cowboy exited the stable. "I thought I heard voices out here."

"I was just telling Lily and kids they should join us for our cookout," said Clint.

Noah eyes seemed to narrow. "What cookout?"

"Son, you know we always have family dinners."

"Yes, sir, but they're usually on Sundays."

"Or any other time that suits us." Clint scowled. "Especially when the weather is as nice as it is today. So, if you all would care to join me back at the house…" With that, he started up the gravel drive.

Colton and Piper sent her pleading gazes.

"Go ahead." Lily watched the two kids rush after the older man. They were growing more fond of him by the day.

"We'd better join them, you know," said Noah.

She reached for her tablet and clutched it in both hands. "What about our meeting? Unless you think we could talk over dinner." Far away from all those horses. That would be the best of both worlds. She'd get the information she needed and a good meal, too.

Noah shrugged. "We could try, but with the whole family here, an in-depth conversation isn't likely."

"I see."

"Of course, we could always slip back inside the stable and talk. The kids would be occupied——"

"No way." She held up a hand. "I'm not going to be responsible for keeping you from a family meal." *Nice cover.*

"All right then." He eyed the single-story house that sat farther up the drive. "I guess we'd better join them."

She thumped the tablet against her leg, still torn. "Let me put this in the car."

Though it wasn't a long walk, she decided to seize the only opportunity she'd had all day. "What drew you to rodeo?"

He stared out over the green, cattle-dotted pasture as gravel crunched beneath their steps. "I suppose it was a combination of things. To a boy growing up on a ranch, it looked like the coolest job ever. So I started honing my roping skills. Calves at first, then I worked my way up to steers. Mama taught me everything she knew about horses. Next thing I knew I was bronc riding, then bull riding——"

A gentle breeze had her hair brushing against her cheek.

She tucked it behind her ear. "Weren't you afraid?"

He lifted a shoulder. "At first, I suppose. But once I got good at things, I wanted to be even better."

"'Bout time you made it, bro." A tall, dark-haired man who looked very much like both Noah and his father stepped off the expansive wooden deck as they approached the cedar home. "We're getting hungry."

The corner of Noah's mouth lifted. "Lily, this is Andrew. The *annoying* brother."

"Hey…" Andrew smiled her way. "It's nice to meet you, Lily."

"Good to meet you."

"You must be Colton and Piper's mom?" A woman with blond curls and a definite baby bump approached and reached out her hand. "I'm Megan's mom, Carly Stephens."

Lily briefly took hold.

"And my wife," Andrew was quick to add, his pride as evident as it was heartwarming. Every woman should be so blessed.

"When are you due?"

The woman smoothed a hand over her flowing shirt. "September 17, give or take. You know how that goes."

She recalled her son's past-due arrival and Piper's earlier-than-expected appearance. "I certainly do."

Colton came toward her then with a cute strawberry blonde girl she guessed to be Megan. "Mom, can I go to the stable with Megan? She wants to show me her horse."

Lily shared a glance with Carly. Saw the stealthy head shake that would have gone unrecognized by anyone except another mother. "Has Megan checked with her mom?"

The grinning girl stepped toward Carly. "Can we?"

"Can you what?" Clint joined them then with the blonde from the restaurant at his side.

Lily smiled her way. "Hello, Hillary. Good to see you again."

"Are you overwhelmed yet, Lily?"

Noting about a half a dozen people still unknown to her, she had to admit— "A little, yes." And while she would have welcomed this type of event any other time, tonight it only meant that the meeting she needed to have with Noah wasn't going to happen. Her questions would go unanswered. And if Noah continued to be as busy as he was today, she might never get the information she needed.

Noah usually enjoyed family dinners. But this one was different. Because according to his brothers, the invitation had only gone out today, *after* Noah offhandedly mentioned to his father that Lily would be coming by tonight.

He eyed the old cowboy sitting on the opposite side of the wooden picnic table. It seemed ever since Andrew and Matt both got married last year, his father had grown increasingly eager to marry off the rest of his sons. And for whatever reason, he seemed to have his sights set on Noah.

But as far as he was concerned, his father was wasting his time. Noah already had a wife. And even though Jaycee had left this world, he'd vowed to love her forever, and that's exactly what he intended to do.

His gaze inadvertently drifted to Lily sitting beside him. With her reddish-blond hair and sparkling green eyes, she was, indeed, pretty. Just not Noah's type. Even if he were in the market for a wife, Lily was too much of a city girl for his tastes. Not to mention her less-than-enthusiastic feelings about horses and that she was only in Ouray for the summer.

However, she had agreed to help promote the rodeo

school. Something he knew nothing about, so it was in his best interest to tell her whatever it was she was so eager to know in order to get the school off on the right foot.

He stuffed the last bite of his hamburger into his mouth and dusted off his hands. It shouldn't be that bad. After all, the rodeo school was something he could get excited about. Without rodeo, he didn't know where he'd be. And while he might have headed back into the arena with a death wish, God had used it to show him that He still had a purpose for Noah. And Noah intended to follow that calling. This world was filled with hurting people. If he could help even one of them…

"Mom," Colton came up behind them. "Me and Megan are done eating and her mom says it's okay for us to go to the stable, if it's okay with you. Can we?"

Lily pushed aside her paper plate, which was littered with celery pieces she'd picked out of her potato salad, and dabbed her mouth with a paper napkin. "Yes, you may. But I want you to be on your best behavior. I know you're familiar with the stable, but Megan has been here a lot longer than you have." She smiled up at Noah's niece, who stood beside Colton. "You do what she says. Okay?"

"I will," said the boy, and the two kids were off like a shot.

Lily peered up at Noah then. "I assume you're all right with them going."

"Yes. But, if you have reservations, we could always join them."

"Oh, that's not—"

"Maybe we could finally have that discussion about the rodeo school."

She hesitated a moment. "Or we could find a quiet place around here. I mean, what about Piper?"

"She can go with us." Turning, he eyed the pony-tailed blonde giggling with Matt's daughter, Kenzie. "However, she looks like she's having a pretty good time here." He faced Lily again. "Besides, I think a tour of the stable is in order."

"Why?" She looked almost appalled. "What does a tour of the stable have to do with rodeo?"

He puffed out a laugh. "For starters, it's where I spend most of my time. It's where we train students, at least until the other building is complete."

Her deep breath gave him the feeling she was trying to talk herself into it.

"Okay. Let me check with Piper." Standing, she moved to the other table and smoothed a hand across her daughter's back.

The girl looked up at her mother.

"Noah and I are going to the stable. Would you like to go with us?"

The little girl frowned. "But Kenzie's dad said they're going to have s'mores."

Noah looked to the other side of the table, to Matt and his wife, Lacie. "Would you two mind keeping an eye on Piper while Lily and I run down to the stable?"

"Not at all." Standing, Lacie reached for the kids' plates. "The two of them are having a good time."

"We won't be long." Lily waved to Piper, then turned and ran into another of Noah's siblings. "Oh!"

Noah caught her elbow. "Lily, this is Jude."

Her eyes went wide. "Just how many brothers do you have?"

"I'm the fourth of five Stephens' sons," offered Jude. "And it's nice to meet you."

Lily looked from Noah to Jude, who also had their father's dark hair and eyes. "Did they just clone you guys? Because all of you kind of look the same."

Jude laughed. "Not all of us." He eyed Noah. "She hasn't met Daniel yet, has she?"

Just then, the brother in question slapped him on the back. "Did I hear my name?"

"Lily," Jude started. "This is Daniel, the baby of the family."

She simply stared at the only blond, blue-eyed brother. "I guess that debunks my cloning theory. How did you—"

"Break the mold?" Daniel shrugged. "The world couldn't have handled it if they'd all been as good-looking as me."

"Oh, brother." Jude rolled his eyes. "Don't let him con you, Lily. Daniel just ended up with all of our mother's genes because Dad's finally ran out."

Noah checked his watch. At this rate, they'd never make it to the stable. "Gentlemen, you're going to have to excuse us. Lily and I have work to do."

She smiled at his brothers. "It's been a pleasure."

Twilight settled around them as they descended the steps, the air still as they started toward the stable.

"Four brothers." Lily shook her head. "I can't imagine."

"Why?" Hands in his pockets, Noah glanced up to a rising moon. "Don't you have any siblings?"

"No. I'm an only child."

"Really?" Gravel ground beneath his boots. "Now there's something I can't imagine."

She chuckled. A sweet sound he found himself longing to hear again. "Then I guess there's one thing we have in common."

Lily retrieved her tablet before heading inside with Noah.

He breathed in the comforting aromas of horse and hay. Here, he was at home.

"We built this structure a few years ago so we could offer riding lessons year-round." He moved past the lobby, toward the training arena.

Opening the cover on her tablet, Lily followed him on the same path she'd taken almost daily to observe Colton's lessons. "Why can't you use this arena for the rodeo school?"

"Too small." Turning to face her, he perched an elbow atop a fence rung. "The two buildings will be attached by a walkway, though, since the horses will still be stabled here."

She made a few notes before looking at him again. "Who designed the new arena?"

"I did. At least the general layout."

"I'm impressed." Her fingers moved over the screen once more.

"Don't be. I've been in a lot of arenas over the years. Everything from small to large, indoor and out. I know what works, and I know what we need."

She cocked her head. "Sounds like you're an expert."

He lifted a shoulder. "Perhaps the only thing I'm an expert at."

"Besides rodeo itself."

"It's what I know." He turned. "Follow me." He aimed for one of two wide corridors lined with stalls.

As they rounded the corner, Lily stopped. "Where are we going?"

"I thought I'd show you a few of the horses."

"That's...not necessary." She fidgeted with her necklace. "Really, I—I don't need to see them."

He moved closer. "I'm not talking about riding them, Lily." He studied her. Saw the flicker of fear in her eyes. "I promise, you'll be fine. I'll be right with you."

After a long moment, she nodded and started walking again.

Hoping to put her at ease, he said, "Why don't you ask me some of those questions you said you had."

"Um, okay. Uh, what drew you to the rodeo?"

He looked at her. Saw her cast a wary eye at each and every horse they passed. "You asked me that earlier. When we were walking to the house."

"I did?" She met his gaze. "Yes, that's right."

He stopped her then. "Do you always get this nervous around horses?"

Her head bobbed. "Chalk it up to a bad experience when I was a kid."

"What happened?"

Her gaze searched his, and he saw her anxiety ease for a moment.

Hugging the tablet against her chest, she said, "My mother loved horses and used to dream of me becoming a championship English rider. So, when I was four, she bought me a horse." Lily looked away then. "I can still see him staring down at me with those ominous dark eyes. Right before he bit me."

"He bit you?"

"He did. Then while I was still crying, my mother hoisted me into the saddle. Of course, the horse wasn't having any of that and promptly bucked me off, leaving me with a broken arm and a strong determination never to get on a horse again."

Noah could hardly believe what he was hearing. No parent should force their child to do something they were afraid of. Coaxing was one thing, but to put her in the saddle while she was still crying…

Briefly lifting his hat, he raked a hand through his hair. "No wonder you made yourself sick at the thought of riding."

Lily rolled her eyes. "Please, don't remind me."

"I have to say, I commend you for not placing your fears on your children. And just so you know, your mother was wrong to put you on that horse. These animals—" he motioned to the stalls on either side of them "—are very good at sensing things, including fear."

"Guess it's a good thing I didn't ride with you then." Her laugh was a nervous one. "You must think I'm a complete idiot."

"Absolutely not." Arms crossed, he rocked back on his heels. "Though I do believe I could help you overcome your fear."

"Ha! I highly doubt that."

His brow shot up. "Is that a dare?"

"More like extreme skepticism."

Lowering his arms, he looked into her green eyes, knowing he shouldn't care. What should it matter to him if she was afraid of horses? After this summer, she'd likely never be around them again.

Unfortunately, he did care.

"That's too bad. Because I've never been one to back down from a challenge." Just then, he spotted Colton and Megan coming down the aisle. "You know, both of your kids seem quite enthralled with horses. Wouldn't it be nice if you could ride with them?"

"What are you guys doing here?" Colton asked as he approached.

"Just going over some stuff about the rodeo school." While Lily appeared calm and collected, the way she looked at her son, as though seeing him through different eyes, had Noah wondering if he'd gotten through to her. Did she want to learn to ride or even try overcome her fear?

"My mom's going to help Noah promote the rodeo school." Colton's pride was evident as he shared the news with Megan.

"That's cool," said his niece. "Because Uncle Noah is the best teacher ever." She reached her arms around his waist and squeezed him tight. "Right, Uncle Noah?"

He looked down at her. "If you say so, kid."

Megan released him then. "Come on, Colton. Let's go get some s'mores."

As the two trotted away, Lily smiled up at Noah. "The best teacher ever, huh?"

Heat crept up his neck. "If you believe an eleven-year-old."

She seemed to contemplate him for a moment. "You really think you can help me overcome my fear?"

"I do."

"In that case..." She held out her hand. "I think you've got yourself a deal."

Chapter Five

By the next morning, Lily was ready to back out of her deal with Noah. Sure, he might be good with horses, but did he really think he could help her overcome her fear?

Last night he'd said he could. But what if he couldn't? And what would her children think when they found out their mother was afraid of horses? Would they look at her differently? After all, she was supposed to take care of them. Protect them. Would they wonder what else she might be afraid of or think she's a coward?

Lily shook the torturous thoughts away and concentrated on the pancakes she was making for breakfast. Because despite her agreement with Noah, she still didn't have enough information to contact even a local newspaper regarding an interview. What she needed was a good hook that would make everyone in the state, if not the country, want to interview Noah and learn about the rodeo school. The only way to come up with that hook was to dig and find out what made Noah tick and why the rodeo school was so important to him.

After dotting one side of the pancakes with blueberries, she flipped them. They gently sizzled as the fruity aroma reached her nose, awakening her appetite.

Spatula in hand, she waited. How had Noah managed to turn the tables on her so easily last night? Not that he'd distracted her. It was being around all those horses that had made it difficult to think about anything except getting bitten or trampled, leaving her stammering and unable to concentrate.

She couldn't allow that to happen today. If only there was some way to get Noah away from the stable.

Maybe they could all go to lunch. Lily, Noah and the kids. Or better yet, she could pack a lunch for all of them. They could have a picnic at the park. It was supposed to be another beautiful day, and the views from the park were positively breathtaking.

Of course, if he was as busy today as he had been yesterday...

No, she was going to remain optimistic. If God wanted her to talk with Noah, He'd pave the way.

Armed with renewed determination, she loaded Colton and Piper into the SUV and set off for the ranch well before the rising sun broke over the mountain hugging the eastern edge of town. Colton had a job to do, and she would not allow him to be late. She wanted to instill a sense of responsibility while he was still young.

When they arrived, Colton ran on to start cleaning stalls while she and Piper found Noah sitting at the desk in the office, his back to them as he attached consent forms to clipboards.

She watched him curiously. "Why don't you have somebody to do that for you?" He was busy enough without a lot of little tasks consuming his time.

Only when he jerked his head in her direction did she realize that she'd probably startled him.

"Sorry. I should have knocked or at least said hello first."

"Nah." Wearing his usual jeans, work shirt and boots, he stood, sending his chair rolling across the concrete floor. "Actually, you're just the person I was hoping to see."

"A kitty." Piper spotted the calico sprawled atop the desk.

Noah glanced her way. "That's Patches." He looked at Lily then. "She's harmless."

Lily looked up at him. "Why were you hoping to see me?"

"What are you and the kids doing for lunch today?"

Her hand went to her hip. "Okay, that's weird, because I was going to ask you the same thing."

"No kidding?" He continued into the lobby with an armload of clipboards.

She followed him, determined that she would have the information she needed by the end of the day. "Yes. I was thinking that, since it's going to be another pretty day, we could have a picnic lunch at the park."

"Hmm…" He slid each clipboard over a hook on the rustic wooden wall. "That does sound like a good plan." Task complete, he faced her. "However, I know of someplace better than the park. And with a lot fewer people."

She like the sound of that. Less chance of being interrupted. "Wonderful. Where?"

"You'll just have to wait to find out."

"Seriously?"

"Do I look like I'm kidding?"

No, he definitely did not. She simply preferred to know these things so she could plan accordingly.

"You're just going to have to trust me, Lily."

Her gaze shot to his. Trust wasn't something that came easy to her. One of the downsides to being wealthy. People always expected something from her.

It's only lunch.

Yes, it was. A picnic at that.

"All right. I'll be here at noon with the food."

"What's on the menu?" Cowboy hat tilted back, Noah lifted a brow.

She sent him a smirk. "I guess you'll just have to trust *me*."

When she and Piper returned at noon, an excited Colton met them out front.

Under a cloudless sky, he rushed to the driver's-side door, all smiles, as she pressed the button to roll the window down.

With no sign of Noah, she wondered if there was a problem. Had he gotten busy again and needed to cancel? Then again, her son wouldn't be smiling if that were the case.

"Guess what, Mom?"

"What is it?"

"Noah said we get to ride to our picnic spot."

Lily found herself at a loss for words. Ride? As in a horse?

And to think, Noah actually had the nerve to tell her to trust him. As if simply putting her on a horse was going to help her get over her fear.

When the tall cowboy emerged from the building a moment later and came alongside her son, she was fit to be tied.

"I was telling them the good news." Colton was beyond excited. "That we get to ride horses to our picnic spot."

Lily remained silent behind her sunglasses, though that didn't stop her from glaring at Noah.

"Now let's not get too excited here." While Noah appeared to address all of them, those dark eyes remained fixed on her. "Colton is only partially right."

Lily waited for him to continue, fearful she might say something she shouldn't.

"The *kids* can ride while you and I take old Duke for a walk."

"Who, or should I say what, is Duke?" *Lord, please let it be a dog.*

"He's my horse."

"Of course he is." She undid her seat belt, killed the engine and rolled up the window before opening the door.

Noah backed out of the way as she moved to the rear of the vehicle to retrieve the basket of food. "Since it's such a nice day, I thought this would be the perfect opportunity for him to get out of the stable for a while. Away from the other horses."

She paused, her hand on the button to close the hatch. "He doesn't like the other horses?"

"Nah." He waved off her concerns. "They don't bother him. He just likes a little freedom now and then."

Lily swallowed against the tightness in her throat. "Then I guess you guys had better bring those horses out so we can be on our way." She glanced at Noah. "To wherever that may be."

"Great. The horses are already saddled, so, kids, if you will follow me."

Before he walked away, Lily said, "I do have one request."

"What's that?"

Head cocked, she clutched both hands around the basket handle. "Actually, it's more of a demand."

His gaze narrowed.

"That I do not leave here today without the information I need to move forward."

The corners of his mouth tilted upward. "You got it."

A few minutes later, Piper came around the side of the stable on a black-and-white Shetland pony, followed by Colton on the chestnut-colored horse he used for his lessons and—

"Oh, my."

Noah led his horse toward her.

Her head tilted back as she took in the massive black animal.

"Isn't Duke like the most awesome horse you've ever seen, Mom?" Colton beamed from atop his horse.

"He's *giant*." Piper stretched her arms as high as they would go.

"He is that." Lily took a step back.

When she did, the animal looked down at her with big black eyes. Her knees began to shake. Her pulse raced, and she felt like that frightened four-year-old girl again.

"I'll take this." Noah grabbed the picnic basket from her hands and tugged on the reins. "Come on, gang. Let's go."

They walked up the drive, past the barn and the house and into the pasture where cattle grazed in the distance. All the while, Lily made sure to keep a safe stretch of grass between herself and Duke.

"You know, Lily—" Noah looked her way, which was about eight to ten feet right of where he walked "—it makes it kind of hard to carry on a conversation when you're all the way over there. I mean, do you hear how loud I'm having to talk?"

She marched through the high grass. "I didn't want Duke to feel crowded."

"Don't you worry about Duke. You're not gonna bother him."

Maybe not, but he certainly bothered her.

A familiar sound touched her ears then. "Do I hear the river?"

"You sure do." A smiling Noah picked up the pace. "It's also our picnic spot."

"Awesome!" Colton fist-pumped the air.

Piper clapped. "Yay!"

Drawing closer, Lily could see it for herself. The way the Uncompahgre stretched to their right and left, winding as it went. The mountains in the distance were the perfect backdrop, with only the slightest slivers of snow still clinging to their peaks.

While the kids dismounted and Noah tethered their horses, Lily closed her eyes, stretched her arms wide and allowed the sun's warmth and the sound of rushing water to wash away her worries. This place was absolutely perfect.

When she opened her eyes, Noah stood before her. "Did I disappoint?"

She couldn't help but smile. "Definitely not."

"Good. Now, if you don't mind—" he held up the basket "—I'd like to see if you kept your end of the bargain."

"I hope you like liverwurst." After the walk she'd just had with Duke, it was hard not to tease him.

"Liverwurst?" Noah's look of horror told her she'd achieved her goal.

"Oh, yes." She took the basket from him and set it on the ground in the shade of a large cottonwood tree. "It's one of my favorites." Lifting the basket lid, she pulled out a blanket, shook it open and spread it on the ground.

"Liverwurst?" He smoothed the edges, his face still contorted.

"Oh, wait." Finished, she stood and touched a finger to her chin. "We were out of liverwurst. I brought ham and cheese and pimento cheese sandwiches."

He looked at her, his expression blank. "You know, Lily, I'm a pretty levelheaded guy. But right now, I'd like nothing more than to toss you into that river." He poked a thumb over his shoulder.

She stiffened. Surely, he was just playing. "You wouldn't."

"No, but I'd like to."

She turned toward the water, where Colton and Piper were running back and forth. "Kids, come eat." Glancing over at Duke, who was happily eating the grass while his reins lay on the ground, she addressed Noah. "Aren't you afraid he'll wander away?"

"No."

Well, that was a bit disconcerting. However, as they ate and laughed, she felt herself relax, despite the animal's presence. And when the kids went off to play again, she knew she finally had her chance.

Kneeling, she neatly tucked the empty plastic containers into the picnic basket, daring a peek at the long-legged cowboy who had stretched out on the opposite corner of the blanket, eyes closed with his hands tucked behind his head. She'd never seen him so relaxed. Not that she'd ever seen him uptight, but he looked different. Peaceful.

Who could blame him? She took in their surroundings. She'd been privileged enough to travel the world, yet the more time she spent in Ouray, the more she realized how much she enjoyed the simple things.

She checked on her children one more time. Seeing that they were busy feeding the horses handfuls of grass, she said, "You awake over there?"

"Yes, ma'am." Noah lifted one eyelid. "Just waiting for you to start pelting me with questions."

"In that case…" She sat down and made herself comfortable. "What made you decide to start the rodeo school?"

Noah wasn't used to opening himself up to people. Unfortunately, if he didn't, Lily wouldn't be able to do her job. And there was nothing he wanted—needed—more than for the rodeo school to be a success. Which meant he'd better answer her question.

He rolled up on one elbow. "Rodeo is my passion. I've been in love with it and with horses my entire life. But more than that—" He paused, knowing he needed to choose his words carefully. Or just get to the point. "Those two things helped me heal after my wife died."

Lily's brow furrowed, and her shoulders drooped as though she felt his pain. "How did she die?"

It had been a long while since Noah had talked about Jaycee's death. Though it was never far from his mind. He'd never forget walking into their cabin and finding her unconscious on the floor. He never got to talk to her again.

Not that he was going to share that with Lily. Still, if it hadn't been for Jaycee, he never would have even considered a rodeo school. Once upon a time, it had been her dream. She'd been a barrel-racing phenom, earning her own share of awards. At the time, he wasn't really interested in rodeo. Mostly because he didn't understand. Until she was gone and he experienced firsthand just how beneficial training and working with horses could be.

"She'd suffered a miscarriage. The doctors said later that she had developed an infection that turned into sepsis." If he had monitored her more closely, he might have seen the signs. Sure, she was sad, but he hadn't had a clue she was sick.

"I am so sorry, Noah. To go from the joy of expecting a child to losing both the baby and the woman you loved." She clenched a hand to her chest. "I can't begin to imagine how difficult that must have been for you."

"I had some pretty rough days. And ended up coping the only way I thought I could. By returning to the rodeo circuit and working 'round the clock. Practicing, trying new and different techniques, all in an effort to become the best rodeo champ ever."

Her smile was a sad one. "From what I've read, you succeeded."

"I suppose." Sitting up, he snagged a piece of grass. Rolled it between his fingers. "Course, it didn't hurt that I had a death wish. I figured I'd already lost everything..." He dropped the grass and looked her in the eye. "Which brings me to my second, more understated, reason for the rodeo school."

He twisted around to check on Colton, Piper and the horses. Assured that everyone was safe, occupied and a good distance from the river, he continued, "Rodeo, horses in particular, played a huge role in helping me work through the grieving process."

Hands clasped, she cocked her head, the breeze tossing tendrils of her long ponytail over her T-shirt–covered shoulder. "How so?"

"Not only are horses good listeners, they're very intuitive. They respond to the emotional state of those working with them."

"Meaning…?"

"We might think we're acting normal, but if we're grieving, impatient or angry, a horse will know and respond accordingly." He drew up one knee and hooked an arm around it. "While I don't want the rodeo school to be one of those therapy-type places, I'd eventually like to create an avenue to help kids dealing with grief."

"I have no doubt you would be very good at that. Just look at the changes you've brought about in Colton." Her troubled gaze drifted to her son. "This past year, he's had all sorts of behavioral issues." She looked at Noah again. "As you witnessed that first day when he tried to steal the horseshoes. But I've seen changes in him since he's been working with you."

"Why do you suppose he was acting out?"

She shrugged, eyeing a pair of birds chattering in the branches above. "I can't say for certain, but I think it has a lot to do with his father's lack of interest. Wade Davis doesn't have a lot of time for his children."

"Wait a minute." Noah dropped his leg and sat up straight. "Did you say Wade Davis?"

"Yes."

"The billionaire oilman?"

Her expression bordered on embarrassment. "That's the one."

Noah again looked for the kids as he tried to wrap his brain around that bombshell. Lily was married to Wade Davis? But she was so kind and unassuming, while Davis was an in-your-face, it's-all-about-me kind of guy. How on earth had those two ever gotten together?

He shook his head. "Doesn't he realize that his kids are the greatest treasure he could possess? That they're his legacy?"

"Unfortunately, no." She dusted crumbs from her gray T-shirt.

Noah watched the children as they took turns tossing rocks into the water. Colton and Piper were great kids. And their father ought to be ashamed of himself for turning his back on them. "I'm sorry, but your ex-husband has no idea what he's missing out on."

Following his gaze, she said, "I would have to agree."

He looked back at Lily. Saw the resignation in her eyes.

"Things don't always turn out the way we think they will, do they?"

He studied her a moment. "No, they don't." Pushing to his feet, he held out a hand to help her up. "But with your assistance, I'm sure the rodeo school will turn out even better than I imagined."

She smiled in earnest then. "I sure hope so."

"Come on." He nodded toward the river. "Let's go wrangle these kids so we can head on back."

"You two look like you're having fun," she said as they approached.

"Here, Mommy." Piper held out a well-rounded stone. "You need to skip a rock, too."

Her mother examined it. "Piper, honey, you need a flat rock for skipping." She eyed the water's edge. "Like this one." As she bent to pick it up, her foot slipped. "Ah!"

Noah reached out to catch her, but the grimace on her face said he was too late.

While she clutched her ankle, he hauled her back a few feet before crouching to her level. "How bad does it hurt?"

Her face contorted. "At the moment, pretty bad."

He carefully pulled off the low-heeled ankle-high boot and rolled up her skinny jeans as much as he could to discover that some swelling had already set in. "We're going to need to get some ice on this right away." Lifting his head, he let go a whistle.

"What was that for?" Lily's pain-filled eyes met his.

"Duke."

"Duke?"

"Yep." He stood as the horse came alongside them. "Good thing we let him come with us, because there's no way you're making it back to the house on your own."

Lily's gaze darted between him and Duke. "What do you mean?"

"It means that unless you want to be laid up for a week or more, Duke's gonna have to carry you back."

"Carry me?"

Noah would have had to be blind to miss the way Lily glared at him, but there was no other choice. He had to get her back to the house and get some ice on her foot. "Well, I'm certainly not up to the task."

"It'll be okay, Mom." Colton laid a hand on his mother's shoulder. "Duke can handle it. He's a good horse."

"I'm sure he is, sweetheart, but I should be able to—" She struggled to stand until Noah reached out a helping hand. "See." She straightened. "I should have no problem—" One step was all it took and she was groaning again as her foot protested against the weight.

"Sorry, Lily, but it looks like Duke is your only ticket out of here."

Her nostrils flared. "Something I'm sure you're just thrilled about."

He took a step back. "You think I planned for you to get hurt?"

"No, but I'm sure you're enjoying this nonetheless."

He knew it was the pain talking, but that didn't mean he had to take it. "Look, I know we don't know each other very well, but I am not the kind of person who takes pleasure in other people's pain."

Her shoulders sagged again. "I'm sorry. I know you're trying to help me." She sent him a pleading gaze. "But isn't there another way?"

He eyed the kids. "You two go grab the basket and the blanket."

They took off without question.

Looking down at Lily's sad face, he wished he could accommodate her. But he couldn't.

"There is no other way, Lily. But I know that you can do this. You're a strong woman. And I'll be with you every step of the way."

Chapter Six

First she threw up in front of Noah, then she foolishly slipped and twisted her ankle. Could she possibly embarrass herself any more?

Lying on the lounge chair on the wooden deck of her cabin, Lily stared up at the leaves fluttering in the trees. Then to be forced to ride a horse… While Duke had been gentle enough, the only thing that had kept her from going into full-blown panic mode was knowing that her children were right there watching her.

She shook her head. At least nothing was broken.

Once they'd made it back to the stable yesterday, Clint drove her to the medical clinic in Ridgway for an X-ray, despite her insistence that she could drive herself. After all, she didn't need her left foot to drive. Of course, walking was another matter. After Dr. Lockridge determined it was only a sprain, he wrapped her ankle and sent her home with a pair of crutches and instructions to keep it iced and to stay off it unless absolutely necessary for at least two days. Longer if it still hurt.

She smiled thinking about Clint and the entire Stephens family. He'd brought her and the kids straight home, telling her they'd deliver her car later since she wouldn't be needing it. Then Carly and Lacie, Noah's sisters-in-law, brought dinner for her, Colton and Piper, while Jude, an Ouray police officer, was so kind to stop by and tell her he was working the night shift, then gave her his cell number in case she needed anything. Later, Noah had showed up, bearing ice cream and an apology for not taking her to the clinic himself. As if he needed to do that. The guy was busy enough without having to worry about her. Still, it felt good to know that someone cared.

The Stephens family was one loving and giving bunch. She wasn't sure she'd ever experienced anything quite like them before. Certainly not from her own family. Well, except for her grandma Yates.

Now, as she contemplated pizza delivery for tonight's meal and waited for Clint to return with Colton and Piper—he'd picked them up earlier and taken them to the ranch for their lessons—she read over the notes she'd made on her tablet, realizing she'd had a rather productive day. She'd researched the media outlets she wanted to contact for interviews, worked up a rough draft of the press release and jotted down multiple ideas for the grand opening event itself. Amazing what she could accomplish when she was forced to be still.

Just then, she heard gravel crunching under tires. She checked her watch. Ten after six. Anticipating Clint with the kids, she closed her tablet, grabbed her crutches and carefully made her way back into the house. By the time she arrived at the front door, she heard the sound of footsteps on the wooden stairs outside and Piper chatting excitedly about something.

Her heart stammered when she opened the wood, iron and glass door to discover Noah escorting her kids, a large brown paper sack dangling from each hand.

"We brought dinner," announced Piper.

"That's a pleasant surprise." Suddenly wishing she was wearing something other than sweatpants and a baggy T-shirt, she stepped out of the way to allow them entry.

"It's enchilada night at Granny's Kitchen." He gestured to the bags, his biceps straining the sleeves of his T-shirt. "We've got enchiladas, beans, rice, chips, salsa…"

The aromas had her stomach rumbling. "Sounds delicious." She closed the door and led him into the well-appointed galley kitchen. "Will you be joining us?"

Setting the bags on the granite countertop, he grinned. "I was hoping you'd ask."

While he emptied the bags of their foil to-go containers, she leaned one crutch against the counter, opened the cupboard and took hold of four plates.

"I'll get those." He intercepted her and set the plates on the counter.

Frowning, she cast him a sideways glance. "I'm not helpless, you know."

He looked down at her. "I do. However, my mother raised me to be a gentleman."

Heat crept into her cheeks. "She'd be very proud of you then." She moved to the silverware drawer. "I'm glad you're here, actually. There are several things I'd like to go over with you."

"Such as?" He removed the lids of the containers.

"Just some ideas for the rodeo school."

"Oh, so you weren't just sitting around, eating bon-bons today."

She gathered knives and forks. "Sitting around, yes. Bonbons, no. Instead, I took the opportunity to go to work for you." Shoving the drawer closed with her hip, she eyed him again. "So if you could hang around a bit, I'll show you what I came up with."

"Not a problem, since Dad'll be bringing my truck by. Oh—" he reached into the pocket of his jeans "—here are your keys." He held them out. "I parked your SUV in the drive, but I can put it in the garage if you prefer."

"No, the drive is fine." She set the silverware atop the plates and reached for the keys. Her fingers brushed against the palm of his hand, sending warmth through her fingertips, straight up her arm and directly to her heart. Try as she might, she couldn't remember a time in her life when someone had been so kind to her.

Closing her fist around the keys, she stepped back, refusing to read too much into it. Noah was a kind man. It was the way he was raised, and that's all there was to it.

After they'd finished their meal, the kids opted for a movie while Lily and Noah relaxed on the deck to go over her notes.

Sitting on the same chaise where she'd spent most of her day, she brought up the first page on her tablet. "This is a list of media outlets I plan to send press releases to. I believe we should get at least two or three interviews out of this. Some by phone, perhaps."

In the lounge chair beside her, he seemed to squirm. "About those interviews. I'm not real comfortable talking with reporters. Even when I was on the circuit."

Of course he wasn't. Noah wasn't the kind to brag or talk about himself. "I understand. Which is why we'll be sure to keep the focus on the rodeo school. But let's face it, if you wanted to further your career, whatever that may be, would you rather take lessons from someone who's dabbled in the field or a seasoned pro?"

"The pro, of course. But what if the interview turns personal?" He folded his hands atop his stomach. "I'm not planning to tell everyone what I told you yesterday."

"Noah." She set her tablet on her lap and faced him. "What you shared with me was to give me a better understanding of you so I can figure out how best to promote the school. And I'm glad you told me, because I think that propelled my work today."

"But what if they ask personal questions?"

"And they're apt to, believe me." She caught his horrified stare. "Sorry. I guess I've dealt with too many society columnists. Especially after Wade and I split. Speculations, accusations…" Resting her head against the back of the chair, she saw the first stars in the sky.

"What really happened?" He leaned closer. "Between you and Wade."

She studied him, realizing Noah was someone she could confide in and trust to keep the story to himself. "Honestly, things began to change when I started going to church again after a rather long absence. He said I wasn't *fun* anymore." Lifting a shoulder, she continued, "Things came to a head when my mother passed away. We were in Salt Lake City. Wade left right after the funeral because he had to get back for business reasons." She eyed her clasped hands. "At least that's what he said. But when I came home a day earlier than he expected, I found him in bed with another woman—who also happened to be my best friend."

Noah let go a sigh. He reached for her hands and gave them a squeeze. "Lily…"

She savored the comforting touch.

"I always think no one can understand what I went through after Jaycee died. But I have a feeling you get it better than anyone."

"To a point, yes." She faced him. "And having a recording device shoved in front of your face when you're going through something like that doesn't make things any easier."

"Sounds like you've had a lot of experience."

"More than I ever wanted, that's for sure." Which meant she might be able to help him. Releasing his hand, she sat up straighter. "What if I coached you? Gave you some tips on how to direct the interview to your advantage instead of letting them lead you."

He studied the night sky, pondering the suggestion. Nodded slowly. "I like that idea." He met her gaze. "I'll help you overcome your fear of horses and you help me conquer the interview."

"We'll be unstoppable," she teased.

"You got that right." He smiled.

Looking up at the stars, she let go a laugh. "Look out, world, here we come."

Lily was not the woman Noah had thought she was.

Two days after dinner at her place, he eased Duke from the rocky trail that wove down the side of the mountain into the grass-covered pasture, glancing over his shoulder to make sure the five riders behind him were still doing all right. Lily wasn't just any city girl. Thanks to a little internet research of his own, he'd discovered was a socialite. Born into wealth, married wealth... She was Colorado's version of those rich women you see in magazines. Yet she seemed so... normal.

With a warmer-than-usual midday sun overhead, he continued toward the stable. Saturdays were historically one of their busier days for trail rides. People came into Ouray for the weekend, looking for a change in scenery, an escape from city life or both. Like Lily. Only she was ready to escape for the entire summer.

He shifted in the saddle, the leather creaking. "Everyone doing okay back there?"

"We're doing *great*," said the young girl whose enthusiasm reminded him of Piper.

"Except it's almost over." Her teenaged sister eyed the stable ahead.

Sad to say, her disappointment was music to his ears. "I take it you enjoyed yourself then."

"Yes, sir," they said collectively.

Scanning the mountains to the south that surrounded the town of Ouray, he wondered how Lily's foot was doing. Thanks to an AWOL employee, yesterday had been another busy one, so he hadn't had a chance to stop by and see her. Not that he needed to. Still, there was a part of him that felt responsible for her sprained ankle. If they'd gone to the park as she'd suggested...

He waved off an annoying fly. Most people who lived in Colorado had at least heard of Wade Davis, the outspoken businessman who'd inherited a nice chunk of change from his late father, then gone on to accumulate his own fortune in the oil industry. Davis was a man who loved the limelight. And Lily had been married to him.

Tilting his hat back, Noah scratched his head. For the life of him, he still couldn't figure that one out. Davis and Lily were as different as night and day.

Not so unlike you and Jaycee. True. Yet while Jaycee had been content to live a simple life, her family had always looked down on him, even going so far as to blame him for her death. His chest tightened. Wasn't it enough that he blamed himself?

He shook off the unwanted memories, grateful they were approaching the stable.

After saying goodbye to his group, he took Duke around to the side of the building for a drink of water, then went inside to grab a bottle for himself. Savoring the cool air in the storage room, he tugged a rag from his back pocket and wiped the sweat off his neck, praying today's heat was just a fluke and not an indicator of what was to come.

His phone buzzed in his pocket. He pulled it out to see the name Marshall Briggs on the screen. Marshall was an old friend from his rodeo days, but he hadn't talked to the fella in at least two years.

He pressed the button and put the phone to his ear. "Hey, Marshall. How's it going?"

"Not too good, I'm afraid."

The muscles in Noah's shoulders knotted. "Why? What's up?"

The man who'd been one of Noah's mentors let out a breath. "You haven't heard about Cody, have you?"

"Chandler?" Noah had mentored the up-and-coming kid, who now appeared to be ready to shatter some, if not all, of Noah's records. "No. What about him?"

"Bull got the best of him in Reno last night."

Noah blinked a few times, knowing what his friend was saying, yet not wanting to believe it. "Is he...?" He couldn't bring himself to say the word.

"Late last night."

Running a hand over his face, he sank into one of two wooden chairs near the door. Set his water bottle on the concrete floor. Cody was the best of the best. He had a wife, a new baby... "What happened? Cody was setting up to be an all-round world champ."

"He hesitated. Bull got to him before he could get up." Marshall paused. "You know as well as I do that there's a risk every time we head out there."

Yes, but that didn't make things any easier. Especially when it was someone so young and yet so experienced.

His mentor continued, "Best we can do is pray for his family and know that he died doing what he loved."

Cody might have been doing what he loved, but Noah had no doubt that Cody's wife held her breath each and every time he burst out of that chute. Just like Jaycee had done with him. Until they decided to have a family, anyway. He'd walked away then, disappointed yet unaware his retirement would be so short-lived.

He cleared his throat. "How is Cheryl holding up?"

"Not so good."

Tossing his hat onto the stainless steel work table, Noah shoved a hand through his hair. He knew exactly how Cheryl felt. As though her heart had shattered into so many tiny fragments it could never be put back together. Like the simple act of breathing was suddenly too much. And feeling the burn of anger and wanting to rail at God for taking away your reason for getting up in the morning.

His eyes fell closed. He pinched the bridge of his nose. *God, be with her as only You can.* "Any word on funeral arrangements?"

"Not yet. I'll keep you posted, though."

"Thanks, Marshall." He ended the call and leaned his head against the wall. As he stared up at the wooden rafters, one question played through his mind. Why? It was a question he'd asked hundreds of times before. Now here it was again. And while he didn't have an answer, he knew Marshall was right. With bull riding, there were no guarantees. Unlike most jobs, you challenged death every time you went off to work. This time, Cody wasn't coming home.

"There you are."

He jumped at the sound of Lily's voice. Scrambled to his feet. "You're here."

"I am." Leaning on her crutches, she looked at him suspiciously.

"Did you drive? Aren't you supposed to be resting?" His rapid-fire questions surprised even him.

"Foot's better. Yes, I drove. I'm still taking it easy, but I wanted to tell you—" She tilted her head. "Are you all right, Noah? You look like you're upset." She was on to him.

He couldn't let that happen.

He did his best to shrug off Marshall's phone call. "Naw, I'm not upset." He stooped to pick up his water bottle and uncapped the lid. "A little overheated, that's all." He took a drink. "Just got back from a trail ride."

"Ah." With her fingers wrapped around the handgrips of her crutches and her bad foot lifted slightly, she straightened. "That makes sense. It's toasty out there today."

"Especially when you're on top of a horse and there's no shade." He took another drink, emptying the bottle. "I guess the ankle's feeling better?"

"Much."

"You should still sit down, though." He motioned for her to take the seat he'd just vacated.

"I'm okay. Really."

"Where are the kids?"

"Your father talked them into joining him for a Popsicle."

He felt the corners of his mouth lift. "I'm guessing he didn't have to do much talking, did he?"

"No, not at all."

He grabbed another water. "Want one?"

"No, thank you."

He unscrewed the lid. "You wanted to talk to me?"

"Yes." Again, she watched him, as though knowing something wasn't right. "I heard back from one of the media outlets I contacted. The *Denver Post*, no less."

An hour ago, he would have been impressed. Now?

"They're going to be in the area and would like to set up an interview with you for this coming week. Tuesday, preferably."

"That soon, huh? You must have really sold them."

"Well, that is part of my job."

"Yeah." Except when he'd brought her on board, Cody was still alive. Now he was gone. How could Noah think about, let alone talk about, teaching others—young people, no less—to put their lives on the line in the name of fun? Because it wasn't always fun. Cody and Cheryl had learned that the hard way. And neither Cheryl nor her child would ever be the same.

Chapter Seven

Lily awoke frustrated Sunday morning. Something was bothering Noah. And whatever it was had kept him from giving her a definitive answer on that interview.

Her irritation grew as she stirred the eggs in the skillet. She understood that he was busy. However, time was not on their side. Saturday would be July Fourth. Meaning there were only two months left until Labor Day. Not to mention she had to be back in Denver by August 15. If Noah wanted this grand opening to be a success, he needed to stop dragging his feet.

She scooped a serving of scrambled eggs onto a plate. "Colton. Piper. Breakfast."

Today wasn't about Noah, though. Or the ranch. This was Sunday. A day of rest and worship. Even if they were on vacation—albeit an extended one—they still needed to have their spiritual tanks filled. That meant going to church. And afterward, they were going to drive down to Ironton, an abandoned mining town one of the locals had told her about. The kids seemed eager to check it out. They were already asking if they could pan for gold in the river.

"Thanks, Mom," said Colton, taking his plate. To her surprise, he hadn't balked or argued when she woke him up. She was pleased with the changes she'd seen in him since he'd been working at the ranch. He was more respectful and seemed to have a good work ethic. Thanks to Noah.

She spooned eggs onto Piper's plate, wondering, yet again, what was troubling Noah. Because she highly doubted it was the heat, as he'd claimed.

Since her ankle wasn't one hundred percent, they drove to Restoration Fellowship, a small brick church she'd been eyeing on their nightly walks around town. Still using her crutches so as not to risk putting too much weight on her bad foot, Lily made her way with the kids up the walk, past a large fir tree, to the solid wooden doors where an older gentleman awaited them.

"Welcome to Restoration Fellowship."

"Thank you." She hobbled past the man, taking in the narrow foyer. "It's nice to be here." Especially since she'd missed worship services the past two weeks. She glanced up the long, dead-end hallway.

The older man must have sensed her confusion, because he said, "Just make a left midway down the hall, and the sanctuary will be straight ahead."

When they rounded the corner, there were two more gentlemen carrying on a conversation. The closest one, a very tall man with thick, dark hair, had his back to her.

The shorter man facing them paused, smiled and said, "Welcome to Restoration Fellowship."

The tall man turned their way. "Good morn—"

"Noah?" Colton's expression went from moderate interest to full-blown excitement.

"Hey, guys." Noah scanned the three of them. And

though he wore a hint of a smile, whatever had been bothering him yesterday still lingered in the lines that creased his brow.

"What are you doing here?" Piper stared up at him, looking somewhat perplexed.

"This is where I attend church." His attention shifted to Lily then, and she took a step back. This was not the cowboy she was used to seeing. The man standing before her now, sporting a pair of stone khakis and a tailored, untucked blue shirt that complemented his physique as well as his eyes, had her a little off-kilter. "I'm glad you could join us."

"Well, look who we have here?" Clint's voice sent the kids' excitement level even further up the scale.

Lily turned to see him approach with a stylishly dressed Hillary at his side, once again raising Lily's suspicions that the two were more than just friends. Not that there was anything wrong with that. Clint was a widower. His children were grown. Why shouldn't he be allowed to find love again?

Her children hung on the older man's every word as he told them how long he'd been coming to this church and how happy he was to see them here.

"Dad, you're creating a bottleneck." Noah motioned to the people waiting behind them.

"Hmm." The older man jerked toward the people in question. "Sorry 'bout that." He took hold of Piper's hand and nodded for Colton. "Let's go get us a seat."

Next thing Lily knew, she and her children were in a cushioned pew, surrounded by the entire Stephens clan, except for Carly, who was holding down the fort at her bed-and-breakfast. Not exactly what Lily had envisioned when she woke up this morning. Especially the good-looking man sitting on the other side of Piper.

Still, the pastor's message about how God uses all things for good struck a chord. While her life had been a privileged one, she'd known her share of difficulties. Yet, now she was able to look back and see how God used even some of the worst events in her life to not only grow and strengthen her, but to bring her to places she'd never expected.

Kind of like coming to Ouray. If it hadn't been for Colton's behavioral issues, she probably wouldn't have been so determined to get the kids away from Denver. As a result, Colton's bad attitude seemed to have disappeared. Her children were happier than she'd ever seen them.

Her gaze inadvertently drifted to Noah. He'd played a big role in those changes. And seeing him here today only bolstered her awareness.

Straightening, she again faced the pulpit. Good thing they already had plans for today. Because the last thing she needed was to find herself at the ranch, being bombarded with wayward thoughts. Her life and her children's lives were in Denver. Something that was not about to change anytime soon.

After the service, she met the pastor, then led her children outside as they again chatted with Clint. The sky was a gorgeous blue. Birds were singing. The sun was warm. A perfect day for exploring.

"Say—" with Hillary at his side, Clint clapped his hands together with a smile "—why don't you all come on out to the ranch today? We'll have lunch, and you can help us get the old farm wagon ready for the parade on Saturday."

Lily cringed.

"The Fourth of July parade?" Colton's green eyes sparkled.

"That's the one," said Clint. "You kids planning to attend?"

They nodded eagerly.

"Mom showed us a book with a bunch of pictures," said Colton. "I can't wait to see the fire-hose fights."

"Oh, you don't want to miss those." Clint nudged his cowboy hat—one that was far more pristine than the one he wore at the ranch.

Lily was still trying to come up with a polite way to bow out when Noah approached with his brothers Jude and Daniel.

"What's going on?" He eyed his father as if he knew he was up to something.

"Lily and the kids are going to join us for lunch."

She nearly choked. She hadn't agreed. Nor did she plan to.

"Clint Stephens—" Hillary elbowed him "—you're getting ahead of yourself again. Poor Lily hasn't been able to get a word in edgewise to say if they will or won't be joining us."

"He has a habit of doing that." Noah glared at his father.

The older man looked embarrassed. "Sorry, Lily. The kids and I got a little excited talking about the parade."

"That's all right, Clint." Not that he wasn't making it extremely difficult for her to say no. Especially with her kids staring up at her with those hopeful expressions. "I thought you kids wanted to go to Ironton today and do some exploring."

"That was before Mr. Stephens invited us," said Colton.

"Please, Mommy," Piper begged.

How was she supposed to say no to that?

"I guess we could do Ironton another day." She squinted against the sun. "But what about the trail rides?"

"Closed on Sundays," said Clint.

She nodded. Maybe the wagon would be outside or at the barn instead of the stable. In which case, she really would enjoy helping. After all, a small-town Fourth of July parade was one of those simple pleasures she wanted her children to participate in.

Again, she looked at her kids. Their wide eyes full of expectation. As far as they were concerned, a new adventure awaited. And she couldn't say no to that.

Her gaze drifted to Noah.

No matter how badly she might want to.

Noah wasn't in the mood for company, let alone participating in something that was supposed to be fun. Instead, he wanted to escape from everyone and everything. Yet here he was, on the deck of the ranch house, the aromas of grilling meat wafting around him as he listened to the happy chatter of Lily, Colton, Piper, Hillary and his family, while he barely held it together. Didn't they realize that the news about Cody still had him in a tailspin?

Of course they didn't. Because he never told them.

Dad offered up a brief prayer before telling everyone to come and get some food. As usual, his father manned the grill while Hillary, Carly and Lacie saw to all of the side dishes.

Noah peered at the spread, surprised. Was that barbecued chicken? Dad always served beef.

His gaze drifted to Hillary. She must've encouraged the old cattle rancher to stop being so stuck in his ways.

Falling in line behind Lily at the food table at the far end of the deck, Noah couldn't help noticing the way she tried to balance a crutch with one hand and her plate with the other. And though he didn't want to help, didn't want to interact or do anything else that might encourage her to start up a conversation, his mother had taught him to do what was right.

"Let me help you with that." He took hold of her plate. "Just tell me what you want, and I'll get it for you."

She looked up at him, surprise darting back and forth in her green eyes.

He supposed he couldn't blame her. Not when he'd barely said two words to her all day. Throw in his behavior yesterday and—

"Thank you," she finally said.

When both of their plates were full, they sat with Piper at one of the picnic tables while Colton joined Megan.

"I really enjoyed the service today." Lifting a forkful of her broccoli salad, Lily watched Noah suspiciously across the table. As though she knew something wasn't right.

"Me, too." He inched farther under the shade of the table umbrella, glad he'd forced himself to go this morning. The uplifting and encouraging message was just what he needed. Even if he couldn't imagine any good that could possibly come out of Cody's or Jaycee's deaths.

Though Lily didn't say any more, he could feel her gaze probing him, looking for answers as to why he was being so standoffish. Not that it was any of her business.

Why do you feel guilty then?

Because he had yet to give her an answer on that interview. How could he, though, when, as of right now, he wasn't even certain he wanted to proceed with the rodeo school? Not after yesterday.

What about all your plans? Your dream? You put your savings into that arena. Are you going to let it all go?

His passion had definitely waned. And right now he wasn't sure he'd ever get it back.

"Everyone, make sure you save room for dessert." Dad took a seat beside him as Hillary eased next to Piper.

"So, Clint—" Lily wiped her hands on a paper napkin "—is that the wagon you're planning to decorate?" She pointed to the old farm wagon sitting across the way, beside the barn.

"Sure is." His father cut a bite of chicken and shoved it in his mouth.

"Have you always used it in the parade?"

"For the last few years we have." Dad reached for his water cup. "It's a way to advertise the trail rides."

"I see." Lily set her plasticware atop her nearly empty plate. "In that case, why don't you consider using it to advertise the rodeo school instead?"

"Hadn't thought about that." His father tore a slice of bread in half. "Sounds like a good idea, don't you think, Noah?"

He chewed his last bite of chicken, his irritation growing. He didn't want to be here. Didn't want to think about advertising of any sort. What he wanted was to saddle Duke and find a quiet place in the woods where he could be alone to collect his thoughts. "I guess."

"That reminds me." Lily shoved her plate out of the way. "Do you have a website?"

Noah shrugged when his father deferred to him. "A basic one for the trail rides and riding school. Hours, contact info…"

"Nothing for the rodeo school?" Her brow puckered as she continued to watch him.

"No." Unable to look at her, he focused on the half-eaten pile of coleslaw on his plate. A few days ago, he might have benefited from this conversation. But things were different now.

"Not even some info on the existing website?"

He shook his head and blew out a breath, longing to escape. He wasn't in the mood to talk business.

"In that case, I highly recommend that you have a separate website for the rodeo school. And that you get it up and running ASAP. If we're advertising, people need to know where they can go to get more information."

Tension clamped down on his shoulder muscles. "Look, it's hard enough managing the basic website we have. I don't have time to come up with another one. Let alone in six days."

"I get that, Noah."

His gaze darted to hers, as though longing for someone to understand. He didn't want to let anybody down. However, the thought of moving forward with rodeo school, something that only yesterday he'd been eagerly anticipating, now terrified him.

She continued, "But in today's world, you can't just

hang out a sign and expect people to come running. An internet presence is vital."

"Lily has a good point." Hillary wiped her fingers. "I know that whenever I hear of something that interests me, the first thing I do is look the business up on the internet."

"You would." Dad frowned.

Hillary glared back. "I may be a middle-aged grandmother, but I'm still one hip chick."

"Middle-aged?" His father lifted a brow. "You planning on living till you're a hundred and twenty?"

His sparring partner sent him a smug grin. "If not longer." She returned her attention to Lily and Noah. "I'm not an expert in web design, but I am rather tech savvy. I keep up the website for Granny's Kitchen and even redesigned it a few months ago. I'd be happy to come up with a website for the rodeo school."

"Hillary, that'd be great." Lily's enthusiasm only amplified Noah's agitation. "We could get some pictures from Noah's rodeo days, a bio…"

Sweat beaded his brow.

"That's a great idea, Lily. Could you help me come up with ideas for the content?"

His heart thundered against his chest.

"Absolutely."

Fists balled, he pushed to his feet, his breathing ragged. "Enough!"

Looking around, he saw everyone staring at him. His brothers, sisters-in-law, nieces… Lily and her children.

He'd lost control. Something he hadn't done in a very long time. And he owed them an explanation.

"There's not going to be a rodeo school."

Chapter Eight

Lily's heart went out to the man standing in front of her, no matter how much she didn't want it to. This was her fault. She'd pushed too hard. Noah wasn't a businessman. He was a cowboy who loved horses and being outdoors. Her role was to help him. Instead, she'd driven him over the edge.

Clint stood. Laid a hand on his oldest son's shoulder. "What's got you so upset?"

Noah's eyes closed momentarily. When he opened them, he scanned the faces of his family before zeroing in on Lily. "If you'll please excuse me."

He turned then, the sound of his boots hollow against the wooden deck until he stepped to the ground and continued down the gravel drive toward the stable.

The lump in Lily's throat threatened to strangle her. The way Noah had looked at her. The pain and anguish in his eyes and the lines etched on his face. Why hadn't she noticed them earlier? Instead, she just kept hammering, as though the entire rodeo school hung on advertising and a website.

"What happened, Mommy?" Piper's blue eyes were filled with confusion, her bottom lip slightly pooched.

She wrapped an arm around her daughter. "Noah's just feeling a little overwhelmed, that's all." Except that wasn't all. She was certain of it.

Memories of yesterday moved through her mind. His strange behavior when she found him in the storage room. His features had been filled with distress. Much the way they'd been only moments ago.

Hillary inched closer. "You all right, honey?"

"Of course." Out of the corner of her eye, she saw Noah's niece Kenzie approach.

"Piper, want to play ponies with me?" The child pointed toward the other table and pile of colorful plastic horses.

Her daughter's eyes widened. "Can I, Mommy?"

"Sure, go ahead." She watched her walk away before returning her attention to Hillary. "Would you mind keeping an eye on my children? I need to apologize to Noah."

"Well, yes. If that's what you feel like you need to do." Warmth mingled with confusion in the older woman's deep brown eyes.

"I was rude. This was supposed to be a fun day, and I ruined it by talking business."

"You were just trying to help. We both were."

"Yes, but for all my help, I only succeeded in making him want to give up his dream." She stood. Took hold of her crutches. "I don't know how long I'll be gone."

"Doesn't matter. The kids'll be fine."

She passed Clint on her way off the deck.

"Where are you headed?"

Fearing he'd try to stop her, she kept moving. "To apologize to your son."

By the time she made it to the stable, she was ready to toss her crutches. They might take the pressure off her foot, but they sure slowed her down.

Inside, the smells of horse and hay gave her pause. She had no idea where Noah was, but her first guess would be with Duke. That meant she had no choice but to head for the stalls.

Her palms began to sweat.

You're doing this for Noah.

With a bolstering breath, she headed down the main corridor before veering off at the row of stalls where they kept Duke.

Save for the occasional sound of horses, the place was silent.

"Noah?"

Somewhere farther down, a horse nickered. But there was no sign of Noah. Unless he was ignoring her. Continuing past the first two animals, she again called his name.

This time he appeared from Duke's stall. "What are you doing here?"

She moved toward him as fast as she could, though it felt like a snail's pace.

Stopping in front of him, she again noticed the deep lines etched in his brow. His drawn lips. And the unmistakable sorrow in his eyes.

"I wanted to apologize for being so tough on you back there."

Hands on his denim-clad hips, he watched her for a moment before looking away. "I'm a cowboy, not a china doll. I know what tough is, and trust me, you weren't tough."

"Then why would you give up your dream?"

He looked everywhere but at her then, not saying a word.

"You don't have to tell me," she finally said. "But I wish you would."

Still nothing. Not so much as a grunt. He just stood there, engrossed in the rafters, walls, horses, floor…

"Okay. I've made my apologies. I'll leave you alone." She turned and started back up the aisle, disappointment weaving its way around her heart. *God, whatever's bothering Noah, please help him.*

"One of the cowboys I mentored—"

She turned at the sound of his voice. Moved toward him.

"Cody Chandler was his name."

"Was?"

He gave a slight nod. "He was killed in the arena Friday night."

Her body sagged with grief. For Cody, for Noah. "I'm so sorry."

"I haven't told anyone because I'm…conflicted."

"About?"

He stared at the overhead lights. "I taught Cody everything I know. Yet I'm still here and he's…"

Reaching for him, she squeezed his forearm.

He laid his free hand over hers as though welcoming the touch. "How can I teach others, knowing that they could end up like Cody?"

She chose her words carefully, knowing that nothing she could say would suddenly make things better.

"You said Cody was killed in the arena. What does that mean, exactly?"

"Bull riding." He patted her hand before lowering his own. "He was thrown but didn't get out of the way in time."

Her insides cringed at the image that formed in her mind. He didn't need to tell her any more.

She cleared her throat. "I may have misunderstood, but I was under the impression that the rodeo school was more about horses and roping than bull riding."

"It is. But students will expect to be exposed to some bull riding."

"Can you use one of those mechanical bulls? You know, like in *Urban Cowboy*."

Not only did the corners of his mouth tilt upward then, he actually grunted out a laugh. "*Urban Cowboy?* Seriously?"

"What? I figured that's how you guys trained."

"It is. But that's kind of an insult. I mean—" he stepped back, held his arms out "—do I look like John Travolta to you?"

She lifted a brow and pretended to study him. "Well, you do have dark hair."

"If it wasn't for that bum foot of yours, you just might find yourself on top of a horse right now."

Suddenly grateful for her klutziness, she dipped her head. "When I first asked you about the rodeo school, why you wanted to do it, you said that rodeo was your passion. That it had helped you and you hoped to use it as a means to help others dealing with grief. Has Cody's death changed all of that?"

He thought for a long moment. "No. I just don't want

to encourage people to go out there, thinking it's all fun and games."

"First of all, that's not your MO." She leaned on her crutches. "I've seen the safety measures you take around here. How serious you are about training. But rodeo is a sport. And just like any other sport—football, baseball—there are risks. You know that. I'm sure Cody knew that."

A long moment ticked by before he said, "How'd you get so smart?"

"I'm simply reminding you of things you already know. The rest is up to you."

His nod said he understood. "How did you manage to make it down here, anyway? Past all these horses." He gestured up the aisle.

"Sheer determination, I guess."

"Because you thought you owed me an apology?"

"Yes, but now that I know you can take it…"

While he chuckled, she felt rather embarrassed.

"I need to go check on Colton and Piper." Turning, she again hobbled up the aisle, praying Noah would come to the decision that was right for him. That he would pursue God's will, whatever that may be.

Approaching the practice ring, she heard Noah call her name. She turned to see him jogging up behind her, smiling.

"Hey, would you mind letting that reporter know that Tuesday would be fine for an interview?"

Her grin was instantaneous. "Of course. But what about the coaching we discussed?"

"We've got two days. I'm ready and willing whenever you're able."

* * *

"Cody Chandler was killed over the weekend after being thrown from a bull." Duff Hinson, a sports reporter from the *Denver Post*, watched him intently, recording device in hand. "You mentored Cody. Is there anything you wish you would have told him? Anything that could have prevented this tragedy?"

Noah sucked in a breath, grateful to Lily for reminding him why he'd wanted the rodeo school in the first place. Not to mention the coaching she'd given him for this interview, preparing him for such a question.

"Cody's death is a tragedy, and my prayers go out to his wife, Cheryl, and their little girl. But rodeo is a sport that, just like any other sport, has its risks. Every cowboy knows that coming out of the chute. Yet, despite all of our training, life still happens. That's when we have to step back and remember Who's in control."

Duff lowered the recorder and smiled. "That should do it then." He tucked the device into his pocket. "Thank you, Noah." He shook his hand. "We'll just get a few photos and be out of your way."

The photographer took one of him with Duke in the arena.

"Can we get one of you instructing a student?" Duff eyed the staff that had gathered, but Noah had a better idea.

"Colton?" The boy had been sitting beside Lily, watching intently the entire time. "Is Sonic still saddled?"

The kid leaped to his feet. "Yes, sir."

"Why don't you grab him so we can give these fellas a demo?"

Colton was off like a flash.

He eyed one of his employees. "Jackie? Would you mind putting a calf in the pen?"

"You got it, boss."

Once everyone was in place, he walked through his plan with Colton. "I know you haven't practiced roping with a real calf yet, but for the sake of their pictures—" he nodded in the direction of the newspaper guys "—I'm going to let you give it try, okay?"

The boy looked skeptical. "I don't think I can do it."

"That's all right, I'm not expecting you to. They just want some pictures."

The kid's smile reappeared as determination squared his shoulders. "I'll do my best."

"That's all any of us can do," said Noah.

He watched as Colton walked toward the pen. Then cringed when he tripped and fell face-first into the dirt. "You okay?"

The boy hurried to his feet, face red, but still laughing. "Yeah."

Inside the pen, he climbed atop his horse. And though this was only for show, Noah couldn't help noticing how seriously Colton approached the challenge. He had his rope coiled perfectly. He eyed the calf in the next pen, then the arena.

Noah was rooting for the kid. There was a first time for everything, after all.

Finally, both pens opened, and Colton was off. He swung his rope. Sent it airborne.

Cheers erupted from onlookers, with Lily's being the loudest. He'd done it. Colton had roped his first calf.

Pride swelled in Noah's chest as he hurried toward the photographer. "I hope you got that."

"I did," the man said.

"Good, because I want a copy."

Colton practically flew from his horse. "Did you see that?" He rushed toward Noah, giving him a massive hug.

Leaning into the boy, he said, "You did great. I'm proud of you."

And when Colton stepped back, the look he gave Noah was unlike anything he'd seen before. A look that filled him with emotions he'd never known.

Lily rushed in to congratulate her son. "You did it!"

"Can I call Dad?" The boy watched her, expectant.

"Sure." She handed him her phone and waited as he dialed.

Finally, "Dad, guess what?" His smile faltered. "But it's important." A moment later he beamed. "I roped my first calf."

Lily's nervous gaze darted from Colton to Noah.

"That's it. Isn't that cool? I did it all by my—" His exuberance evaporated. "Well…yeah. I wanted—" A moment later Colton ended the call, thrust the phone toward his mother and sprinted across the arena.

Concern filled Lily's eyes. "I need to go after him." She pushed past Noah.

"You're not going alone." He was right behind her. "Dad," he hollered, "keep an eye on Piper."

With his father's thumbs-up behind him, he bypassed a hobbling Lily in the aisle and waited for her at the front door. "Any guesses what happened back there?"

She pushed up the sleeves of her lightweight sweater. "Yes. His father dismissed him once again."

Anger fueled Noah as he stepped into the bright sun. "You start here and work your way up to the house. I'll check the barn and the rest of the immediate area." Yet, when they met at the house a short time later, neither had seen hide nor hair of Colton.

Lily was beside herself. Her brow puckered with worry while a tear spilled onto her check. "Where could he have gone?"

He scanned the area around them. "I don't know." He met her gaze then. "However, I do know every square inch of this ranch." He gripped her shoulders. "We're going to find him."

She nodded quickly.

"You wait here or at the barn. I'm going to take the UTV and search the pastures. I'll call you just as soon as I know something."

"Okay." More nodding. "And I'll let you know if he shows up here."

He hurried to the utility vehicle they used to get around the ranch and fired up the engine. With one last glance toward Lily, he was off.

Where could Colton have gotten to so fast?

His grip tightened around the steering wheel. *God, please lead me.*

Moving through the pasture behind the house, he noticed a thin strip of recently flattened grass. He followed it into the woods, his gut tightening as he realized where it led. That's when he spotted Colton, sitting on the porch of the cabin Noah had shared with Jaycee.

He swallowed hard. In the past twelve years, he'd done little more than drive past the building. Even then, he didn't dare look.

Then he recalled Lily finding him in the stable the other day. Working her way past all those horses to get to him.

If she could face her fear, he could, too.

He killed the engine and sent Lily a text that said, Found him, before continuing up to the cabin.

He sat down beside Colton on the top porch step. "How did you manage to get out here so fast?"

The kid shrugged, refusing to look at him.

"Mind telling me why you ran off?"

Colton hung his head. "I wasn't mad at you guys. It was my dad."

"What about your dad?"

"He was too busy to listen to me."

A breeze rustled the leaves overhead.

"But I heard you tell him you roped your first calf."

The kid looked up at Noah then, his eyes swimming with tears. "He said, 'You called me for that?'" He lowered his voice to mimic his father. "And that he didn't have time for my nonsense." The tears fell then.

Noah's blood boiled. How could any parent treat a child that way? He understood busy, but surely the guy could have spared a minute or two for his son, especially when it was obvious how excited Colton was about his achievement.

"Perhaps you caught your father at a bad time." Was he really defending the guy?

"There's never a good time with him."

Noah wasn't sure he'd ever been this angry. No kid should feel this way, no matter how large your bank account. "You know, I've been thinking. How would you like to ride alongside me in the Fourth of July parade?"

Colton's head popped up. He sniffed and wiped at his face. "You mean, like, on my own horse?"

He nodded. "We'd need to check with your mama first, but you and Sonic have been getting on pretty good. You're becoming quite the horseman."

"I am?"

While Noah wasn't stretching any truths, he was amazed at what that little bit of encouragement did for the boy. Now he was beginning to understand why Colton had been so difficult when they'd first met.

"You sure are. All that practicing you've been doing has paid off. I'm proud of you." He didn't think the kid's grin could get any bigger, but it did. "However—" he stood "—your mother was quite worried about you, so we'd best get on back."

"Yeah. She worries a lot."

"That's because she loves you."

Another grin told him that Colton knew he was speaking the truth.

Turning to leave, Noah gave the log cabin a final once-over, noting how much it had deteriorated and feeling somewhat sad. A different kind of sad, like the place had been forgotten. Probably because he'd wanted to forget. After Jaycee's death, he came back here once, grabbed everything that didn't remind him of her and never darkened its door again.

He looked down at Colton. "How did you find this place?"

"I saw it on one of our rides. What is it, anyway?"

"It used to be someone's home."

The kid looked up at him. "Whose?"

"Mine."

"Why don't you live here now?"

How could he even begin to explain something he couldn't quite understand himself?

He placed an arm around the boy's shoulders. "That's a story for another day. Come on, your mother is waiting."

Chapter Nine

Colton was safe, and the Fourth of July had finally arrived.

Excitement bubbled inside Lily. Between the photos they'd seen and everything people had told them, she'd been anticipating this day for weeks. And her kids? The way they'd been counting down, one would think it was Christmas.

Today they'd get to experience Ouray at its best. From the parade to the fire-hose fights to the fireworks and everything in between.

Standing on the front porch of Carly and Andrew's historic bed-and-breakfast Saturday morning, Lily was grateful that, for this one day, she wouldn't have to worry about going to the ranch. Not that she didn't like the ranch. On the contrary, she found it quite beautiful. Especially that spot near the river where Noah had taken them for their picnic that day. That was, before she went and ruined everything by twisting her ankle.

Now that her foot had healed, though, she knew it was only a matter of time before Noah would decide to execute his plan to help her overcome her fear. And she didn't want the possibility of having to ride a horse hanging over her head and ruining her good time today.

"You have a beautiful home, Carly." While Piper hurried down the porch steps, Lily gave the gracious Victorian a final once-over before starting down the front walk.

"Thank you." Noah's sister-in-law absently laid a hand atop her growing baby bump. "As I like to say, Granger House Inn isn't just our home, she's a member of the family."

Lily pressed a hand to her chest as she met the woman's gray-blue gaze. "Oh, I love that." She again surveyed the sea-foam-green house with its large porch and intricate millwork. "I hope you use that line in your promotional material."

Carly smiled as they continued into the yard. "Ever since the fire I have." During their tour, she'd told Lily about the fire that had ravaged a portion of the home early last year. Something that had ultimately brought her and Andrew together.

The nicker of a horse drew Lily's attention to the next drive, where Colton and Megan sat atop their respective steeds. Noah had decked the kids out with boots, chaps and Stetsons, making them look as though they'd come straight from the rodeo. Perfect advertising.

Noting the grin on Colton's face, Lily thought back to Tuesday evening when Noah returned with him after he'd bolted from the stable. While she'd been scared to death, her son was beside himself with excitement, begging her to let him ride with Noah in the parade. As if she could have said no. Not when she was so happy to see him. However, learning of how his father had treated him had her wanting to wring Wade Davis's neck.

Her gaze drifted to Noah, who was sitting tall in his saddle. They'd only known him a couple of weeks, yet he'd taken the time to listen to Colton. And then, later, let her know in no uncertain terms that he was not happy with her ex.

Those are his children, he'd said. *They deserve to be cherished, not brushed aside like pesky flies.*

His actions and his words had endeared her to him. And that scared her. Especially since she found herself spending more and more time with him.

"Sorry I'm late." Hillary hurried up the walk wearing a pair of denim capris and a sleeveless white button-down shirt.

Clint went to meet her. "Thought maybe you'd chickened out."

The blonde's dark eyes narrowed. "Clint Stephens, since when have you ever known me to be a chicken?"

Lily leaned toward Carly. "They're more than just friends, aren't they?"

"Definitely. I'm just waiting for Clint to figure it out."

Lily couldn't help laughing. "Well, if there's one thing I've learned this week, it's that Hillary is quite a dynamo. Thanks to her, the rodeo school now has a top-notch website." She gestured to the vinyl banner on the side of the wagon.

"Hey, that looks great."

"We ordered it online, using the website header Hillary designed. And thanks to overnight shipping—"

"All right, gang." Clint waved everybody in. "Time for us to get in line."

"What about Lacie and Kenzie?" Carly glanced up

and down the gravel street as a sheriff's vehicle pulled up. Lacie climbed out and made her way toward them while Matt released Kenzie from the back seat.

"Sorry about that." Dressed in navy shorts and a flowing red ruffled tank, Lacie eyed the little girl. "Someone had a hard time deciding what to wear this morning."

Carly smiled at the dark-haired girl in Matt's arms. "Sometimes those things just can't be rushed."

Noting the cuter-than-cute stars-and-stripes short ensemble, Lily added, "I think your outfit is perfect, Kenzie."

Matt set her to the ground. "You have fun, and I'll see you later today."

"Okay, Daddy." The five-year-old hugged him before turning her attention to Piper. "Want to sit by me on Grandpa's trailer?"

"Sure."

The two took off for the trailer, where Andrew and Daniel lifted them into the bed.

"Guess we'd better load up, too," said Carly.

"I'll be right there." Lily crossed the drive to where Colton waited, careful to keep a safe distance between herself and the horses. "Are you ready?"

"I'm more than ready." He nudged his cowboy hat back, the way Noah often did. "This is gonna be so cool."

After a year of nothing but negative attitude, she appreciated seeing her son so happy and eager to participate in something. "You do what Noah tells you to do out there, all right?"

"I will."

"He'll do fine," said Noah.

"Of course he will. He has a good teacher." Shielding her eyes from the midmorning sun, she looked up at Noah, her heart doing a weird flippy thing that had her quickly shifting her attention to Megan. "You look great, sweetie. Have fun out there."

Hurrying to join the others in the wagon, she felt heat creep into her cheeks. Unfortunately, it had nothing to do with the sun and everything to do with one ruggedly handsome cowboy.

By the time the parade began, though, Lily wasn't sure she'd ever felt more energized. Sitting in the back of the hay bale–lined farm wagon with Piper, Kenzie, Lacie, Daniel, Carly and Andrew, she peered out over Ouray and all the visitors and townsfolk that lined Main Street for the annual Fourth of July parade.

At the front of the wagon, Clint was all smiles, sitting atop the bench seat, reins in hand, steering them along the parade route. Hillary sat beside him, waving and tossing candy to the spectators. A true family affair.

As an only child, these were the kind of moments Lily used to dream of. And while she and her kids weren't part of the Stephens family, Clint and his sons had not only invited them in, they'd made them feel welcome. And she found herself wishing it didn't have to end.

Looking left and right, Lily tried to take it all in. The festive decorations, the aroma of smoking meat wafting from the Elks Lodge up the street and the sound of an airplane engine as a biplane zipped across the crystal clear sky, leaving a curlicue contrail and cheers in its wake.

This was going to be the best Fourth of July ever.

Later, after games at the park and lunch at Andrew

and Carly's, they all returned to Main Street for the fire-hose water fights.

"Mom." Colton's green eyes were alight with something between joy and mischief. "Megan says we'll get really wet if we watch from the street." He pointed to the north and south end of the intersection where a barricade had been set up to block vehicles. "Can I?"

"I don't know." While she was certain the idea sounded enticing to her son, especially on such a hot day, she deferred to the other adults, particularly Carly. "What do you think?"

"Sure." Carly held a hand over her eyes to block the sun. "But stay together and keep in mind that there's a lot of pressure coming out of those hoses."

"Enough to knock both you kids over," added Noah. "So I wouldn't get too close."

"We won't," they responded in unison before running off.

"Famous last words." Noah chuckled, leaning closer. Close enough for Lily to smell the faint aroma of his soap. "I meant to ask you, how do you feel about your ex running for state senate?"

Lily practically spewed the water she'd just taken a sip of. "What?"

His brow puckered in confusion. "You mean you don't know? It was all over the news this morning."

She blinked. "I haven't turned on the news since we've been here."

"In that case, Wade Davis is running for state senate."

"Why?" She stared blankly, searching her mind for some clue as to what could have compelled Wade to do such a thing. He'd never had any political aspirations before.

I won't be able to take the kids this summer. My associates and I are working a deal that's going to require my undivided attention. Was that what he was talking about?

"He is in the oil industry," said Noah. "Perhaps he's got some ulterior motives."

"I can guarantee it." Because Wade Davis had motives for everything he did. And they were usually self-serving.

She thought about her children. Wade could have at least given her a heads-up so she could prepare them. Even though they weren't apt to run into any reporters here in Ouray, they needed to be aware. And what if Wade wanted to take them on the campaign trail? Use them as pawns in his latest game?

No, she refused to dwell on it. She took another drink and recapped the bottle. "I know one thing for sure."

Noah's shoulder touched hers. "What's that?"

"He won't be getting my vote."

"I kinda figured that. And if I lived in his district, he wouldn't get mine, either." His easy smile had her heart racing.

Fortunately, the fire-hose fights began, and it wasn't long before she found herself thoroughly engrossed. Who knew such a thing existed? Teams of people aiming fire hoses at each other, trying to knock each other down. She loved each and every minute of it.

"What are we doing next?" Colton was soaked to the bone when he and Megan rejoined them.

Her brow lifted. "You mean *after* you change your clothes?" Fanning herself with a flyer someone had handed her, she watched Megan continue on to find Carly.

"Well, if I remember correctly—" Clint eased alongside Noah "—the activities are in a lull until the fireworks."

Colton smiled. "I have an idea then."

"Let's hear it." Lily waited.

"We could go horseback riding at the ranch."

Her breath caught in her throat.

"And this time you could go with us, Mom."

"Oh, I'd like that," injected Piper.

Lily's hand went to her neck. This wasn't supposed to happen. This was her day away from the ranch and horses.

Her stomach churned. *God, what am I going to do?*

Noah recognized the glassy look in Lily's eyes. Her tremulous smile. And if he didn't do something fast, she'd find herself in the midst of another full-blown panic attack, like that first day when she came to the stable with her kids.

Except they weren't at the stable. They were in the middle of Main Street, surrounded by hundreds of people.

What should he do, though? He couldn't keep enabling her. Granted, her fear was valid, but why was she so afraid to tell her kids? Sure, they were young, but they'd understand, wouldn't they?

He cupped a hand around Lily's elbow, hoping the touch might snap her back to her senses. "That's not a bad idea, Colton. I don't know, though. What do you think, Lily?"

Looking up at him, she swallowed, her expression nowhere near as carefree as it had been only moments ago. "I—"

"Colton!" Everyone but Lily turned at the sound of Megan's voice. And though it was Colton's name she called, she seemed to address all four of them. "Aunt Lacie invited me to go to the hot springs pool with her, Uncle Matt and Kenzie, and she said you and Piper could come, too."

Just the reprieve Lily needed. That was, if Colton went for it. The kid had fallen in love with horses, though, and had been talking about another family ride for some time.

Lacie approached then. "Just wanted to let you guys know that it was my and Matt's idea to invite the kids." She looked from Colton to Piper. "Have you two been to the hot springs pool yet?"

Piper squinted up at the Lacie. "I've been wanting to go, but Colton always wants to be at the ranch."

"Oh, I see." Tucking her long caramel-colored hair behind her ear, Noah's sister-in-law knelt beside the little girl. "Well, you're more than welcome to come with us even if your brother decides not to."

Piper's blue eyes went wide and shifted to her mother. "Can I go, Mommy? Please, please, please." She prayed her hands together.

Slowly emerging from her stupor, Lily regarded her daughter first, then Lacie. "You—you're sure you don't mind?"

"Not at all. Kenzie loves playing with Piper."

Behind Lily, Dad rubbed his chin. "You know that place is going to be packed—"

Hillary shushed him with an elbow to the ribs then smiled. "My granddaughters love the hot springs pool. Especially now that they've added those new slides."

"They have water slides?" Colton's interest was suddenly piqued.

"You mean you haven't seen them?" Megan looked at Colton in eleven-year-old disbelief.

He shook his head.

"You really need to come with us then." She nodded very matter-of-factly.

Lacie glanced at the sun still high in the western sky, then her watch. "Matt gets off work in about thirty minutes. That should be just enough time for everyone to gather up their suits and towels and meet over at our place."

Smoothing a hand over her red-and-white-striped tank, Lily regarded Matt's wife. "That's very nice of you to do this. Thank you."

"Not a problem. It's not like we have to entertain the kids. Matt and I will just sit back and watch."

"Yeah, if you can get Matt off the slide." Not that Noah wouldn't do the same thing. Those things were fun no matter what your age. He turned his attention to Lily's son. "What do you say, Colton? Horses or hot springs?"

The kid scuffed a sneaker over the concrete sidewalk, trying to be nonchalant. All the while his eyes were alight with excitement. "I guess the hot springs would be kinda fun."

"Kinda, huh?" Noah ruffled the boy's wet hair. "Come on. Let's head over to your place so you two can gather your stuff."

After dropping the kids by Matt's a short time later, Noah and Lily strolled Ouray's side streets, savoring the quiet before heading to Andrew and Carly's for an evening barbecue and fireworks. Of course, the time alone also gave Noah an opportunity to address the elephant in the room.

"You almost had another panic attack when Colton brought up horseback riding."

Lily nodded but kept her focus on an ornate Victorian home.

"I get that you're afraid. But do you think it's fair of you to keep lying to Colton and Piper?"

The glare she sent him was filled with indignation. "I wouldn't lie to my children."

"Ever hear of lying by omission?"

Again, she studied the house. Not to mention the trees, fences…

They eased around a corner, the silence between them heavy, filled only by the sound of gravel crunching beneath their feet and the chirps of broad-tailed hummingbirds swarming a nearby feeder.

Yet for as much as he wanted to let it go, he couldn't. "You're not being straight with them, Lily. As far as those kids are concerned, you enjoy horses and riding every bit as much as they do."

Though her gaze remained fixed straight ahead, her features relaxed. "You think so?"

"I know so. Didn't you hear Colton? He didn't want to go riding today just to ride. He wanted to go riding with you. Something he didn't get to do the last time." Noah stopped then and turned her to face him. "You said you'd let me help you. And now that your foot's better, it's time for you to hold up your end of the deal." He hesitated, choosing his words carefully. "Either that, or you're going to have to tell Colton and Piper the truth."

She let go a sigh. "I know you're right. It's just…" She lifted a shoulder. "I can't tell my children I'm afraid.

They look up to me. Count on me to be there for them, to take care of them. If I tell them I'm afraid of horses, they'll lose faith in me."

"No, they won't. Not if you tell them why you're afraid."

"But they'll think I—"

"Lied to them."

She lowered her head. "I guess you're right."

Touching a finger to her chin, he encouraged her to look at him. "I don't want to be right, Lily. I want to help you. But to do that, you have to be willing to step out of your comfort zone and accept that help."

"And therein lies the problem." She pulled away from his touch.

"What?"

"Leaving my comfort zone. It's so…comfortable."

He couldn't help chuckling. "Are you always this difficult?"

"No. I usually like trying new things."

"Such as?"

She shrugged. "Zip-lining, sushi—"

"Wait a minute." He held up a hand. "You'll eat raw fish that could have who knows what in it, but you're afraid to get on a horse?"

At least she had the decency to look embarrassed. "I know it sounds silly—"

"Oh, it sounds more than just silly."

She was quiet for a moment. Then, "What would be truly silly, though, is to tell my children the truth when I haven't even made the effort to overcome my fear." She looked him in the eye. "If you're still willing to help me, I'm ready to accept your help."

His smile was instantaneous. "Then I'll see you Monday morning."

Standing there in the shade of an aspen tree, he searched her pretty face, feeling his heart swell with something that hadn't been there in a long time. Respect? The thrill of a challenge? Or something else he was too afraid to name?

Chapter Ten

To say Lily was nervous when she pulled into the ranch Monday morning would be an understatement. Yet for all of her anxiety, she had one thing going for her. Determination.

Noah was right. She either needed to overcome her fear of horses or come clean with her children. Only problem was, now that she'd resolved to overcome her fears, what might Noah expect from her? Would he make her get on Duke again? Or perhaps some other horse?

She wasn't sure she was ready for that.

Small puffy clouds dotted an otherwise blue sky as she got out of her SUV.

"Mom, do you think maybe we could go to the hot springs tonight?" Colton emerged from the back seat. "Megan said they're open until, like, ten. We could go after dinner."

She chuckled, tossing her door closed. And to think Megan practically had to twist his arm to get him to go the first time.

"I think we can arrange that." After today, she'd probably be ready for a good soak.

"And I can show you all the cool stuff." Piper took hold of her hand as they started inside.

"Oh, I'd like that."

"Good, you're here." Clint was waiting for them just inside the entrance.

"We are, indeed."

"Noah was called away on an emergency, but he'll be back soon." His gaze bounced between her and the children. "In the meantime, he asked me to work with Piper on her riding while Jude helps Colton with his roping skills."

And what about her? Was she supposed to wait for Noah? Not that she minded. Anything that delayed her having to get on a horse was fine by her.

"Oh." Clint twisted her way. "And Noah suggested you help Megan feed and brush the horses."

Feed and brush? That would involve getting up close and personal with the horses. Touching them. Or worse, the horse might touch her. With its teeth.

She cleared her throat. "What kind of emergency did he have?"

"Equine rescue."

She wasn't sure what all that entailed, but having witnessed Noah's passion for horses, she was certain he was the right man for the job.

They were still in the lobby when Megan came around the corner. "Good morning."

"You're going to help my mom?" Colton seemed confused, if not disgusted, by the notion.

"No." Megan's response was very matter-of-fact. "She's going to help me."

"Why?" He looked from Megan to Lily.

Megan shrugged. "Because Uncle Noah said so." Turning toward Lily, she said, "Are you ready?"

"As ready as I'll ever be." She followed the girl, wondering if she had any idea just how true that statement really was.

After Megan armed Lily with two buckets of feed, they continued down one of the corridors lined with stalls.

"You like helping your uncle Noah?" She followed the girl.

"Uh-huh. It means I get to be around the horses."

Hmm... Too bad Lily couldn't say that. "You like them, huh?"

"Oh, yeah."

When they finally stopped, Lily read the wooden sign attached to the outside of the stall. "So this horse's name is Cookie?"

"Yes, ma'am." Megan slid the wooden and metal door to one side. "She's sweet, but she likes to eat a lot. Do you want to brush her or feed her?"

Neither, really. "I don't know. What do you think?"

The girl grabbed a long, oval brush that hung just outside the stall and handed it to Lily. "Just brush it across her back and sides. She'll like it."

"That's good to know." Because the last thing she wanted to do was make this horse mad.

She eyed the tan-colored animal for a moment. *God, please don't let this creature hurt me.*

With a bolstering breath, she set the brush on the horse's back and made a couple of short strokes.

The horse let go some kind of sound that had Lily taking a giant step back.

"Did I do something wrong?"

The girl smiled, shaking her head, sending her strawberry blond ponytail swaying back and forth. "No, that means she likes it."

Lily let go the breath she'd been holding. "Okay, good." Resuming her position next to the horse, she started brushing again, this time using longer strokes.

"Miss Lily, could you help me with the feed bucket?"

"Of course, sweetie." Still holding the brush, she reached for the bucket with her free hand. That's when she felt it. Cookie was trying to bite her other hand.

She jerked it away, letting out a loud yelp as she dropped the bucket to the ground, toppling it, spilling the feed.

"She tried to bite me!" Lily's heart pounded against her chest.

Megan laughed. "She wasn't trying to bite you. She was looking for a treat."

Lily clasped her hand against her chest. "She what?"

The kid continued to giggle. "That's why her name is Cookie. She's always looking for a treat."

"Oh." Feeling more than a little foolish, Lily slumped against the wall. "Megan?" She tried to slow her breathing.

"Yes, ma'am?"

"I'm going to trust you to keep this little episode just between us. Because if Colton gets wind of this, I'll never hear the end of it."

Megan finally stopped laughing. "It's okay, Miss Lily. I promise not to tell."

"Thank you, sweetheart."

After sweeping up the spilled feed, the two continued on to the next horse. And though Lily did her best not to make a fool of herself again, she was no more comfortable than before.

They were on their way back to the feed room when they heard Clint yell for Jude. The urgency in his voice was unmistakable.

She turned to see Clint moving quickly down the corridor, toward the side of the building.

"What's going on?" she asked as he passed. "Is something wrong?"

"Noah's back."

Jude jogged past her then, bypassing his father and continuing toward the large garage door–style opening at the side where they moved the horses in and out of the building.

Still confused as to what all the hoopla was about, she gathered the kids and followed.

She leaned toward Megan. "Do you have any idea what's going on?"

"Uh-uh."

Outside, they stood in the shadow of the stable as Noah opened the back of a small horse trailer.

Peering inside, she was able to make out a lone horse.

Noah eased beside it. "It's all right, girl." His voice was gentle and filled with compassion. "Come on. I'm not going to let anybody hurt you."

Hurt her? What was that all about?

Several minutes passed and nobody moved. Not Clint, not Jude. Everyone, including the hands, just stood there at the side of the building, watching and waiting. Even the air was still.

Lily pulled Piper against her, uncertainty and curiosity plaguing her mind. What was going on?

When the horse finally emerged, Lily's heart nearly stopped.

The animal looked nothing at all like the powerful, intimidating creatures she was used to seeing. This horse was emaciated, its hair matted and baring what looked like open wounds. Its hooves were deformed.

"What happened to it?" Colton's gaze remained riveted to the horse.

"She's been neglected," said Noah. "From the looks of things, for a pretty good while."

"Poor horsey." Piper leaned into Lily, her bottom lip protruding.

"That's so sad," said Megan.

Noah eyed his father and brother. "We need to start her on antibiotics right away."

"I'll get things set up." Jude rushed past Lily and the kids on his way inside.

"Call the vet, too," Noah hollered after him.

Try as she might, Lily couldn't stop staring at the pathetic creature. Its dark eyes were almost…lifeless.

"Dad, help me get her inside." Noah held on to the horse. And no wonder. The poor thing struggled for each step.

Lily's stomach clenched at the sight. She might not be a fan of horses, but how someone could treat any of God's creatures this way was beyond her comprehension.

Noah continued to coax the horse. Patiently. Gently. The intensity in his eyes was like nothing Lily had ever seen before. "I've got you, girl. You're gonna be all right."

Had truer words ever been spoken? Because anything or anyone in Noah's care was in good hands. So why did she find that so difficult to accept?

Noah felt like a heel the next morning. He'd promised to help Lily yesterday. To at least begin to help her overcome her fear of horses. Instead, he'd spent all of Monday focused on this rescue horse. What else could he do, though? When these calls came, you had to do whatever needed to be done. If he'd ignored it, he'd have felt even worse.

Yet thoughts of Lily continued to plague him. The way she'd hung around all day had him wondering if she wasn't waiting for him to be done with the horse and start working with her. Perhaps feeling as though she'd taken second place. And to a horse, of all things.

Noah wasn't used to breaking his promises. But in this case, he hadn't had much of a choice. He hoped Lily understood that. She seemed to, but then, maybe she was simply being polite.

From his bed of hay in the corner of the horse's stall, he looked up at the pitiful creature. With so much going on—trail rides, lessons and prepping for the rodeo school—he really didn't need the addition of a rescue animal right now, but there was no way he could have turned it down, either. It's a wonder this poor girl was even standing.

If he lived to be a thousand, he'd never comprehend how people could be so cruel. Didn't they realize that animals had feelings, too?

Especially horses. When they were neglected or abused, their wounds went beyond the physical. And while the emotional scars might not be visible, they had the power to leave an animal unable to trust ever again.

Thoughts of Lily again played across his mind. She'd been betrayed by someone she'd trusted, too. And he'd witnessed just how difficult it was for her to take him at his word. At first, it had bothered him that she'd questioned his integrity. Now, though, he had a better understanding.

He leaned his back against the wooden wall, contemplating the horse. Earning this gal's trust would be the hardest part of his job. Because judging by the look in her eyes, she'd all but given up.

For the moment, though, he'd focus on her immediate physical needs and pray the mental recovery would follow.

Movement outside the stall brought him to his feet. He was surprised when it was Lily's face that appeared on the other side of the door. She'd had to walk past a lot of horses to get here.

She wrapped her long fingers around the bars. "How's she doing?"

Approaching the door, he noticed that Lily looked tired. Her green eyes weary. As though she hadn't slept well. Her long reddish-blond hair had been pulled into a ponytail that trailed down her back.

"The vet gave her some electrolytes, but I still haven't been able to get her to eat."

"That's not good, is it?"

"No. Even though she can only have a very small amount every few hours, her body badly needs the nourishment." Realizing Lily had to stand on her tiptoes to see, he reached for the door and slid it aside. "You can join me."

She did but never took her eyes off the horse. Nor did

the horse take her eyes off Lily. Both appearing more cautious than afraid.

"Where are the kids?" He made more space for her.

"Your dad intercepted them. Asked them if they wanted to ride out with him on the UTV to check cattle."

"I imagine they were all over that."

Lily's laugh was soft. "Yes, they were."

He continued to watch her, seemingly unable to stop. "We didn't get a chance to talk yesterday. Did you help Megan with the horses?"

Still transfixed by the horse, she said, "I did."

"And?"

"No panic attacks, if that's what you're getting at." Hands tucked in the pockets of her jeans, she rocked back on the heels of her boots. "And only one momentary freak-out."

"What happened?"

The pink in her cheeks heightened when she finally met his gaze. "I...thought one of the horses was trying to bite me."

"Uh-oh." That would only add to her anxiety.

She scrunched her nose. "I may have made a little noise before Megan informed me she was simply looking for a treat."

"Ah." He relaxed then. "That would be Cookie."

"That's the one." Her focus returned to the horse. Like a mother watching a sick child. "Do you take in rescue animals very often?"

"Only when necessary." He swiped a sleeve across his brow. Having been here all night, he was coated in grit and probably didn't smell that great, either. "It's been a few years since we've had one."

"What's going to happen to her?" Removing her hands from her pockets, she started to reach toward the animal, then withdrew.

"Only time will tell. For now, we tend to her immediate health needs."

A horse nickered somewhere down the aisle, and another echoed in response.

"I feel sorry for her." Lily briefly glanced his way. "First to be treated so horribly, then to be taken to a strange place with people you don't know."

"It'll take time to earn her trust. She's been hurt, so trusting won't come easy."

"Looks like she and I have something in common." Again, Lily reached out a hand.

He took hold of it, directing her toward the animal's head. "Let her smell you. Then you can stroke her nose."

Fear flickered in Lily's eyes, but only for a moment. She took a step forward and did as he instructed.

He watched the silent exchange between horse and woman. As though each recognized their own fears in the other.

"You're a good girl." Lily cooed, stroking the animal's muzzle. "But you need to eat, sweetheart. Otherwise you won't get well."

Her words surprised Noah. They didn't sound at all like someone who was afraid of horses. But of a mother talking to her child. And he had the strangest feeling the horse was responding.

Reaching behind him, he grabbed a small handful of alfalfa. "Lily?"

When she looked his way, he held out the feed.

"See if you can get her to eat this."

She stared at him for a long while.

He understood her hesitation. But if the horse would respond to her...

Slowly, she held out her free hand, allowing him to give her the feed.

Returning her attention to the horse, she again stroked its nose. "Shall we try eating a little something? Not too much, just a little." She brought her other hand to the animal's mouth. "I hear this is good stuff." Her voice was sweet. Almost childlike.

Noah was pleased when the horse sniffed the alfalfa. Encouraged when she didn't turn away. And he had to clamp his mouth shut to contain his excitement when the horse began to nibble.

Lily turned wide eyes his way, her smile one of amazement. "She's actually eating," she whispered.

"I know," he whispered back, reaching for another handful.

The horse ate that, too.

"You did it, Lily." He moved alongside her, wrapping an arm around her shoulders. "You got her to eat."

But Lily's focus was still on the horse. "Good girl." She ran a hand up the animal's nose. "Doesn't it feel good to get something in your tummy?"

After a few more minutes, she stepped away. "I'd like to help take care of her. If that's all right."

Speechless, he simply stared at the amazing woman before him. Not only was it all right, he had a feeling it would benefit her as much as the horse. And in the process, perhaps he could find a way to earn the trust of both.

Chapter Eleven

Lily wasn't sure why she wanted—perhaps even needed—to care for this horse, yet something had compelled her. Maybe it was the desire to prove something to herself. That she was stronger than her fears.

Of course, when she'd made that decision yesterday, her children weren't with her. Now?

"What's her name?"

Inside the stall, she looked from the malnourished rescue horse to her daughter, who was crouched in the corner, drawing hearts in the dirt floor with a piece of hay. "She doesn't have one yet." At least, she didn't think so. She'd only heard Noah refer to the animal as "the rescue."

"We should give her one then."

Lily scooped a small amount of food from the pail she'd left outside the door.

Somehow, the horse must have known what she was doing, recognized the sound or something, because when Lily turned around, those big, dark eyes were fixed on her. And though they weren't menacing or anything, it was still a little unnerving.

She swallowed hard as she moved slowly toward the horse and the plastic bucket attached to the wall.

Midway, the horse bumped her arm with its nose.

Lily felt her eyes widen as memories again flew to the forefront of her mind.

While some of the feed spilled onto the floor, the remainder went flying through the air when Lily jumped. At least she managed to silence her scream before it escaped.

Standing, Piper giggled, wrapping her arms around her middle and doubling over. "You looked funny, Mommy."

How embarrassing.

"She startled me, that's all." Lily glared at the animal that was now eating the feed off the floor. That's when it dawned on her. The horse wasn't trying to get to her—she simply wanted to eat.

Boy, did she feel like an idiot. "You're hungry, aren't you, girl?" She stroked the animal's head, knowing that was a good sign.

She promptly grabbed another small scoop, this time managing to get it into the feed bucket. And as the horse continued to eat, she couldn't help smiling. Who would have imagined that, with all of Noah's knowledge and love for horses, she'd be the one to get the animal to eat?

They'd spent the rest of yesterday going over how to care for the horse. Small feedings every few hours, water, tending her wounds and plenty of TLC.

Strange, for as much as she disliked horses, she found the loving part the easiest. Probably because this animal needed so much of it.

"Mommy?"

"I'm sorry, Piper. What is it?"

"We need to give the horse a name."

She took a step back, tugging her daughter with her, giving the animal space. "Okay, what do you think we should name her?"

"We could give her a princess name, like the twin horsies Megan showed me. She named them Elsa and Anna."

"I see." Lily wondered how the guys felt about that. "In that case, two princess names are probably enough." Leaning against the wooden wall, she continued to watch as the rescue finished the food and moved to the water. *Good girl.*

Turning to face her daughter, she said, "Do you have any other suggestions?"

The girl's face contorted. "Let me think."

"All right. And while you do that, I'm going to check this horse's wounds." When she'd first seen the animal, she'd thought it was covered in sores. Yet once Noah gave her a good washing with some medicated soap, Lily realized that most of what she'd thought were wounds was actually dirt.

Approaching the horse, she began to second-guess herself. Maybe she should wait and do this when her daughter wasn't here to watch her. She'd already made a fool of herself once. She'd hate to do it again.

Smoothing a hand down the animal's side, she winced at the defined outline of each and every rib. *This is so wrong.*

"You know, Piper, when this gal stepped out of that trailer yesterday, I never would have guessed she had such a pretty honey-colored coat. Would you?"

Her daughter gasped. "That's it, Mommy."

She must have missed something. "What's it?"

"Her name." Piper moved closer with no fear whatsoever. "Honey."

Lily looked from Piper to the horse. The color of the hair, the animal's seemingly sweet disposition… "I think it's perfect. We'll have to run it past Noah, though."

"Run what past me?" He appeared in the doorway of the stall, his cowboy hat tilted back, his work shirt dusty.

"Honey." Piper beamed and practically bounced out the word.

He looked confused. "You're going to run past me with honey?"

The girl giggled. "No, silly. The horse. Her name should be Honey."

"Oh." He eyed the animal a moment. "It fits." He again looked at her daughter. "Honey it is then. Good job, Piper." He held out his fist.

The girl bumped it with her own. "Mommy helped, too."

"Well, in that case—" He turned his attention to Lily. "Good job, Mom."

"Mommy?" For whatever reason, her daughter was suddenly wearing a pouty face.

"What is it, sweetie?"

"I'm hungry."

She wasn't surprised, given that the child had barely touched her eggs this morning.

"Well, guess what, kiddo?"

Tilting her head, Piper looked up at Noah, curious.

"Miss Hillary just brought us a big ol' pan of cinnamon rolls from Granny's Kitchen."

Her daughter's blue eyes flickered back to life as she licked her lips. "I like cinnamon rolls."

"Why don't you run on up to the office and get one then." He watched as she darted out of the stall. "And make sure my dad doesn't eat them all."

"Wash your hands first," Lily called after her. When she turned back around, she observed how much more rested Noah appeared this morning. "You sure made her day."

"I do what I can." He eyed the horse. "How's it going in here?"

Shoving her hands into the back pockets of her faded jeans, she decided not to tell him about the little mishap with the feed. "Good, I think. She seemed quite eager to get her food."

"I'm glad to hear that. Have you checked her wounds?"

"No, I was just about to."

"Good. Why don't you go ahead and do that while I'm here?"

Great, another opportunity to potentially embarrass herself.

"Oh, and I talked to the farrier." He retrieved the equine first-aid kit from the wall just outside the stall. "He's going to try to get out here this afternoon or tomorrow to start working on her—on Honey's hooves."

She glanced down at the animal's misshapen feet. "That is kind of gross."

"I know." He opened the plastic box. "It's also not good for the horse." Pulling out some gauze pads and a tube of ointment, he handed them to her. "I'm ready when you are."

Hmm...how much time do you have?

Taking the items into her hand, she drew in a bolster-ing breath and moved to Honey's hindquarter.

"Any sign of blood?"

"A little, maybe." She stood on her tiptoes for a closer look.

"Wipe it with the gauze. Any blood will show up there."

She loosened a couple of squares from the stack, pressed them against Honey's hair and started to wipe the wound. The horse's skin twitched beneath her fingers.

Honey jerked her head in Lily's direction.

"Oh, my!" Her hands shot into the air. She dropped everything and pressed her back against the wall, her heart beating like a bass drum against her ribs. "What just happened?"

Noah reached for Honey's halter, shaking his head. "That was my fault."

"Your fault?"

"Sorry about that. I should have held on to her so she couldn't jerk like that."

"Why did she jerk?" Lily cautiously bent to pick up the gauze and ointment.

"Your kids ever fuss when you're doctoring a scrape or cut?"

"Yes." She rose slowly, her hands shaky.

"Same thing. Honey here was simply reacting."

Lily shook her head, trying to understand. "So, you knew she was going to do that?"

"Suspected, yes." His matter-of-fact response grated her already frazzled nerves.

"You suspected she might do something yet you

not only didn't hold her, you failed to warn me?" Her breathing intensified.

He scratched his head then, looking rather sheepish. "When you put it like that…"

"How could you do that to me?" She took two steps in his direction, her gaze narrowed. "You know better than anyone how terrified I am of horses."

"I said I was sorry."

"Well, sorry doesn't cut it, buster." She poked a finger into his chest. "I trusted you and you—"

He took hold of her wrist and stared down at her, an annoying grin tugging at his lips.

"Let me go." Her nostrils flared as she glared up at him.

"You trust me?" He smiled in earnest now.

"*Trusted.* Past tense." She yanked her hand free, tossed the items at him and continued out the stall door before looking back. "I won't make that mistake again."

Noah watched Lily storm up the corridor with determined steps that quickly ate up the distance.

She'd trusted him? And he'd let her down.

He quickly closed the stall door and took off after her. Somehow, he had to make this right.

You should have held on to that halter.

"Lily!"

She didn't even slow down. Instead, she made a left at the arena, probably headed for the door then her vehicle and back to town.

He picked up pace, dirt pounding beneath each booted step. He'd just reached the arena when Jordan Stokes, one of his hands, met him.

"Hey, boss."

"Not now, Jordan." He continued past the lanky college-aged kid.

"Williams hasn't shown up, and his student is waiting."

Reluctantly, Noah slowed as Lily ducked into the front office. Probably to grab Piper.

He turned slightly. "Has anyone heard from him?"

"He called Amber to say he had a flat tire. We're just wondering what to do with his student in the meantime."

"Can you cover until he gets here?"

The kid shook his head. "I've got some folks saddled up and waiting to go out on the trail."

Noah heard the door open then. He twisted to see Lily and her daughter disappear behind it.

"Tell the student I'll be right there. I have to take care of something first."

"Sure thing, boss."

Noah jogged toward the door and threw it open. Just in time to see Lily driving away.

His heart sank. Any other time he would have gotten in his truck and gone after her, but unfortunately, that wasn't an option now. He let the door close and started back toward the arena.

The riding lesson was almost over when his absentee instructor finally arrived, meeting him in the arena.

"Sorry about that, boss." The remorse in Seth Williams' eyes was hard to miss.

Noah gave him a nod. "It's all right, Seth. Life happens." And although the timing of his flat tire couldn't have come at a worse moment, it wasn't the kid he was upset with, just the circumstances.

He eyed the student, then his employee. "I'll let you take over." With that, he left them and headed back to check on Honey. Best he could hope for now was to catch Lily when she came to pick up Colton from work later. And then pray she'd at least hear Noah out.

Approaching the stall, he noticed the door sitting open. Strange, he thought for sure he'd closed it. He peered through the bars.

"I'm sorry I ran out on you like that." Lily stood inside the stall, gently stroking the horse's muzzle.

He took a step backward, his mind racing. She'd come back. When? And why hadn't he seen her?

He leaned forward just enough to continue to watch.

"After all, I said I'd take care of you." She looked into the animal's eyes. "Of course, you probably didn't think I was doing a very good job when I hurt you. I wasn't trying to. But sometimes we have to endure a little pain before we can heal."

Pulling back again, he wondered what he should say. He could apologize profusely or act like nothing ever happened. Or settle somewhere in the middle. Though he wasn't quite sure where that was.

Whatever he decided, at least Lily was here.

He took a deep breath and continued into the stall, as though he didn't know she'd returned. As if the sweet lilac aroma of her perfume wouldn't have tipped him off.

She turned at the sound of his footsteps. "Noah." She didn't appear to be upset anymore. Though she didn't seem to want to look him in the eye, either.

"You're back."

Her nod was subtle as she stepped away from the horse, wrapping her arms around her middle as she moved toward the back of the stall.

He followed her. "Lily, I'm sorry for what happened

earlier. I don't know why I didn't hold on to Honey's halter. All I know is that I didn't, and for that I am truly sorry. I never meant for you to be frightened."

She still refused to look at him. She just kept nodding, staring at the dirt-covered floor. How was he supposed to interpret that?

After a long silence, her green eyes finally met his. "I accept your apology. But I owe you one, too."

Okay, now he was confused. "For...?"

"Overreacting."

"I'm not so sure about that. I mean, given what happened to you when you were younger, it's understandable."

"That doesn't give me the right to blame you. I mean, what if you hadn't been here? She—" Lily gestured toward the animal "—would have reacted the same way."

"True. But as you pointed out earlier, I could have warned you."

Falling quiet again, she leaned against the wooden wall. "I'm madder at myself than anything." She lifted her gaze. "I really do want to help this horse. After what she's been through, I have no doubt that she's every bit as afraid and distrusting of humans as I am of horses. So in reality, her reaction to me treating her wound was the same thing as me startling when she reared her head back."

"I hadn't thought of it that way..."

Pushing away from the wall, she moved to Honey's side and ran a hand over the horse's neck. "I don't want her to be afraid of me. So from now on, at least where Honey's concerned, I'm going to have to check my fear at the door."

"You want me to put a bucket out there?" He pointed

outside the stall, a grin tugging at the corners of his mouth. "For your fear. Wheelbarrow, maybe? Eighteen-wheeler?"

"Stop." She smiled then. Exactly what he'd hoped to achieve.

Joining her beside the horse, he said, "You know I'll do whatever I can to help you."

"I appreciate that." She sucked in a breath. "For now, though, I think Honey and I need to get to know each other a little more. Start building that trust."

"I think that's a good idea." And as he absently rubbed the horse, he found himself wondering if he shouldn't do the same. Get to know Lily more and start rebuilding that trust.

Chapter Twelve

Lily had never been so eager for a worship service to end. Though it had nothing to do with the pastor's sermon and everything to do with the oppressive heat that seemed to have overtaken Ouray the last two days.

Since most places in the town were not air-conditioned, including Restoration Fellowship, they relied on ceiling fans, open windows and the cross flow of air to keep things cool. But the air coming through those windows today felt more like a furnace.

Standing in the shade of the large fir tree in front of the church, Lily fanned herself with this morning's bulletin while she waited for the kids. They had yet to join her because they were too busy enjoying their conversation with Clint. She had to find a way to escape this heat. At least until sundown.

Maybe there was movie theater nearby.

No, that would be too much like their life in Denver. She wanted something out of the ordinary. Something they couldn't do in the city.

She fanned harder. There was always the hot springs. Not that she or any one of the hundreds of other people there would want to indulge in the actual hot portions of the pool. Perhaps they should consider the reservoir over in Ridgway. That was bound to be cooler. And on a day like today, probably every bit as crowded as the pool.

Maybe a trek into the mountains. Someplace nice and secluded, just her and the kids, where she wouldn't be distracted by a certain good-looking cowboy.

She let go a sigh. No matter what she decided, she'd still need to stop and check on Honey. She was pleased with the way the rescue horse was coming along. Something she supposed she could say about herself, too.

Never had she been more ashamed than when she walked out of the stable on Wednesday. Yet, since then, things had been different. She'd been different. She felt stronger, more confident. As though she might really be able to overcome her fear.

The small congregation continued to file out of the sweltering building until she finally spotted Colton and Piper with Clint. Seeing the three of them together, the enormous smiles on their faces, always warmed her heart.

The patriarch of the Stephens family was like the grandfather her children never had. With her parents and Wade's father gone and his mother's aversion to children, Lily often felt bad that Colton and Piper weren't able to experience that special grandparent-grandchild bond like the one she'd had with her grandma Yates.

When Lily was growing up, there were times when she'd spent more time with her than her own parents. Her grandmother was the one who'd told her about Jesus and how He died for her sins. She'd taught Lily to cook, to crochet and even how to do laundry. Something Lily's mother never would have done because, as far as she was concerned, laundry was the maid's job.

Lily shook her head. Lois Yates had had money, too, yet she knew and appreciated the value of a dollar. Having grown up poor, she always said, *Why would I waste perfectly good money paying someone for something I can do myself?*

Only one of the reasons she'd loved her grandmother so much. She was in high school when the woman passed away, and she still remembered feeling as though she'd lost her best friend.

Watching her children now, she suspected that their bond with Clint was something they'd miss when they returned to Denver. Perhaps even more than the horses.

Just then she saw Noah leave the building with Jude and Daniel. All three of them were grinning from ear to ear. The trio sneaked up behind their father and the kids before Noah continued toward her.

"We have an idea," said Noah.

The smiles on their faces had her lifting a brow. Because whatever they were contemplating had them pretty excited. "What's that?"

He waited as the kids drew closer. "What would you guys think about spending the afternoon by the river out at the ranch?" His gaze bounced between Colton and Piper. "My brothers and I could show you how we used to cool off when we were kids."

"You mean, like, swim in the river?" Colton's eyes were wide, his face red from the heat.

"More like splash and play, but yes."

Lily paused her fanning and leaned toward him. "That river water moves pretty fast. Are you sure it's safe?"

"Absolutely. The snowpack is gone, so things have calmed considerably since that day we were there. Besides, we're not going to be in the main part of the river."

She eyed a couple with a toddler as they passed. "Then...where will we be?"

"There's a little fork that breaks off at the bend. It's deep enough to sit in, cool off and play around, but without the current."

"When we were younger—" Jude gestured toward Noah and Daniel "—and the weather was like this, we practically lived there."

Noah turned his head slightly so only she could hear him. "The water's still mighty cold, though."

"Ah. Thanks for the warning," she whispered.

Addressing the group again, Noah continued, "If that sounds like something you'd be interested in, we could make a day of it. Build a fire to roast some hot dogs, maybe make some s'mores later..."

"I'm in," said Colton.

"Me, too." Piper bounced up and down.

"Don't forget about me." Clint raised his hand.

"Where's Hillary?" Lily was used to seeing her and Clint together.

"She's working today, but I'll see if she can join us later."

Everyone looked at Lily then.

Cooling off in the river on a sweltering day like this did sound enticing. So why did it bother her so much? Given all the time she'd been spending at the ranch, one would think she'd be used to it by now.

Perhaps that was the problem. She was getting *too* used to being around a certain cowboy. Making her heart long for things that, until recently, she'd considered off-limits. Things like a second chance at love. Which was foolish, given that she and her children had to be back in Denver in a month. Because wherever her kids were, she'd be there, too.

Unfortunately, Noah's idea was the best she'd heard all day. And since she was planning to go check on Honey, anyway…

She tucked the bulletin inside her Bible. "You had me at s'mores."

"Good." Noah rubbed his hands together. "Why don't you and the kids go change and grab whatever you think you might need, and we'll meet at the ranch."

"Okay, but do you think we could take Honey with us? You know, give her a chance to get some fresh air and exercise. That is, unless you don't think she's up to the walk or that the heat would be too much for her."

"No, I think that's a great idea. There's plenty of shade where we'll be. And now that the farrier's seen to her hooves, yeah, we can give it a try."

"Good. I think she'll appreciate the change of scenery." And so would Lily. But she'd best keep her mind on her children and Honey. Otherwise, there was no telling where her heart might lead her.

Seeing Colton and Piper's flushed faces in church this morning, Noah knew he had to do something to help make the heat more tolerable for all of them. Once he mentioned it to Jude and Daniel, it didn't take long to come up with a solution.

Now as he stood in the shade of a large cottonwood tree, clad in swim trunks, listening to the sound of children's laughter, he knew he'd made the right decision.

For them as well as him. And he hoped to make this day memorable for all of them.

He couldn't remember the last time he'd spent a day on the river, just having fun. But being out here today, playing and goofing around with his brothers and Lily's kids had him feeling like a younger man, instead of a forty-year-old ex–rodeo champ. Perhaps it was the freezing-cold water that had renewed him. Or the pretty blonde feeding Honey a few feet away.

He shook his head in disbelief. Lily might not know much about horses, but she knew how to love. And that rescue horse needed love.

In only five days under Lily's care, Honey was eating regularly. Her eyes flashed with life, and she was always on the lookout for Lily.

But the biggest change of all was that Lily actually seemed comfortable around the horse. Even in the stable. And whether it was working with Honey or sheer determination that had brought about the transformation, Lily and the horse had formed a special bond. Understanding each other in a way no one else could.

He sucked in a breath as a blast of freezing-cold water hammered into his back. Turning, he spotted a grinning, swimsuit-clad Piper holding one of the water soakers he'd grabbed from the house. A move he was now regretting.

Retrieving another soaker from the bucket, he followed her into the water. "Oh, so you think that's funny, huh?"

Even as he dipped the tip into the water and pulled back the plunger to fill it, she continued to laugh.

"Let's see how you like it." Afraid of hurting her, he took aim at her legs and fired.

She squealed and tried to run away, but to no avail. The water hit his target.

Without missing a beat, the little stinker shot right back at him, this time hitting him smack-dab in the middle of the forehead.

He dropped his soaker and clutched his pretend wound before stumbling to the bank and collapsing on the ground. He stayed there, unmoving, until he heard footsteps approaching. Small footsteps.

With a roar, he sat up, scooped the little girl into his arms and tickled her.

She wriggled. "Stop." And giggled. "Stop."

He quit then, allowing both of them to catch their breath. Yet, as he watched the water drip from her two blond ponytails, he wondered if this was what it was like to be a father. The joy, the playfulness, making memories... How he wished he'd had the opportunity to find out.

Colton approached then. "Can we go exploring?"

"Sure." He set Piper on the ground and stood. "We used to do that all the time."

"Cool." The kid eyed his mother. "Hey, Mom?"

She stroked the horse one last time before heading their way. "What's up?"

"Want to go exploring with us?"

Shoving her hands into the pockets of her denim shorts, she said, "Sounds like fun."

Dad, Jude and Daniel emerged from the water, and Noah suddenly felt as though he'd gone back in time.

"You guys want to come with us?"

Jude shook his head. "Wish I could, but I need to get ready for work."

"And I need to run up to the office to check on some

equipment." Daniel draped a towel around his neck. "I'm taking a group for an all-day rafting trip on the Gunnison River tomorrow."

"That sounds exciting." Lily looked more than a little fascinated.

Noah's baby brother was the adventurer in the family. He traveled all over the world white-water rafting, snowboarding and who knew what else. For some reason, though, he'd decided to stay home this summer. And Noah kind of enjoyed having him around again.

"It can be." Daniel looked from Lily to her children. "You should check out our tours sometime."

She smiled. "I just might have to do that."

"I reckon I'll head on out with these two." Dad waggled a thumb between his two youngest sons. "We'll leave you all one of the utility vehicles so you can haul everything back to the house." His gaze moved to Lily. "Mind if I take Honey back with me? One less thing you'll have to worry about later."

"No, not at all. Thank you, Clint. And I'm sorry Hillary couldn't make it today."

The older man waved a hand. "Aw, I'll see her soon enough."

"Well, tell her I said hello."

"Will do." He waved as he started toward the horse.

Lily looked at Noah and her children and shrugged. "Guess it's just us then."

Noah threw on a T-shirt and flip-flops as Colton took the lead while his sister did her best to keep up.

They were almost to a wooded area when Colton stooped and started picking at the ground with his fingers.

"Whatcha got there, Colton?" Noah moved closer. "A rock?"

"I think it's an arrowhead." The boy continued to dig.

"Man, I used to search high and low for those when I was your age. My father always told me there weren't any, but—"

"I got it." The boy stood. "It is an arrowhead." He held it out to Noah.

He took hold of the triangular, rough-cut piece of rock and let go a chuckle. "It sure is. Humph. Just wait till the old man sees this."

"Can I keep it?"

"Of course you can." He handed it back to Colton, thoughts of fatherhood again plaguing his brain. Making him wish for things that would never be. He cleared his throat. "It'll be your souvenir of our day on the river."

He shook off the emotion as the four of them continued into the woods. A breeze rustled the leaves on the trees as birds sang sweetly overhead, flitting from branch to branch.

"You know what I like most about Ouray?" Lily glanced his way, the ground crackling beneath her canvas shoes.

"The charming cowboys?" He grinned, hoping to lighten his mood.

Her brow lifted. "Close, but no."

"I give up then." He eyed the children as they ran ahead.

"Ouray makes me feel...normal. As though I'm okay just the way I am."

Hands stuffed in the pockets of his trunks, he said, "I guess I'm not following you."

"My entire life, all I've ever wanted is to have people accept me for me. Not for what I have or what I could do for them. Not Lily the real estate mogul's daughter or Wade Davis's wife, but just me. And aside from my grandma Yates, just me has never been good enough. Not for my mother, not for my husband." She paused. "Have you ever been in a room full of people and still felt alone?"

That he could relate to. "Just about every time I went into the arena."

Her smile was one of understanding.

"What's that place?"

He glanced up to see Piper pointing. Only then did he realize they were at the cabin. His cabin. His home. The place he'd avoided for the past twelve years.

Why hadn't he paid better attention to where they were headed?

Because you were enjoying yourself.

"What a cute cabin." Lily approached the neglected log home. "That lilac bush smells amazing."

He recalled the day he and Jaycee had planted it. It was one of her must-haves for the house because she loved the smell of lilacs. Now it had overtaken the entire north end of her beloved home.

Lily stepped onto the porch as though taking in every detail. "Was this somebody's home or, maybe, a hunting lodge?"

"Noah said it was his house." Colton looked from his mother to Noah.

"Can we go inside?" asked Piper.

His mind swirled at the thought. All the memories he'd locked inside, not wanting to ever see them again.

His insides twisted and turned. He began to sweat even though he felt cold.

How could he say no without sounding like a jerk? "I, uh, I don't have a key."

Liar. You know there's one hidden behind the outlet cover.

Obviously sensing his unease, Lily urged her children off the porch. "That's okay, kids. Perhaps Noah can show us another time."

There would be no other time. Of that, he was certain.

Yet, rather than telling them why, he'd lied. *What kind of guy does that just because he doesn't want to do something?*

A coward, that's who. Someone who had no respect for others or placed no value on trust. Someone like Wade Davis.

Well, Noah was no coward.

Forgive me, Lord.

"Wait." He held up a hand to stop them. "There's a key behind the outlet cover by the door if you'd like to let yourselves inside. If you don't mind, though, I'll stay out here."

"That's all right." Lily came alongside him, understanding in the green depths of her eyes. "We don't need to see it."

He thought about the beautiful river-rock fireplace and hand-carved beams. Building this house had been a labor of love, and he'd enjoyed every minute of it.

Pride sparked inside him once again.

He glanced at Lily, smiling. "I built it myself."

She looked from him to the house. "Now I'm intrigued."

"Three bedrooms, two baths." Suddenly curious as to what she might think of it, he nodded in the direction of the cabin. "Go ahead and have a look. I'll be here when you're finished."

Her gaze searched his for the longest time. Finally, "We won't be long."

"This is so cool."

Noah couldn't help chuckling when he heard Colton's echo from inside, even if it was his usual comment whenever something impressed him.

A short time later, Lily closed the door and returned to his side. "You are a man of many talents, Noah Stephens. The craftsmanship in there is beyond anything I've seen before. It's truly beautiful." Her words wiped away his anxiety.

"Thank you." Looking down into her green eyes so filled with life and love, he couldn't help thinking about what she'd shared with him as they walked. "Earlier you said that just Lily has never been enough. Well, I've spent a good bit of this summer with who I believe is just Lily, and you know what I think?"

"What?"

"Not only is she enough, I think Lily's perfect just the way she is."

Chapter Thirteen

Lily stood in front of the washing machine the next morning, staring at the rain streaking down the window. How could today be so gloomy when yesterday had been perfect in every way?

She eyed the small pile of swimsuits and shorts. Okay, maybe not every way. But, thanks to Noah, they'd sure made the most of what would have otherwise been an unbearable day.

One by one, she tossed the clothes into the washer, recalling the look on Noah's face when they were at the cabin. Like a scared little boy who'd been left all alone. It was then that she realized that it wasn't just any cabin. It was the home he'd shared with his wife. And given all of the photos she'd seen when she went inside, the memories that still lived there were too much for him to bear.

Reaching the bottom of her laundry pile, she spotted the jacket Noah had wrapped around a chilled Piper last night, after the sun set. She picked it up, brought it to her nose and inhaled. It smelled of fresh air, horse and masculinity. Just like Noah.

How sweet it had been to see him so playful with her daughter. But the sight of him holding a sleepy Piper as they sat around their little campfire, roasting marshmallows, was what really got to her.

I think Lily's perfect just the way she is.

His words played through her mind for about the fiftieth time this morning. And once again, she found herself wondering what it would be like to have the love of a man like Noah. Someone who appreciated her for who she was, instead of trying to turn her into someone else. Someone strong and caring who adored her children and actually wanted to spend time with them.

A clap of thunder brought her to her senses. She tossed the jacket into the washer, closed the lid and pressed Start, mentally kicking herself. Even if Noah was over his wife, which he obviously wasn't, what was the point? They'd be heading back to Denver in a month. And Noah was no more likely to come there than she was to stay here.

It was time for her to get the kids up to head to the ranch, anyway. Aside from their lessons and seeing after Honey, she'd received emails from two magazines, *Cowboy News* and *Rodeo Magazine*, wanting to schedule interviews with Noah. Meaning she had no choice but to talk with him about timing before she responded.

Yet, when they arrived at the stable, Noah was eager to get going with the kids' lessons, which was fine by her. Her thoughts from earlier this morning had her feeling rather embarrassed. Not that he knew any of them, but still…

While Piper's instructor worked with her, Lily made her way down to see Honey. She'd checked on her before heading back into town last night, concerned that the day's heat might have been too much for her, but she didn't appear any worse for the wear. If anything, she seemed happier. Perhaps because she'd had the opportunity to get out of the stable and enjoy the outdoors for a while.

Looking left, then right, she observed the other horses as she passed their stalls. Some watched her, while others were oblivious. Mr. Withers always nodded when she walked past, and Dakota did this weird thing with his mouth, as though he was smiling real big.

She stopped in her tracks.

She was actually looking at the horses. Not keeping her eyes to the ground as she would have a week ago. She was learning their names, their habits.

Leaping into the air, she did a fist pump. "Yes!"

Suddenly aware that she might not be alone, she slowly scanned the area, relieved when she saw no signs of anyone.

She continued down the aisle, listening to the varying intensity of rain on the metal roof. She found the sound rather soothing, so long as the rain didn't fall too hard. Then it was just plain loud.

"Good morning, my Honey girl." She slid the door aside. "How are you doing today?"

The horse nickered her own greeting as Lily stepped inside.

"Did you sleep well?" She stroked Honey's muzzle. "You were probably worn out from that long walk yesterday, weren't you?"

The horse flicked her ears.

"And now you're hungry." Over the past week they'd gradually increased the amount of food Honey received, as well as the length of time between feedings, and it seemed to be paying off. The animal was actually showing signs of plumping up, though she still had a long way to go.

After Honey was squared away, Lily returned to the arena, eager to talk with Noah about the interviews. His first one had been very well received, at least judging by the number of inquiries they'd received via the website. Something that had her thinking.

Once the rodeo school was up and running, perhaps Noah should consider some sort of a summer camp. That way he'd be able to bring in students from across the nation as opposed to the region.

Seeing that lessons were still going strong, she continued on to the front office. Maybe Clint was there.

Instead, the place was empty. Not to mention messy.

She moved to the desk, noting the empty clipboards. Of course, with the rain, there were no trail rides this morning. Still, Noah should have someone to take care of these little things, freeing him up for all the other stuff he did. Like running a business.

Locating the consent forms, she attached them to each of the clipboards, hung them on the wall in the lobby and then organized the desk. At least that would make things a little more efficient.

"I wondered where you were."

She turned as Noah walked into the office.

"Did you do this?" He pointed to the desk.

She lifted a shoulder. "I needed something to pass the time."

"Lily, you have no idea how much I appreciate that. Sometimes I feel like I'm on my own here."

Uneasy with his praise, she said, "I need to talk to you about something."

"Okay. And then I have something for you."

Something *for* her?

She briefly explained about the magazine interviews. "For now, they'll be for their online versions. However, it could lead to an entire spread in an upcoming issue."

"I like the sound of that." He paused. "At least, I think so."

"It's a good opportunity."

They looked at the calendar and came up with a handful of dates she could offer the magazines.

"Oh, and before I forget." She grabbed her tote bag from the chair, pulled out his jacket and handed it to him. "I washed it, so you're good to go."

"Thanks." He set it aside and took hold of her elbow. "Now come with me."

She couldn't help noticing the way he grinned as they walked in the direction of the arena.

"Where are the kids?"

"Piper's helping Colton put Sonic up, and then I told them they could get a snack from the storage room."

"That ought to keep them busy for a little bit."

He nodded, opening the gate to the arena. "You've been doing very well with Honey this week, and I've observed that you're much more relaxed, even when there are other horses around."

She stepped inside, recalling her little happy dance a short time ago. "I've noticed that, too."

With the sound of rain on the roof filling the momentary silence, he led her across the arena to where a lone horse still remained. "I was thinking, perhaps, we might try building on that." He stopped beside the horse.

She eyed the animal, then Noah. "What do you have in mind?"

"I thought maybe you could try a short ride."

Her heart skipped a beat, but she quickly recovered. "I don't think I'm up to that just yet."

"Okay." Seemingly confused, he shifted from one booted foot to the next. Tilted his cowboy hat back. "Then what if you tried sitting in the saddle for a few minutes?"

She swallowed hard. Helping Honey was one thing. She wasn't as robust as this horse. What if this one didn't like her?

Stop this nonsense, Lily. You're overreacting. Her mother's words taunted her.

"Come on, Lily, give it a try." Smiling, Noah patted the animal. "Checkers is a good horse. Mild mannered."

Her gaze drifted past him, searching for her children. They were nowhere in sight.

She looked at the horse. Her pulse raced. She knew she needed to do this eventually. And that she'd come a long way. But— *You're acting foolish, Lily.*

Was she? Like when the horse bit her and she cried? Had she been foolish when that same horse sent her crashing to the ground, breaking her arm? Even Noah had understood her fears.

"Lily…" He leaned closer, his smile teasing. "Come on. Don't you trust me?"

Her gaze darted to his. Why did he have to say that? She did trust him. But what about the horse? What if it didn't like her? Or sensed her fear? She'd heard Noah say countless times how good horses were at sensing a person's feelings. If she got on this horse with apprehension and fear pulsing through her veins, there was no telling what could happen.

So tell him.

And have him think her a fool, too?

She watched him for several moments, silently begging him to understand. When he didn't, she shook her head. "I'm sorry, I just can't."

Then, with disappointment blurring her vision, she hurried away.

All of this rain was getting depressing.

Oh, who was Noah kidding? His moodiness had nothing to do with the weather. Lily didn't trust him. And the knowledge of that, coupled with gray skies and daily rains, had made this one miserable week.

Trail rides were down to mornings only and, with the ground growing more saturated by the day, things weren't looking good. If the rain kept coming—which was likely, given southwestern Colorado's annual monsoon season—things would soon be too slick to risk taking the horses up the mountain.

Sitting at his desk, he thumbed through a stack of invoices and packing slips for items that had been delivered for the new arena. But for the life of him, he couldn't locate the one for the chutes he'd ordered. They were supposed to have been delivered last week, yet he had no record.

He reached for his cup of coffee, knocking it over. With a loud growl, he sprang from his chair, sending it rolling across the floor. He quickly snatched all of the paperwork out of the way before grabbing a rag to sop up his mess.

Seemed he was good at making messes lately.

He tossed the rag aside. Why wouldn't Lily trust him?

Because you messed up, remember?

When he forgot to hold Honey's halter. But he thought they'd worked that out. Evidently he'd thought wrong. He'd barely seen Lily this past week. Sure, she still brought the kids and cared for Honey, but she'd virtually ignored him. And that hurt.

Pacing, he jammed his fingers through his hair. How long had he known Lily now? Four, five weeks? He should not be hurting. They were barely more than acquaintances.

Actually, she knows more about you than most people.

That was his fault for not keeping his mouth shut. Something that only served to further frustrate him. Lily was leaving in a few weeks, and his heart belonged to Jaycee.

He could not keep dwelling on this. He had a business to run. Meaning he needed to find out where those chutes were.

Turning, he marched out of the office and headed next door to the new arena. Perhaps Andrew, who was also his contactor, would know something.

"Andrew!" he hollered as he entered the large metal structure. The word echoed throughout the empty building.

"Over here."

The sound of power tools filled the space as he strode toward the far end of the building, ready for something to finally go his way.

"What's up, bro?" Andrew lowered his hammer.

"There were some chutes that were supposed to be delivered last week, but I can't seem to find any paperwork on them. Have you seen them?"

"Chutes aren't coming until next week."

"What do you mean? I scheduled them for last week so I'd have time to inspect them before they were installed."

"Sorry 'bout that." He swiped a sleeve across his brow. "I changed it to next week for fear they'd be in the way."

Noah's blood pressure ratcheted. "Who are *you* to go changing my deliveries?"

"*I'm* the one who has to find a place to store these things so they're not in our way." He motioned a hand across the space. "We're still building here, you know."

"Yes, I know. You're building for me."

Andrew sighed. "Look, I'm sorry I didn't check with you before I changed the delivery date. Next time I'll be sure to do that."

"Next time?" His voice echoed again. "There'd better not be a next time, brother."

Andrew pulled back. "What's got you so stressed out?"

"I can't imag——"

"Noah?"

Andrew nodded, indicating he should turn around.

When he did, he saw Lily standing a few feet away. Dressed in jeans, a gray Ouray T-shirt and rubber boots, she appeared timid. And though it killed him to admit it, his insides tangled at the sight of her.

"Is everything all right in here?"

Noah and Andrew exchanged a look before Noah said, "Yeah. Everything's fine."

She clasped her hands in front of her. "Well, they

didn't sound fine." She glanced left then right before taking a step closer. "I could hear you next door."

Sure, he was mad, but had he really been that loud?

"Noah, I need your help with something. Honey's having a problem."

He cut his brother a parting glance.

Noah and Lily had entered the stable a few moments later when she said, "I finally heard back from the magazines I told you about regarding the interviews."

He'd all but forgotten about that. "And?" Following Lily around the corner, he caught a whiff of her lilac perfume.

"*Rodeo Magazine* will be here next Thursday, and the other will be the following Monday."

He fought to gather his thoughts. "That should give me time to regroup between interviews." He paused outside Honey's stall. "So what's the problem?"

"Um…" She poked her head inside the stall. "Honey's out of food."

He simply stared. "Did you really need me for that?"

"No, it was just an excuse to get you away from Andrew."

Suddenly realizing how irrationally he'd been behaving, he chuckled. He'd been taking his frustrations out on his brother, much like when they were younger. "I guess I was acting rather juvenile."

"Um, yeah. So what's the real problem?"

"Real problem?"

"Yes. Something's obviously bothering you. Because the man I saw in there was not the Noah I know."

He crossed his arms over his chest. "Then maybe you don't really know me."

Shifting, she said, "Maybe. But I don't think that's the case."

A silent moment ticked by, the two of them in an apparent battle of wills.

Looking away, he leaned against the opposite stall. "You must have been busy this week. Haven't seen you around here much."

Now she refused to make eye contact. "I guess I was hiding." She opened the stall door.

"Hiding?"

She looked at him then. "I walked away from you last week without any kind of explanation. Leaving you with the impression that I don't trust you."

Did that mean— Straightening, he moved closer, eager to know. "Do you? Trust me, that is?"

"I do."

The tension in his shoulders eased.

"It was the horse I didn't trust." She continued, "But at the time I was too afraid to tell you."

"I don't get it. If you trust me, why were you afraid?"

She shrugged. "I don't know." Her gaze lowered momentarily then bounced back to his. "No, that's not true. I do know."

He waited for her to continue.

She squared her shoulders. "All my life people have discounted my feelings. 'Lily, don't be silly. Lily, you're overreacting.' I got good at keeping things to myself."

Relief and sadness mingled as he reached for her hand. "Lily, I don't ever want you to be anything but real with me."

Her nod was quick. Too quick. She turned away and tried to break free, as though she didn't believe him.

But he refused to let go. He wanted her to understand that he wasn't like those other people.

Still holding her hand, he waited for her to look at him.

When she finally did, he smiled and said, "Just Lily is my friend, and I like her just the way she is."

Chapter Fourteen

Sitting at the desk in Noah's office late Wednesday morning, Lily stared at the Ouray visitor's guide, longing to see more of the San Juan Mountains. Since the first time her friend Kayla had mentioned that Ouray was the jeeping capital of the world, she'd been intrigued. The thought of traveling old mine roads built almost a century and a half ago and seeing a landscape that had been virtually untouched by man had sparked her desire to spend the entire summer here. And yet there was still so much she hadn't seen.

Then again, when she planned this trip, horseback riding had never entered her mind, let alone roping lessons, riding lessons, promoting a rodeo school and caring for a neglected horse. Not that she was complaining. Because even though her plans might have changed, there was plenty of good coming from those changes.

Still, if she could find the time…

"Mommy, look." Her daughter gestured to the stack of clipboards now complete with consent forms.

"Thank you, Piper." She closed the booklet and set

it aside. "You did a very good job." Lily had been trying to help out in the office more.

"What's going on?" Noah strode into the office just then, with Colton not far behind.

"Just taking care of some paperwork for you." She pushed away from the desk and stood. "How was the trail ride?" The rain had stopped Monday afternoon, leaving plenty of sunshine and pleasant temperatures in its wake.

"Good. Soggy in a few low spots, but we were able to make it onto the mountain."

"Yeah and we saw some bear tracks." Colton's green eyes were wide. Since there were only three people in the group, Noah had invited him to go along.

"But no bears," Noah was quick to add before addressing her again. "What have you two been up to?"

"Not much." She picked up a piece of paper from the desk. "Travis Vasquez's mother called to say he won't be able to make his lesson today or anytime in the near future." She held out the paper, meeting Noah's gaze. "Apparently he has mononucleosis."

"Mono? The kissing disease?"

"Eww." Piper's face contorted as she petted Patches the cat.

Lily chuckled. "I…think I've heard it called that."

"You mean you can get a disease from kissing?" Colton looked from her to Noah and back, and she wasn't sure if she should be alarmed by his interest or not.

"That's right, Colton." Noah sent her a stealthy wink. "So you'd better watch out." Grinning, he continued, "Looks like I'll be able to work with both of you kids this afternoon then."

Lily bit her lip, her gaze drifting to the sunlight pouring through the window. "How's the weather looking? Any clouds?"

"Nah, they're saying it's supposed to be another nice afternoon."

"Hmm…" She eyed the visitor's guide, wondering if all the tours for this afternoon were already full. If not, maybe they could get in. Otherwise, she could drive down to—

"Did you ever take the kids to Ironton?"

She looked up, realizing that he'd caught her daydreaming. "No, I haven't found the time. However, if you wouldn't mind—" she mustered her best smile "—I was thinking I might see if we could get on a Jeep tour for this afternoon."

"A Jeep tour?" Colton whined. "What about my lesson?"

Noah grinned. "I've got a better idea."

Seemed no matter what she suggested, he always had a better idea. And while he had yet to let her down—

"What if I took you all to a place that's off the beaten path?"

Curiosity lifted her brow. "What do you call off the beaten path?"

"Someplace the tours don't go."

She liked the sound of that. "Go on."

"You like wildflowers?"

"I *love* wildflowers."

"I imagine with all this sun—" he motioned toward the window "—they're quite brilliant."

"Flowers?" Her son appeared more than a little chagrined.

Noah glanced his way. "Did I mention a couple of really cool glacial lakes, too?"

"Ooh, can we go swimming?" Piper beamed.

"Okay, so how do we get to this place?" Lily crossed her arms over her chest. "Rent a Jeep? Unless your truck can make it?"

"Truck's too wide. And our chances of finding an available rental Jeep are slim to none with this weather." He wasn't building a very good case.

"So what are we supposed to do?"

"Not to worry." He pulled his phone from his shirt pocket. "I'll simply call Matt to see if he'll swap vehicles with me for the afternoon."

Lily was afraid to get her hopes up. Yet a little over an hour later, they had grabbed a round of hamburgers at Granny's Kitchen and picked up the Jeep and were on a dirt road weaving their way into the mountains.

Since they'd removed the vehicle's top, the sun shone down on them, warming Lily's skin as well as her heart. This was even better than she'd imagined, and she could hardly wait to see where Noah was taking them.

Through sunglasses, she eyed the cowboy-turned-tour-guide in the driver's seat. With his Broncos ball cap, aviator sunglasses and stubble lining his jaw, he looked even more rugged than usual. Throw in the muscles straining the sleeves of his T-shirt, and any woman would swoon.

However, she'd seen the kind, wounded heart that beat inside Noah. The one that longed to help hurting people as well as hurting horses. The one that still grieved the loss of his wife. And that made it more and more difficult for her to resist him.

But resist she must. For her children, if not herself.

Because August 15 would be here before they knew it, and then it would be back to life as usual, which sounded rather unappealing at the moment.

The engine groaned as the road grew steeper, and Noah came to a stop.

"Is there a problem?" Because this narrow road would be a really bad place to break down.

He adjusted the manual gearshift. "No, just switching over to four-wheel drive."

She let go a sigh. "That's good."

"Don't worry, Lily." His smile was reassuring. "You won't be disappointed."

They continued on, winding around a wall of dark gray rock that stretched toward the blue sky, while on the opposite side, a knee-shaking drop-off led to a valley blanketed with white-barked aspens and deep green conifers.

Colton poked his head between the two front seats. "Did they really used to bring mules down this road?"

"They sure did." Noah eyed the boy in his rearview mirror, both hands firmly on the steering wheel. "Back then it was the only way to get supplies to the mines and to bring the ore down, so they had to build these roads."

"They built them?" Colton peered down at the road. "How?"

"Dynamite."

"Whoa..."

Did Noah know how to capture the boy's interest or what?

"Yep, they dynamited out large chunks of the mountainsides all over this area, allowing them to create these roads we still travel today."

"Now that's cool." The kid leaned back in his seat, smiling.

"If you get an opportunity," Noah hollered over the engine, "you all should stop by the museum in town sometime. They've got a mine display in the basement where you can see and learn all sorts of stuff."

They moved on up the road, waving to other vehicles as they passed. Something that was very precarious in a few of the narrower sections and made Lily more than grateful that it wasn't her doing the driving.

When they finally turned off the main road, the first thing she saw was a relatively wide stream in their path. Fortunately, there was also a bridge.

Noah revved the engine, eyeing the stream. "Think we can make it, gang?"

"Yay!" cheered the kids.

Lily jerked her head toward him. "You're not seriously considering going through that, are you?"

"It's part of the experience."

"But what if we get caught in the current?"

"You're right. I'd better get a running start." With that, he put the vehicle into Reverse then, before she knew what was happening, they were moving head-long into the water.

She shrieked when the cold water splashed against her skin and couldn't help laughing at the sight of her children doing the same.

"That was cold," giggled Piper when they came to a stop on the other side.

"Yeah, but it was fun," said Colton.

"Things are going to get a little bumpier now." Noah eased on the gas. "So you might want to hold on."

He wasn't kidding, either. Moving into the woods, it

felt as though they were bumping from one boulder to the next, making it impossible for her to take any pictures of the wildflowers lining the trail.

The air smelled of fragrant firs and earth as they picked their way up another rocky rise, then crept back down, only to repeat it one more time. Mud went flying and the back end of the Jeep came down hard, jolting them to an abrupt stop.

Everyone went silent. The only sound was that of the engine and some birds chattering nearby.

Noah adjust the gearshift. Eased off the clutch. Yet they didn't move.

He tried again, but to no avail. The tires continued to spin.

Hopping out, he rounded the vehicle, his brows drawn together.

Not a good sign.

Finally, he stood in front of them, hands perched on his denim-clad hips. "Sorry, guys, but it looks like we're stuck."

"Stuck?" Surely he was kidding.

"Stuck," he confirmed.

Her shoulders sagged. Now what were they supposed to do? It wasn't like roadside assistance could make it up here to help.

Disappointment wove its way through her. What about their destination? The wildflowers, glacial lakes and her off the beaten path?

Instead, they were stuck.

There was no way Noah was going to let Lily down. He'd promised to take her someplace special, and that's exactly what he intended to do. After all, this wasn't his first trip into the mountains.

Eyeing his passengers, he said, "Don't worry. We'll be on the road in no time."

"How?" Lily unhooked her seat belt and stood on her seat, batting a tree limb out of the way. "Are you going to push us out?"

Smiling, he took in the space around them, the position of the wheels. "While I appreciate your faith in me, that would not be a viable option. Fortunately, we have a winch." He moved toward the vehicle.

Lily was beside him in no time. "At the risk of sounding like a city girl, what's a winch?"

"That thing right there." He pointed to the spool attached to the front of his brother's vehicle, with a cable coiled around it.

She looked at it then back at him. "What does it do?"

"Gets us out of the mud." Reaching toward the contraption, he released the clutch. "Colton, would you grab that yellow strap from the back of the Jeep and bring it to me, please?"

"Yes, sir." The kid hopped out of the vehicle.

"Piper, would you mind keeping your mama company over there for me?" He pointed to a nearby rise.

"Okay." She unhooked her seat belt and jumped down.

"Good girl."

"Is this the one?" Colton came toward him, holding up the strap.

"That's it."

In no time, he and Colton had a length of cable pulled out and hooked to the strap Noah had looped around a tree several feet away.

"All right, gang. Looks like we're ready to roll."

With Lily and the kids standing a safe distance away, Noah attached the controller and turned the power on.

"Would you look at that," he heard Lily say. "That thing is pulling the Jeep right out."

"Cool," said Colton.

"Yay for Noah." Piper jumped up and down as the vehicle came to rest on solid ground.

He couldn't help chuckling. Having them around did wonders for his ego.

He turned off the power and faced his audience. "Anyone ready to see some lakes?"

They hurried back and piled into the vehicle while he disconnected everything.

When he returned to the driver's seat, he looked at Lily. "The journey is always better when there's a little adventure involved."

"Well, it was definitely a learning experience." She hooked her seat belt. "And I'm sorry I doubted you. But now I'm ready to see some wildflowers."

"All right then." He shifted into gear, making a mental note to approach this section with a little more caution on their way out.

A short time later, they emerged from a forest of conifers into an alpine meadow covered with wildflowers in every color of the rainbow. Yellows, pinks, purples, reds and blues.

Lily's gasp was like a tickle on his ear. "Stop, please."

He readily complied as she stood on her seat, camera at the ready.

"This is incredible." She glanced down at him. "I've never seen wildflowers like this. So brilliant. So abundant." Her camera clicked multiple times.

Peering up at her, he said, "Can I move on up to the lake?"

She immediately dropped back into her seat, her smile almost childlike. "Yes, please."

She looked so cute. Like a kid with a long-awaited gift.

They continued through the meadow, its delicate floral fragrance wafting around them.

"Whoa…" Standing, Colton clutched the roll bar as they approached the lake. "How did the water get so blue?"

"Pretty cool, huh?" Noah brought the Jeep to a stop and turned off the engine. "It has to do with something called glacial, or rock, flour. It's so light that it stays suspended in the water. The sunlight reflects off it, giving the lake that unmistakable turquoise hue."

Lily's feet were on the ground in an instant. "I've lived in Colorado all of my adult life, and I've never seen anything as beautiful as this place." She twisted left then right, snapping pictures.

"That's because you've never been to Ouray." He lifted Piper out of the vehicle as Colton jumped out the other side, then set her on the ground and watched her take off after her mother and brother.

Drawing in a deep breath, he took in the unmatched beauty of his surroundings. He hadn't been up here in years. Silver Basin was more brilliant than he remembered. The flowers, the lake…all of it above the timberline and hidden by craggy gray peaks. Here, his worries seemed to fade away.

Under a gorgeous blue sky, he looked around, surprised to discover they were the only people there.

Something that could change at any moment, so they'd best take advantage of it.

"Come on." Approaching the water, he motioned for Lily and her children to follow him. "Let's walk around the lake." A task easily achieved since the upper lake wasn't that big. And the lower lake was even smaller. He'd show them that one on their way down.

"How come nobody's here?" Lily walked beside him as the children ran on ahead through vibrant green grass and over chunks of gray rock that had broken free of the mountains to dot the landscape.

He shrugged. "Like I said, off the beaten path. Not that it's always this way."

Her smile was beyond contented as she tried to take in every aspect of the area. "If I lived here, I think I'd come up here as often as I could, just to get away."

"Funny, my mother used to say the same thing."

"Did she come up here a lot?"

"As often as she could." He dodged around a large rock. "Which, I'm sure, wasn't near as often as she would have liked. This was her favorite place to escape."

"Your mom had good taste." Lily paused in front of a spruce to take some pictures of Colton and Piper tossing rocks along the water's edge. "Though with five boys, I can't imagine what she'd want to escape from." Lowering her camera, she sent him a knowing look that made him smile.

They began walking again.

"What was she like?"

Lily's question was unexpected. Yet, he knew it was because she cared. And it had been a long time since someone cared about him.

For a moment, he gazed at the sky, trying to gather

his thoughts. "She was devoted to her family. Loved Jesus and horses. Was an amazing cook." He glanced toward Lily. "And I never saw a better example of a marriage partnership than the one between my dad and her. The ranch had been their dream from the time they first started dating in high school."

"Aww…" She paused to take another picture.

"They both grew up in town, but Dad loved old Westerns and Mama loved horses. So they started with one small tract of land when they got married and then added to it over the years."

"It must have been hard for your father when she passed away."

"It was hard for all of us, but yeah, he struggled." He shoved his hands into the pockets of his jeans. "Poured himself into the ranch, either to help keep her legacy going or simply to occupy his mind."

Lily looked up at him, tucking her long hair behind her ear. "How did she die?"

"Cancer." Unable to look at her, he stared up at the jagged peaks, blinking.

"It's obvious how much she meant to all of you."

"She was an amazing woman, all right. Had to be to put up with my father and us boys."

Lily puffed out a soft chuckle as they found themselves near the Jeep again.

"She knew how to keep all of us in line, including my father." He spied the kids running into the meadow. "Only one of the reasons we adored her so much."

Lily blinked several times. "What was her favorite wildflower?"

"Columbine, of course." Reaching down, he plucked one. "Though she was partial to anything purple or blue." He handed the flower to Lily. "You remind me of my mother in some ways."

She tilted her head. "I'm guessing the part about loving horses isn't one of them."

He felt himself grin. "No. But your commitment to your children, your determination to bring them up with morals and values, your faith… The two of you would have been fast friends."

She studied the flower in her hand. "That may be one of the nicest compliments anyone has ever paid me."

Staring down at her, his pulse quickened as emotions he hadn't felt in a long time wove their way around his heart. Emotions he hadn't felt since Jaycee died. Emotions he'd vowed to never feel again.

He took a step back.

"Hey, Mom!" Colton's voice had her turning around. "You gotta come see all these flowers."

Smiling, she said, "Well, now there's something I never thought I'd hear him say." She took off in the direction of her children.

He watched the three of them, his stomach twisting in knots as one thing became as clear as the water in these lakes.

Bringing Lily up here was a bad idea.

Chapter Fifteen

Lily stared out of the office window, grateful to Noah for taking them to Silver Basin. In part because her children had yet to stop talking about it. That and the fact that the rain had returned the next day, harder than it had been before. This time, the showers weren't relegated to only the afternoons. Instead, it had rained all day and all night for the past five days. Add that to what they'd received the week before, and everything was drenched, meaning no trail rides, no Jeep tours...

No wonder Noah had been so moody.

At least they were getting a small reprieve this morning, allowing her children to play outside for a while. For some reason, they found stomping around in the mud in their rubber boots fun.

Since Noah and Clint had gone off to help someone at a neighboring ranch, Lily had the office to herself, giving her the perfect opportunity to address the freshly printed VIP invitations for the open-house event. They now had demonstrations planned for the event—roping, barrel racing, bronc riding—as well as photo ops with Noah, cake, balloons...

She licked another envelope. If only she could talk him into getting a mechanical bull.

Reaching for another invitation, she prayed she and the kids would be able to make it back out here for the event. Labor Day was a long weekend, after all.

"Mom!"

"Mommy!"

The calls came simultaneously.

She pushed away from the desk and hurried into the lobby before her children decided to track mud everywhere. "What is it?"

Colton huffed and puffed as though he'd been running. "There's a calf in the pasture, and he's all by himself."

"He's crying." Piper pouted.

Slipping out of her shoes and into her own rubber boots, she said, "Let's go have a look."

She followed them out the door and up the drive, dodging puddles as she went until they reached the barn. Sure enough, in the middle of the muddy pasture, a cute little black calf stood unmoving, repeatedly calling for his mother.

Hands on her hips, Lily scanned the area, but she didn't see any cows.

"We have to save him, Mommy."

"Save him from what, Piper? Maybe his mama left him there on purpose and told him to stay put until she got back."

"But what if she forgot about him?"

Lily bit back a chuckle. "His mama won't forget. So I suggest we wait until Noah and his father get back and let them handle it."

Her children looked at each other, seemingly satisfied with her response.

"Can we keep playing?" asked Colton.

"Yes, you may. But try not to get too muddy, all right?"

"We won't."

Ha! She headed back to the stable. Like that was going to happen.

The phone was ringing when she stepped inside. She hastily stomped her boots on the mat before rushing into the office to answer it.

"Abundant Blessings Ranch."

"Yes, this is Lauren Pearson with the *Grand Junction Daily Sentinel*. I'd like to speak with Noah Stephens."

The *Grand Junction Daily Sentinel* was one of the newspapers she'd sent a press release to. "I'm sorry, he's not available at the moment. This is his publicist, Lily Davis. Is there anything I can help you with?"

"We're looking at doing a brief article on the rodeo school. Would you be able to answer a few questions?"

She wheeled the chair closer to the desk and sat down. "I'll do my best."

While the questions were easy enough, they dragged on forever. Glancing at the clock on the wall, Lily realized twenty minutes had passed and she hadn't heard so much as a peep from her children. They were either having fun or getting into trouble. Maybe both.

"Ms. Pearson, I thank you for your interest—"

"Mommy!" Piper cried as she swung the door open. "Help!"

"I'm sorry, I need to go." Lily hung up the phone as her daughter hurried into the office, tears streaming down her face.

"Colton fell into the river!"

"What?" She felt the color leave her face as images of her son being carried away by the current filled her mind.

Piper grabbed her hand and tugged her toward the door. "Hurry, Mommy. He slid down the bank, and he can't get out."

With all the rain, the river was rushing fast and furious.

She had to get to Colton now.

"Come on." She pushed through the door and aimed straight for the UTV parked on the side of the building. "Hop in, Piper." She threw herself into the driver's seat and reached for the ignition. "Where's the key?" Her gaze darted around the vehicle. She hastily checked the glove box. Nothing.

"We could ride Duke?"

"Piper, I don't know how to saddle a horse."

"He's in the arena. Noah left him there."

Lily did not want to ride Duke. But she couldn't afford to waste any more time, either. She had to find her son.

"All right. Let's go."

Lily sprinted ahead, led Duke out of the arena and brought him outside before lifting Piper into the saddle.

She stroked the animal's muzzle. "Noah trusts you, so I guess I'm going to have to, too, Duke. Help me get to Colton."

With a deep breath, she put her foot into the stirrup, climbed into the saddle behind her daughter and urged Duke in the direction of the river.

The horse moved swiftly, his muscular legs eating up the distance faster than she expected.

Why had she let the kids play outside alone? She

should have been watching them. She squeezed her eyes shut. *God, please let Colton be all right. Keep him safe. Don't let the water take him under.*

Approaching the river, the roar of the current heightened her anxiety. She pulled back on the reins. "Where is he, Piper?"

"Over there." She pointed. "By the tree."

Lily guided Duke to the tree then dismounted, dragging Piper with her. "Colton?"

"Here!"

Her gaze combed the muddy riverbank until she spotted him clinging to a tree limb. She rushed to where he was and dropped to her belly, the sodden earth soaking her shirt and jeans as she tried to reach him.

He was too far down. She tried to push her body out farther, tried to grab him, but it was too far. She'd risk going down, too.

"Hurry!" her son cried.

God, help me. I don't know what to do.

"Mommy?"

Turning, she saw her daughter pointing to the coiled rope attached to Duke's saddle.

"Hold on, Colton. I'll be right back." Lily leaped to her feet, sprinted toward the horse and grabbed the rope. She tied one end to the tree and then stretched it so she could send the looped end down to Colton. But the rope was too short.

She looked around, her breathing ragged. There was nothing close enough.

Her gaze drifted to Duke. The animal was massive. If he could hold Noah, surely he could support the weight of her son.

Knowing that was her only hope, she quickly untied

the rope from the tree and returned to the horse, eyeing the saddle horn. She'd seen Noah, Colton and the other cowboys do this at least a hundred times. *Think, Lily.*

She had to climb into the saddle to reach the thing. When she did, she twisted the open end of the rope around the horn a few times, then cinched it under the last loop, praying it would hold.

Dismounting, she led the horse closer to where her son held on for his life and lowered the looped end toward Colton. "Can you hold on to the branch with one hand long enough to grab the rope with your other?"

He glanced down at the rushing water, then back to her. "I—I think so."

She could see the fear in his eyes. He'd already been there so long. He must be exhausted, his muscles spent. *God, please don't let my boy fall. Give him strength.*

Her grip tightened on the rope as she waited for him to take hold. All the while never taking her eyes off her son. "You can do this, Colton. I know you can."

He nodded and, in one swift motion, let go of the branch and stuck his free hand through the loop before wrapping his fingers around the rope.

"Good job." The rope was taut. The length perfect. "Now the other hand."

Again, he nodded and, after a moment, he moved his left hand from the branch to the rope.

"Okay, good. Now hold on while I pull you up." But the more she tugged, the more her feet slipped beneath her. *God, help me!*

She straightened, the horse coming into her periphery. "Keep holding on, Colton," she yelled over the sound of the river.

A handful of steps and she was beside Duke. "Piper,

stay back." She thrust herself into the saddle, took hold of the reins and pulled with all her might.

The horse took one step back. Then another and another.

"It's working!" Just like the Jeep up on the mountain. "Hold on, Colton!"

A few moments later, he appeared over the edge of the bank, his knuckles white as he continued to cling to the rope.

Lily's heart pounded. "Attaboy, Duke. Just a few more steps." She continued backward until her boy was on solid ground, then jumped down and rushed to his side.

She drew him into her arms as he tossed the rope aside. "Thank God you're okay." Setting him away from her, she smoothed a hand over his wet hair, surveying him to make sure he wasn't hurt. That's when she saw the tears streaming down his mud-streaked cheeks. "Oh, it's okay, baby." She clutched him to her again, her own tears falling as his arms wound around her waist. "You're safe. I've got you."

"I'm sorry, Mom. I know I shouldn't have come down here."

"No, you shouldn't have." She kissed his forehead. "But we can discuss that later. For now, let's get you back to the stable."

Clouds had filled the sky at some point during the ordeal, and the rain started to fall again as the kids climbed atop Duke. Lily took hold of the reins to walk the horse.

"What are you doing, Mom?" Her son was covered in mud. "You can get up here, too."

"There's not enough room in the saddle."

"That's okay. You can sit in the saddle with Piper, and I'll sit back here." He patted the spot just behind the saddle.

She knew Duke could handle the weight, but, "We can do that? I mean, he won't try to buck you off or anything?"

Her boy smiled then. A smile she'd never been happier to see. "No. We're not going that far, anyway."

"All right then." She climbed behind her daughter and felt Colton's arms around her waist. Relief washed over her along with the rain. By the grace of God, she'd done it. She'd saved her son. God had given her the strength and the wherewithal to do what she needed to do, including getting on a horse. She found she actually didn't mind it too much, especially now that Colton was safe.

Perhaps riding was within her realm of possibility, after all.

Noah watched the wipers on his father's pickup slap back and forth across the windshield, the gray skies a perfect match for his mood. "Just what we need. More rain."

Dad clutched the steering wheel. "Not like it's unexpected this time of year."

A sports car whizzed past them then, going well over the speed limit. And on a wet road, no less.

His father growled. "Everybody's in a hurry."

That's precisely why they'd spent the last few hours at Jim Osborn's ranch. Some idiot flying down the highway last night lost control and took out a good hundred feet of fence. Every rancher knows that cattle on the highway spells bad news for everyone, so Noah and his father had packed up early and gone to help put up a temporary barrier in order to avoid such a problem.

Now they were headed back to Abundant Blessings, where he'd no doubt have to face Lily again. After all, she had agreed to hold down the fort while they were gone. Still, since their trip up to Silver Basin, he'd been trying to keep things a little more businesslike between them. Call it self-preservation. But he'd made a vow. One he intended to keep.

Perhaps he could knock the kids' lessons out early, giving them no reason to hang around. Not that they ever really needed a reason. They'd simply become a part of everyday life at the ranch, and, as much as he didn't want to, he liked having them there. All of them.

He supposed he could make himself scarce by working in the new building. Now that the chutes and pens had been installed, his vision was starting to come to life. He'd be able to find plenty to keep himself busy and away from Lily.

Dad turned into the ranch, the truck rumbling over the cattle guard. "Want me to drop you at the stable?"

"Nah. I need to grab a fresh shirt."

They were almost to the house when his father leaned closer to the windshield. "Is that what I think it is?"

Noah looked up. "It can't be." He blinked once. Twice. "Lily's on a horse?"

"Not just any horse. That's Duke."

Noah puffed out a disbelieving laugh. "You have got to be kidding me." He smiled, wondering what could have convinced her to do that. In the rain, no less.

Yet there they were. Lily, Colton and Piper all riding Duke.

"I gotta find out what's going on." He piled out of

the dually before it had come to a complete stop and jogged through the mud until he met them just beyond the house.

Lily smiled down at him, her long hair wet, her shirt and jeans covered in mud…and he felt something shift inside.

He continued to stare up at them, despite the rain pelting his face. "What are you doing?"

"Oh, you know." Lily lifted a shoulder. "It's such a beautiful day, thought we'd take a ride."

Well, his day had indeed gotten brighter. "No, seriously."

"Colton fell into the river." Piper was nothing if not candid. "But Mommy saved him."

Noah's chin dropped.

Lily nodded her confirmation while Colton appeared rather sheepish.

"What's goin' on?" Dad joined them.

"Colton fell into the river."

"Do you have to keep saying that, Piper?" Her brother frowned.

She twisted to look at him. "I'm just telling the truth."

Noah bit back a laugh. "Why don't we get out of the rain and you can tell us the whole story."

"Good idea," said Lily.

They heard a calf bawl.

"Aww, look, Mommy." Piper pointed across the pasture. "He's still there."

"Hmm… Doesn't look like he's moved." Lily looked left and right. "No sign of his mama yet, either." Her gaze lowered to Noah and his father. "The little guy's been crying all morning." She eyed the calf again. "Do you think he could be stuck in the mud?"

"It's possible." Dad studied the situation. "Guess I'd better go see if I can help the little fella."

"Can I come?" Colton straightened.

"Sure." Dad waved the boy down. "You're already muddy."

Colton swung his leg over, then paused. "Is it okay, Mom?"

She grinned. "Go ahead."

"I want to come, too." Piper started to get down, but her mother stopped her with a hand to her shoulder.

"It's all right," said Dad. "She can come."

Noah helped the girl down and watched her run off through the mud before returning his attention to her mother. "How about you? You want to help, too?"

"I think I'm good." She stroked Duke's neck. "But I am curious about what they're going to do."

"Dad'll just pick the calf up. Move him someplace safe, then wait for his mama to come for him."

"What if she can't find him?" Spoken like a true mother.

"She'll find him." He took a step back. "You comfortable riding Duke back to the stable or you want me to take over?"

"I think I'm good."

Actually, he was surprised just how relaxed she seemed to be.

She urged Duke forward, and Noah walked alongside them. "By the way, where do you keep the keys to the UTV?"

"In my pocket." He tugged them out to show her.

Looking down at him, she lifted a brow. "A lot of good they did me there."

"So what happened?"

All the way to the stable and on to Duke's stall, she explained what had transpired.

"You should have called me." He removed the horse's saddle and moved just outside the door to set it atop its stand.

"There was no time." She paced a few feet away, no doubt reliving everything in her mind. "All I could think of was that I had to get to Colton. Fortunately, everything turned out all right."

When she looked at him, he saw the angst in her pretty green eyes. Only then did he realize what she must have gone through. How terrified she must have been.

And he hated that he hadn't been here to help her. He clenched his fists, longing to take her into his arms and comfort her. To be that one person she could lean on.

But he couldn't.

He shoved his hands in his pockets and took a step back, dirt grinding beneath his boot. "You overcame your fear and got on a horse to do it."

Her smile grew wide. "I did."

"How was it?"

She studied Duke for a moment. "Not nearly as frightening as I thought it would be."

"I think you were already frightened."

"You'll get no argument from me there." Rubbing her arms, she turned away. "I've never been so scared. And not knowing what the situation was…" Her voice cracked. "It felt like everything was moving in slow motion. I was so afraid I wouldn't make it. That he'd—"

She let go a sob. Her shoulders shook, robbing him of whatever resolve he might have had.

Closing the short distance between them, he moved in front of her and took her into his arms. "Let it out, Lily. It's okay, I've got you."

Her body melted against his as she continued to cry. "I was so afraid." She hiccuped.

"I know." He rubbed a soothing hand across her back. Her hair was wet against his cheek and smelled of something tropical. "You did everything right, though. And you saved your son." He felt her nod against his shoulder. "You were very brave."

She stilled then and sniffed as she pulled away. "I was, wasn't I?" Her watery eyes found his, testing his strength.

He cleared his throat. "If moms received medals, you'd be first in line."

Smiling, she said, "Just having my son here is reward enough." She stepped away then, breaking whatever connection they'd had. It was a connection he didn't want, but it had him wondering if he could overcome his fear and allow himself to love again.

Chapter Sixteen

Lily had, indeed, been brave yesterday. When Colton was in danger, she had gotten on a horse and she'd saved him. Question was, could she bring herself to ride again? In a normal, everyday setting, without the threat of losing one of her children propelling her into action, could she do it?

There was only one way to find out.

Having dropped Colton off at the ranch earlier and with Piper playing at Kenzie's, she pulled up to the stable, contemplating not only what she hoped to do today, but all that had transpired yesterday. Between almost losing her son and then being held in Noah's capable arms, savoring his warmth, drawing from his strength, she wasn't sure she'd ever be the same.

The memory of his embrace seemed to have taken up residence in her mind and had her thinking how nice it would be to have a companion. Someone to share life's joys and help bear the struggles. A safe place to land when things got tough.

Was she a fool to think of him as anything more than a friend?

Yes, yes, she was. Hadn't she already gone over that with herself multiple times? Noah's actions were nothing more than those of a friend. Friends comforted each other.

But do friends whisper sweetly in your ear?

Why was she doing this to herself? Her children needed her. Yesterday had driven that point home, loud and clear. Besides, she'd be going back to Denver in a few weeks, so she might as well do herself a favor and keep her heart in check.

Especially since her little plan to test herself involved Noah's help.

She waited for the rain to let up before making a run for the stable. Unfortunately, the wet conditions meant any riding would have to be done in the stable, where Colton would likely see her.

Lily paused at the wooden door, watching drops of water fall sporadically from the overhang. What if she freaked out again? What if she couldn't do it?

I can do all things through Christ who strengthens me.

The verse from Philippians, chapter four, gave her hope. God had given her both the physical and emotional strength she'd needed to save Colton. Why would He stop now?

Inside, she shrugged out of her rain jacket and placed it on a hook just inside the office before seeking out Noah. She found him in the arena, still working with Colton on his roping skills. Perhaps she should have him teach her how to rope. That way, if she ever found herself in a situation similar to yesterday—which she had better not—she could simply lasso her children.

She waved as she passed, then continued on to see Honey.

The horse watched her as she approached, something Lily was getting used to. Not to mention the way the once-neglected animal seemed to stomp her feet, as though she was excited to see her.

"Good morning, my Honey girl." She slid the door aside. "How are you doing today?"

Honey nickered her response, a sound that never ceased to delight Lily. This once-neglected horse had come a long way in the past few weeks. She was actually starting to get some meat on her bones, which once seemed as though they might poke right through her skin. Her eyes shimmered, and she just seemed happy.

Retrieving the brush from the wall outside the stall, Lily swiped it over Honey's much-improved coat. "Does that feel good?"

The horse bobbed her head, making Lily chuckle.

"You're getting good at communicating with me."

"Lily?"

She turned at the sound of Noah's voice. "In here."

He placed a hand on either side of the stall's opening. "How's it going?"

"We're just enjoying a little rubdown." She continued to brush.

"No, I mean how are *you*?" He moved inside the stall. "Have you recovered from yesterday?"

"I think so. However—" her hands stilled, and she stepped back "—I need your help with something."

"Anything."

Her thumb ran across the bristles in her hand. "I need you to set me up with a horse."

"Set you up?"

"To ride. Or at least attempt to."

"Attempt? What about yesterday?" He stared down at her, confused.

"That's just it. I need to prove to myself that what happened yesterday wasn't a fluke. That I really can ride a horse without panicking."

"I get it." He crossed his arms over his chest. "You think you were only able to do it because of the circumstances."

"Exactly."

"Are you sure you're not overthinking this? You seemed pretty relaxed yesterday."

"That's why I need to find out." Her eyes drifted to the stall's dirt floor. "And I'd prefer Colton not see me."

"In case you fail."

Lifting her gaze, she nodded.

"Let me see what I can do." He left her then and, about fifteen minutes later, sent her a text message.

Colton is helping Dad in the barn. Meet me in the arena.

With a deep breath, she gave Honey a final nose rub. "I'll let you know how it goes."

Approaching the arena, she saw Noah waiting for her with the same dappled gray horse he'd tried to get her to ride a couple of weeks ago. Checkers.

She closed her eyes. *I can do this.*

Noah smiled as she came alongside him. "You can do this, Lily. I know you can." His faith in her had her smiling back, albeit rather nervously.

He stepped away. "You know what to do. Don't talk yourself out of it."

Her mind rewound to yesterday. Knowing Duke was the only way for her to get to Colton had gotten her into the saddle the first time. After that, it was pure necessity.

And everything turned out fine.

The ride back had even been somewhat enjoyable. The three of them talking while they meandered along. Once her blood pressure returned to normal, Lily had realized horseback riding was kind of fun. From atop Duke, she'd had a better perspective. She could see things she wasn't able to see on the ground. Such as that abandoned calf.

She reached for Checkers's saddle. Shoved her foot in the stirrup and pulled herself up.

"How does that feel?" Noah watched her.

Good question. She waited for the panic to set in. The sweaty palms. The churning stomach.

Nothing.

"I…think I'm okay." She reached for the reins. Nudged the horse's sides with her heels.

Checkers started walking at a snail's pace.

"Nudge him again," Noah coaxed.

She did. Then she felt Noah's eyes on her all the way around the arena.

Pride swelled inside her. With God's help, she'd done it. She'd overcome her fear and was actually riding a horse.

She made another lap at an even faster clip. "Woo-hoo!"

After one more round, she and Checkers came to a stop beside Noah.

Hands slung low on his hips, he grinned up at her. "How was it?"

Where did she begin? "Freeing. Exhilarating. Amazing."

"So you enjoyed it."

"Very much."

He held out a hand as she dismounted. Then refused to let go once her feet were on the ground. "Do you have any idea how proud I am of you?"

She lifted a shoulder. "If it's even half as proud as I am of me..."

"I'm just sorry I can't take credit for helping you."

"What do you mean? You got Colton out of the way and readied the horse. You encouraged me."

"But you had the determination. You wanted to prove something to yourself, and you did." The feel of his fingers against hers, the intensity of his gaze... "I think you deserve a reward."

"A reward?"

Still holding her hand, he tugged her across the arena. "Yes, and I know just the thing." He led her from the stable into the new building. But unlike the last time she'd passed through the corridor that connected the two, the metal walls were now covered with the same rustic wood they'd used in the stable.

"When did you do this?" Not only did it warm the space, it visually tied the two buildings together.

No response. Instead, he continued up the corridor until it ended at the arena.

Her mouth dropped open. Though she'd been in there once before, the day she found Noah and Andrew arguing, she hadn't paid much attention. "This place is huge." She eyed the metal rafters that spanned the ceiling. This arena was double, maybe triple the size of the one in the stable.

He veered left, past a handful of stalls that were also new and lined with the same rough wood. Approaching the far end of the building, she saw the pens and chutes.

"Where are you taking me?" Couldn't he at least let her look around? Maybe give her a tour of new place?

Finally, he stopped beside something covered in a blue tarp and let go of her hand. "I was going to wait until later to show you this, but I think you deserve to see it now."

She couldn't imagine, but, "Okay."

"Close your eyes."

Her brow lifted.

Arms crossed, he stared down at her. "I'm not removing the tarp until you close your eyes."

"Oh, all right." She covered her eyes. "Satisfied?"

"Give me one minute."

The rustle of the tarp had curiosity mingling with excitement.

"Okay, you can look."

Lowering her hands, she waited for her eyes to adjust.

Staring at the red barrel-shaped thing with straps, she couldn't— She burst out laughing then, realizing what it was. "A mechanical bull?" She looked at him now. "But I thought you said they were an insult."

"No, comparing rodeo cowboys to the cowboy wannabes in *Urban Cowboy* was an insult. Besides, this isn't mechanical."

"It isn't?"

"No. See the handle back here?"

She twisted to see. "Oh. Sure enough."

"Are you ready to get on?"

"Me?"

Moving so close that she could smell the woodsy scent of his soap, he lowered his head until his mouth was right by her ear. "Come on, Lily. Don't you trust me?"

She couldn't help smiling as she looked up at him. The twinkle in his browner-than-brown eyes. The teasing tilt of his lips. She did trust him. Perhaps too much. Definitely more than she'd ever wanted or expected to. And no matter how hard she tried, she seemed powerless to resist.

One more interview and he was home free.

That was, unless Lily scheduled something else. Which wouldn't surprise Noah in the least. The woman was the best thing that ever could have happened to the rodeo school.

He could hardly believe that the grand opening was just a little over a month away. And, honestly, he wasn't sure he'd have been able to pull it off if God hadn't brought Lily into his life. Sure, he could have managed a cake and some balloons, a few tours of the facility. But Lily had created an entire event. One that was certain to draw people in and make sure everyone knew about The Rodeo School at Abundant Blessings Ranch.

"What are you grinning about?" His father eyed him over his cup of coffee Monday morning.

"I'm not grinning." Sitting on the opposite side of the table in the ranch house kitchen, he sipped his own brew as the first rays of sunlight appeared outside the window over the sink. Lord willing, they'd have another dry day, making it two in a row.

"All right, then something's got you *smiling*."

"Just thinking about the rodeo school."

"The rodeo school or the woman helping you with the rodeo school?" The old man shoved his last bite of toast into his mouth.

"Dad…" Could he not just drink his coffee in peace?

He rested his forearms on the wooden tabletop, eager to turn the tables. "I haven't seen Hillary around much lately."

"Her daughter, Celeste, has had some pretty bad morning sickness, so Hillary's been helping out with her two girls and one-year-old boy. Not to mention making sure things are running smoothly over there at Granny's Kitchen."

"Sounds like she's got her hands full."

"She can handle it. The woman thrives in chaos." He stared into his mug, falling unusually silent for a long moment. "You know…you and me…" he met Noah's gaze, his brow creased. "We were blessed to have been loved by a couple of mighty fine women."

Noah leaned back, stretching his legs out in front of him, uncertain where Dad was going with this conversation. "Can't argue with you there. Mama and Jaycee were the cream of the crop."

Dad shifted in his seat, tilting his cup one way and then the other, looking intently at whatever was left inside. "Lately, God's been showing me that there are other good women out there that need the love of a good man. I reckon that's why I've been spending so much time with Hillary."

Noah drew his legs back as he sat up straight. "Dad, are you thinking about getting married again?"

The old man held up a hand. "Now let's not go jumpin' the gun. All I'm sayin' is that I'm starting to realize that my feelings for Hillary are more than just… friendly."

Man, did he understand that. Better than he ever thought he would. Envisioning Lily as more than a friend seemed to be getting easier by the day.

"Do you think Hillary feels the same way?"

"I can't say for certain, but I believe so. She's very cautious when it comes to matters of the heart." He looked right at Noah. "Her ex-husband left her for another woman when Celeste was just a little girl. And I expect it left a pretty big scar."

"Humph." Noah's grip tightened around his mug until he feared he might break it. He eased up. "Wade Davis cheated on Lily."

"Your mama always said that women who've been betrayed like that have a lot of love to give. They're just afraid to give it for fear they'll get hurt again." Dad stood and moved to the coffeepot beside the sink to refill his cup. "I expect Lily's one of those women. The way she dotes on those kids and that rescue horse. She's a keeper, all right."

She was that and more. "I'm not sure the rodeo school would be a reality without her."

His father returned to his seat. "Lily's a good woman. She deserves a good man. And those kids..." Steam rose from his cup. "They need someone they can look up to."

Noah raised his mug. "I agree. I just don't think I'm that man." No matter how much he'd allowed himself to think about it.

"I do."

A quick intake of breath had him choking on his drink. "How can you be so sure?"

"Because for the first time in ages, you're happy—I mean genuinely happy. And it's got nothing to do with the horses or the rodeo school. It's because of Lily and her kids."

"And in case you've forgotten, they live in Denver." Ready for this conversation to be over, Noah shoved away from the table. "I've got an interview to get ready for." He went to his room down the hall and grabbed a fresh shirt for the interview, as well as another pair of boots before heading down to the stable.

Dad was falling in love with Hillary. Noah supposed he shouldn't be too surprised. Since the two former schoolmates had reconnected a year and half ago, they'd spent a good bit of time together. It was nice to see the old man getting out again.

Yet the notion of his father remarrying had never crossed his mind. It was hard to imagine him with anyone but Mama. Still, Hillary seemed to fit right in. She certainly knew how to keep his father in line. Yet despite their banter, there were little things Noah had noticed that said she cared about Dad. Like the way she looked at him. As though he was the most important person in the world.

But loving posed the risk of losing. Noah had experienced both. He'd lost his wife, child and mother. He wasn't sure he could go through that again.

He unlocked the front door to the stable and flipped on the lobby light as he entered. Just as he'd done every other day for the past two and half years. And then he'd usually stay until well after dark. That was, until he met Lily.

Tucking his fear aside for a moment, he allowed himself to wonder what it would be like to have someone to come home to. Someone to talk to other than his father or brothers. Someone to discuss his day with and take just as much interest in theirs. It had been so long since he'd had that, he'd all but forgotten.

He thought about all of Lily's ideas for the rodeo school and grand opening. They made a good team.

And the kids… Colton and Piper were great. Colton had grown so much. In the short time he'd been here, he'd gone from being a smart-mouthed kid too eager to grow up to a respectful, happy-go-lucky boy truly experiencing his childhood.

After depositing his shirt and boots in the office, he roughed a hand over his face. He needed to stop thinking and get to work. Otherwise he'd only succeed in driving himself crazy.

He eyed his watch and went to check on the horses. His hired hands would be here soon, and he hoped he'd have at least one more opportunity to go over things with Lily before the reporter arrived at eleven. Of course, she'd tell him he already knew the answers to whatever they might ask him and then tell him to speak from his heart, but he still worried he might put his foot in his mouth.

His phone vibrated in his pocket as he approached Honey's stall. His heart beat faster when he pulled it out to see Lily's name on the screen.

He pressed the button. "Good morning."

"Morning." She sounded tired.

"You all right?"

She yawned. "I was up with Piper most of the night. Poor kid's got some sort of stomach bug."

"Is she okay?"

"She will be once whatever it is runs its course." She blew out a breath, and he could picture her running her fingers through her long waves. "Things seem to have settled in the last couple of hours. She's asleep now, so that's a good sign. However, I'm afraid I won't be able to make it out there today."

"No, of course not." He toed at the dirt. "Piper needs you."

"Thank you for understanding. I just pray that neither Colton nor I will catch it. Or you, for that matter."

"No, I'm sure I'll be fine. You just concentrate on Piper."

"Call me after the interview. I want to know how it goes."

"I will." Tugging open the door to Honey's stall, he added, "Tell Piper I hope she feels better. And if you need one of us to come get Colton, just let me know."

He ended the call and moved toward the horse, feeling more than a little conflicted.

How on earth was he going to get through this interview without Lily?

Chapter Seventeen

Lily felt bad that she hadn't been able to be there for Noah's interview yesterday. While she knew he was perfectly capable of doing it on his own, she also knew that he liked having her there for moral support. So, now that Piper was back to her usual bubbly self, Lily had invited Noah to dinner at their place tonight to, hopefully, make up for her absence. Or at least ease her conscience.

Standing in the kitchen, chopping tomatoes for a salad, she peered through the wall of windows overlooking the deck where Piper was coloring at the table while Colton practiced with the rope Noah had given him.

A few months ago, she never would have envisioned such a scene. Yet, there it was. Had her children ever been this content?

Their lives were so different here than they were back in Denver. There, the kids spent most of their time inside the house. In Ouray, they were almost always outside, living life and experiencing new things. Especially when they were at the ranch. From the animals to playing in the river to exploring… Those were memories they would cherish forever. And probably miss when they got back home.

No doubt about it, life was just better here. For her and the kids. Who would have thought that small-town life would fit her so well? Yet, here she felt more relaxed. Probably because she didn't have to worry about living up to someone else's expectations. She was free to be herself. Just Lily. She rinsed her hands, dreading the thought of returning to Denver in a couple of weeks. So much so that she'd even entertained the idea of moving to Ouray.

What was holding her back then? Aside from the custody arrangements with Wade and how impossible he could make such a move if he chose to.

She reached for a towel. Noah. Or more to the point, her growing feelings for him. What if those feelings weren't reciprocated? He was still in love with his late wife. Was he capable of loving someone else?

"Noah's here." Colton rushed through the living room to the front door with his sister on his heels.

They must have seen his truck pull up.

She hurried into the bathroom, finger combed her hair and added a swipe of lip balm.

Why are you primping? It's not like this is a date.

Eyeing herself in the mirror, she frowned. "Oh, be quiet."

Both kids were clamoring for Noah's attention by the time she got to the door. At least she was pretty sure it was Noah. This wasn't the cowboy she was used to seeing. He wore a pair of stone-colored shorts and a blue button-down shirt with the sleeves rolled up to the elbows. His cowboy boots had been replaced by flip-flops, and there wasn't a cowboy hat in sight. Instead, his thick dark hair looked slightly damp, as though he'd just showered.

Making her wish she'd primped a little more.

"Look at the picture I made for you." Piper waved the paper in front of him. "It's a horse, and I colored him to look just like Duke. Want to color with me?"

"Come watch me practice," said Colton. "You can show me—"

"Hey, you two." Hands on her hips, she glared at her children. "Noah is our guest. He's here for dinner, not to entertain you."

Behind them, Noah shrugged. "It's okay. I really don't mind."

Her gaze drifted from him to the kids. "All right. But if you give them an inch, they'll take a mile."

"I'll consider myself warned. But first—" he moved toward her and held out a brown paper gift bag "—this is for you."

Wrapping her fingers around the handles, she simply blinked. "For me?" Her heart raced as his hand brushed hers.

"Ouray may not have any flower shops," he said, "but we do have some of the world's finest chocolate."

Her brow lifted as she peered inside. "Mouse's?"

"The one and only."

She lifted out a small box. "I love that place. And you're right. Their chocolate is amazing." She hugged the box to her chest. "Thank you."

"I like their cookies," said Colton.

"Their chocolate mice are my favorite." Piper rubbed her tummy and licked her lips. "They're yummy."

Lily looked at Noah. "I may have to hide these."

While he joined the kids on the deck, Lily pulled the

homemade lasagna out of the oven, then put in the garlic bread to brown. She couldn't believe he'd brought her a gift. *And does he look amazing or what?*

She nudged the thought aside, grabbed plates and silverware, and went outside to set the table.

"I like this view." Noah leaned against the wooden railing. "The way it looks down on the town."

She moved beside him. "That's the main reason I chose it." Her gaze lifted to the Amphitheater, the grayish rock formation that curved around the eastern edge of the town. "Sometimes, after the sun sinks behind the mountains, but before it actually sets, it casts these incredible shades of rose, orange and purple over the Amphitheater."

"Alpenglow."

Her gaze moved to his. "What?"

"The colors. It's called alpenglow." He turned so his back was against the rail. "Some natural occurrence having to do with particles in the air."

"Whatever it is, I absolutely love it."

Midway through the peach cobbler she'd made, the conversation turned to business, and Colton and Piper made themselves scarce while she and Noah lingered over coffee.

"This is just a random thought." She set her cup on the metal tabletop. "Something to think about for the future." Twisting toward him, she continued, "But have you ever thought of adding summer camps to the mix? Like two-or three-week-long rodeo camps where people from just about anywhere, looking to hone their skills, could come and train and immerse themselves in rodeo." She shrugged. "Of course, you'd have to provide room and board for something like that. Still, it would be an opportunity to reach people beyond this region."

"I'd never thought of that, but it's not a bad idea." He sat up straighter. "It would definitely be an opportunity to expand the school." He grew quiet then. Contemplative. "I really appreciate it when you throw out ideas like that."

"You do?"

"You have a fresh perspective that challenges me." His hand covered hers. "I like that."

"Mom?"

She turned to see Colton poking his head out of the door.

"Piper's asleep."

"Okay. I'll get her." She picked up her plate as she stood. "You need to get ready for bed, too, Colton. You have an early day tomorrow."

"Yes, ma'am."

Noah reached for her plate. "I'll take care of the dishes. You go take care of Piper."

Gratitude filled her as her gaze drifted to his. "Thank you."

His smile warmed her, but not nearly as much as the look she saw in his deep brown eyes. A look she'd not seen before. One of longing. Hope.

She stepped away for fear he'd be able to hear her heart pounding. "I won't be long."

After settling Piper, Lily went to check on Colton. He was already in bed, his wilderness comforter pulled up to his neck.

"Mom, do we have to go back to Denver?"

She eased beside him, wishing she could say, "No,

of course not," but decided to play the adult instead. "Well, it's where our home is. Your school. Friends."

Lying on his back, he lifted a shoulder. "We could get a house here. I've seen lots of them for sale."

"What about your friends?"

"I can make new ones. And I already have one friend."

"Who's that?"

"Megan."

"Oh, yes." She adjusted his covers, amazed at how his thoughts mirrored her own. "What about your father?"

Colton was quiet for a moment. "It's not like we ever see him. Even when we do go to his house, he's hardly ever there."

A pattern Wade wasn't likely to change.

Smiling down at her boy, she brushed the hair off his forehead. "Moving is a big decision. One I can't make without praying about it, because a lot of things would have to fall into place." Such as custody issues.

His green eyes filled with hope. "Will you? Pray about it, I mean?"

She pondered his words. While she'd hoped and wished, she had yet to pray. Something she really ought to do. "I will."

"Promise?"

"Pinkie promise." She held up her little finger.

He hooked his to it and squeezed. "Thanks, Mom." Sitting up, he hugged her.

She kissed his cheek. "Good night, sweetie."

Returning to the main part of the house, she found the kitchen void of any dishes and Noah again on the deck. "Sorry I took so long." She joined him at the railing, taking in the multitude of stars twinkling in the sky as the cool air whispered over her arms.

"Everything all right?"

"Yes. Just a little…strange."

"How so?" Keeping one elbow on the rail, he faced her.

"Maybe *strange* isn't the right word. More like *unexpected*." She met Noah's gaze. "Colton asked me if we had to go back to Denver. Seems he'd be just as content to stay in Ouray."

"And what about you?"

She again studied the stars. "I've been happier here than I've been in a long time. It's as though we were just existing in Denver. But here…we're alive."

He stroked her arm with the backs of his fingers. "I know what you mean. I've felt a lot more alive since you've been here, too."

Her heart cartwheeled in her chest. Looking up at him, she swallowed hard. "You have?"

Straightening, he cupped her cheek with his hand as he threaded his fingers into her hair and leaned toward her.

Closing her eyes, she drew in a deep breath, anticipating his kiss. He smelled of coffee and fresh air. Then his lips met hers, and possibly for the first time in her life, she thought she might swoon.

His arms found their way to her waist, and he pulled her closer, deepening their kiss. This was too good to be true. He wanted her to stay in Ouray. Wanted to—

He abruptly pulled away, leaving her lost in a romantic haze.

She opened her eyes as he released her.

His face was marred with confusion and pain. "I'm

sorry, Lily. I can't do this." With that, he whisked past her and into the house.

She turned around just in time to see the front door close.

What just happened?

Touching her fingers to her still-throbbing lips, she wandered into the house and dropped onto the sofa, her heart breaking as she struggled for answers.

One thing was obvious. Noah didn't want her.

So why did she still want him?

Her cell phone rang in the kitchen. Like a fool, she hoped it might be him and hurried to grab it. Instead, her attorney's name appeared on the screen. Why would he call her so late?

She shook her head to clear the fog from her brain before answering. "Geoffrey?"

"Lily, if you're not sitting down, I'd advise that you do so now."

That was rather cryptic. "Why? Is there a problem?"

"You could say that."

She racked her brain trying to comprehend what he was saying. "Go on."

"Wade is suing for full custody of Colton and Piper."

"Wait, what?" Since when was Wade interested in being a father?

"There's a photo that has surfaced showing Colton on the ground, as though he was bucked from a horse."

"Bucked from a horse? That never happened."

"I'm afraid it gets worse, Lily. Wade is claiming that you're an unfit mother. That you've put the children in danger, so he wants immediate custody and has managed to secure a preliminary hearing for Friday."

She rubbed a hand over her forehead and through her hair. "That's only three days from now."

"I know. Which is why I'm going to suggest you come back to Denver as soon as possible so we can go over things. Just let me know when, and I'll clear my schedule."

When the call ended, Lily staggered to the couch, her body shaking. Why was this happening? First Noah, now this. If she lost her kids…

A sob caught in her throat.

Her world was falling apart.

Noah was a fool.

How could he think about having a relationship with Lily when had yet to say goodbye to Jaycee? Yet, he'd kissed Lily, anyway. Then left without so much as an explanation.

Pulling up to the ranch house, he contemplated turning around and going back. But he wasn't sure he could face Lily until his conscience was clear.

Inside the house, he barely spoke to his father as he passed through the living room. Once in his room, he opened the top drawer of his dresser and pulled out the note his mother had written to him shortly before she passed away. A note he hadn't even known existed until last year. Instead, it had been tucked away until his sister-in-law Carly stumbled across it.

He sat on the edge of his bed, opened the card with a columbine on the front and read.

My dearest Noah,
The first time I held you in my arms, I knew I was
created to be a mother. You were my sunshine on

cloudy days, always quick with a smile. But that smile faded when Jaycee died. As though a part of you had died with her.

You were a good husband. You loved Jaycee with everything you had. Though that doesn't mean you can't love again.

Your loyalty is one of your greatest traits, but, someday, God may bring a woman into your life who makes you smile once more and infiltrates your thoughts at the most unexpected times.

He looked up. Even Dad had said it was nice to see him happy again. Was it really because of Lily? She definitely seemed to find her way into his mind on a daily basis. Morning, noon and night. He was helpless to stop it. Perhaps because he didn't want to.

He continued to read.

Allowing yourself to love her won't mean you love Jaycee any less. You just have to let go of the past. Weeping may endure for a night, but joy cometh in the morning. You deserve joy, my son. So much joy.

When he'd first read this letter a little over a year ago, he'd been touched by his mother's sentiment. Now her words smacked him in the face. She was right. It was time to let go of the past.

But how?

He tossed and turned most of the night until just before dawn. Then, as though a bolt of lightning had struck him, he knew just what he needed to do. Something he'd put off for twelve years.

He gathered a few clothes and some canned goods from the pantry and wrote a note to his father, explaining that he was going to the cabin, asking him to cover things at the stable and begging him not to let anyone know where he was. He set it beside the coffee maker before heading out the door.

The road to the cabin was overgrown, barely wide enough for his truck to get through anymore. Something he'd need to remedy.

When he reached the cabin, he stepped out of the cab, allowing the sun's rays to warm him as he stared at the abandoned house. When he'd first left, shortly after Jaycee's death, his mother had taken care of it. Until she got sick. Since then, Dad checked on it occasionally, making sure there were no major issues.

Noah wasn't sure how long he stood there, remembering the life he and Jaycee had built here. The dreams they shared and looked forward to expectantly. Dreams that came to an abrupt end the day she died. But the memories they'd made here remained. Good memories that he'd all but forgotten because he'd allowed them to be overshadowed by the bad.

That had to stop.

After turning on the power to the house, he made his way up the steps and onto the wooden porch. It was still solid, though it could use a good power washing and another coat of stain.

He drew in a deep breath as he unlocked the door and stepped inside. The room was dark and smelled musty. Shoving aside the curtains on either side of the door, he opened the windows, allowing the fresh air to flow in.

Funny, the living room was much smaller than he

remembered. Though it looked just the way it had the day he walked in and found Jaycee lying on the floor.

A lump formed in his throat, but he swallowed it away. The last time he was in here, he'd taken only what was his and left everything that reminded him of her behind. As though not being surrounded by Jaycee's things could diminish her memory.

Moving past the leather sofa, he picked up a framed wedding photo from the bookshelf, recalling how excited he'd been to make Jaycee his wife. It wasn't long after that he'd made the decision to leave the rodeo and come back here to start a family. So many plans. Plans that died right along with Jaycee.

For years he'd begged God to take him, too. Every time he got on the back of a bronc or bull. Until he finally realized that, maybe, God still had him here for a reason. That's when the idea for the rodeo school first took root.

God, thank You for bringing Jaycee into my life, even if it was only for a short time. She taught me what it meant to love.

He continued through the house, opening curtains and windows, flooding the space with sunlight. Light that revealed the signs of neglect. How could he do that to Jaycee's memory?

Well, not anymore.

He rolled up the sleeves of his work shirt and went outside. After locating a pair of trimming shears in the shed out back, he attacked the overgrown lilac bush and brought it under control. Next, he brushed away cobwebs from the outside of the house and cleaned the windows, removing twelve years' worth of haze.

Inside, he moved from room to room, wiping down

walls, dusting, scrubbing floors and vacuuming. After making sure the washer and dryer were still in working order, he stripped linens from beds and took down dust-laden curtains.

The sun was setting when he finally sat down on the porch with a bowl of canned chili. The once-forgotten cabin looked more like a home now. A place Jaycee would be proud of.

A place he actually wanted to be.

Waking up in the cabin the next morning, Noah felt like a new man. Good thing he'd hung on to that container of coffee he found in the cupboard yesterday.

Lifting his cup, he took another sip. A little on the stale side, but it would do.

He wandered through the house, thoughts of Lily peppering his brain. What was she doing? Had she brought the kids out for lessons? Had she come to check on Honey? He should have called her, told her what he was doing.

After locating a box in one of the closets, he gathered all of the photos around the house and placed them in it. He didn't need them to remind him of Jaycee. She would live in his heart forever. But it was time for him to move forward.

Standing in the hallway, he studied the two secondary bedrooms. Why were they so small? Okay for a baby or small child, he supposed, but Colton and Piper would need more space. Peering into the so-called master, he realized that it wasn't much better, except that it had its own bathroom. He couldn't expect Lily to live—

A smile split wide across his face when he realized what he was contemplating. And for the first time in twelve years, he felt his heart truly beat. A pounding, strong and vibrant, as though it had finally broken free of the grief that had held it captive.

He fell against the wall. "I love her. I love Lily." Why had it taken him so long to realize it? "God, I don't know how, but I have to make this right."

He rushed outside to his truck. He had to find Lily.

It was just after noon when he reached the ranch house and burst through the mudroom door.

"Dad?"

"Noah, just the person I need to see." Carly met him as he moved from the mudroom into the family room.

"I can't talk right now." He moved past her. "I need to find Lily."

"You're going to Denver?"

His steps slowed. He turned to face her. "What are you talking about? She's in town."

"No, Lily left for Denver yesterday." Carly reached for a stack of papers on the end table beside the sofa. "She asked me to give you these flyers for the grand opening."

"Denver?" He sank onto the couch. *Why would she go back now?*

"Yeah." Carly set the papers back down again. "She seemed pretty upset, too."

He buried his face in his hands. *Because of me.*

"Noah!" Dad rushed in from the adjoining kitchen. "Lily's on TV." Remote already in hand, the old man turned up the volume.

Looking at screen on the other side of the room, Noah saw side-by-side photos of Lily and her ex-husband.

"Billionaire businessman-turned-state-senate candidate Wade Davis is suing for custody of his two children after a photo surfaced earlier this summer, showing his son grimacing in pain after being bucked from a horse," the announcer said.

Standing, Noah stared at the image on the screen. "I remember that. He wasn't bucked off. He tripped and fell."

"And came up laughing, as I recall," said Dad.

"Davis appeared before reporters—" the announcer continued as they cut to a clip of Wade Davis.

"The welfare of my children is my top priority. I cannot risk having them put in danger."

"Danger?" Noah started to pace. "This guy is out of his mind."

A picture of Lily flashed on the screen as the announcer again spoke. "The children's mother, Lily Davis, daughter of late real estate mogul Gunther Yates, refused comment. The former darlings of Denver are due in court tomorrow."

He turned away. Lily had trusted him, and he'd let her down. *Why did I have to walk away?*

Dad came alongside him. "What are you going to do now?"

Chapter Eighteen

Lily sat at the front of a Denver courtroom Friday morning with her attorney by her side as they awaited the judge's arrival. Across the aisle, at a duplicate table, her ex-husband eyed her smugly.

He hadn't changed. This lawsuit had nothing to with being a father. It was about his political campaign and appearances. He thought that if he played the doting father, it would garner him more votes. Lily was certain of it.

Her stomach churned. Her only defense was the truth. She'd done nothing wrong. That photo they were trying to use against her, to prove her an unfit mother, was a lie. Something taken completely out of context. And if needed, she had witnesses who would confirm that.

Still, Wade's self-satisfied grin rubbed her the wrong way.

Standing, she crossed to where he sat. "Why are you doing this, Wade? You know I would never put my children in danger, just like you know that picture doesn't portray the real story." Arms crossed, she cocked her head. "How did you get it, anyway? Did the photographer offer it to you? Was he looking to pad his wallet?"

Wade leaned back in his chair, one side of his mouth lifting in amusement. "You seem awfully worried, Lily. Is there something you'd care to tell me?"

Anger sparked inside her, but she tamped it down, unwilling to give him the satisfaction.

Out of the corner of her eye, she saw the doors open at the back of the courtroom. Corrine Davis, Wade's current wife and Lily's former best friend, walked in. The woman Lily had once been foolish enough to share all of her secrets with was as beautiful as ever in her perfectly tailored navy pantsuit, though her shoulder-length hair was a shade blonder than Lily remembered.

With a final look at Wade, Lily returned to her seat, not wanting to cause a scene.

Corrine paused beside her husband, almost glaring at him, then continued around that table toward Lily.

Her heart beat faster. What could Corrine possibly have to say to her? Would she call Lily an unfit mother and pretend to care for Colton and Piper as if they were her own?

Stopping in front of their table, she nodded in Lily's direction before pulling a plain manila file folder from her leather Salvatore Ferragamo tote and handing it to Lily's lawyer. "This is for you."

Her gaze moved to Lily. "I'm sorry, Lily. For everything." With that, Corrine turned on her Jimmy Choo heel and moved across the granite floor, past Wade and his attorney, back down the aisle and out the door.

Weird.

Lily leaned toward her attorney. "What did she give you?"

Only then did Geoffrey open the file just enough for him to peer inside.

"Well...?" She waited anxiously.

He straightened. Then sent her a smile. "Excuse me, please."

She watched as he stood and made his way to the other table. What was going on? And why wasn't Geoffrey sharing anything with her? He did work for her, after all.

"Some information has come to light that you two might be interested in." He handed the folder to Wade's attorney.

The man opened it so that both he and his client could see its contents.

Yet, she was being kept in the dark.

The lawyer riffled through the papers, and Wade's eyes went wide. Wade and his attorney exchanged looks. Then he slumped back into his chair, a scowl on his face as his attorney closed the folder and handed it back to Geoffrey.

Lily's lawyer returned to her side as the judge entered the courtroom.

"All rise for the honorable Judge Rawlings."

Standing, Lily leaned toward Geoffrey and whispered, "What's going on?"

The judge gaveled in. "You may be seated." The older, fatherly-looking man took his seat behind the bench.

Geoffrey grinned. "Let's just say that a leopard doesn't change his spots," he whispered.

"What?" All of these ambiguities were about to drive her crazy.

"First order of business, Davis versus Davis," said the judge.

Wade's lawyer stood. "Your Honor, counsel requests permission to approach the bench."

"Permission granted."

Wade's attorney moved forward and spoke to the judge in hushed tones.

The suspense was killing her.

A few moments later, Wade's attorney returned to his seat as the judge gaveled once again.

"The case of Davis versus Davis has been dismissed."

Now Lily was really confused, and she couldn't help but wonder what her ex-husband was up to now.

"Dismissed? Geoffrey?" Standing, she watched as he gathered his papers.

Finally, he met her gaze. "Corrine is filing for divorce."

Lily didn't think it was possible, but she found herself even more puzzled. "Why?"

"Let's just say there was a third party involved. And some photos confirmed it."

"A third— Oh. Oh…" So Wade was cheating on Corrine. Now it all made sense. The dismissal, Corrine's apology.

Despite everything, though, she felt sorry for her old friend. The sting of betrayal hurt on many levels.

Again, she eyed her ex-husband across the aisle, a new sense of determination flooding through her. The more she discovered about this man, the more she felt the need to protect her children from his self-serving antics. And protect them she would.

She approached him once more. "That didn't turn out so well for you, did it, Wade?" Laying her hands atop the table, she leaned toward him. "Well, it's about to get worse, because not only will I be seeking full custody of my children, I can assure you that I will receive it."

Moments later, with Geoffrey at her side, Lily exited into the large granite lobby and blew out a breath. *Thank You, Lord.* Not only had He vindicated her, He seemed to be paving the way for her and her children to live the life they'd been praying for.

She faced her attorney. "Thank you for everything, Geoffrey. I appreciate—"

"Lily."

Her pulse raced. It couldn't be.

She turned to find Noah standing behind her with his cowboy hat in hand. He wore a pair of dark-wash jeans, ostrich boots and a slate blue polo shirt that highlighted his dark eyes every bit as much as his bulging biceps.

She swallowed hard. "What are you— How did you know I was here?"

"Carly said you'd gone back to Denver. The news report said you were due in court today." He shrugged. "I took my chances, because I couldn't let you go through this alone."

Her mind still reeling, she said, "That—that's sweet." She rubbed her temple. "Noah, this is my attorney, Geoffrey Forester. Geoffrey, Noah Stephens."

While they shook hands and exchanged pleasantries, Lily tried to gather her thoughts.

Geoffrey touched her elbow. "I'll leave you two alone."

She nodded. "Thank you, Geoffrey."

"Are you okay?" Noah watched her as Geoffrey strode away. "You don't look so good."

"Yes, I'm fine. Just a little overwhelmed." Could this day possibly get any crazier?

"Here, let's sit down." He gestured to a wooden bench along the wall. "How'd it go in there?"

She lifted a shoulder. "It was over before it began." She told him all that had transpired and that the case had been dismissed.

"That's excellent news."

"Yes, it is." She dared to meet his gorgeous dark gaze. "What are you doing here? I mean, if you're feeling guilty about the other night, it's okay, I get it. You didn't have to come all the way to Denver."

"I did feel guilty, but not for the reasons you might think."

She cocked her head, daring to hope as she waited for him to continue.

"I love you, Lily. Of that I couldn't be more certain."

Tears of joy pricked the backs of her eyes.

"But I wasn't free to tell you until I'd let go of the past."

Finding her voice, she said, "Your steadfast love for Jaycee is one of the things I admire most about you."

"I never thought I'd love again, Lily. Until I met you." He took hold of her hand. "You are my future. You, Colton and Piper." Reaching into his pocket, he pulled out a velvet box and dropped to one knee. "Please say that you'll marry me."

Oh, boy, things had just gotten crazier.

"I'm willing to forgo the rodeo school and live in Denver until the children graduate from high school. I just want to be with you."

She touched a hand to his cheek. "The fact that you'd postpone your dream makes me love you all the more."

He smiled up at her.

"But the kids and I have already decided that we

want to make Ouray our home." She shrugged. "I'll have to tie up some loose ends here, but, Lord willing, we'll be there in time for the kids to start school."

"Well, I know of a nice little cabin, just outside Ouray. You and the kids are more than welcome to stay there."

The joy in her heart spilled into a smile. "I'd like that, but we should discuss this marriage thing with the kids before I give you an answer." Her cheeks heated. "Although I'm pretty sure I know what they're going to say."

"In that case…" Standing, he tugged her to her feet, gazing down at her as though she was the most special person in the world.

She pressed a hand against his chest. "I love you, Noah."

"I love you, too. With all of my heart." As he smiled down at her, she pushed up on the toes of her pumps and kissed him without reservation. This was the man she'd longed for. And even though she'd given up on her dream of true love, God had fulfilled it, bigger and better than she ever could have imagined.

"Here's to Noah and a successful grand opening." Dad lifted his cup of lemonade.

"Hear, hear," echoed the rest of the family lining the deck on the Saturday evening of Labor Day weekend.

Noah wrapped an arm around Lily's shoulders and pulled her close. "None of this would have been possible without this woman by my side." He peered down at her, making her heart flutter. Hard to believe that in just a little over a month, she would be his wife. She could hardly wait.

Wade had not contested her petition for full custody of the children, though she had agreed to grant him visitation. He'd also decided to pull out of the race for state senate. Given all that had transpired in his personal life over the past few weeks, his polling numbers had dropped significantly. Lily prayed he might use this time to reevaluate his life and his choices and turn over a new leaf.

"Lily," Noah continued, "you took a grand opening that would have been mediocre at best and turned it into an event I never would have thought possible."

"Yeah," said Colton. "We might even be on TV." Thanks to a couple of reporters who'd shown up, referring to the grand opening as a not-to-be-missed event.

"Hey, great job with the calf roping out there, Colton." Jude patted him on the back.

Lily was so proud. The kid had ridden his heart out and hit the mark on his first try.

"I still can't believe how many people came." Andrew shook his head. "It was standing room only in there."

"Lily and I calculated somewhere in the neighborhood of four to five hun…dred—" Seemingly perplexed, Carly laid a hand on her husband's arm. "I think my water just broke."

"What does that mean?" Colton's face contorted.

Clint moved toward his daughter-in-law. "It means these two had better get going, because they're about to have a baby."

"What do I do? Do we have enough time to make it to the hospital? Are you in pain?" Andrew's rapid-fire questions were accompanied by a look of terror. Understandable, Lily supposed. Since Megan wasn't his biological daughter, he'd never experienced the whole childbirth thing before.

"I'm fine," Carly assured him. "Though I don't know for how much longer, so yes, we should probably go to the hospital."

Andrew looked at his father.

"Well, don't just stand there gaping, boy. You heard the woman." Clint pointed toward their vehicle. "Get her to the hospital."

Megan hugged her mother. "I can't wait. My first campout *and* I'm going to be a big sister. All in the same night."

With Andrew and Carly on their way, Lily helped Lacie clean up the paper plates and plasticware from dinner, while Clint and Hillary gathered the kids for their big campout—which the two had planned a week or so ago and that probably signaled the next step in their relationship, considering Hillary's granddaughters, Cassidy and Emma, were among the campers. Daniel had helped them set up tents near the river earlier today and get the firepit ready. All they had to do now was show up.

Returning to the deck, Lily joined her fiancé while Lacie stood in front of her husband to watch the group.

"Just look at them," said Lacie. "They're going to have so much fun."

Matt wrapped his arms around his wife's waist. "I just hope we don't get a phone call in the middle of the night to come and pick her up because she misses us."

Noah placed his mouth beside Lily's ear, sending shivers down her spine. "Care to take a ride with me?"

"Mmm…a sunset ride sounds delightful." Not to mention romantic.

After seeing the children off, they headed to the stable for Duke and Checkers.

"I can't wait until Honey is strong enough to be ridden." She climbed into her saddle. "Not that you're not a good horse, Checkers." She patted the animal's neck. "Where do you want to go?" She eyed her intended. "The cabin?"

Since returning to Ouray, she and the kids had been living in Noah's cabin. Something that was much more practical, considering they spent most of their time at the ranch. That was, when the kids weren't in school.

Of course, their new rural life had presented a few adventures. Such as the morning they woke up to find a coyote in the front yard. She'd had to convince Piper that it was not a dog and she could not play with it. Fortunately, it ran away.

"Actually, I have someplace else in mind." The spark in his dark eyes had her curious.

"You lead then." Holding on to the reins, she followed him the short distance through the pasture, beyond the barn, admiring the way he looked in the saddle.

"I've been thinking about your idea of summer camps."

"Really?" This was the first time he'd mentioned it.

"We're still talking a ways down the road, but what if we had at least one that was dedicated to kids struggling with grief or loss?"

"That's always been a part of your dream." And she'd seen the positive effect horses had on Colton.

"I know something like that would involve counselors and such, but I think I'd like to explore the possibility." He smiled as they came into a small wooded area that had a natural clearing in its midst. "And speaking of possibilities." He looked her way. "What would you think about building a home here?" He eased off Duke before coming to help her down.

"Building? What about the cabin?"

"Lily, I love that cabin. But we both know that it's way too small for all of us. It's barely big enough for you and the kids. Once I move in, we'll be on top of each other. Not to mention as the kids get older."

"I suppose things are a little tight." And while she didn't want anything near as large as the monstrosity she'd shared with her ex-husband, a little extra space never hurt.

"It's closer to the stable and the rodeo school. And if you look through here—" he tugged her a few feet over and turned her just so "—we'd have a spectacular view."

Though the sunlight was dwindling, she could still make out the unmistakable silhouette. "Ouray. Mount Hayden's peak, anyway."

"That's it." He stepped away, gesturing. "We could do a big porch that wraps around the entire house."

"Could we have a log home?"

"If you like. One story or two?"

"Hmm… I suppose a two-story home would afford us a better view." She pointed toward town.

"Or just a two-story wall of windows on the front."

"Ooh, now that would be a view. And we'd need at least four bedrooms."

"For a guest room?"

She slowly lifted her gaze to his. "Or a nursery." She hadn't broached the subject of more children before, but she knew Noah would be an amazing father. Besides, she'd always hoped for more kids.

His Adam's apple bobbed as he blinked several times.

She reached for his hand. "How would you feel about that?"

"I..." He blew out a breath. "I'm not going to lie. It kind of scares me."

"Then we don't—"

"But I also think a baby—" Taking a step closer, he cupped her cheek, weaving his fingers into her hair. "Our baby—" he grinned "—would be pretty exciting, too."

She smiled up at the man who would soon be her husband. "Then let's pray about it and see what God has in store."

"Good idea." Lowering his head, he kissed her. Soft and tender...then he abruptly pulled away. "If it's a girl, we have to name her Joy."

She liked that, but— "Okay. Why?"

The way he stared at her made her feel cherished. Something she'd never felt before. His hands moved to her waist. "Because that's what you've given me, Lily. You, Colton and Piper have taught me to live again. And I'm so glad God brought you into my life." He pulled her to him. "I love you. Today. Tomorrow. And for the rest of our lives."

Once more, he pulled her into his embrace. A place where she was safe. Where she could be herself. And where just Lily was a perfect fit.

* * * * *

WE HOPE YOU ENJOYED
THIS BOOK FROM

LOVE INSPIRED
INSPIRATIONAL ROMANCE

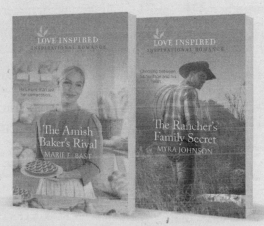

Uplifting stories of faith, forgiveness and hope.

Fall in love with stories where faith helps
guide you through life's challenges, and discover
the promise of a new beginning.

6 NEW BOOKS AVAILABLE EVERY MONTH!

LIHALO2021

Arleta had tossed and turned all night ruminating over Sovilla's and Noah's remarks. And in the wee hours of the morning, she'd come to the decision that—as disappointing as it would be—if they wanted her to leave, she'd make her departure as easy and amicable for them as she could.

"Your *groossmammi* is tiring of me—that's why she wanted me to go to the frolic," she said to Noah. "She said she wanted to be alone. And if I'm not at the *haus*, I can't be of any help to her, which means you're wasting your money paying me. Besides, her health is improving now and you probably don't need someone here full-time."

"Whoa!" Noah commanded the horse to stop on the shoulder of the road. He pushed his hat back and peered intently at Arleta. "I'm sorry that what I said last night didn't reflect the depth of my appreciation for all that you've done. But I consider your presence in our home to be a gift from *Gott*. It's invaluable. Please don't leave because of something *dumm* I said that I didn't mean. I was overly tired and irritated at—at one of my coworkers and… Well, there's no excuse. Please just forgive me—and don't leave."

Hearing Noah's compliment made Arleta feel as if she'd just swallowed a cupful of sunshine; it filled her with warmth from her cheeks to her toes. But as much as she treasured his words, she doubted Sovilla felt the same way. "I've enjoyed being at your *haus*, too. But your *groossmammi*—"

"She said something she didn't mean, too. Or she didn't mean it the way you took it. If I know my *groossmammi* as well as I think I do, she felt like you should go out and socialize once in a while instead of staying with her all the time. But she knew you'd resist it if she said that, so she turned the tables and claimed she wanted the *haus* to herself for a while."

That thought had occurred to Arleta, too. "*Jah*, perhaps."

"I'm sure of it. I can talk to her about it when—"

"*Neh*, please don't. I don't want to turn a molehill into a mountain." Arleta realized she should have spoken with Noah before jumping to the conclusion that neither he nor Sovilla wanted her to stay. But she'd been so homesick yesterday, and she'd felt even more alone after she'd listened to the other women implying how disgraceful it was for a young woman to work out. Hannah's lukewarm invitation to the frolic contributed to her loneliness, too. So by the time Sovilla and Noah made their remarks, Arleta already felt as if no one truly wanted her around and she jumped to the conclusion they would have preferred to employ someone else. She felt too silly to explain all of that to Noah now, so she simply said, "I shouldn't have been so sensitive."

"*Neh*. My *groossmammi* and I shouldn't have been so insensitive." Noah's chocolate-colored eyes conveyed the sincerity of his words. "It can't be easy trying to please both of us at the same time."

Arleta laughed. Since she couldn't deny it, she said, "It might not always be easy, but it's always interesting."

"Interesting enough to stay for the rest of the summer?"

Don't miss
Hiding Her Amish Secret *by Carrie Lighte,*
available May 2021 wherever
Love Inspired books and ebooks are sold.

LoveInspired.com

LIEXP0421

LOVE INSPIRED

INSPIRATIONAL ROMANCE

UPLIFTING STORIES OF FAITH, FORGIVENESS AND HOPE.

Join our social communities to connect with other readers who share your love!

Sign up for the Love Inspired newsletter at **LoveInspired.com** to be the first to find out about upcoming titles, special promotions and exclusive content.

CONNECT WITH US AT:

Facebook.com/LoveInspiredBooks

Twitter.com/LoveInspiredBks

Facebook.com/groups/HarlequinConnection